FOREWORD

After 127 years of service to Colorado, we often say at Denver Rescue Mission that, "We stand on the shoulders of the saints who came before us." Without the men and women who sacrificed and who had a heart not only for Jesus but for the poor and homeless we serve every day, there would not be a Denver Rescue Mission. These folks who worked so hard for others, were much like all of us and certainly like Jim Goodheart. These were regular people who made mistakes, who were flawed, who had their own ups and downs, and who were not always perfect. Timothy Browne, the great grandson of Jim Goodheart has shared a fictional account about a man who provided leadership to what is now Denver Rescue Mission at a critical time in its development. I truly believe that Tim has given us a taste of just what life was like at the Mission during Jim's life. Praise God that He used Jim for good!

Brad Meuli
President/CEO
Denver Rescue Mission

FOREWORD

My Grandpa, Jim Goodheart was a very dear man. We had many happy times together when I was a youngster. When I was five-years-old, we played together with a neighbor's dog that we taught to sit and stay, teaching me to give animals love.

Grandpa Jim let me go fishing with him and my dad. What fun and success we had together in the high mountains above Coal Creek Canyon. When I was able to "sleep over" in Grandpa and Grandma's house, my Grandpa Jim would ask me "who is your Savior." I've never forgotten that Grandpa lived a life of love, kindness, and joy that touched me and his many friends.

Sometimes Grandpa would ask me to sit on his lap for a "story." The story he told me was always the same, "Once upon a time—there was a great big one time." Then off to bed I'd go giggling about the "big story." I will never forget my dearest Grandpa and the lessons learned. I'll love him forever.

Virginia Goodheart Browne
Granddaughter of Jim Goodheart

FOREWORD

The internet age offers amazing opportunities for new friend-ships that would likely not have developed prior to its invention. During my assignment as the deputy commander (we call them Director of Operations) of the 96th Bomb Squadron in northwest Louisiana, I searched the web for bits of 96th Aero Squadron history, our unit's progenitor. Through this search, Tim and I met as he conducted research for this book. Tim and I learned we shared much more than just interest in the squadron as we were both devoted followers of Jesus Christ. Like Tim's grandfather, James Goodheart, I grew up in a devout, but legalistic Christian home. And, like James, a loving friend led me to my own Larimer Street as a young adult. The obstacle in James' path to the Lord was alcohol. Mine was intellectual doubt. Like James, the person who helped bring me back to Christ became a life-long partner (my wife, Wendy, though an apologetics ministry called Alpha). And, finally, again like James, I began to serve in lay ministry, albeit mine was part time as I continue to fly bombers. Now flying the B-52 Stratofortress, the current 96th looks fondly upon its contribution to bringing World War I to an end as they flew Breguet 14B.2 bombers. The unit's chant "First to Bomb!" harkens back to WWI when the unit was the first American squadron to drop bombs on an enemy. Other Americans had dropped bombs from aircraft before, but they had done so as a part of other nations' military units. James Goodheart witnessed it all, and his involvement with the 96th during WWI was my main draw to this book, initially. However, as I read, I became immersed in Joe's ministry, Ada and Donny's pain turned to bumpy happiness, and the struggles and successes of the Sunshine Rescue Mission. Most of all, the constant devotion to Jesus Christ as Savior resonating throughout the book, exhibited by real people of all walks of life - warts and all, is the greatest reason to read on through the story of Larimer Street. I hope you find your Larimer Street, if you are in need. Jesus is there for you.

In Christ,
David Leaumont
First to Bomb!

FOREWORD

My grandfather. Jim Goodheart. For years I heard stories about Jim Goodheart, from my father and sisters. Indeed, we still have the little portable organ that my grandmother played at the jail and on the sidewalk outside the Mission to lure people into the services. I have seen some of the newspaper articles that abound about him and he appears in history books about Denver. He became the fodder of a newspaper war between *The Rocky Mountain News* and *The Denver Post*, with one for and one against him. He was undoubtedly a controversial figure, but this book is about the personal side.

I am honored that that my nephew, Timothy Browne, asked me to write a forward. Also, I am delighted that he has taken so much interest in Jim Goodheart that he was prompted to write *Larimer Street*. The story is enthralling, and the book clearly shows all the good that he did, and why he was named the first chaplain of the City of Denver. However, it is fitting that Timothy writes about his flaws as well as his virtues. No person is without flaws and to portray him otherwise would be a disservice. He was a man of deep faith, but we also know he struggled with alcohol addiction his entire life.

It is hard to get into the mind of another person, but Timothy Browne had attempted to do just that by using a first-person voice in this historical novel. He has definitely captured the sense of Denver's skid row, Larimer Street, at the turn of the previous century. It is ironic that Larimer Street has become a trendy area in Denver attracting tourists and locals alike. And the descendant of the Sunshine Rescue Mission still lives on as the Denver Rescue Mission, albeit in a different location, on Lawrence instead of Larimer, and not far from the baseball stadium, Coors Field, where the Colorado Rockies play.

Despite his struggles with faith and addiction, and maybe partly because of them, God used Jim Goodheart to help hundreds and probably thousands of people. He could set an example of one who, by the grace of God, was saved from addiction. Following in my grandfather's footsteps I was inspired to give my life to God and was ordained 45 years ago as an Episcopal priest. I only hope I have touched a fraction of the many lives that Jim Goodheart helped.

Reverend Donald P. Goodheart
Grandson of Jim Goodheart

CALL TO ACTION

Author Timothy Browne:

Dr. Nicklaus Hart Series

Maya Hope
The Tree of Life
The Rusted Scalpel
The Gene

Literary Fiction

The Book of Andy

Please visit:
AuthorTimothyBrowne.com

You can start the Dr. Nicklaus Hart Series with
Maya Hope for free by signing up to receive updates
and information on upcoming books by Timothy

Follow Timothy on Facebook
@authortimothybrowne

An Epic Tale of Love, Faith, and World War I

LARIMER STREET

A NOVEL

TIMOTHY BROWNE

USA TODAY BEST-SELLING AUTHOR

To: Mom-Virginia Mae Goodheart Browne

ACKNOWLEDGMENTS

Writing *Larimer Street* took me right to the heart of Denver, to the edge of the Western Front in World War I, the deadly 1918 Spanish Flu pandemic, and most importantly to the lives of my great-grandparents, Jim and Ada Goodheart—the true authors of this story.

Jim's struggles and ultimate victory with his fidelity to God challenges me to continue to fight the good fight. I hope it does the same for you, my dear reader. And most of all, I pray that Jim and Ada's story fills you with hope. The kind that comes from the knowledge of God's ever-loving kindness and grace given to us, over and over and over again.

Thank you to my dear friends and editors Burney Garelick and Erin Healy for your care and love of this story. Your humor and TLC are fuel to my creative fire.

Thanks to Stefano at Peye Nymi for a beautiful cover.

Thank you to my mother, who kept letters, articles, Bibles, pictures, sermons and so much more, locked away for such a time as this. Thank you for trusting me with Jim and Ada's story.

To my beta readers and proofreaders, Julie, Lynne, David, Sarah, Michelle, Paula, and Glenn. Thank you for diving into the story and helping to flush out areas that were not clear. And mostly, I thank you for your encouragement to continue to write.

To my wife, Julie, our boys, and their families. Thank you for your constant encouragement and love. I wrote this for you and future generations...that you may know the love of the Father.

"Famed is the name of the sculptor who can
Fashion mere earth to the pattern of man.
Greater is he who can shape shattered men
Into the form of the human again."
-Unknown Poet to Jim Goodheart

ACT ONE

DEATH

October 1, 1907

I cy pellets pummeled the hospital windows, impatient for answers.

"She'll be dead by morning, more than likely," the man in the bloody scrubs said. "I'm sorry." With reverence, he removed the surgical cap from his head and held it against his heart, as if he paid his last respects at her funeral. Patches of gray stubble peppered his cheeks, and dark circles underlined his haggard eyes.

Cruel, harsh words for this man pawed at the back of my tongue. I swallowed them and glared at him in disbelief until the pungent, antiseptic smell of the hospital choked me. Nearly doubling over, I steadied myself on Ada's bed frame, then looked at her and knew what he said rang true: her face had turned white as a ghost and her body stiffened with misery. If not for her perpetual, agonizing groans, the nurses would have surely pulled the sheet over her head and transported her to the basement morgue.

"I'm afraid we've done all we can. She's now in God's hands."

The surgeon wouldn't look me in the eye. I followed his gaze to his shoes—as tired and worn as the man and covered in blood, Ada's blood.

Ada's groans intensified, crescendoing from the depths of her soul. My mind went blank, but my body echoed her pain, threatening to turn my bowels to mush.

Mush—that's how the surgeon had described Ada's insides. Her gut had twisted on itself and gone gangrenous. He'd removed yards of her small intestine and sewed the ends together. It was a new procedure, one that had little chance of working, but the only alternative to stitching her up and signing her death certificate.

My body trembled involuntarily, soaked with sweat and tears, and I clutched her bed frame to stop the room from spinning. I stared at my wife helplessly, and she answered with another loud moan.

I looked back at the surgeon. "Have any of your patients survived this surgery?"

His head shook slowly but decisively.

"There is nothing more we can do?"

I glanced at my mother-in-law standing in the corner with our son, Donny, and she returned a look of utter disdain. This was somehow my fault. Her stoic sneer—that stinking I-told-you-so sneer that said Ada should have married Jimmy from down the street; Jimmy, who became a successful lawyer—and the smell of mothballs from her ratty fur coat magnified my nausea. God, how I hated that smirk. She stared at me through angry eyes, daring me to speak, then wrapped her tattered fur coat arms around Donny: seven years old and not understanding any of it.

I frowned at the surgeon, who hadn't answered my question. Instead of speaking, he snapped his fingers at the young nurse, who pulled a syringe from her smock pocket and thrust a needle into Ada's thigh and injected a clear fluid.

"We'll make her comfortable with morphine," the surgeon said. "I have nothing more to offer..." His words trailed off. "You should go home and get some rest. You can have the funeral home pick her up in the morning."

Ada's mother spoke for the first time. "I'll arrange to have Lawry's funeral home pick up *my daughter*. They are faithful members of First Baptist. My daughter's service *will* be held at the church." Her hostile glare gave no room to argue. She would command her daughter's final hours.

She could not control our lives, and it galled her. But it never stopped her from loudly vocalizing her displeasure during our ten short years of marriage. On the day of our wedding, I overhead her complaining to Ada: "Why do you want to marry that boy? For Lord's sake, Ada, you might as well go and marry a writer or artist or musician if you prefer to live a pauper's life."

She didn't have a say in Ada falling in love with a no-good, traveling grocery salesman, a boy whose shadow seldom darkened the steps of a church, and a Scotsman to boot. But she certainly planned to take control in Ada's death.

That was okay. She could do what she wanted now.

The nurse and Ada's mother looked at me.

What were they waiting for? Curse it all to hell. I had no right to protest. Her scorn seemed to spread to the nurse, accusing me of being a lousy husband and killing her myself. Hadn't they heard the surgeon say that this sort of thing just happens? He had suggested the malady came as an act of God. The bowel can just twist, he'd said, even the ancient Egyptians recorded it, and it's as deadly now as it was back then.

I turned to Ada and knelt by her bed. Her gasping breath smelled of decay and death. I grasped her cold hand. As the end came near, I took heart knowing that whatever afterlife existed, she'd be welcomed into it with loving arms.

"Ada?"

She answered only with haunting groans as though her spirit had left already, and she no longer remained conscious of the torturous agony of her body clutching the shreds of life.

I rose to my feet and touched her lifeless and leathery face. "Ada, I'm so sorry. I love you so much. Please forgive me."

Leaning in, I pressed my lips to hers, only to be assaulted by the smell of rotting bile flowing from her mouth into mine. I wanted to spit but swallowed instead. The vile bitterness set my gut on fire, and I stumbled from the room as fast as I could.

Partway down the hall, I couldn't hold it back and let the contents of my stomach spill into an alcove. Gagging and retching, again and again, clinging to whatever would keep me upright, and then, catching my breath, I looked up. I had supported myself on a statue—a statue of Jesus. I knelt at the foot of a marble Jesus hung on the cross. He had a look of agony that matched Ada's.

"You punishing me?" I wept. "I'm sorry for all the hell I've done, but please don't take it out on her. Leave her in peace and give it to me, for God's sake."

Maybe this omniscient God knew. Perhaps my mother-in-law knew. Surely Ada did. She knew I had not been trustworthy in my thoughts or deeds.

I dropped to my knees, and my head fell into my hands. My stomach threatened to retch again. "Can I ever be faithful?"

I felt the statue's eyes bore into my soul with conviction.

"You let her live, and I'll change," I promised. "Let her live, and you can have my miserable life."

The cold tile stung my shins, and I pushed myself up. "Damn it all to hell," I muttered. "I need a drink."

2

JAIL

October 23, 1907

Excruciating anxiety rolled like thunder through my heart, and I worried it would rupture at any moment. My hands shook violently as I tried to still my pounding head, but the pain only intensified. The room spun, and I wished for death. I lay immobile and closed my eyes. My stomach wanted to heave again, but I kept still, knowing that if I moved, I would live. Something I preferred not to do.

I understood the source of the suffering and my mind wrestled with my body—the one wanting to die, the other struggling to survive.

A little hair-of-the-dog would ease my agony and settle my hangover.

"If you sonsofbitches would just give me a drink!" I croaked.

My call for aid raised a ruckus.

"Someone shut that weasel up before I reach in and strangle him myself," a nearby voice snarled.

"Give him a pistol and put us all out of our misery," another yelled.

I allowed my eyes to squint, wary of bright light, but fortunately, I lay in the shadows. Trying to open them wide, I could barely see the outline of the man behind bars in the cell next to mine. From what I could make out, he looked like a gorilla pacing in a small cage. Maybe he was the ape I had stopped from killing me by breaking a perfectly good beer mug over his noggin.

I almost grinned as glimpses of the fight flickered through my murky mind. It all came back. I'd been on a bender for weeks—long enough that time had lost all meaning. I'd run from the hospital and hit every bar in Chicago. The rage in my chest exploded with every shot of whiskey and pint of beer until my drunken mind formulated a plan to end my miserable life. I put it into effect, leaning against the bar to search the joint for the biggest brute, one I didn't stand a chance of defeating. When I saw him, I hoisted up my pants, swaggered up to him, and queried with pickled confidence, "Hey, mama's boy. How's your mum?"

He raised the brim of his tweed cap and looked at me with confusion.

I threw the first verbal blow. "Say hi to her from Jim Goodheart. My friends tell me she whinnies like a well-ridden horse."

The big man turned to me. His eyes narrowed, and he straightened his spine.

I spread my legs, thrusted my hips, and threw my arm up like I'd lassoed a wild stallion.

I can't honestly say what came next. Probably the raucous laughter of the man's companions, then his thunderous roar high above my six-foot frame, and then his huge fist smashing my cheek like a sledgehammer splitting a log.

The blow sent me across a table that crashed under my weight. The curtain fell on my conscious mind, only to rise immediately. Fully anesthetized by liquor, my brain reviewed the horrific scene. The big man leaped on top of me with his grizzly bear paws around my neck, squeezing the air from my body.

I wanted to die. God, how I wanted to die. It hit me like a punch to the gut—Ada was dead! It hurt so much. Drinking the pain away hadn't worked. The pain grew like a tumor, infecting my being with loneliness, hopelessness, and despair, unlike anything I could honestly describe.

Until that moment, I had never understood how someone could take his own life. But I now knew how it could happen —when pain overtakes you—when the pain of living is worse than the pain of dying. When you've given up on yourself. I heard the suicide demon whispering when I ran from the hospital, but now he screamed in my ear that I was better off dead.

So I surrendered. I would not fight any longer. I did not know what the afterlife held, but it had to be better than the hell I'd landed in. At thirty-six, I'd never given much thought to death or the divine. Only hacking out a living for Ada and me, keeping food on the table and a roof over our heads— scraping by with my own wits and hard work.

I looked into the eyes of my executioner. I may have even smiled, urging him to finish me off.

That was my mistake.

My assailant must have sensed my resignation, figuring it was no fun to beat a man who wouldn't fight back, and as my body went limp, he loosened his grip on my neck.

Much to my surprise, even though my mind desired death, my body fought for life. My eyes spied a beer mug on the floor within reach of my hand, my lungs gasped for breath, and my compressed vocal cords croaked out, "You stupid ass."

Before he could react, my fingers grabbed the mug's handle, swung high and fast, and brought the heavy glass down hard on the man's skull.

With a crash, a thud, and a spray of blood, I unleashed all hell.

That's the last I remembered until I woke up in jail, cold and shivering and in more pain than I've felt in my life.

If my assailant paced in the cell next to mine, I could back up to the bars and let him reach in and snuff out my miserable existence, as I had hoped he would. But my moral compass clicked in. After all, I had nothing against this guy, and I really didn't want to put his life on the line for my errant ways.

I shook my aching head to clear my mind. I was the caged animal. Worse, I had become a raging beast trapped by circumstances of my own making. If they let me out of this wretched cell, I would end my life as soon as possible. It would be for the greater good.

My sense of smell awoke, and I gagged on the combined stench of vomit, body odor, and overflowing toilets. My body screamed with pain as it twisted for comfort on the hard wooden bench I lay on. But I didn't know if I had the strength or the will to sit up.

A nightstick clanged against the bars, reverberating in my brain and jolting me upright.

"Goodheart...you better clean yourself up. Your father is here. You've made bail."

The mention of my father jerked me up from the bench. "Oh...crap."

The jailer slammed the cell block door behind him, and I ran my hand over my head. Blood and vomit matted down my hair, and one eye opened only partway. Someone had stuffed my swollen nose with tissue.

James G. Goodheart, father of twelve, brick mason, contractor, Republican—and I couldn't decide which seemed worse, US Deputy or Methodist Preacher—had come to get me.

Stink…he had made the long journey by train from Bloomington to Chicago via the C&A Railroad. This was going to be bad.

I heard his baritone voice and the cacophony of keys unlocking jail doors. What sounded like civilized banter stopped when my father and the jailer entered the cell block. That's when I heard the prisoner in the adjacent cell sneer, "Now you're getting an ass-whoopin'."

US Deputy Pastor Goodheart's boots stomped across the wooden floor and stopped in front of my cell. Somehow, my legs and spine snapped me to attention, but my head hung in defeat. I couldn't look at him.

"Jimmy, come out of the shadows and let me look at you," he demanded.

I'm not sure how my legs compelled me forward, but I stood face-to-face with the man I feared and loved equally. With my head still bowed, I raised my eyes to his.

He stared at me, pursed his lips, crossed his arms, and nodded slowly. Then he sucked in a deep breath and let it exhale slowly from his nose. The weight of his stare fell as heavy as a ton of bricks, and just as I thought my legs would buckle, he broke the silence.

"Mr. Loar came to our house three days ago. They have Ada with them."

I just nodded. I figured they'd bury her in their family plot in Bloomington.

"The Loars are taking care of *your* son."

His emphasis stung. I tried to apologize, but neither my mouth nor my brain would cooperate.

"My Lord, Jimmy, you look like death warmed over. How in the world did you get yourself like this?"

In a flash, the man went from US Deputy to Preacher to Father, a father who had failed his duty. His shoulders drooped with regret. Then he looked into my eyes and reached through the bars for my shoulders. "Son, you have eleven brothers and sisters, and your mother and I could have given any of you eight boys my name. But we held it for you. The day we christened you, your mother looked at me and said, 'James...this is the one.'"

He sucked in another long breath and blew it out. "Damn, what a mess you've made. In your thirty-six years, we have spent more time on our knees for you than all of your siblings combined." He dropped his hands from my shoulders.

I rarely heard him swear. His disappointment in me speared my heart, and I wept.

"Men are carrying furniture out of your house," he said. "There's a foreclosure note on the door."

He reached into his jacket pocket, pulled out a paper, and thrust it into my hand. "I've paid your bail and bought you a ticket to Denver. Maybe you can clean up your life with your brothers, John and Luke."

I looked at the train ticket and then at my father and finally found my voice. "I'm so sorry, Father."

He nodded, hesitated, and reached for my arm again. His eyes bore into my soul as he searched for the right words.

"Son, honor and faithfulness are gifts you give to yourself."

He withdrew his hand and walked away, but turned back. "The Loars ask that you don't try contacting Ada."

The words hit me like a locomotive, and I grabbed the bars. "What? Wait…what do you mean?"

Father stopped dead in his tracks, turned and crossed his arms. "You really don't know?"

"Know what? Father, please tell me."

He took two more steps to the exit and said over his shoulder, "She survived, you damn fool. While you've been stuck in a whiskey bottle, your wife fought for her life and won."

3

CARBOLIC ACID

November 12, 1907

No use dyin' with two bits, I decided, turning the quarter over and over between my fingers. I shivered and thrust my hands deep in my trouser pockets to keep warm from the cold. Only a quarter remained of my miserable life. It'd come time to spend it and make way in the world for a better man.

Father had escorted me to the train aimed toward Denver and made it clear that Ada and her family wanted no part of me. My wife's rejection burned worse that the money in my pocket and the desire for one last drink.

"James Goodheart," I announced to no one, "I should have been born a Macbeth."

A woman walking down the sidewalk, her parasol shielding her from the icy drizzle, glared at me.

This was my cue, I thought, bowing theatrically and dropping an octave to my stage voice. "Out, out brief candle! Life's but a walking shadow, a poor player that struts and frets his hour upon the stage and then is heard no more…"

The woman huffed at me, lifted her long skirt with one hand, stepped off the curb, and crossed the muddy street.

"It is a tale told by an idiot, full of sound and fury, signifying nothing," I called after my audience of one, as though I commanded the finest stage in Denver, surrounded by adoring fans. Shakespeare always rolled off my tongue whenever booze filled my veins. Theater was my first love, although I could never overcome my stage fright. But now that I'd decided to end my life, I felt confident and gregarious and with no fear, my heart leaped with joy.

Bowing, I peeled off my black porkpie hat and extended it to the thunderous applause that roared in my mind.

"Thank you, thank you," I shouted, waving my hat.

"Derelict!" a voice scoffed behind me.

A foot thumped my extended derrière, kicked me off the curb into the street, and my liquor-infused legs couldn't catch up to my falling torso. I ended up on my hands and knees in the middle of Larimer Street, the thoroughfare running through the heart of downtown Denver.

The lamps of a motorized roadster aimed for my head. Before I could react, the driver blasted the horn and swerved the car, missing me by a fraction, crushing the brim of my hat still in my hand. I heard the driver swear and accelerate the gasoline engine as he roared by.

I staggered to my feet, noting the rip in my trousers and the cherry-red scrape on my knee, but I suffered no pain. The whiskey had anesthetized me. I stumbled forward, nearly colliding with a team of two Clydesdales hauling a wagon of beer kegs. They pulled up short to avoid me. Their nostrils flared, and their shod hooves clipped against the newly paved street.

One horse reared, missing my chest with his mammoth hooves, making me stumble again and fall backward into a puddle of rain and horse piss. I waved my tortured hat to the man with the reins.

"Well done, young man," I declared. "I can think of no better way to depart this dreadful earth than at the mercy of my favorite ale."

"Get out of the street, you fool," the man yelled back, tightening the reins on his prancing horses.

"I've been called much worse," I hollered back, "even by my family. So let go the reins and end my miserable life, you scoundrel. The roadster missed me, so it's up to you."

The man yelled obscenities while I lay there waiting. But just as I praised the god of horses, two pairs of hands grabbed me by my arms and hefted me to my feet. I nodded at the two young men as they dragged me out of the way so the beer wagon could get through. As it passed, I rapped my knuckles against a keg.

"Awww, the sound of heaven," I crooned, trying to get my rescuers to join in the merriment.

The young men let go of my arms. I turned to them, staggered two steps, bowed again and tipped my hat. "Thanks for nothin', my fine young sirs."

They waved me off and jumped onto a passing streetcar. Sparks flashed from the electric discharge in the overhead wires, and ozone stung my nose as the extension arms snapped across a junction.

I slapped my hat against my thigh and returned it to my head, giving it a rakish turn in honor of a splendid performance. I could see the reviews: *Great actor plays miserable wretch with aplomb! Will death get his victory in the last act?*

I shivered and hugged my body as it rained. Of course. It was mid-November, with the rainy season underway. It fell harder, soaking my shoulders and bubbling the puddles on the street. I shuddered against the cold westerly wind coming from the Rocky Mountain front.

"Could be snow by mornin'," I said to a passing gentleman, who ignored me and hurried on his way.

I shrugged at his back and sighed. Why should he even acknowledge a tramp like me? I patted the bottle in the jacket pocket over my heart—my final cure remained intact after a rambunctious day of drunkenness. The black glass bottle contained carbolic acid. I'd found it in the bathroom of the flophouse where I'd rented a room two nights ago when I got to Denver. The disinfectant with a blood-red label marked with skull and crossbones had become the preferred method of offing oneself, or so the papers said. According to the article, "There is certainly nothing pleasant about the manner in which it saps the vital spark from the human body, for the agonies it inflicts are probably the most acute that a human being can endure."

It quoted a man who survived accidental ingestion of the poison. "The first feeling was similar to that induced by the application of anything extremely cold upon a delicate spot, only to be succeeded by a terrible burning sensation." The man survived only because of dumb luck. When he was sure he would die, he downed two shots of whiskey, perhaps to give himself a happy send-off. He did not know that the whiskey would neutralize the deadly liquid. His recovery prompted the government to require the label of carbolic acid to include this advice: "ANTIDOTE—Give draughts of Brandy or Whiskey; then an emetic of Wine of Ipecac or Salt and finally Epsom Salts or Castor Oil."

As much as I'd enjoy a final shot of whiskey, I would not make his mistake. I deserved every bit of the suffering and severe death. That's what my brother told me. I had thought I could make a fresh start of it in Denver, returning on my father's ticket to lay bricks with my brothers. John had bailed me out of scraps before, but I was still young and foolish when I'd moved to Denver the first time seventeen years ago.

"Now just foolish," he'd said when I showed up at his house with an empty wallet and bruised face, and he refused to give me a hand.

I looked down Larimer Street. Many of the brick buildings had John's, Luke's and my sweat in their mortar, something our father and grandfather would be proud of, carrying on the legacy that Pop and Grandpa both laid down for us as masons. But things had changed. John had changed.

All of John's youthful mercy had disappeared, and he hissed exceptionally cruel words: "After falling back into the pit of drunkenness, leaving your wife and son in Illinois, and losing all sensibility and integrity, you deserve to die. And the sooner, the better."

My oldest brother's rejection became the last straw. The time drew near.

Maybe if I had accepted the teachings of the church and the principles my father taught, I could see this end as a new beginning. But I'd never truly believed any of that nonsense I'd endured during Sunday school and long prayers of grace at the dinner table. Besides, if God existed and met me at the pearly gates, I was certain He too, would reject me. I knew where I headed, but I hoped they'd been wrong about the burning lakes of sulfur.

A goggled man riding a newfangled bicycle zipped past me. It had a gasoline motor that loudly propelled the front tire. I grabbed my chest to slow my racing heart. My life would not be stopped by anyone else. It was mine to take, and I had a plan.

Union Station stood about four blocks from Larimer

Street. I'd bypass the station and go to the railroad yard, where plenty of abandoned boxcars sat idle for me to hide in and finish my wretched life and suffering. The police had already warned me to keep "below the dead line"—to keep my head down and out of trouble. Because they were on to me, there was no use going to my final destination until after dark, when I had a smaller risk of encountering coppers. Ending up in jail again would just prolong my agony.

The ragtime chords from a piano and shouts for more libations poured out of Gahan's saloon on the corner. I wondered if a real pianist or the player piano with its scrolling paper played so elegantly.

The grip of remorse tightened around my belly, thinking of how Ada played the piano so beautifully. I'd miss that this Christmas and wondered if Ada would hear of my death—or if she'd even care.

I staggered toward the saloon, not knowing if I'd make it past the muscle-bound bouncer at the door, but I still had the quarter in my pocket and not about to let that go to waste. Another drink or two would steady my resolve and allow the night to darken.

Approaching Gahan's, I steadied my gait and straightened my spine to impersonate a fine gentleman. The wary-eyed bouncer sat on a wooden stool at the door. He slapped a leather sap from hand to hand, reminding the clientele to stay in line. The burly bouncer stood when two patrons stepped to the door. He required them to open their jackets to prove they carried no weapons.

As the bouncer sat back down, he shot a glance toward me and turned up his nose at my soiled and torn trousers. He frowned and slapped the club harder against his palm. His look let me know I wasn't acceptable clientele, so I turned away to shelter under the awning of the building next door.

How I wished for a smoke.

A man escorting a lady in a fine dress and matching parasol strolled down the sidewalk but cut a wide arc around me.

"Could you spare a cigarette?" I asked.

"Piss off, ya bum," the man scowled, and the lady averted her eyes and sniffed.

From the corner of my eye, I saw the bouncer spring from his seat. My heart leaped, thinking he aimed for me, but I breathed a sigh of relief when he entered the saloon to quell the sounds of a ruckus inside.

Now was my chance.

I brushed the rain from my shoulders, removed my hat, and stepped into the saloon. The bright lights dazed my eyes, but the room felt warm and dry and a comfort to my chilled and wet body. I moved to the right, behind the poker tables, and faded into the cigar smoke and the crowds watching the high-stakes games. A woman beside me shot me a scornful glance and covered her nose with a lace handkerchief. The rain had soaked my woolen suit, and I probably smelled like a wet dog that had rolled in a puddle of horse piss.

I winced an apology and sidestepped her, pulling my porkpie hat over my forehead to shield my face from the bouncer who now escorted a man by his collar to the front door. I'd be next if I wasn't careful. Making my way to the darkest corner of the bar, I nodded to the bald bartender with a handlebar mustache. He wiped his hands with a white towel and eyed me with caution until I produced that quarter from my pocket and spun it on the bar.

He saw I could pay and stepped close enough to hear my order, but not close enough to smell me. "What'ya have?" the paddy yelled in an Irish accent over the piano and lively crowd. *What's a man to have for his final drink?* Whiskey was my drink of choice, but a beer would last longer. The barkeep grew impatient at my hesitation and glanced toward the muscle man at the front door.

"Beer…I'll take a beer," I said and added, "please." *No need getting the bouncer involved.* I slid the quarter down the wooden bar, and he stopped it with a slap. The Irishman grabbed a mug from under the counter, topped it off until foam spilled over and slid it to me. I breathed a sigh of relief when the keep turned to other customers. But when he didn't return any change, it reminded me why I'd stopped drinking at Gahan's when I laid bricks with my brothers years ago. This high-class, two-bit saloon remained as one of the few left on Larimer. With the economy so poor, most drinking establishments had dropped to one-bit where you could get two drinks for a quarter. *Oh well, it will be dark soon.* I put my foot on the bar rail, making sure I didn't knock over the brass spittoon on the floor, and took a swig of the brew.

"Hi, darling," a sweet Irish voice came from behind. The words were wrapped in strong, sweet perfume. "Looks like you could use some TLC."

I turned to see a woman with curly red hair, wearing a yellow peasant dress cut low to show her cleavage. I averted my eyes. When she rested both arms on the bar, her breasts bulged, making them impossible to ignore.

"Aren't you a tall, dark and handsome chap? I'm thinkin' you'd make a perfect fit." She giggled and looked down between her cleavage.

I didn't understand but followed her eyes. Her ample flesh was pleasing, but I forced my eyes from her chest to her face. Her mouth opened, and she smiled. To my surprise, she had a full set of teeth. Then I saw her kind blue eyes.

"See anything you like?" she teased. "I might have to bed you for free with that fetchin' look you got goin' on."

I laughed and sipped my beer. "You're a mighty pretty lady."

"Oh, aren't you the charmer…most folks don't call me a lady." She laughed. "Why don't ya let me take some of that stress off your face." She moved closer but stepped back immediately. "Oh darlin'." She wrinkled her nose. "We'd needin' to get you a bath 'fore we do anything."

"Yeah, sorry," I said, looking into my beer. "Little down on my luck."

"Well, ol' Pixie here n'ver seen no layer of filth that a hot bath can't fix. Only cost you a buck," she said, surveying my sorry person from head to foot. "Tell you what. I'll throw the bath in for free." She stepped back to me and grabbed my jacket to make me look at her.

When she grabbed my jacket, her hand must have brushed the bottle of carbolic acid, because she let go and stepped back. "Hey, mister, you know the rules. No other moonshine in here 'sides what you pay for." She shot a glance toward the bouncer.

"It's not booze," I protested.

"Prove it, or I'm callin' Lance over."

"Pixie, or whatever your proper name is, you don't want to know."

She started toward the front door, but I put out my arm to block her path. "Okay, okay…please," I pled.

She stopped, turned, crossed her arms, and fixed her blue eyes on me, giving me one last chance. I took the bottle from my jacket and held it out so only she could see the label.

Pixie's shoulders dropped, and her attitude softened. "Oh, darlin', you don't want to do that." She pushed the bottle deep into my pocket. Ignoring my smell and depravity, she reached for my face and held my cheek. "I've served more last drinks than I want to know about." I saw sadness in her eyes. "Please don't be the next."

She'd extended the first bit of kindness I had in months, and I didn't know how to react. I took my mug and drained my beer.

"There's no amount of bad luck that's worth doin' that." She moved to catch my gaze. "Let ol' Pixie getcha another beer and we can talk about it." She gestured to the barkeep, but I tried waving him off. I had no money. I had no one— not my wife or my son, not my brothers—I had no job. I'd lost it all.

"Sean, pour the man another," she said and slid the mug down the bar with ease.

The barkeep stopped the glass. "You got more money?" he asked, looking at me warily.

I shook my head and looked at Pixie. I followed her eyes to the bouncer making his way toward me.

"Oh, hell," she said and grabbed me by the jacket. "Don't you go an' do it."

The bouncer's meaty hands gripped my collar. "Come on, ya arse. I'd figured you'd snuck in."

"Lance, no!" Pixie shouted. She put out her hand to stop him.

Before the bouncer dragged me out, Pixie touched my shoulders and looked at me with those kind blue eyes. Then she brought her face to my ear. "It's Mary MacDougall," she whispered. "Be a good bloke for Mary, won't you?" She kissed my cheek.

4

DARK NIGHT OF THE SOUL

I swear my feet never touched the floor of Gahan's bar. Somehow, within seconds, I found myself sprawled head-first on the cold, hard, wet surface of Larimer Street and it all went black.

When I came to, I had no idea how long I'd been lying there, but my teeth were chattering, and I shivered, colder than I'd ever been in my life. My head throbbed like the bouncer split it in two. I touched my face and looked at my hand, awash with blood. As I wiped it on my sleeve, the sight and smell of blood gave me to understand I'd survived, and I hated that. It wasn't my plan.

With angry adrenaline, I pushed myself up to all fours, wincing as the cold steel of the streetcar rail stung my hands. If the trolley had still been running, I'd be dead. I wondered why death did not come for me. It seemed I would have to do it myself. I patted my jacket, searching for the weapon that would do me in, and found the bottle of poison in my pocket. Half expecting it to be smashed, I sighed with relief that this elixir had survived.

I took stock of my position, glancing around warily. The night had grown dark, shrouding the street lights in a heavy mist. Traffic had all but disappeared except for a lone motorist or two. A commotion stirred at the corner.

"Oh, bloody hell. The coppers," I muttered.

Two street patrolmen confronted a drunk, trying to confiscate a parcel that probably concealed a jug of whiskey. One cop snatched the bag and sent it flying into a trash can. Indeed, it held a bottle that shattered the silent night.

I mustered all the strength left in my body to stagger to my feet, no longer sure if the split in my head made me woozy or the fact that I'd been drinking for the last three days and couldn't remember my last meal. Either could contribute to my unsteadiness. Even a man facing the green mile gets a decent meal. But too late for food, and my journey less than a mile—four blocks up Larimer and then north, four or five more blocks to the rail yard—I aimed my feet in that direction, away from the cops. At last, the final act had arrived. Alone in the boxcar, I'd drink the deadly poison and enter the great unknown.

The drizzle turned to rain. I swiped my bloody brow and wondered what men on death row thought. Were they filled with remorse and regret for the things they'd done? Or were they numb to the reality that their life neared the end? I fell somewhere in between regret and numbness. Even though I had murdered no one, my demons tortured me just the same. My life didn't amount to a capital crime. I'd just drunk it away, losing all that I'd worked for and all that I held dear.

I glanced over my shoulder, stepped up to the curb and onto the sidewalk. Maybe the mist concealed them, or perhaps they'd turned around, but the police were no longer in sight. I pulled my jacket tight over my chest. It helped little, and I shivered against the chill.

"Shoot," I scolded myself, "I lost my hat." My head ached from the cold, but it was more than that. My son loved that hat. Little Donny would pull it over his seven-year-old head, so it almost covered his eyes, grinning from ear to ear. He got that joyful smile from his mother. I pictured Ada sitting next to Donny, playing peek-a-boo, raising and lowering the brim of the hat. It had taken Ada a while to get used to that hat. She'd hated it at first; she'd wanted me to buy a more conserv-ative fedora. "For heaven's sake, a bowler would even be better than a porkpie," she'd scolded.

Maybe the universe thought me worse than a murderer. I'd abandoned my family. By the time I learned Ada lived, I'd lost my job, they'd hauled my furniture away, and a foreclo-sure notice hung on the front door of my house. I tried not to remember the look that my mother-in-law shot me as she stomped her foot and cursed the day I was born. They would all be glad to see the end of me. But what about Donny? Would he understand? Would he forgive me for what I was about to do?

I passed a saloon and paused to look inside. Only three patrons hunched over their drinks in the dark and dingy tavern. "Yup, fellers, better get it while you can," I called. The barkeep glared at me with a look that said there'd be no drinks on the house, and I wasn't welcome. Probably that bouncer from Gahan's had spread the word.

I trudged on, and with each step, my legs grew heavier. I looked at the street signs. EIGHTEENTH and LARIMER. One more block to go until I'd turn north up Nineteenth. I reached for my head; maybe if I kept bleeding, the poison would be unnecessary. A dark curtain slowly fell over my consciousness.

I stepped off the curb and fell on my ass. Maybe I'd just rest a spell—so tired now. I lifted my foot to empty my shoe that had filled with rainwater when I noticed a hole worn clear through the leather sole.

Alcoholic bile spewed out of my mouth, and I fell against the sidewalk. So dizzy, I couldn't sit up, so I rolled onto my side, resting my head against the base of a lamp post—down for the count. What's more, I'd let down everyone in my life, most of all my Christian father. I hoped Pop would never hear the details of my demise. Just a year ago he'd told me that, while he took pride in my achievements as a salesman, he wished I'd grow closer to God.

"God," I scoffed. "That's a good one." Even if God existed, I was sure He, too, had abandoned me.

An intolerable sense of self-disgust flooded me. Yet the angst of dying warred with the torment of living. I looked at my hands. They no longer seemed a part of me. I closed my eyes and inhaled and exhaled.

I tried surveying my senses. My repulsive odor—a mixture of wet wool, horse excrement, and vomit—faded. Too tired to open my eyes, I couldn't see. I didn't feel the cold but instead felt a curious warmth. If death knocked, I welcomed it.

But I could still hear. I'd heard this before. What was it? It seemed to come from miles away—swelling and fading. I tried to capture the familiarity. I got it—the rhythmic plunking of the keys. Had I ended up back at Gahan's? I licked my lips, but the melody roused something deeper than thirst for drink.

I kept listening. The sound drifted in, softer than Gahan's player piano. It had an airiness…a lightness, a memory…

Faces floated through my mind like clouds of smoke from my father's pipe—my father's face, Donny's, Ada's, and my mother's. My mother mopped the fever of rubella from my face with a cool cloth—and she sang to me…but that was a long, long time ago. Maybe I stood on the staircase to heaven, and my mother had come to take me to the afterlife. Her voice buoyed my spirit.

Then she stopped, and I saw Ada tickling the keys. She turned to me, smiled, and sang:

"Are we weak and heavy-laden,
Cumbered with a load of care?
Precious Savior, still our refuge—
Take it to the Lord in prayer."

She played louder and encouraged me to sing along, so I complied.

"What a Friend we have in Jesus,
All our sins and griefs to bear."

5

RESCUE

"Boss, open your eyes."

The singing had stopped. I heard the rough command. Is that you, God? Wait, but He was boss, not I. Swirling in the ether of alcohol and sweet memories, I couldn't tear myself away. In my barely conscious coma of whiskey and ale, I thought I'd passed through the gates of hell. I stayed on my side waiting, willing my senses to scout it out. The stench of rotten-egg, burning sulfur hadn't reached my nose. I didn't hear agonizing screams of damnation and torture. But I heard that request again.

"Boss, open your eyes," it pleaded.

I studied the sound. The voice sounded non-threatening. Had someone else joined me in this boxcar? I couldn't remember the last few moments of my life. I must have made my way to the loneliness of the train, but try as my mind did, I couldn't remember putting the black bottle of carbolic acid to my lips and swallowing. What if my father was right all along and there was a God to meet me in the afterlife? What if, through some divine mistake or the prayers of my wife and family, I'd made it to heaven?

"Boss?" the voice repeated.

The call came soothing and gentle. It floated between my ears. It sounded almost joyous.

With my eyelids clamped tight, I strained to part them. The vague light from the lamp post veiled the apparition hovering above me, like an angel or a shadow.

"Where...?" I uttered through cracked lips and parched throat. The carbolic acid must have burned my mouth when I swallowed it.

The apparition put a huge hand behind my head, tipped it up, and put a tin cup to my lips. I swallowed reflexively. The cool water soothed the back of my throat.

The vision moved back, so it appeared as an outline of a human.

"Who are you?" I croaked, straining to define its features. When I could make out a face, my jaw dropped, and I pulled back in shock. Not only was this human smiling, it had white teeth framed in black skin.

"You look as if you've seen a ghost," he said.

"Michael? Gabriel?" I asked in all sincerity.

"No," he chuckled.

"Je...Jesus?" My teeth chattered.

He guffawed with a wide-mouthed laugh. "No wonder you look so surprised," he said. "A black Jesus! That might even surprise me." He laughed even harder. "But if you want to meet Jesus, you'll have to step inside."

My mind swirled in confusion. I looked around in the darkness and it surprised me to discover that I remained on Larimer Street. It still smelled of sewage and urine, and I was still alive. I couldn't do anything right.

"We need to get you inside, or you'll be froze and stiff by

mornin'."

He eased my body into a sitting position. My head pounded. I tried to speak, but my teeth chattered so hard I couldn't get a word out.

Studying this apparition, I decided he really was a man— an elderly black man. I heard him say he would get me inside. I tried to protest, but without effort, he put his arms under my legs and back and lifted me, grinning all the time. He smelled of tobacco and smoke, and his body radiated heat. I shook with cold and clung to his warmth.

"You're near hypothermic, Boss. We gotta getcha warmed up," he said, and carried me across a threshold into a bright room. My eyes blinked, adjusting to the light. When I could see clearly, I could tell this was no flophouse or saloon. It seemed more like a meeting place with rows of chairs, only a third of them filled with people.

The black man set me down gently on a folding chair in the back of the room. He found a couple of blankets and wrapped one around my shoulders and the other around my trembling legs.

"We're gonna need to getcha out of those wet clothes. You need a bath and a hot meal, but for now, let me fetch a cup of hot coffee. Then you get the pleasure of listening to Reverend Driver."

Reverend? What kind of afterlife hell had I fallen into? I didn't need no reverend. My eyes squinted against the bright light, and my body shook uncontrollably. No one else in the room paid me much attention or even seemed to care. To tell the truth, they all looked as bad as I did, ragged men down on their luck and wanting to die.

The black man returned with a smile and a cup of steaming coffee. He extended it to me, but my outreached hand trembled.

"That won't do." He pulled the cup back. "You'd just go and spill it all over yourself and get some nasty burns."

He sat in the adjacent chair, lifted the cup to my lips with one hand, and steadied my head with the other.

The coffee burned the roof of my mouth and the back of my throat, but I didn't care and begged for more. It tasted sweet, like it had three lumps of sugar the way I liked it. I drank greedily, craving the warmth and the fuel.

As soon as my hands had thawed, I grasped the cup. That's when I noticed the black man's hand. The first two fingers of his right hand were missing and a nasty scar took their place. But the gruesome sight didn't stop me from guzzling the coffee.

"Boss, don't you go and drink that cup clean," he warned. "We got plenty where this came from, and you do yourself no good replacing the whiskey in your blood too fast." He laughed.

I must have had enough presence of mind to know he was right, and I lowered the cup to my lap. I wanted to ask about his fingers when a short man in a black suit stepped up to a wooden podium in front. The man cleared his throat.

"That's Reverend Driver," my rescuer whispered and adjusted the blanket around my shoulders.

"I want to talk with you tonight," the Reverend began, "about the greatest sinner the world has ever known, the chief of sinners, the Apostle Paul. Paul had been given authority to take the Christians and cast them into prison and torture them as he chose. He was present when Stephen was stoned to death and stood by and sanctioned every movement of those who were stoning him. Paul was a man who exercised authority. He was a politician. He was well educated. He had all the worldly prosperity that man can long for. He wasn't in need of a meal or a place to sleep."

The Reverend adjusted his wire-rimmed glasses and examined his audience. I surveyed them as well. They didn't look like they paid much attention, with most slumped in their chairs, fast asleep.

The Reverend was not put off and continued. "This man, Saul of Tarsus, whom we now know as the Apostle Paul, was on his way to Damascus," he said, "with letters in his pocket empowering him to bind and persecute any and all Christians, whether they were men or women, and bring them to Jerusalem. As he journeyed along the road and came in sight of the city of Damascus, suddenly there shined round about him a light from heaven, causing him to fall to the ground." The Reverend straightened his spine and looked up from his notes. "Oh, the brilliance of God's love is so great that it will shine into the hardest and blackest heart and brighten it up!" He looked back at his notes. "And the voice of the Lord spoke to Saul, saying, 'Saul, Saul, why persecutes thou me? It is hard for thee to kick against the pricks.'"

I looked at my rescuer with confusion. Where was I? What was this place? Who were these people?

The black man misunderstood my look. "What 'kick against the pricks' means is this," he explained. "A farmer uses a pointed spear to prod oxen when plowing. If the oxen kicks at the goad, it drives the spear point deeper into its flesh…the more an ox rebels, the more it suffers."

My questions would have to wait. I nodded, finished the rest of the now warm coffee, and looked back at the man in the black suit, who continued to speak.

"And Saul said, trembling, 'Who art thou?' and the voice said, 'I am Jesus who thou persecutes. Arise and go into the city.'"

The Reverend cleared his throat and looked directly at me. I sat up straight and locked eyes with him as he spoke.

"Although the sinner is wallowing in crime and down to the lowest depths, it is only the voice of God when He speaks to the sinner's heart, that can say, 'Arise, thy sins be forgiven thee.' Now then, you may be a great sinner, you may have committed all the sins that are on the calendar and known to man—murder, adultery, robbery and the rest of the sins that the world looks at, from its mortal eye, as most horrible…but you cannot be a greater sinner than the chief. Paul was the chief of sinners, and the Lord saved him. So, there is great hope in this salvation for all who will accept."

I tried looking away, but the Reverend's stare held my eyes.

"There was a slave named Onesimus who became disobedient and ran away from his master, Philemon," the Reverend continued. "Philemon was an old business partner of Paul's. Onesimus came to Rome, probably staggering around the streets of the city with no money in his pocket or food to satisfy his hunger. Coming across Paul, Onesimus told him his history and how he had run away from his master, Philemon. Paul told Onesimus, 'Now, my brother, you can't lead a good life until you make all things right so far as it lieth within you. I am going to send you back with a letter to my beloved partner, Philemon, asking him to release you.' Onesimus put the letter in his pocket and went back to his master, expecting to be locked up, but Paul said another thing in this letter: 'If thou count me, therefore, a partner, receive Onesimus as myself. If he hath wronged thee, or oweth thee ought, put that on mine account.'"

The Reverend stepped from behind the podium with his Bible in his hand and took a step toward his audience.

"Now isn't that a picture of what Jesus Christ does for us?" he whispered with intimacy to make sure we understood. Then he spoke louder. "He took upon himself our sins, and bore them for us, and He, when enduring the agony of the cross, as He 'poured out His soul unto death' said, 'Father forgive them, for they know not what they do. If they owe thee ought, oh, Heavenly Father; if thou counts me worthy as thou only begotten Son, though many their sins may be, place them on my account, and let them go free.'"

The man took another step forward, stood ramrod erect, stretched his arms straight out from his sides, and formed a crucifix. With his Bible clutched in one hand, he intoned, "Jesus is saying those very words tonight."

The Reverend continued to speak, but I stopped listening and put my face in my hands. How does a man fall into such a deep pit as I had found myself? What a wretched man I'd become. Images of home wound through my mind—Christmas, Thanksgiving—such joy and happiness. I cursed alcohol. My love of drink was the root of my destruction. How many times had I landed in the slammer, drunk and disobedient? It had cost me everything, especially my family. My body shook under the weight of my sins.

Ada and Donny…how I loved them.

I wanted to curse out loud with remorse and pain, but the words wouldn't leave my mouth. Did I truly want to die or just be done with the pain? Mother and Father preached that God wooed the repentant soul, but I quickly learned I couldn't keep the long list of rules. I wished God might have mercy upon me. The alcohol numbed the pain, but never took it away…a poisonous cure.

I didn't know what to do, so I dropped my hands and looked up in despair.

The Reverend had returned to the podium. "I want to ask you one thing—what if the next few years bring no more to you than the last few have? I know you are suffering, but you have gone no farther down in sin than I have gone. Some of you have never gone so far. Perhaps you never will. Perhaps you will have to go farther. Maybe you will have to lose your arms, your eyes, everything before you come to yourself. But tonight, I bring you a message out of God's Word that you can be free in the twinkling of an eye. Up to this time, you haven't made the world a much better place by living in it. If everyone lived as you have, it wouldn't be safe for humanity to be out on the streets, day or night."

"Amen," the black man shouted and laughed.

"Maybe this is a picture of you." The Reverend looked at me. "But that can change right now. I know in that soul of yours, many of you can hear the voice of Jesus, saying, 'Follow me.' You can hear His voice saying, 'I will be with you when you walk through the valley of the shadow of death. I have been to see the Father, and if you owe Him ought, He has placed that upon my account. Thou shalt go free.'"

He put down his Bible, stepped from the podium, and raised his arms. "Come forward and be free," he whispered, and when no one stirred, he raised his voice. "Come forward and be free!"

Growing up, I only knew staunch legalism of God's acceptance—clean up first and then you might be acceptable to the Lord. This new message of grace grated across my familial beliefs. My mind had no intention of urging me forward, but my heart had other ideas, making my legs stand and walk. When I'd walked halfway to the Reverend, my mind started screaming to sit back down. But my body couldn't stop. I had to go forward. The only other course pointed down, and I couldn't go much farther in that direction.

The man in black smiled like a proud father and welcomed me with a long embrace. "Bless you, my son."

My knees gave way, and I collapsed.

6

DELIRIUM

My body made its way through delirium with caution. My ears rang with a shrill buzz, and my brain swam in a tsunami of confusion. My neck seeped with sweat. My breath came slowly. Every muscle in my body ached, even the hair on my head hurt.

My mind slowly came to its senses. I still didn't know what had happened to me. Whether I was alive or dead. Where the hell had I landed? Nothing made sense. My heart pounded with the ferocity of a freight train. My body seemed frozen and immovable. I panicked—what if they'd buried me alive? I tried to yell, but my voice didn't work.

My God, help me! What kind of terrible hell had I fallen into? The buzzing in my ears grew louder. Dark thoughts crowded my mind. Everything erupted too loud and shined too bright. I tried to raise my hands to cover my face, but my arms wouldn't move.

I panted hard, like a wolf that had lost its prey, and waves of nausea swelled up my throat, making me gag and spit up bile. The vile mixture slopped over the edge of a bed. "Oh God," I moaned and wiped my face on the sheet.

A sheet, a bed…I'm in a bed. Ada died in a bed. I'm dead. I wailed and struggled to move.

Then my ears took charge, awakening my consciousness to a song.

"Swing low, sweet chariot. Coming for to carry me home…"

It came rhythmic and haunting and soothing. I lay my head back, closed my eyes, and listened. Ada didn't die. She'd survived. Father told me. Ada had returned to her parents' home. I wanted to go home. The song began again. I understood that the home in the song wasn't a house with a fire in the hearth and supper on the table. Home was heaven. The song brought healing.

Until the singer sang the song again and again, over and over, like one of Donny's wind-up toys. I gritted my teeth. My head throbbed and my eyeballs ached. Finally, I couldn't stand one more refrain, and my eyes popped open. I raised my head enough to see the back of a large black man across the room. The singing came from him, and he swayed to the song and danced with a mop, slopping its wet fibers back and forth across the floor.

I tried to yell at him to stop. My vocal cords could only moan, but it made the man turn and smile.

"Look who's back from the dead," he said, leaning his mop against a set of bunk beds and walking toward me. I watched his eyes trace the stream of green bile from the bed to the floor. "And makin' more work for an old man."

"Sorry about that…I thought I'd died," I rasped, finally able to make words.

"Oh, you lost your life all right." The man laughed loudly,

making my ears buzz and my belly ache with fire. He shook his head. "That is fo'sho. Mmmm, mmm, mmm."

I couldn't understand his joy at my travail and tried to move my legs off the bed. He put his hands under my arms and pulled me to a sitting position. That's when I saw that two fingers were missing from his hand, and in their stead lay a heavy pink keloid. My brain clicked in. I knew this man. He'd given me coffee.

"You're the man that brought me in…"

I wondered if I should thank him. Instead, I looked around the room. Bunk beds, neatly made with gray wool blankets and pillows, crowded the space. "Where am I?"

"Welcome to Living Waters Mission," the man said, stepping back and bowing like a player introducing a second act.

Mission? I frowned. What did that mean? I scrutinized the room. All the beds were bunk beds except the one I occupied. "Whose bed is this?"

"That'd be mine. We were completely full, but for Lord's sake, we couldn't have you sleepin' on the floor. We couldn't leave you out to freeze to death neither."

"Where'd you sleep?" I asked warily, hoping we hadn't shared this bed.

"On the floor. At least they're clean. I make sure of that," he said without rancor. I searched his eyes. They were dark, rimmed with gray, but kind and not disapproving. The whites of his eyes had yellowed with time. His head was bald except for scruffs of gray on each side that flowed down to his cheeks in thin patches of black and gray stubble that couldn't hide severely pockmarked skin. Deep crevices chiseled his brow, and crow's feet tracked a torturous life.

He wore a clean, white button-down shirt with the top three buttons undone. The wrinkled shirt had never seen a hot iron. He wore no undershirt and small dark rings, like cigarette burns, marred his hairless chest.

When I realized he watched me stare him down, I tried to look away. But instead of anger, his face broke into a broad smile, displaying the white teeth I had seen before. But now I saw he lacked a few.

My head spun, and my mind reeled with confusion. My consciousness still tried putting the pieces together. Images from Gahan's clicked through my mind…a woman…with red hair…beautiful red hair. She smiled and treated me kindly. Who was she? She'd disappeared, and I flew through the air and landed on the cold, wet street.

I remembered the carbolic acid and felt for my front breast pocket where I'd secured the bottle. There was no bottle or pocket in the gray cotton clothes I wore.

I glanced back at the black man. "Am I in jail?"

His head fell back, and he roared with laughter.

I panicked. I thought I'd gone mad. "Is this an asylum? Please let it be prison."

With a huge grin, the man raised his arm and declaimed, "All at once the prison doors flew open, and everyone's chains came loose." He put his hands on his hips and looked at me cockeyed. "You a funny man, James Goodheart," he said. "You gonna fit right in."

I didn't know what he meant or how he knew my name, but his laughter and nonsense made my head pound. I fell back on the bed as if someone had knocked me out cold. Another fleeting image clicked…heavyweight boxing champion Tommy Burns using my head for a punching bag. No, not Tommy Burns. My brothers, John and Luke, teaching me to box and punching me silly until Mother stopped them.

The scene in my mind changed. A man in a black suit

smiled at me. The Reverend? No. Maybe the mortician that buried my younger sister when I was ten.

I inadvertently put my hands to my face. To my surprise, they didn't stink. They were clean. They smelled of roses, like the Pear's-brand soap Ada loved so much. Ada. What had I done? My shoulders slumped under the weight of my guilt— abandoning my wife and son. Tears rolled down my cheeks and wet my clean hands. This was clearly no dream. I sat up with a start. "My God, what have I done?"

Large, warm hands grasped my shoulders. "James, we gotta get you something to eat. The death of the ego is painful. You got a fight ahead of you."

I looked into the man's eyes for clues and wished he'd stop talking nonsense.

"Besides, no more rest for the weary. Everyone's gotta pull their weight 'round here."

I stretched my neck and tossed my head from side to side as though I had just awakened from a nightmare. "What day is it?"

"It's the Lord's day," the black man almost sang. "And you're working the front door tonight."

"Sunday?" I said, trying to remember when I'd arrived in Denver.

I pushed my hair back and only then realized how badly my hands were shaking. I held them out in front of my eyes. The more I tried to steady them, the more they quaked.

"Them be the alcohol tremors," the black man explained. "You've been out for three days. Seen 'em kill a lesser man. Now get up so I can finish my job."

He took my arm, wrapped it around his shoulder, and hefted me to standing. I wasn't sure my legs would support me, but he braced my weight and helped me take a few steps.

Once I steadied myself, I straightened my spine and

looked at the scarred face of the old black man. I remembered
the keloids where his fingers used to be. "You the one that
cleaned me up?"

He just smiled back.

"Thank you," I said, meaning it.

"Sometimes a fella just needs a break." He shrugged.
"Now it's time to pass it on."

I took another step, but my knees buckled, my stomach
rumbled, and bile came up and out again. I would have
collapsed if he hadn't caught me.

"There you go again, making a mess for me." He shook
his head, still in good humor. "Mmmm, mmm…I swear God
pulled you out of a mighty deep pit, James."

I wiped my mouth with my sleeve and steadied my
resolve not only to stay upright but to change my life. Tentatively, I took five steps forward without falling.

"Um," I said, "how come you know my name? What do I
call you?"

"Joseph, Joseph Jackson," he replied. "Some people call
me Joe, and some people call me Jackson…you can call me
anything, but don't call me late for dinner." He laughed at his
own joke.

He hadn't answered my first question, but I decided it
could wait. I licked my dry lips. "Joe," I asked, "you think I
could have some water?"

7

SALVATION

Sunday - November 17, 1907

C hicken-neck soup, a slice of fresh bread, a cup of coffee —the best medicine a guy could have in my condition. Even the company wasn't bad. Joe introduced me to the staff as I joined them at the table. Only one man shook my hand while the others just nodded and went back to slurping their soup. I didn't think they were rude, so much as preferred to keep to themselves. I understood the heavy dose of oppression that ruled the room and filtered through like strong body odor. Quiet worked for me. I sipped my coffee and felt better.

Joe excused me from doing dishes that first day. Instead, he took me outside and sat me on a wooden stool beside the front door.

"All you need to do is welcome people inside," he told me and patted my shoulder.

"Uh…" was all I thought to say.

"No worries, James. Everybody pulls his weight, like I

told you. Invite the folks inside. Tell 'em soup's served promptly at noon, and Reverend Driver preaches after that."

He started back inside, but not before flashing me a broad smile. "I'm glad you're here, James. You're a new man now." He half saluted me with his two good fingers and smiled again.

I felt better, but I sure as hell didn't feel like a new man. My legs ached as though I'd walked to Denver all the way from Bloomington. My head reeled as if someone had whacked me with a two-by-four, and my hands wouldn't stop shaking. I tucked them under my armpits to keep them still and warm. I shivered in the cold, brisk air.

"Sure wish I had my hat," I said to a passing gentleman wearing a fedora and dressed in an elegant suit. He ignored me.

When my old wool suit had dried, I'd gladly shed the gray prison garb and put on my clothes. It didn't matter they smelled of horse piss, and my blood stained them. They reminded me I existed one short step from Larimer's gutter, and I'd better mind my p's and q's.

"I'm supposed to sit here and welcome people in," I said to no one. "Is that what he said? Those are my instructions? But how can I do that when I don't even know what this place is?"

I looked behind me at the window near the door. I saw large letters painted in blue, peeling and faded. LIVING WATERS MISSION. Underneath in smaller letters it read, All Are Welcome.

"What in the world does that mean?" I exclaimed.

A passing streetcar grabbed my attention as a gaggle of young hooligans climbed onto the back of the trolley, pulled the electric extension arm from the overhead wire, and brought the car to a screeching halt. A fat man with an even fatter cigar lumbered from the driver's seat, yelling obscenities at the boys, who yelled back and taunted him with fists. One dropped his trousers and flashed him a moon.

The driver grumbled and walked to the back of the street-car. With his attention focused on the overhead wires, he almost slipped in a pile of horse dung. He caught himself, but I heard the squish from my stool.

"Sonovabitch," the man fumed and threw his cigar down in rage, causing it to erupt into a shower of sparks and ash. He glanced at his shoe but kept walking, shaking his leg like a wet cat, which made the boys roar with laughter. "Rotten urchins," the driver snarled.

Finally, he pulled on the rope hanging from the extension arm and reattached the coupler to the wire with a snap and a spark. He returned to his seat, and the streetcar went on its way. I watched its journey as it passed the Windsor Hotel across the street and continued west down Larimer.

I sat up straight and sucked in the cold, fresh air. Then gazed at the Rocky Mountains off in the distance, topped with glistening snow, towering like guardians thrust into the brilliant blue, mile-high sky. I shivered. No wonder it was so cold today; the wind slid off the Front Range, and I couldn't see a single cloud from my stool. I wished this mission, or whatever it was, sat on the south side of the street where the sun warmed the bricks. But typical of Denver's weather, in a matter of minutes it could go from cold as the North Pole to warm enough to shed your jacket.

Automobiles and horse-drawn wagons maneuvered for position on Larimer, dodging men and women crisscrossing the street. I laughed to myself, recalling Henry Ford's quote about his soon-to-be-released Model T, which people were calling a Tin Lizzie. When questioned about his new mode of transportation, Ford said, "If I had asked people what they wanted, they would have said faster horses." I liked Ford and knew the automobile was here to stay, but I found it hard to imagine a world without horses. Although it seemed to happen right under our noses. A few of the new automobiles looked like someone had cut the horses apart from the buggy, and the buggy moved by magic. Others were unimaginable creations from the future, with fancy designs of brass and steel, shiny and polished and fit for royalty.

The street clock struck eleven chimes, and I stretched my neck to clear my head. I'd read in the Bloomington newspaper about the Russian scientist Pavlov and his dogs. When Pavlov rang a bell, the dogs came running. When the street clock struck, people came running—toward me! I braced myself. What had Joe said? That I needed to welcome everyone? I felt like a welcome mat about to be trampled and clung to my stool. But before things got out of hand, the surging mob turned into an orderly line outside the Living Waters Mission.

A passage from John Donne tripped off my tongue.

"Perchance he for whom this bell tolls may be so ill, as that he knows not it tolls for him; and perchance I may think myself so much better than I am, as that they who are about me, and see my state, may have caused it to toll for me, and I know not."

I regarded the man who had beaten the crowd to the front of the line, hoping for applause, but he made no acknowledgment of my performance. He looked Indian.

"That's okay." I grinned. "That's the usual reaction I get from my audiences." Still no response. Maybe he didn't speak English. I'd never been this close to an Indian fella. His feet were bare, and his torn canvas trousers smelled of urine, and his breath stank of cheap whiskey. His tattered shirt hung from his skeletal frame. But if the cold affected him, he didn't acknowledge it.

I shuddered, not with cold so much, as with guilt. As sorry as I'd felt for myself the last month, the pathetic specimen standing before me made me so ashamed that I wanted to run. Why this man hadn't died of starvation or hypothermia was beyond me.

My brain begged for alcohol.

A firm, warm hand grabbed my shoulder. "Hey, boss, you did pretty well, I'd figure. Look at all these fellas you bringin' in. Even got 'em all lined up and orderly."

I turned to see Joseph smiling at me, fighting back a Cheshire Cat grin.

As if on cue, I raised my voice and recited, "'Please would you tell me,' said Alice, a little timidly, for she was not quite sure whether it was good manners for her to speak first, 'why your cat grins like that?'"

But Joseph's grin faded, and he cocked his head at me like alcohol withdrawal affected my state of mind.

"It's from a play we did in high school," I explained sheepishly. "*Alice in Wonderland.*"

His smile returned. "You an actor or something?"

His question filled me with cynicism and remorse. "No… no. Always wanted to be one though."

"Well, looks like you got quite the audience here," Joe said, waving his arm down a line of men that stretched around the corner.

That's when it hit me—the clock had struck eleven chimes —almost noon. Lunchtime. That's why these men waited in line. Here I was, so full of myself I didn't get it until now. I felt I should apologize.

Instead I asked Joe, "You feed all these men?"

"Lunch and dinner."

"Where'd they come from? Who are they?"

Joe smiled his toothy grin. "They are me and you…lots of

heartache in this group, mmm, mmm, mmm. Just like you and me. Been this way in Denver since the silver crash of '93. Hard twenty years, that's fo'sho."

"1893," I repeated. I lived in Denver before that, working with my brothers in the heyday of a building boom that had ended. No wonder my brother John sulked in such a foul mood.

A burly man with a large mustache and cowboy hat who elbowed his way to the front of the line interrupted my thoughts. He shouted loud enough to make me jump.

"Why's the injun going first?"

The men in line remained still and silent. Joseph's smile disappeared and the muscles in his neck tightened.

"You know, what I need right now is some General Custer toilet paper," the cowboy yelled, egging the men to join his taunt. But no one moved or spoke.

"Yeah, General Custer toilet paper takes no crap off any redskin." He roared with laughter and poked the man behind the Indian. "Oh, come on, that's funny."

I didn't know Joseph's age. I figured seventy, but I'd never seen an old man move so fast with such determination and force. One minute, he stood next to me. The next minute he had the cowboy by the scruff of his neck, and with super-human strength, hurled him into the street, where he skidded through fresh piles of horse poop.

"Anyone else need a lesson in civility?" With veins popping out on his forehead, Joseph turned to the men in line. They stood up straight and looked at him with fear and gratitude.

The cowboy picked himself up and huffed off, endeavoring to have the last word. "You injun-lovin' son of a whore."

"You come back when you've learned some manners," Joseph replied, dusting his hands.

In the five steps to the door, Joseph transformed back to his tranquil self and smiled at me. "Just givin' him the lovin' hand of Jesus." He laughed. "He'll be back for some humble pie when he's hungry enough. Seen it all the time."

I nodded, still astonished at his strength.

The Indian spoke for the first time. "Thank you. You take one like me here?"

Joseph smiled at him.

I couldn't take my eyes off Joseph. I'd never seen a man go from humor to rage to compassion in a tick of the clock.

"Oh yes. You are welcome here," he told the man.

"What cost? No money have," the Indian murmured, not looking at us.

Joseph laughed. "It'll cost you nothing. Oh, but it's gonna cost you everything." He patted the Indian's shoulder and went inside.

The black man seemed to talk in more riddles than I did. I just shrugged at the perplexed Indian, who started to step away from the line. I gently blocked his departure with my arm. "Stay put," I said. "What he meant was it'll cost you an ear-beating." I smiled, not sure he caught my meaning, but pretty sure he understood they would feed him.

I looked down the line, and no one met my eyes. These men were lost in hopelessness, beaten down. Some were held together in rags, while others wore well-tailored suits that had seen better days. The men in line were diverse—Italians and Mexicans, whites and blacks, old and young—a cross-section of the world waiting in line for a meal. I realized then that poverty is the great equalizer.

The organist had pumped out "Amazing Grace," and someone had wound up Reverend Driver, thumping the men with a fire-and-brimstone sermon. But, sneaking a peek through the door, I saw it didn't light a flame in anyone. The way he carried on wasn't the way I would do it if they put me in charge. I turned away and went back to my stool. These men needed hope. Life had already done its best to beat them up and drag them down; they already knew about hell.

Hell was feeling so bad about yourself that you'd be willing to drink a bottle of carbolic acid to end the pain. Hell was losing your family because you couldn't save yourself from the bottle. Hell was looking your father in the eye and feeling the weight of his disappointment. Larimer Street was hell, and I'd landed smack dab in the middle of it. I might as well be thrashing in the rivers of sulfur.

I shook my head thinking how I'd left Ada and Donny, and the black curtain of depression and suicide dropped over my mind. *What a miserable scoundrel you are, James Goodheart.*

That's when I saw her. I suppose most men would have noticed her breasts, but I spotted her smile first thing. She'd come out a side door of the five-story Windsor Hotel across the street and smiled at two men passing on the sidewalk. Yes, even though I had been drunk out of my mind a few days ago, I knew it had to be her—the same smile and canary yellow dress. Her red curls flowing from an elegant, royal-blue chapeau tilted just so with Paris flair. Its beaver-fur brim matched the collar of her royal-blue cape and gloves. Her cape flowed behind her like a parasol catching the wind.

The vision of her warmed my mood, raising the dark curtain of depression as she stepped into the sunshine and off the curb. She hiked up her dress, revealing shapely ankles as she carefully maneuvered around the piles of horse dung.

A blaring horn blasted my ears. An automobile, a red

Model K, headed straight for the woman, screeched and swerved, then motored on.

I jumped to my feet, relieved when I saw her standing there fuming at the menacing driver. I didn't know whether to sit back down or approach her. What if it wasn't her? If it was, and she didn't recognize me? If it wasn't her, well, a damsel in distress deserved my assistance.

Before I got through playing the indecisive Hamlet, she headed straight for me, and when she reached my side of the street, she looked at me and smiled.

I could hardly believe it.

I walked to the curb and extended my hand to assist her as she stepped up.

"Thank you, fine sir," she said, dropping hold of her dress and taking my hand.

The scent of her delicate perfume encouraged my brain to remember her name. "Hi, Mary," I said tentatively.

"You're so sweet to remember my name, but you never told me yours," she said and fluttered her eyelids over her exquisite blue eyes, which were exactly the same blue as her hat, cape and gloves.

Maybe I'd got up too fast or still recovering from the alcohol tremors, but my knees felt weak, and my tongue turned thick.

"J…J…James," I stuttered.

She smiled a most mischievous smile and asked, "Shall I call you J…J…James or just James?"

I could tell by her tone she teased me, and I relaxed. "James will do," I said without stuttering.

"Well, James, I thought you might want your hat back."

I hadn't noticed the parcel she carried, but like a magician pulling a rabbit out of a hat, she produced my porkpie out of a sack.

I stared in disbelief. Could it really be my beloved hat? It looked clean and new.

"How did you…? Where did…?" My tongue tied again.

"There you go again with that stammering. You're going to give a lady a complex." She pursed her lips and fanned her face with a gloved hand.

I must have looked befuddled because she gave me the first rational explanation I had in days. "I gave Lance such a tongue lashing for throwing you out the other night that I made him promise to keep track of you. He saw you get hauled into the mission. I figured if you survived, you'd be needing your hat." She pushed it into my hands.

I accepted it, checking the inside. Yep, I recognized my handwriting on the label. "My hat!" I grinned and put it on my head. "Thank you." I tipped it at her, and she curtsied.

With a tilt of her head, she indicated the door of the mission. "Looks like you got more than your hat back."

"Well, uh, yeah, I guess so." I didn't know why I became so embarrassed to be standing outside some religious institution where I didn't belong.

"Well, I'm glad you're here. Still here, maybe I should say. Been praying for you every day." She said, patting a small gold cross on a chain around her neck.

She said that about praying with such conviction that for a moment, I forgot her profession. Then it came back, and stupid words fell out of my mouth. "Didn't you have an Irish accent the night I met you?"

Her cheeks turned red, and her eyes turned sad.

She looked at me. I could see the wheels turning in her brain. She started to speak but stopped. Then, as though she were playing a part on the New York stage, she twisted a button on my shirt, and said with the familiar brogue, "J… J…James, come by Gahan's to-nuhight and hove a droft with ol' Pixie, and you'll meet me Irish." She thumped my chest, picked up her dress, turned, and walked away.

I wanted to apologize, but my tongue got tied. I watched her spine straighten and her chin rise as she headed up Larimer Street.

PROPHECY

Midnight

"You did good today, James," Joseph said, reaching across the table with his deformed hand to grab my arm. "Next thing you know, you'll be runnin' the place."

I huffed through my nose and shook my head, knowing that would never happen. I tried to pull my arm away. I had done nothing but sit on a stool and smile at woebegone men who shuffled through the door for lunch and dinner. What good was that?

Joseph must have read my mind. "These men haven't seen a friendly face for a while, and sometimes a smile is the best medicine."

It neared midnight, and the men lucky enough to secure a bunk were mopping the floor and cleaning the kitchen. Someone sang softly. I couldn't make out the words until Joseph joined in at the next chorus:

"Follow the drinking gourd, follow the drinking gourd.
For the old man is a-waitin' to carry you to freedom.

Follow the drinking gourd."

I listened to the haunting lyrics. I wanted more coffee and started to get up, but Joseph still held my arm. I tried excusing myself when I saw in his eyes that he was somewhere else in another time. As he sang and tapped the rhythm with a finger of his good hand, a cloud of sorrow claimed his face. His hand fell from my arm onto the table, and he stopped singing. I waited silently as he disappeared into himself. After a few moments, he returned with a sigh and a nod. Whatever had oppressed him seemed to lift.

I stared at him, waiting, and I guess he felt the need to explain.

"That song always gets me. Takes me right back to my home in Mississippi."

The nation abolished slavery in 1865, so I tried doing the math to figure his age when he beat me to it.

"I'm sixty-seven. Spent my first twenty-five years as a slave. Picked me a whole trainload of cotton before they let me go free," he said with more pride than bitterness.

He caught me looking at his scarred hand.

"I'd just turned nineteen, and one of the white girls was raped. We all knew who done it. Wasn't one of us slaves, that's fo'sho." He lifted his deformed hand and studied it from side to side. "I'm just glad I got the pruning shears and not the noose. I think the owner knew I had nothin' to do with the rape and felt remorse. 'But a price has to be paid,' he told me. Probably why I was one of the first slaves he set free."

I sat horrified, sad, and embarrassed, but I wanted to know more. "How did you make your way to Denver? You have a family?" I asked.

The old man's eyes cleared and squinted at me, and he broke into his familiar grin. "That's a story for another day.

Besides, I'm supposed to be helping you. How did *you* make your way to Denver?"

How skillfully he turned the question back to me. I half-smiled and answered. The words tumbled out of me. "I came to Denver in 1890 and worked with two of my brothers, John and Luke, laying brick. We put a whole lot of blood, sweat, and tears in the bank blocks on Seventeenth," I said, sounding as though we'd built the entire financial district with our bare hands.

Joseph cocked his head with suspicion.

"Well, we had a hand in the Equitable Building," I explained. "It stood as the tallest and most expensive building in the city at the time." My chest puffed with pride. "I remember the day we topped the brick on the ninth story. It was the first of April, and my friends helped me play my finest April Fool's Day prank ever. They distracted my brother John while I took a precarious position on the ledge. When John returned, he saw me balancing there and scowled. He said, 'Get your arse off there before I come knock you over, you fool.' That's when I performed my most elegant bit of acting to date. I waved my arms like I'd slipped, and feigning a look of horror, I fell from the edge. You should have seen the look on John's face when he arrived at the lip and saw me dangling merrily from a rope my cohorts had secured around my waist." I shook my head. "I think if John had a knife in his hand, he would have cut the rope. I bought lots of beer to smooth that one over." I laughed. "To tell the truth, I'm not sure he's ever forgiven me. I guess the joke was on me because the rope left a burn on my back." I stood, turned, and lifted my shirt to prove the point.

Joseph winced and smiled but didn't seem entertained.

I sat down and changed the subject. "Kind of sad to see the city in such disrepair," I said, looking at the mission room. It was in as dire a need of upkeep as the down-on-their-luck men who washed dishes and mopped the floor. "Where do the women go?"

"The women's mission is on Thirty-First and Lawrence," Joseph said. "It's run by Reverend Joshua Gravett. He's the pastor of Galilee Baptist Church and runs both the missions." Then he turned the conversation back to me. "Why'd you leave Denver?" he asked.

I sighed with the memory. "I had a girl back home. I went to work for Reid and Murdock as a traveling grocery sales-man...I was third from the top," I added with pride. "We married three years later and moved to Chicago."

"Kids?"

"A son, Donny. He's seven."

Joseph nodded without judgment.

"I'm told she wants nothing to do with me." The words choked me. But I judged myself, and the verdict was guilty, and it flooded me with shame—no amount of bricks or groceries could cover it.

All this talk made me tired. I leaned back in my chair and yawned. "I may head over to Gahan's for a beer."

"You know, James, you're a free man. You can do as you please. But I wonder how's that been working out?"

His question stabbed me. I didn't answer.

"You do whatever you want, James. But I don't think booze has been a good mistress. You wishin' to be her slave again?"

I found myself unable to look him in the eye, although judgment didn't seem to come from him, but from the pounding of my own heart.

"You also need to know that if you go back to drinkin', there won't be a bed here for you."

I masked the pounding with a sneer, looked at him, and

asked, "You mean God won't like me anymore?" I regretted the smart-ass comment, but it was the understanding of God I'd grown up with.

"So you *do* believe in God?" Joe asked.

Heat rose in my ears and spread to my face. "I suppose I do after being beaten over the head by my father about the importance of fidelity to God as the ultimate virtue. I found I wasn't exactly a good rule follower."

"That's what you think fidelity means, huh?"

"I…guess," I stammered, realizing I'd never stopped to think about the word, only that it sparked anger.

Joe thrust out his lower jaw and bobbed his head. "I suppose if my relationship with Him was based on duty or obligation, I might be feelin' the same. I'm thinkin' it's more of a privilege livin' in His great story. Gotta believe and trust in something."

"But when I hear Driver preach, I hear my father's condemnation."

Joseph just smiled. "The hollerin' Reverend Driver, he means well. All you got to know is God already loves you. Always has, always will, that's fo'sho. Your behavior has nothing to do with that." He looked back at the men mopping the floor. "We, on the other hand, have no grace for that sort of behavior."

"So God will just make my life miserable?"

"Oh, I think you can do that on your own." He laughed loud enough that the men stopped mopping and looked at us. "Amazes me we're so quick to blame God for the stuff we do to ourselves."

One of the men refilled our cups with coffee. Joseph looked at him, smiled, and looked back at me. "I've heard people on the street call Living Waters the refuge for derelicts.

Guess that's how they see us." He shook his head. "I'm not sure I've met one derelict since I've been here—"

"Until me, huh?" I thought I'd finish his sentence and stood, but he ignored my comment and finished it himself.

"Down on their luck maybe, made stupid mistakes fo'sho, but derelict, I don't think so." He sipped from his cup, then continued, "Somehow I think we got it all backward. We thought coming into this life as sinners, we had to strive and work to right the wrong we've done, only to find out we never can. We can never be good enough, smart enough...holy enough. But what if we lived our lives through victory—what if we lived our lives as God sees us? Someone's already paid the price." He held up his deformed hand. "Yes, sirree, you can go and drink all you want. Nothin' goin' to change the way God sees you. But you think that's the best God has for you?"

Sweat ran down my neck. I sat back down, ashamed and bewildered.

"Jim Goodheart, I see you much different than that," he laughed. "Mmmm, mmm, mmm...be running the place before no time."

———

Yep, it was Denver all right. Earlier, at breakfast, the sun glistened, but when I returned from the bathroom, the weather had turned nasty. Sleet hit the side of the building with such force I thought the front window would give way.

A sane man would not have opened the door, but I'd hardly slept a wink, and I needed fresh air to clear my head. My sleeplessness had less to do with the cacophonous choir of snores and farts and more to do with my restless mind, tossing and turning with thoughts of guilt and redemption.

I'd hurt Mary, and I had to make amends. I squirmed in my seat during the Reverend's sermon last night and didn't catch every word, but I caught the drift. It was about judging people, even yourself, and you had to start with penitence if you were going to get your life back on track. I'd start by writing a letter to Ada. Of course, I'd never know if her mother would give it to her. My mother-in-law was mean as a rattlesnake. I reached for the mission doorknob, wondering if I could ever apologize to that woman.

When I opened the door, sleet hit me with a vengeance. The storm bellowed in full force. I held on to my precious porkpie with one hand as the wind tried to jerk the door from my other. Then glanced back at the men inside eating their oatmeal and heard them caterwauling and cursing me for exposing them to the gale.

I stepped into the squall, pulled the door shut, and stood to get my balance in the wind. "What a stupid idea," I said to the storm. I figured I should have thought this through, as I wasn't even sure I could find her. I'd seen her come from the Windsor Hotel across the street yesterday and hoped I'd get lucky today.

Even on this blustery day, Larimer Street bristled with activity. People lucky enough to have a job would not let a little weather stop them from doing it. They hunkered under umbrellas and pushed on.

I led with my head and hat diagonally across the street to the main entrance of the Windsor. They may not even let me into the place. Seventeen years ago, I'd entered with enough for one drink and a cigar in the Windsor bar. It cost me a whole week's pay, but I had to see the three thousand silver dollars embedded in the floor and the four holes in the ceiling put there by Calamity Jane. The same bartender that gave Calamity a shot of whiskey had poured mine. He told me that all the lady wanted was a drink. When he reminded her that Denver had outlawed serving booze to women, she shot up the place. "That's when I figured she was no lady," the bartender had laughed.

Now I dodged automobiles and thought about my father and his verbal assault against the horseless carriage. He swore they had come from the devil himself and would be a blight on humanity. I knew I'd have to add Father to the list of reparations…and my brothers…and my mother. I caught my breath. "This might take me a while," I said to the storm.

The five-story Windsor shielded me from the wind. Nevertheless, the rain soaked me from my fifty-yard dash, and I thought about trying to find Mary on another day. The way I looked, drenched from head to toe, I didn't belong in a place that had enjoyed the company of famous visitors like Mark Twain, Rudyard Kipling, and even President Teddy Roosevelt. Then I remembered my father's admonition: "If you could just put all that energy and drive looking for your next drink into doing good, you could make something out of yourself."

Resolve filled my chest as I bounded up the steps and through the main entrance, wide enough for six men to walk abreast, like I belonged. It was just as I remembered, with elegant high ceilings, stained-glass rotunda, Italian marble floors, and a grand black-walnut staircase leading to the rooms.

But as I stood and dripped onto the marble floor, I realized much had changed. Long gone were the refined furnishings and the diamond dust mirrors. I took heart at the sight of the fabulous Otis elevator. My brothers and I had been in awe of the magic box rising on a cushion of steam. Then I saw the sign that said OUT OF ORDER. I sighed and glanced around the lobby. Gone were the Rothschilds and Vanderbilts and well-lubricated legislators who never had to stumble through the rough street when they could navigate the convenient tunnel under Eighteenth Street to the Barclay Block, where they held the assembly.

I looked like a wet mongrel, but no one paid me any mind. I guessed that since Denver's financial collapse, bookings of wealthy guests had declined, and the hotel accepted the likes of me.

"Excuse me," a voice said.

I stepped out of the way of a black man pushing a cart full of trash. I noticed a slightly bedraggled bouquet of flowers in his load and reached for it.

The man stopped and glared at me.

"I'm sorry," I said, "do you mind if I take this?"

He shrugged. "Suit yo' self."

I broke off a white rose that still had a tinge of life, peeled off the dying petals, and tossed the rest back into the trash cart. I sniffed the rose to make sure it didn't smell like the refuse. "Thank you, sir," I said and smiled at the man as he pushed the cart away.

I stood smelling the flower when Mary appeared, gliding gracefully down the staircase, her hat and cape in hand. She saw me and smiled. Then, like she remembered she had a bone to pick with me, she looked away.

Undeterred, I stepped forward and said ever so sweetly, "Mary, Mary, quite contrary, how does your garden grow?"

She fought back a grin and looked at the rose I held out to her. She took the flower but glanced at the black man pushing the trash cart and smiled. "I guess it's the thought that counts."

"Mary...I'm...uh..." I started, not accustomed to the apology regimen I had set for myself. She crossed her arms as though she was about to get annoyed.

I swallowed the stutter and spoke clearly. "Look, Mary, I

didn't mean no harm. I know I hurt your feelings yesterday when I said…"

She looked me in the eye. "Just spit it out, James. What are you trying to say?"

"I'm trying to say I'm sorry. I'm sorry all to hell." My shoulders relaxed, and my pounding heart eased. It felt good to say it, so I said it again, "I'm sorry."

"Okay, James, you can quit groveling. I forgive you." She paused, looked around, and lowered her voice. "I know who I am, and it's not what most people see. But a girl's got to do what a girl's got to do to get by. But I'm darn *sure* who I am," she said with dignity and certainty. "What about you?"

I knew what she was asking, but didn't know how to answer, so I said, "I'm not sure what I'm going to do with myself now. Ain't got a lick of money. Guess I'll stay at the mission for a few days until I can figure things out."

"For now, you'd better stay away from the drink. I'm not sure it fits you so well."

I smiled and nodded.

Mary looked me up and down, including the puddle under my feet. "I don't mean to hurt your feelings, but your wet dog smell has got to go. And you're gonna scare away those poor men in the mission stinking like that."

She reached into a small purse she carried with her hat and pulled out a business card. "Kirk is a friend of mine, and he'll get you fixed up. Just tell him, ol' Pixie sent you." She smiled and winked.

I turned the card over and read it. O'Reilly's Laundry and Tailor.

I did not know why she was being so kind to me and didn't know what to say.

"It's okay," she reassured me. "We've all been there. Maybe someday you can pay it forward."

ACT TWO

9

MY KINGDOM FOR A HORSE

July 5, 1909
(Two Years Later)

"Getcha newspaper! Getcha newspaper!" shouted the newsboy. With a satchel full of news hot off the press, he dodged swerving automobiles on Larimer Street.

Enter the Messenger. Well-played, Jimmy, I thought. I knew the boy well. He was a local who'd lost both parents to consumption a year ago—a fairly common tragedy with people from the East coming to Denver for the high-mountain air and the hope of recovery from tuberculosis.

As much as I wanted a paper, I didn't need to wave him over. He'd pass by soon enough. A red roadster pulled to the curb, and the driver gave Jimmy a nickel and received the afternoon *Denver Post.* The boy tipped his cap, and the roadster pulled into traffic and sped off.

I leaned back on my stool posted against the mission door, fighting the urge to close my eyes and grab a cat nap. Lunch had come and gone, and we had the place cleaned up.

The afternoon after Independence Day warmed with a brilliant blue sky, so clear that the Rocky Mountains appeared to tower over the end of the block. And so warm that no one burned coal that muddied up the air. The winds had changed course and blew smoke from the northern factories west and away from downtown.

Even so, on this beautiful summer day, I saw no silver lining, feeling tired and grumpy, as if I was hungover. I knew that was not the case, but very well could have been. Yesterday I really wanted to celebrate the birth of our nation with a shot of whiskey, but I swallowed my craving and made the hard decision not to. This coming November, I would be dry for two years. I didn't want to mess it up. Still, I missed the drink, and not indulging in it made me cranky.

But I persisted, not limiting my decision to remain sober to holidays. Whenever happiness filled my chest and I wanted to celebrate with a shot, I remembered Joseph's warning. He told me that once the demon of alcohol touched a man, he's better off not to let the spirit pass his lips again lest it stoke the flame of desire. My mind argued the point, but my heart knew it to be true.

Resisting was tough. Besides, when you tell a man he can't have something, he wants it that much more. To tell the truth, that flame of desire burned every day, sometimes dimmer, sometimes stronger, but always flickering. I faced a daily battle, one that I thought would grow easier with time. But no sooner did the sun rise than I had to set my mind against it, or I'd soon find my way to Gahan's again. Mary became a big help. I would have loved to visit her at Gahan's, but she knew I would succumb to the drink, and she made it a point to visit me at the mission for a cup of coffee. I have to admit she was the sugar in my coffee, and those visits doubled my pleasure. Not only did I get to see her, but she turned the men's eyes, and I became a celebrity to have such a pretty friend.

Today was her birthday, and I hoped she would come by. I had something for her. It wasn't gold, but I'd driven a hard bargain for it. I'd horse-traded four jars of mustard for a small container of hand lotion. The horse trader, a man I trusted, said it came from Paris and had an exotic French name and sweet aroma. I thought Mary would like it.

"Getcha newspaper, the *Denver Post*. Getcha newspaper!"

Jimmy, the newspaper boy, wore knickers, a button-down white shirt, and a cap. He was remarkably clean and presentable, considering he lived in the boys' home on Lawrence.

"Hi, Jim," he smiled, offering me a newspaper.

I put a nickel in his palm, and he dropped it into the satchel around his waist "Thanks, Jimmy," I said. "You're looking well today."

"Thank you, Jim. Look good, feel good." His smile broadened, and he paused as though he wanted to talk with a man who shared his name and maybe get a tip for that. I enjoyed seeing him; in fact, I felt like I saw my younger self, scrappy and smart.

"Hey, Jimmy, let me give you a tip," I said. "Get out of the business."

He laughed loudly, even though he'd heard the same joke for the last two years. He snickered because he knew what came next. I always smuggled out a treat from the lunch room, an apple or a peach when they were in season. Today his indulgence was even better, a chocolate-chip cookie still warm from its hiding place in my front coat pocket.

Even though our exchanges were frequent, Jimmy glanced around every time, thinking he might get into trouble and have the treat snatched from his hand. It was a sad consequence of being an orphan, always suspicious of getting short changed.

He didn't yet believe he had no worries with the mission and me. The mission tightly controlled the dispensation of every crumb, but the bits they allotted me I could do with as I wished, and the treats I gave him were mine to give.

He accepted the cookie and grinned with thanks. Then it was back to business. He saw a group of prospective customers down the street, nodded to me, and hustled quickly away.

"See ya, Jimmy," I called.

I unfolded the paper on my lap and read the headline: "Shoshone Station Open." The subtext read: "Shoshone Hydroelectric Generating Station begins transmitting electricity from Glenwood Canyon to the Denver area." I nodded at the achievement.

I'd read the article and the rest of the paper later. What I really wanted to see was a small ad in the back. I'd convinced my boss that newspaper ads were the way to go. I'd repeated the old business adage to him, "You gotta spend money to make money." He hadn't agreed until I told him I'd pay for the ad myself, and he could take it out of my wages. I also negotiated a raise of one cent per bottle if the ad sold more mustard. He shrugged, knowing he had nothing to lose if I was wrong.

I'd found the job peddling mustard a year ago and could now pay for my room and board at the mission, put a few cents in my pocket, and even contribute to the plate we passed around after Reverend Driver's sermon.

"Ah, here it is." I folded the newspaper in half and brought it up to my eyes to read the small ad I'd written: "If it's good enough for the St. Louis World's Fair, it's good enough for you!" A picture of a jar of French's Cream Salad

Mustard sat to the right of the text. Below was a picture of a hot dog and under that the following text: "Slather it on your next wiener or sandwich to add some spice to your life."

"Hmmm." When I wrote the text, I was happy with my good humor. Now, seeing it in print, I didn't think it was that clever. The more refined society might be put off by it, and I'd have to put more thought into the next ad. My company made a fine product that was bound to sell, and people needed to know about it. The St. Louis World's Fair had introduced this new condiment that didn't require refrigeration, and I was keen to sell it and make some dough.

The jars of mustard sold for thirty-two cents apiece, of which I got one cent, and if my ad did well, I'd get two. I knew how the grocery business worked, and I would not get rich, but if I could sell mustard, I could sell anything.

I turned back to the front page and read the article headlined: "Elsie Sigel's Murder Still Not Solved." Like most of the country, the murder of the young missionary whose strangled body was discovered in a trunk in New York City's Chinatown fascinated us all. The authorities had found love letters from two separate Chinamen, and the police figured one of them killed her in a fit of jealousy. They were calling it the "chop suey murder." Too many raunchy jokes were coming out of that. I shook my head and said aloud, "Poor girl, having her life dragged through the gutters."

But it wasn't just the murder that set off the fascination, it was the fact that Elsie was the granddaughter of Franz Sigel, the great Civil War general. The murder set off a wave of prejudice against the Chinese, and the *Denver Post*, never shying away from controversy, suggested that the killing was Sigel's own fault for her improprieties.

Over top of the newspaper, I caught the glimpse of a man wearing a canvas miner's cap pacing by, accompanied with the clomp of heavy boots against the sidewalk. The wearer's cadence slowed at the door of the mission, but quickly accelerated past. Out of the corner of my eye I saw the man walk away shaking his head, shoulders hunched. I grinned, knowing he'd be back. Over the last two years as the doorman of the mission, I'd seen it thousands of times: men at the end of their ropes—drowning men grabbing for a life ring.

I could judge the resilience of their will by how many store fronts they passed until they turned back and circled again, and the depth of their depravity by the number of times they walked by before stopping. This young man's stubborn youthful self-reliance had him go three store fronts up and pass by four times until he stopped at the door to the mission.

I crinkled the paper in my lap and examined the boy up and down. He looked about the same age as me when I arrived in Denver to lay bricks almost twenty years ago. A teenager edging toward manhood; his boots had already seen better days, and a sturdy belt where a miner could hang an oil lantern held up his filthy canvas pants. Both this and the carbide lamp that attached to the leather strap of his hat were missing. I hoped he'd left them at the mine but knew better. He'd probably lost both in a poker game. The boy's face was gaunt and thin, stained with ground-in dirt that even the longest bath couldn't erase, and finished with a mustache holding on for dear life. He licked at his dry, cracked lips, revealing that whiskey had been his only drink, but his sullen eyes revealed his deepest thirst.

"I wouldn't go in there if I was you," I said.

The boy flinched with eyes full of fear, like he hadn't noticed me sitting there, and I might assault him and take whatever possessions he had left, which I imagined was nothing.

"What?" he said.

"I was just saying, don't go in there. You might just find something to eat."

He licked his lips again.

"What do they do in there?" he said with hesitation in some kind of Scandinavian accent, Norwegian or Swedish, I guessed.

I sighed and shook my head in disgust. "Oh, *rundbrenner,* you don't want to know. The screams have just recently stopped." I called him a ladies' man. It was the only Norwegian I knew.

"I'm Finnish, not Norwegian." He looked at me as a flicker of life and national pride returned to his eyes.

"What's your name, son?"

"They call me Finn."

"I guess I should have started there." I laughed. "You needing something to eat?"

He nodded. "I haven't ate for three straight days. The thievin' whores and cards have took everything I have."

I looked at the street clock and back at the boy. "Men will line up in another hour for dinner."

Disappointment shadowed the boy's face and his shoulders drooped.

"Young man, that emptiness you feel in the depth of your gut is not only hunger, but it's for something more." I continued, even though the boy's stare didn't leave his boots. "I was in a worse way than you find yourself when I stumbled to this place two years ago. I had no more need of God, than a bucket of rocks." I smiled. "I had drifted into infidelity: thinking I could do many good deeds hoping to merit some peace of mind, still evading direct and immediate surrender."

The boy took one step, but I reached out and held his arm.

"Look, Finn, God is dearer to the heart when He is all the heart has left. You go in and ask for Joe, tell him Jim sent you." He finally looked me in the eye. "I don't have it all figured out either, son. But you can't go trying to change your ways with an empty stomach, now can you?"

I reached down and turned the knob of the door and swung it open for him. Then patted him on the back as he walked through.

I folded the pages and was about to lean my head back for an afternoon siesta when I saw Mary crossing the street in my direction. I smiled, waved, and stood. She must have bought herself a new dress for her birthday. The Prussian-blue silk dress was perfectly tailored to fit her shapely form. She smiled like a high-fashion model on a Parisian runway. Of course I'd never been to France, but I'd read of fashion events in the newspapers and Ada's magazines back home, and I'd been to the World's Fair in Chicago in 1893. I knew things.

Mary's new dress had an empire waist accentuated with a black sash and a chiffon overlay that shifted with her curvy hips as she sashayed across the street. Her tailor designed it with a square neckline, and, sad to say, not enough view of her cleavage. But the silky fabric jostled and bounced with her full bosoms. Her accessories included a black bow tie, a black feather hat and a parasol, all to create a look of refined elegance.

She enraptured me as time stood still, even with the busyness of Larimer Street. The passing parade of people and automobiles lost color and definition, emphasizing the vision in blue coming toward me. I felt a desire stronger than my taste for booze. In my weaker moments, I'd asked Mary if she and I could be more than friends. But she'd always laugh and say, "Ol' Jim, you are such a charmer. You make this old maid feel young again, but you're one of the few genuine friends I have. Can't we get on without muddying the waters? Don't be one of those men that gamble with their fidelity."

I don't know why she took it upon herself to be my moral conscience. After all, Ada lived a long way away, and I didn't even know if she still wanted me. But if Mary had decided that we were better off friends, then I needed to be okay with that.

I steamed with jealousy of the men that kept Mary's company. But every time she mentioned fidelity, I was relieved she had refused my carnal craving. I supposed there was only one woman for me. But there was no law that said I still couldn't admire Mary's ample figure.

As she approached me, I sang with gusto, "Happy birthday to you. Happy birthday to you. Happy birthday, dearest Mary, happy birthday to you." I concluded with a glissando, taking a knee.

It took a lot to make her blush, but as she stepped onto the curb, she fanned her cheek with a white lace hankie. "Jim Goodheart, you're making a spectacle of me. Now you go and stop that."

But I knew she didn't mean it, and I wasn't done teasing. For my next number, I stood up, spread out my arms, and began a chorus of, "How old are you?"

That's as far as I got because she kicked my shin—hard enough to make me stop, but not hard enough to keep me from laughing.

"I'm old enough to know that gentlemen don't ask questions like that," she said without anger.

But it didn't stop my curiosity. "Just kidding," I said and gave her a kiss on the cheek, still trying to calculate her age. I figured from what she'd told me about growing up outside of St. Louis and how long she'd been in Denver that she was in her early twenties, but I knew enough not to ask directly. Instead, I teased, "You look beautiful in your birthday suit."

Fire shot up the back of my neck and inflamed my cheeks.

Before I could stammer an apology, she laughed and slugged my arm. "Wouldn't you like that, James Goodheart!"

I stepped back and took the small container of lotion from my pocket, wishing it were prettier and wrapped in a red ribbon. Feeling like a schoolboy with a crush on the lovely new girl, I knew my cheeks were still on fire. I took a deep breath and said, "I got you this," adding softly, "I wish it was something more."

Mary accepted my present and studied the label. She looked at me, smiled, and said, "Oh, Jim, you shouldn't have. What a wonderful gift!" She gushed as if it were a diamond bracelet.

My shoulders relaxed, knowing that I'd done okay. She opened the lid and sniffed. "It's delightful, James, thank you." She leaned in and kissed my cheek, making my knees wobble.

A loud argument in the street interrupted our afternoon encounter. Such disputes were not unusual in the busy thoroughfare as riders and drivers each thought they owned the right-of-way.

I was about to turn my attention back to Mary when the ruckus intensified and two gunshots rang out. Denver was not Montana or other parts of the wild west, but it was not so far removed, and anxious cowboys often settled their scores with revolvers.

Reflexively, I stepped between the mayhem and Mary just as two more shots exploded—one bullet whizzing by my ear, close enough it nearly clipped some skin, the other ending in a deadly thud.

My heart skipped a beat, thinking the bullet had hit Mary

or me, but then I saw a buckskin mare on the street in front of us stumble and collapse. The rider going down with it, getting his leg pinned under the horse. He pulled frantically while a river of blood gushed from the horse's neck.

I sprung from the sidewalk, gripped the cowboy's arm, and together we dislodged his leg. The shooters scattered like rats in the light.

Hanging on to me for support, the cowboy knelt beside his dying animal. "Oh, Sunshine, don't go dyin' on me," he begged. He looked up at me, hoping I could fix his broken horse, and I said I was sorry. There was nothing else to say.

The cowboy hugged the horse's neck. I watched the animal's chest rise and fall for the last time. "Oh, Sunshine, my poor Sunshine," the man wailed. Then he turned, looked after his assailants, and screamed into the street, "You sons of bitches shot my best horse!"

All I could do was shake my head in sadness and acceptance. After all, this was Larimer Street—home to swindlers, drunkards, and some of the worst thievin' gamblers and cheats you ever laid eyes on. It had more saloons and brothels than Chicago had Italian restaurants, and more counterfeiters and rascals than even New York City. It now had a dead horse named Sunshine laid out in the baking sun. If someone didn't drag it away soon, the rats that were feared by the most feral cats would devour it by morning. Despite it all, Larimer Street was my home.

Joseph and Reverend Gravett exited the mission to see what the commotion was all about. Reverend Gravett, who had started the Living Waters Mission, doffed his hat at the sight of the dead horse and grieving man. "*Requiescat in pace*," he prayed softly. "Rest in peace."

Joseph, in his practical manner, surveyed the scene and

said, "Someone better get a lasso an' wagon an' drag that poor animal out or we's gonna have a heck of a stink."

The four of us nodded in agreement as the Italian came out, saw the dead horse and made the sign of the cross over his chest.

"*Carne di cavalla*," he said and clapped his hands together.

I looked at him, mortified. The mission desperately needed meat, but didn't think any man would appreciate horse stew.

"*Scusami.*" He bowed apologetically and stepped over to help the cowboy.

Joseph and Reverend Gravett greeted Mary, whose rosy cheeks had paled.

She curtsied to them, smiled, and excused herself from the mess.

We watched her walk away, and I had to wonder where each man looked and what they thought as her blue silk figure strutted down Larimer Street. I glanced at Reverend Gravett; he was a man of the cloth, but he was still a man.

Reverend Gravett had more energy than I could ever hope to have. In his early forties, the pastor of the Galilee Baptist Church started the Living Waters Mission seventeen years ago, even though he already involved himself in many other social services. Reverend William Driver did most of the preaching at the mission, but I loved when Gravett took over the pulpit. He'd apparently studied under the great D. L. Moody, and although he was only a few years older than me, he held a great depth of wisdom. He never met a man who wasn't a friend.

Gravett pulled out a pocket watch, flipped open the top and frowned.

"Not sure what we're going to do about the evening

service, boys. Billy's taken ill, and I'm afraid the church is expecting me for an evening gathering."

I looked at Joseph, who grinned at me like that darn Cheshire Cat. Gravett also smiled at me. They were complicit in something, and I had a feeling they'd set me up. The Reverend put a firm hand on my shoulder, and I felt a charge of electricity course through my body.

"You know, James. You've been our doorman for almost two years now," he began. "Reckon you've seen a lot of humanity come and go. Joseph tells me that our numbers are up because of you. Says that few can resist your persuasion and winning smile." He seemed to peer through my eyes into my soul, and, like Joseph, he looked past my iniquities—my shame and guilt. He squeezed my shoulder. "James, I'd like you to share your testimony tonight."

Then he quoted something that sounded biblical. "And they overcame him by the blood of the Lamb, and by the word of their testimony, and they loved not their lives unto the death."

I had no idea what it meant, but I didn't like the sound of it, and my back sweated profusely. Was he asking me to preach? No. He'd only asked me to share my testimony. I could do that. "I...I guess that would be okay," I stuttered, hating that I stumbled over my words already and my stomach rumbled with nausea.

"You'll do fine, James. Just be yourself and tell your story." He released my shoulder, looked at the dead horse, and sighed. "You know we're struggling to keep the doors open," he said with humility. "There are just too many mouths to feed and more every month. So much need." He paused, seeming to get lost in thought. "We either need to close the place or infuse it with new blood. We need some fresh energy and ideas for fundraising."

His gaze fell on me and then on Joseph.

"Joseph here thinks you are just the man to do that."

I frowned at Joseph, but he smiled back. His voice echoed in my ears: "Mmmm, mmm, mmm, be running the place in no time." I shook my head at him. He knew I understood nothin' of the Bible. The Reverend must have known it too. I wasn't a preacher, and for me to stand behind the pulpit could be a disaster. Surely they knew that.

"James, I'd like you to pray about becoming the superintendent of the mission," Reverend Gravett said with great sincerity. "You can study scripture with me and even become ordained if you have the calling." He put his hand back on my shoulder. "I have only one requirement," he said, pausing for emphasis. "You've got to get back to Illinois and make amends with your wife and her family."

I crossed my arms. All my life I'd been picked last. Here, not only had they chosen me for the team, but they asked to lead it. Maybe this was a way to show Ada I'd changed, and she'd consider taking me back. Besides, it was my chance in life to recompense for all the wrong I'd done.

Joseph raised his hands and twisted back and forth between the street and the crumbling entrance of the mission. "All this can be yours," he guffawed.

I looked at the dead horse in the street. "A horse, a horse, my kingdom for a horse," I declaimed without passion, reckoning the mission was all but worth a dead horse. I grimaced at King Richard III's cry for help when his horse was killed in battle, and they left him at the mercy of his enemies.

I didn't realize the room could hold so many men. I figured they'd come to see ol' Jim make a fool of himself after all the ribbing I'd given them at the door. As I got up to speak, I stumbled over a leg of a chair, and the men howled with laughter.

When I got to the pulpit, sweat beaded on my upper lip. I forced myself to smile. Much to my surprise, the men quieted. I took out some notes from my jacket and set them on the lectern.

I scanned the crowd, and every one of my senses came alive. Like being on stage, my heart thumped with excitement and my hands trembled with stage fright, as though I was about to perform Hamlet and couldn't recall the opening lines. I caught a glance of Joseph in the back corner. He beamed like a proud father.

I swallowed hard and looked at the men. The show must go on. "Well, I…" I began, coughed, and cleared my throat. "I guess this place is going to hell in a handbasket. I could sure use a drink about now," I said.

After a few seconds of surprise, the men roared with laughter. A fire lit in my chest, embarrassed by my swearing in the pulpit. But my audience sat attentive, and their reaction bolstered me. I glanced at Joseph and grimaced.

"Reverend Driver has taken sick, and Reverend Gravett has asked that I step into his shoes…a size, I'm afraid, that is much too large for me, but I'm all you got tonight." I swallowed through my parched throat and continued, "There are some in this house tonight with whom I drank whiskey and to whom I dealt the cards. That was a time when you were more prosperous than I. Even today you are richer than I. But richer or poorer, you and I need God in our lives now more than ever…"

10

BLOOMINGTON

August 1, 1909

The ticket seller at the train station took what was left of my savings and pushed my tickets under the scrolled wrought iron window.

"Okay, son, here are your tickets to Bloomington," he said, looking over my shoulder at the enormous clock on the far wall. "Be leaving at one o'clock sharp today." He smiled. I thought the man must call everyone son because, at thirty-eight and with my years of inebriety, I didn't look that youthful.

"You'll take the Denver Pacific to Cheyenne. There you'll catch the Union."

I took it to mean the Union Pacific but didn't ask as train people can be prickly, thinking everyone should know as much about trains as they do.

I thanked him and started to step away, but not before he grabbed my arm. "From Cheyenne, the Union will pull with their new articulated steam locomotive." He made it sound like a real treat. "Gets you there much faster," he explained in simple terms, reading the ignorance on my face.

I thought of Ada's mother's know-it-all attitude and smiled at him. "Great, just what I need," I replied with irony —not so sure I wanted to get there that much quicker.

It had taken me a month to decide to return to Bloomington and to sell more mustard than I usually sold in a year to have enough money for the trip. I still wasn't sure I was ready to face Ada, not to mention her parents, Dr. Nelson Loar and his wife, Olive.

I turned away from the ticket seller and smiled at Mary, who waited patiently on one of the wooden benches. She had come to see me off, and I was grateful. The clock tower above the station chimed twelve, echoed seconds later by the clock on the wall. I wondered why the timepieces weren't in sync. So unusual for train folk. I walked to Mary and smiled, waiting for the tolling to stop before I spoke so she could hear me.

"I've got an hour before boarding. Can I buy you a cup of coffee?" I asked, hoping I had enough money.

"That would be sweet," she said, taking my proffered hand.

She took my arm as we walked into the café, where the hostess showed us to a table in the corner. Mary wore the canary yellow dress that revealed her ample cleavage, and a hush came over the room until we took our seats.

"We'll take two coffees," I told the black waiter in a starched white uniform.

Looking around the room, I witnessed plenty of stares and whispering from self-important men and women, all dressed in their finest travel togs. I could tell they didn't approve of Mary's attire. I looked back at her. She looked out the window at the trains and ignored the officious crowd.

Anger rumbled in my belly. Mary turned to me and saw my expression.

She smiled and said, "Never mind them. Bearing scorn is the unfortunate requirement of my profession."

She turned her gaze on the intrusive patrons, examining each one. I almost laughed out loud when her gaze caused a shift in some of the men, who immediately averted their eyes to their laps. Mary turned back to me, lowering her voice, "Yep, I reckon' I could ruin a few lives right now by waving and calling out names...hi, Larry; hi, Fred. But I suppose it wouldn't be good for business." She laughed.

"I'm sorry," I apologized for all the people in the cafe.

She shrugged. "It's fine. After all, I know most of their secrets."

The sparkle left her eyes. She shook her head and said with quiet anger, "They act so pious in here, but get their clothes off..." She paused and took a breath. "Sorry," she said, touching her cross necklace and pinching it between her fingers.

Maybe because I was leaving, I got the nerve to ask a bold question. "How did you get in the...uh...business?"

She crossed her arms, leaned back, and sighed.

Immediately, I regretted asking. "I'm sorry, Mary, you don't need—"

She put the cross to her red lips and kissed it. "It's okay, James. I know you don't judge me for it. Just some things are hard to face. You know."

Boy, did I ever.

"I grew up on a farm outside of St. Louis in a small town named Festus," she began. "My folks were good people, brought me up right and all, in the Christian faith. They trusted me, and with their blessing, at the age of sixteen I left home and headed to Los Angeles for nursing school. My train broke down in Cheyenne, and we had to spend the night." She pulled her hankie from her purse and dabbed at her eyes.

I wished I had never asked.

But she continued. "They put us up in some flea-infested flophouse. Some fellows broke down my door, stole my money, beat me up pretty bad, and—"

Tears filled her eyes and rolled down her cheeks. She didn't have to finish the sentence.

It took a minute for her to regain her composure, but when she did, she said, "I don't know, I guess I thought I had become damaged goods by then…and I had to make my way somehow."

I swallowed my rage at those men. We sat in reflective silence until the waiter brought our coffee. Then she wiped her tears and sat straight in her chair.

"Thank you," we told the waiter simultaneously.

She smiled at me, her blue eyes luminescent from her tears.

"Just glad I know the truth about myself now. I'm a child of God—Reverend Gravett has taught me that much. Kind of wish I could've become a nurse though." She chuckled. "Come to think of it, I guess I am, sorta."

I laughed with her and raised my coffee cup in a toast. "To nurse Mary."

We clinked cups.

The tower chimed the half hour, and my stomach rumbled with anxiety. I knew she heard it too.

"Sure wish you were going with me."

She laughed so loudly people turned to look. Then she said, "Oh, I do too, Jim Goodheart. I'd love to be there to see you explain our friendship to your wife and her parents!"

I knew she didn't say it to hurt my feelings, but I frowned and swallowed hard. "It's just that I have no idea what I'm getting into. I really do love Ada, you know." I exhaled. "It's hard to explain. I knew it the moment I first saw her that something was different about her. I have written so many apologies and love letters to her that my hand is sore, and I've not heard one word back. I'm not even sure she got my posts. Her mother is a bear of a woman, and she might just tear me to pieces when she sees me."

Mary raised her eyebrows and nodded like an angry schoolmarm with a ruler in her hand. "Maybe you'd do well to crawl up their front steps on your hands and knees and roll over when they answer the door," she teased.

"Yeah, thanks. This is probably a terrible idea," I moaned. "I'll do anything to win her back, and maybe Gravett's offer is enough motivation to face the bear. But it's probably foolish of me to think of running the mission and myself as a minister to boot."

She shook her head and touched my hand. "I think you're gonna make a fine pastor, James. I see it all over you."

"Yeah, that's what Joseph says."

She patted my hand and changed the subject. "Bet you'll be glad to see your son."

"Sure will." I half smiled, reflecting both shame and excitement.

"James," she said with conviction. "Just know we'll all be praying for you." She took my hand and squeezed.

After a moment, she released me and asked, "Is someone going to meet you at the station?"

My stomach rumbled again before I could say, "My father."

Never thought I'd live to see the day my father drove a car. Truth be told, I didn't think I'd survive him driving us back home.

"Gal-blasted machine," he groused as he ground the gears, trying to find the right one.

He'd borrowed the Hudson Roadster from a friend to fetch me from the train. I'd written that I would be happy to take the train to Chicago and another to Bloomington, but he'd insisted I get off at the Peru-LaSalle Station, and he'd drive me home. I dreaded all that time alone with him. I wrote to him many times that it would be more convenient if I took the Pullman. But, in his last letter, he all but ordered me to get off the stinking train at Peru-LaSalle. There was no way I could say no.

I was glad my train had arrived in the morning, and we'd be driving in daylight. While the red roadster had headlamps, I didn't want my father with his failing eyesight driving in the dark.

It was an August day in the low seventies, pleasant for a ride in the open two-seater. The leather seats were reasonably comfortable even with the stiff ride of the Hudson, but there wasn't much room. We would sit shoulder to shoulder for three hours, an uneasy intimacy with the man who I both loved and feared. I sweated like a bricklayer on a sweltering day.

The tension was not all in my mind. We were barreling down a street when a young couple crossed in front of us. I gripped the side of the roadster, trying to will them to stop or my father to hit the brakes.

"Uh…Pop…" I blurted.

"I see 'em, dagnabbit," he snarled, trying to stop the car. "Too many pedals and levers!" He threw his hands up, and I resisted the urge to grab the wheel. The pedestrians wisely stepped back onto the curb, and by whatever fate or luck, he found the next gear, aimed the automobile down the road and headed us toward Bloomington.

I relaxed, took in the countryside, and stole a glance at my father. He'd aged in the two years since I'd last seen him—his eyes were dimmer, and his beard had turned completely gray. He'd always had a stern and chiseled face, and the wrinkles of time did nothing to soften it. His fierce, determined expression hadn't changed from his Civil War picture that hung in the hallway back home and overshadowed my childhood. The caption under the photo read: "Company A, Ninety-fourth Regiment, August 8, 1862," suggesting that his sons stand at attention and salute.

Tomorrow would be forty-seven years since he had enlisted. Using my fingers to count, I realized he would be seventy-nine this year. My heart filled with sadness, thinking he probably didn't have many years left, and I let my shoulder sink into the warmth of his.

But when he flinched and sat up straight, I returned to safe ground. "They're saying that Ty Cobb may win the Triple Crown this year with his batting average, his RBIs, and home runs. You hear he hit another home run last night?" With no windshield, I had to shout, at the same time try not to swallow bugs.

I awaited a reply. I knew Father was not one for idle chit-chat, but his silence unnerved me. He hadn't said a word since he picked me up, except for occasionally cursing at the automobile.

"Better have," he finally scowled. "If you're getting paid five thousand dollars a year to play baseball, you better be hitting home runs."

I nodded. "You think it's going to be Detroit's year for the series?"

He turned his gaze to me and stared so long the roadster edged to the side of the road. Before I could grab the wheel, he refocused and guided the tires back on track. "I got it," he groused.

"So," I tried again, "who's up for the series?" I thought it was safe to talk baseball, a sport that he loved, even though I'd never had much interest in it.

He frowned. He wasn't about to talk baseball with someone who'd never swung a bat. Instead, he sped up and got down to brass tacks.

"Your mother and I have been on our knees about you every night since you left, James." His baritone voice always dropped an octave when he turned serious, something that had probably served him well as a US Deputy Marshall for McLean County. "But I can't say enough how much your letters this last month met us with great joy." I felt his shoulder relax and heard his voice crack. "You've had a great cloud of witnesses surrounding you." He blinked a tear.

Can't say I'd ever seen my father cry. My chest tightened at the trouble I'd caused him.

"I'm sorry, Pop."

When he didn't reply, I didn't know if he'd heard me over the wind or just ignored my apology. "This November I'll be sober now for two years," I shouted.

He nodded and his frown lines deepened. "Your inebriation was probably my fault, son. I'm sorry."

My eyebrows raised and my jaw dropped. I couldn't believe he apologized to me.

He caught my look and chuckled grimly. "Guess the devil had it out for you on account of me."

I looked at him, confused.

"When I turned twelve," he began, "I joined the Juvenile Temperance Society at the church at the urging of my father, who passed away forty-eight hours later. To honor his memory, the society formed the Temple of Honor. We were determined to stop the sale of liquor in Bloomington."

I breathed slowly with expectation.

"Many of us Templars became the city council," he continued. "We passed an ordinance declaring the sale of liquor to be a nuisance and closed every saloon in town. It was a fine day when Abraham Lincoln came to town to assist in defense of the law."

I shook my head with wonder. "I've never heard you tell of this."

"Well, probably because we lost. The judge declared the ordinance unconstitutional and handed a victory over to the liquor interest." He scowled, still angry at the ruling, and swore, "Damn devil…relentless bastard."

It was more swearing than I'd ever heard from his lips.

"But the Lord is victorious," he sang in his next breath, reminding me of Reverend Driver. "He's always victorious," he said defiantly, sounding every bit like himself and lifting an arthritic finger to the sky.

I was glad when he lowered his hand to the wheel but startled when, instead, he patted my leg, glanced at me, and smiled. Then he returned his hand and his attention to steering the automobile.

His voice turned serious. "Is there another woman?" he asked bluntly.

"No," I said without hesitation, grateful that it was sincere and thankful to Mary for keeping me on the straight and narrow.

I felt his body relax as we settled that issue.

"So," he began, his baritone almost singing with warmth, "they asked you to become superintendent of the mission? Good for you, Jimmy, good for you." He patted my leg again.

"Of course, it's not what I had in mind for you. I thought perhaps the pulpit of a proper Methodist church, not skid row in downtown Denver, and certainly not a Baptist." He smiled and turned from the road long enough to wink at me. "But if sinners were good enough for Jesus, I suspect they're good enough for you. If Jesus took a dunking, then I say go for it. We'll still allow you at our table." He chuckled. "The Loars will be happy about you falling into the Baptist camp."

"You talk to the Loars? They know I'm coming?"

"Yes, Dr. Loar and I have been meeting. I visited their house yesterday and they know of the Lord's transformation of you. I think he's satisfied."

"And Ada and her mother?"

My father pursed his lips and tilted his head in thought, then glanced at me with a twinkle. "You know what's worse than a woman scorned?" He didn't wait for my answer. "Two women scorned." He chuckled again.

Sweat dripped down my back.

His levity diminished, and his tone became serious. "Your mother and I will celebrate fifty-seven years of marriage at the end of the month. It hasn't always been easy, especially whenever we lost one of your brothers or sisters."

Of the twelve of us, my parents had lost three of my sisters and two of my brothers.

"I don't know what to tell you except go in with a contrite heart," my father advised, "and maybe an acceptable gift. Hopefully, two years will have put out the fire." He looked at me with his eyebrows raised. "Just be yourself." He paused and then added, "Well, on second thought, best be tucking that smart-aleck, stage-loving side of you out of sight." Then he brightened. "I do know a little boy who's going to be glad to see you."

Fear rose in my mind, but at least I enjoyed one of my first grown-up discussions with my father.

"Pop...I'm not sure I have what it takes to run the mission."

His smile reminded me of Joseph. "Well...it's not up to you, James. Few men would end up in the pulpit if that was the case. God doesn't call the qualified, He qualifies the called. Besides, your mother and I rejoiced at your letter that said that the night you shared your testimony, the Lord brought the highest number of conversions ever in the mission's history. I know the Lord is with you, Jimmy."

"They probably just felt sorry for my stammering," I said.

"You know, James, the Lord loves using the broken."

I said no more and looked at the road ahead, letting the wind blow my hair, and the sun warm my face. It reminded me of Joseph's words about me being a new man. Being here on the road with my father was the first time since I'd stumbled into the mission that I believed it might be so.

We sat in comfortable silence for many miles. Finally, I asked, "Where we headed first?"

"To get you a shave and haircut...and buy you a suit befitting of a pastor. You can't go visiting Dr. Loar looking like that."

11

DON'T POKE THE BEAR

I counted the stairs leading up to the Loars' front door—thirteen, the same number of years Ada and I had been married. My legs turned to jelly, and I thought I would fall. It was as though I would take Mary's advice and crawl up the stairs on my hands and knees, even if I didn't want to. With my father behind me, he inquired as to my well-being, and I pulled myself together.

As we reached the top landing, muffled tones of a piano and gospel hymn emanated from the home. Both Ada and her mother, Olive, played beautifully, but the raspy voice coming from the house sounded like my mother-in-law's, and I assumed Olive was busy chasing away demons before my reappearance.

Father grabbed my elbow for support as he pulled himself up the last step. Then he turned me around. "You look good, son. Try to relax."

I looked at my new patent leather shoes, which were already hurting my feet. Father had insisted on the black shoes and matching suit. But I felt more like a mortician than a returning husband. I wished I could have talked him into the brown tweed, but he wouldn't hear of it, insisting it looked too modern for the Loars.

The Loars were staunch members of the First Baptist Church, and Dr. Nelson Loar was a well-established and extremely respected family physician. He'd delivered half the babies in Bloomington, including our Donny in Ada's own childhood bedroom.

I remembered Dr. Loar that day, as cool as a cucumber while I clenched my hands in the parlor downstairs, awaiting the baby's arrival. When he finally slid open the chamber doors, he wiped his bloody hands on a white towel. It was the first time I'd seen him without his jacket and with his shirt sleeves rolled up over his elbows.

He smiled as he gave me a tight embrace and handed me a cigar. "It's a boy, son!"

I hoped he'd saved some of that jubilation for today.

The wooden landing under my feet creaked, and the music in the house stopped. I wiped my forehead with the back of my hand and stepped to the door, feeling my father's presence over my right shoulder.

I couldn't decide whether to knock or ring the doorbell. In either case, I was sure they knew we were here. I'd seen shadows near the upstairs windows when we drove up.

Might as well go all in. I rang the bell.

It seemed like an eternity before I heard footsteps and saw Dr. Loar's silhouette move past the etched glass sidelight next to the entrance. The door opened quickly, and my father-in-law greeted me with a smile and hardy handshake.

"Jimmy, good to see you!" he exclaimed with the same fervor he had when announcing the birth of my son. "James," he said, reaching past me and greeting my father with a handshake.

"Come in, come in," he welcomed, escorting us into the entry and waving us into the parlor, where I'd anxiously waited for Donny to come into the world.

Olive and Ada were nowhere to be seen. I didn't know if that was good or bad. Nelson slid the French doors closed behind him and indicated for us to sit on the chairs in the bay window.

Dr. Loar stood, crossed his arms, and paced slowly back and forth in front of me. My heart skipped several beats.

"Jimmy, I thank the Lord that you have come to your senses. I know your parents also rejoice that their prodigal son has returned." He winked at my father, dropped one hand and stroked his beard with the other. "But, as Ada's father, I have to say that Mrs. Loar and I were mighty disappointed in your behavior." He stopped, looked at me with stern eyes, and waited for me to speak.

My mind raced to find the right words—excuses and justifications wouldn't do.

"Sir…all I can say is I'm sorry," I pleaded. "I have no argument or defense that can explain my ways." My voice cracked, and I fought back tears. I knew that acting like a sissy wouldn't help my cause. "I'm sorry," I repeated. A Bible verse dropped into mind, one that I'd heard Reverend Gravett say over and over. It fell from my lips unbidden. "'The goodness of God leadeth thee to repentance.'"

The quote seemed to surprise my father and Dr. Loar as much as it did me. It was probably the first time I'd quoted the scriptures.

Dr. Loar dropped his hand from his beard. "This is true, son. This is true."

"Dr. Loar, I have been sober for near two years now, and I make every effort to live a right and wholesome life. I know I'm not worthy of your daughter's mercy and affections, but I do love her and ask for your and your family's forgiveness."

Dr. Loar was a charitable and compassionate man. His body language relaxed, and his smile returned. "Son, you have my forgiveness," he said, turning to the French doors and opening them as though it were a secret signal. "But I'm afraid the rest is not up to me."

Olive marched into the room with Ada a step behind her. Mrs. Loar had gained a few pounds, and she'd pulled her hair into such a tight bun that it raised her eyebrows but didn't turn her smirk into a smile. That darn smirk. *Don't poke the bear*, I reminded myself.

I pulled a silver spoon from my jacket pocket. They made it from the silver mine of Horace Tabor, Denver's silver king. At least that was the story told to me by the man on the street who sold it. Tabor aside, I just hoped the darn thing was genuine silver. Olive collected spoons, and this was the best I could do to win back her favor.

"Mrs. Loar, I brought you this spoon from Denver. I'm hopin' it might fit well in your collection."

She looked at it and back at me without changing her expression. I didn't think she would take it until my father intervened.

"Hello, Olive. It's good to see you again," he said, stepping forward and extending his hand. She offered him a limp hand and then took the spoon from me. Without giving it another look, she put it on the curio cabinet next to the door.

I looked beyond her to see Ada with her eyes cast down. She had her hair in a bun similar to her mother's and wore a white blouse with a high collar and an ankle-length black skirt. My stomach knotted with anxiety; this wasn't going well and wouldn't end well. What a cad I'd been to this beautiful woman who was quiet and modest and always laughed at my silly jokes and sweeping soliloquies. She had made me feel like Charley Chase, the movie comedian and actor. I also missed her ability to make a piano sing and her superb cooking. Even from where I stood, I could smell her perfume. It was her favorite, lavender, and a pilot light of passion sprang to life in my belly.

I searched Olive's imperious face for a sign and looked at Ada for affirmation. No one moved or spoke, so I thought the reunion had ended, and they would banish me. But a ruckus broke out behind Ada. Footsteps raced down the staircase, and the Loars' nanny shouted, "Donald, come back here. Your grandmother is going to…" Before she could finish, Donny burst into the room, almost knocking me over and hugging my waist.

"Daddy, Daddy!"

I couldn't believe he'd grown a foot in my two-year absence, and I suddenly became as enraged at myself as Olive was. *How could I have abandoned this child?*

He released his hold to look up at me with bright eyes. "Daddy, thank you for coming back," he said and re-tightened his grip around my waist and buried his face in my hip, making it clear he would not let me go.

I peeled him from my waist, squatted, and hugged him tightly. His arms almost choked the life out of my neck, but I didn't mind. God, how I'd missed him.

I kissed his cheek, dug into my jacket pocket, and pulled out a model of a locomotive. His face filled with joy as he took the toy from my hand. I couldn't help feeling a twinge of guilt that I hadn't thought of it myself. Mary had suggested at the station that I buy him a present and even loaned me the money. I needed to remember how to be a father again—if the Loars would let me.

Donny examined the engine carefully. Satisfied that I was

actually here, he asked me, "You meet any real Indians in Colorado?"

I looked at Olive, who frowned, and thought about the Indians on Larimer Street.

Ada pushed past her mother into the room and squeezed Donny's shoulders. "We've been studying a bit about the Wild West," she explained and smiled.

I smiled back. I had no words. I wanted so badly to take her in my arms, but a glance at scowling Olive deterred me. Still, the sound of my wife's voice had reassured me that everything was going to be okay.

LABOR DAY PARADE

September 6, 1909
(One Month Later)

Denver's Union Station bustled with excitement as the starting point for the Labor Day parade. It would begin in two hours and work its way down Sixteenth Street to the capitol building. The locals festooned the station with patriotic bunting a year ago to celebrate the Democratic National Convention held in the new Denver Auditorium Arena—the first to be convened in a Western state. The city had kept the streamers in place even though William Jennings Bryan, the state's choice for president, had lost to the Republican, William Howard Taft. Bryan extended generosity toward the silver interests, and that made him a hero to the miners. I figured the city just didn't want to admit their candidate lost and left the convention folderol up in protest or solidarity.

The rumor swirled that President Taft might be in the parade, and the speculation arose whether they needed a larger wagon to haul him, a man of significant substance, or if an automobile could support his more than three-hundred-pound figure.

Either way, it had been a terrible decision to bring Ada and Donny to Denver on Labor Day. If their train didn't arrive on time, we'd get swept up in the parade crowds. Reverend Gravett had been kind enough to provide his carriage and driver, which waited for us in front of the station. I watched the driver from the platform where I stood. I could tell he and the horse were growing impatient. The driver glanced at me and sighed. I shrugged and gave him a look of commiseration.

We'd stop by the mission first, then take them to our new home on Fourteenth and Bannack. *Some home*, I sighed. The small flat was barely a step up from a flophouse, but Reverend Gravett had paid the first few months' rent as a gift to me for becoming superintendent. I hoped the place might be adequate for Ada and Donny, but I knew better. When she saw it, she might just turn around and go back to Bloomington and the comfortable life she had grown accustomed to.

I looked at the clock hanging from the porte-cochère. Their train should arrive any time, and I leaned against a post supporting the awning over the platform. I thought the pole would give me something to latch onto amid the crowd and tried distracting myself with the newspaper in my hand. The headline read, "U.S. Army Signal Corps Buys First Military Aircraft from Wright Brothers." I tried reading the text, but even with the protection of the post, people jostled me, trying to maneuver their luggage through the crowd. I gave up and tucked the paper under my arm.

Ada's letter said they assigned her to the fourth car of the train, and I hoped I had chosen the right place on the platform where her car would stop. If I'd misjudged, it would be next to impossible to find them in this mob.

For days, I had been nervous as a cat surrounded by a pack of coyotes. To make matters worse, my digestion acted up, and I worried I'd have to find a bathroom in all the chaos. I pushed on my stomach, willing it to stop rumbling.

When I'd left Bloomington a month ago, I did not know whether Ada would allow the reconciliation of our family. She had promised that in two weeks she would send me word of her decision. Two weeks to the day, I received the joyous letter —she and Donny would arrive in Denver on September 6, Labor Day.

I pulled off my faithful porkpie, smoothed what was left of my hair, and frowned. I feared all the stress and worry over the last few months left me balding. I also doubted my adequacy of being a father and husband. Half my life had passed, and here I started over. The suit Father had bought me didn't give me any confidence; it made me feel stiff and a failure in my own skin. If I could be a better person, live up to everyone's expectations, maybe Ada would love me once again…Ada and everyone else, including God. But I doubted I'd win back what little respect I ever had from Olive.

Ada's shyness hindered her ability to show affection. *What if she no longer wanted to lie with me?* Did I even remember how to be intimate? Now, while I waited for her train, I grinned, hoping it was like riding a bicycle, but the imagery tickled my funny bone, so I pushed it from my head.

That demon of alcohol, always at my side, spoke loudly in my ear: "You need a drink." I couldn't have agreed more. Then, in my other ear, I heard my father's low baritone voice: "Jimmy, you're in for a battle, but you have what it takes." I have to admit, I really missed my father. We'd connected more in the few days I went home than in my entire lifetime. Sadness pierced my heart as I wondered if I'd ever see him again.

It occurred to me that when he'd seen me off in Bloomington, he may have felt the same sadness. He'd hugged me tightly, and then, with tears in his eyes, he'd held my shoulders, looked me straight in the eyes, and said, "Never let go of Jesus, no matter what you do."

A man bumped my shoulder and jostled me back to reality. He apologized. I smiled at him, and he blended into the crowd. That's when I saw it—the black locomotive rounding the bend, pulling twenty passenger cars, including one carrying my wife and son.

Since Ada avoided public displays of affection, our reunion became slightly awkward when I ended up kissing her hand after she extended it—something I'd never done before. Her blush matched the pink bow on her hat.

By the time we retrieved Ada's steamer trunks from the baggage compartment, pulled them to the carriage, and climbed aboard, the parade had started. We sat in regal splendor, as the driver had peeled back the carriage top, allowing us to bask in Colorado's sunshine and crisp September air. The driver slapped the reins of the horse and pulled away from Union Station.

"I'm afraid it's going to take us a while to get to Larimer," he said. "I guess we've become part of the parade." He looked back at us and smiled.

I wasn't sure about myself, but Ada looked perfect for riding in a parade. A large straw hat with a bow covered her auburn hair neatly tucked into a bun. I smiled at her, and she smiled back, but I could see her slightly nervous look of amazement at all the activity that surrounded us. I admired the new wire-rimmed glasses they had fitted her with. The white blouse and ankle-length skirt appeared to be the same one she had worn at our reunion, but the pearl-encrusted cross broach at her collar and the silver pocket watch hanging from her leather belt were new. I suspected they were going-away gifts from her parents. I had noticed her discomfort walking and attributed it to her new leather cowboy boots, which needed to be broken in. But I imagined the crowd that lined the street believed she was a celebrity.

Donny hadn't left my side since he'd gotten off the train. Even now, he stood on the seat between us with his hand on my shoulder.

Our driver pulled up behind a military band marching with precision. The band led us through the huge steel arch erected three years ago to welcome everyone to the city of Denver. The arch's two hundred lights blazed, turned on for the parade even though the clock atop Union Station chimed high noon.

Donny's mouth gaped as we passed under the arch, and he turned and stretched his neck to see the other side. "Dad-dy," he said, "it says 'Welcome' on the other side, but on this side, it says 'Miz…pah.' What is Miz…pah?"

Wow. My son can read! Then I sadly realized he had turned nine, and I missed his learning-to-read years. Thankfully, I knew the answer to his question. I had noticed the unfamiliar words on the way to the station and asked the driver about it.

"*Mizpah* is Jewish for 'watchtower.'"

"Watchtower?" Donny asked

"The watchtower represents a pile of stones to mark an agreement between two people with God as their witness," I explained. "Jacob, a man in the Bible, took his wives and chil-dren and fled from his father-in-law. When his father-in-law found out, he raged even though his daughters had left volun-tarily. When he caught up with Jacob, he made him promise to watch over his daughters and not take any other wife. The two men erected a pile of stones, a *mizpah*, as a remembrance of this promise."

Lost in my explanation, I finally noticed Donny's attention wandered elsewhere. But Ada had been listening. I smiled at her, and she smiled back. We recognized how appropriate mizpah became to the two of us.

I started to speak when the band struck up a rousing "Battle Hymn of the Republic," and the music swelled among the brick buildings. I chuckled to myself—we were part of the grand parade only because there was no other way to get to Larimer Street. People packing the sidewalks broke into song, accompanying the band. Many of them even waved enthusiastically at us.

I laughed and shouted to Ada and Donny, "Just a little show I put together to welcome you."

Donny's grip on my shoulder tightened, and his eyes widened. Ada brought her hand up to her mouth, trying to cover her grin.

It took us an hour to go the five blocks. The most challenging part was convincing the copper to let us turn left on Larimer. Fortunately, our driver succeeded, and the police officer finally separated the crowd to let us through.

When we stopped in front of the mission, I jumped down from the carriage and offered my hand to assist Ada. She stepped onto the sidewalk and inspected the white, one-story building, the Living Waters Mission. I turned back just in time to catch Donny jumping from the carriage.

I glanced up and down Larimer Street and couldn't believe my eyes. With the excitement of the parade, Larimer seemed like a quiet cul-de-sac with no traffic, no fistfights, no gunfights, and no dead horses named Sunshine. Of course, I was grateful for the absence of all that, but the ubiquitous odor of skid row remained. I winced as Ada sniffed into her hankie. She hesitated, and I thought I might lose her, that she'd step back into the carriage and demand to return to Bloomington.

But she transfixed her eyes on a young girl about the same age as Donny approaching the mission door. The child, one of the many orphans who begged between meals for scraps of bread or fruit, had a bowl-cut, cropped hair—probably chopped by one of the other children. She wore a filthy knee-length peasant dress, dirtier than her bare feet. The somber child, who mesmerized both Donny and Ada, ignored their stares. As the girl grabbed the door to the mission, she paused, remembering her manners. She turned to Ada and curtsied.

I'm not sure I heard right, but the child smiled and said to Ada, "I knews you were comin'." She held out her hand for Ada's, opened the door like she welcomed us, and we stepped through with her.

The main room was empty and dark. I hadn't noticed the pungency of the soap and water we used to clean the floor and tables until Ada stood at my side and I experienced the mission through her eyes.

Pans rattled in the kitchen, and I invited Ada and Donny to follow me. "The staff is working on dinner and looking forward to meeting you."

With orphan in hand, Ada followed me into the kitchen, and as soon as we entered, the five men cooking stopped in their tracks. Joseph sliced potatoes, but he responded immediately. He put down his knife, grabbed a towel from the rack above the countertop, wiped his hands, and offered a dry one to Ada. She took it with ease and smiled at him.

"So mighty glad to make your acquaintance, Miz Good-heart," he said, pumping her hand eagerly.

"You must be Joseph, whom I've heard so much about," she said, glancing around the room at the other men. "Please call me Ada."

"Yes, siree, Miz Ada. I'm Joseph, and you're as refined a lady as James described. It is an honor to have you here." He finally released her hand and put his own on his hips. "You must be starved and thirsty half to death from your travels. Can I get you something to eat...coffee?"

"Coffee would be fine," Ada said, and looked down as the forlorn orphan girl squeezed her fingers. Ada smiled and added, "Maybe something to eat as well."

Joseph had noticed the child and looked to me for permission. We rarely fed the orphans between meals. If we did, they'd eat us out of house and home. Then I caught Joseph's look at Donny, who hid behind my legs. I pulled him around and introduced him.

"How do you do?" Joseph said. "You a fine young man. I suppose we could come up with a cookie or two." He glanced at the orphan and smiled. "And for the young miss as well."

I had no objection. He found a jar and offered cookies to the children.

While Joseph fetched coffee from the urn outside the kitchen, I introduced Ada to the other men, including the chief cook, a short, stout Italian who stood in front of the stove tending three large pots, rocking in a boil.

"*Benvenuto, Signora*," he said. "Welcome."

"Thank you," Ada said. "What are you cooking?"

Using the corner of his dirty apron, the cook lifted the lid off one pot. I wasn't sure if the steam or the smell made Ada step back and put her hankie to her nose. Most likely the vat of chicken necks bubbling to the surface caused the revulsion.

"What is that?" she said bluntly.

Fortunately, the cook spoke very little English, and I stepped in. "Uh…it's dinner. Chicken-neck soup," I said with as much pride as I could muster, hoping she didn't gag. The chef was very sensitive about his cooking. "It's pretty slim pickings around here, we're lucky that the butcher shop sells these to us. It's all we can afford."

Ada focused on the other men, who looked sheepish, as though their mothers had caught them with a girly magazine.

"You all like this soup?" Ada said.

They all looked at the floor.

"How often do you serve this?"

No one answered.

Ada looked at the loaves of bread on the counter. She nodded approvingly until she saw the moldy butter and frowned.

The Italian's face lit bright red. I watched the scene unfold like a slow-motion automobile accident. He started with a string of Italian, intermixed with obscenities, then worked himself up to a full rage until he ripped his apron off without untying it, threw it at her feet, and stormed out of the kitchen.

Oh, God. I've made a colossal mistake. We all stood frozen with only the sound of the boiling vats of chicken necks. Joseph returned to the kitchen, nearly getting knocked aside by the enraged Italian, and stated the obvious, "Who's cooking dinner tonight?"

Ada frowned, crossed her arms and considered the situa-tion. I could see the wheels turning in her brain. I'd never seen her so sure of herself.

"This is Colorado, isn't it?" she said. "Is anyone here a hunter?" Two of the men raised their hands like schoolboys answering the teacher. "All right. Now you two go out and shoot us a couple of deer, and tomorrow I'll fix a meal that'll stick to your ribs. Venison stew."

Ada ignored Joseph and the cup of coffee. She went to the wall where the aprons hung and selected one. She held it to the light and shook her head. It hadn't seen the laundry in a while, but she put it on anyway and rolled up her sleeves. "We've got a lot of work to do, boys."

13

SMALL BEGINNINGS

"What is that, Daddy?"

Someone shook my shoulder. I woke with a start and blinked. My eyelids fluttered to see Ada on the other side of Donny, as he stared out the window from a spot in the bed beside me. Although nice for an old loner like me to wake up with companionship, I had to admit I didn't sleep well, with all three of us on the double-size mattress. I assumed we would make a mat for Donny on the floor in our one-bedroom flat, but when we'd come home from a long night at the mission, I could tell by the look in Ada's eyes that she thought the place looked like a dump and refused to let Donny sleep on the floor. Too tired to argue, it meant that there was no intimate reunion as our son tossed and twisted between us all night long. Still, having him beside me brought comfort.

I pulled Donny close, so his chin rested on my chest. "What's what?" I asked.

"That!" he said, pointing out the window.

"That, son, is our million-dollar view." I lifted my head

to look out the window. "It's the Colorado State Capitol." The stately gold dome rose high above the neighboring apartment building. Truth be told, this was the only splendid view from our humble flat on Fourteenth and Bannock. The rest of our windows looked at the other apartment buildings in much need of repair and paint—that is, if you could even see them. Each flat had a coal-burning stove, so, on a wintry day, about all you could see was black smoke.

"What is a capitol?" Donny asked.

"Where they keep all the scoundrels."

"Like a jail?"

Ada rolled toward us, pulling the blanket tightly around her. "James, don't go and confuse the boy."

I turned and greeted my wife, "Good morning." She just looked at me, and I knew I had to make amends, so I turned back to the window and said, "Donny, that's where they make the laws for Colorado. They gilded that dome with gold leaf just last year."

"Real gold?" he asked. "Wow. Can we go see it?"

The talk of gold even aroused Ada, and she raised her body so she could see the capitol dome.

I smiled at her and said, "Sure, if you and your mother would like."

Donny jumped from under the covers and bounced on the bed between us. "Mother, can we? Can we go, please?"

Ada pulled him down and hugged him to stop the seismic shaking. "We've got a lot to do today. Maybe soon." She rolled him over her and set him on the floor. "Now you go wash up and get dressed, and we'll talk about it then."

He picked himself up and left the room with joyful expectation, taking his mother's maybe as a yes.

I couldn't help but admire her rapport with the boy, an

equal measure of love and discipline. I wondered if I could build such a relationship after all this time.

Ada wrapped herself in the blanket and turned back to me. "He's sure excited to be here…and to see you."

I put my hand on her shoulder, hoping she wouldn't pull away. Last night she had waited until Donny and I were in our pajamas and in bed, and the room darkened before she appeared in her nightshirt. Her ghostly silhouette quickly came to bed and tucked itself under the quilt. I knew most of her modesty came on account of the boy, but some of it originated from fear and uncertainty of me. I realized I had a long way to go to gain her trust, affection, and love.

Now, in the new morning, Ada's auburn hair tumbled down her neck. The last time I'd seen her hair out of her tight bun was in the hospital when the surgeon told me she would not survive the night. *Blasted man.* Leaving the hospital and abandoning Ada represented a horrific mistake. I'd told Joseph the complete story, and he told me not to be so angry at the physician. "He'd just done his job. Besides," Joseph added, "forgiveness goes a long way…even forgiveness for yourself."

A strand of Ada's hair had fallen over her eye, and with my finger, I swept it back. "And how about you? Are you happy to be here…to be with me?"

I thought her slight hesitation gave away her true feelings, but she said, "Yes, of course, James, you are my husband."

It wasn't rejection, but it wasn't an enthusiastic endorsement. I tried reading her eyes, but they gave nothing away. It was simply Ada's nature. She was certainly a fine-looking woman, a capable and strong woman, but no one had ever described her as warm and endearing. Besides, we'd not yet talked through my betrayal, but that time would surely come.

A sense of loneliness crept over me, and even at eight

o'clock in the morning, my alcohol cravings tried slithering in.

My mind beat it down, and I said, "Well, I'm glad you're here and are giving me a second chance."

"Can I make you breakfast?" she asked.

"Sounds good." Not exactly what I'd hoped for, but it sounded like a good idea, and we had a lot to do. My first day as superintendent of the mission started today.

Ada pulled her arms from under the covers, stretched, and yawned deeply. Her nightshirt covered her arms to her wrists, and the neckline almost covered her chin, as if she wore a sign that said, DON'T TOUCH. I'm sure if I got any loving, it wouldn't be until we found a two-bedroom apartment.

Anger and frustration grumbled in my chest. I tried to crush it, but some of it verbalized as, "We can't go running anyone else off today."

"That man has no business in a kitchen," she huffed, very much like her mother. I nearly made the mistake of pointing that out and fought back the urge to call her Olive. In our thirteen years of marriage, I'd done that twice, and each time, it did not end well. Not sure why women hated to be compared to their mothers.

"That soup," Ada continued, "if you can even call it that, is one of the most disgusting things I've ever smelled. I don't want to even imagine the taste."

"That's what they've been serving for years," I said. "Funds have been short, and besides, that's the way they've always done it."

"The way they've always done it," she scoffed. "Isn't that the definition of stupidity? Just keep doing the same thing even though it's not working." She grew angry enough to sit up. "Jim Goodheart, you've always been an optimist. That's why I fell for you. But, husband, open your eyes to the condition the mission is in. It's barely suitable for feeding the rats."

As angry and hurt as I felt, I knew her words struck near reality. Except that the mission survived as one of the few places on Larimer that didn't have a rat problem.

"If I'm going to be a part of this," Ada said, "we're going to do it right. My father taught me that you don't give your scraps and leftovers to the poor, you give them your very best. 'Whoever oppresses the poor shows contempt for their Maker, but whoever is kind to the needy honors God.'"

"That from the Bible?" I knew the verse but couldn't resist teasing her.

"Oh, James, you're impossible." But her expression went from frown to grin.

Her smile returned, but I knew she spoke truth. What I… what we were getting into seemed impossible and insurmountable. I held my head in my hands trying to keep it together. Of course, I'd been honored with all the attention from Reverends Gravett and Driver, as well as Joseph and even the men on the street, but I knew this would not be some cakewalk. I treaded in water over my head. "I don't know where to start," I moaned. "I can't do this by myself."

Ada grabbed my wrists and pulled my hands from my face. "We'll do this together. We'll work like it's all up to us and pray like it's all up to God."

I nodded reflexively.

"James, you're a good man. You can talk a dying man out of his last nickel, and right now, the mission needs funding. You've sold more mustard than Carter has liver pills. Turn on that thinking cap of yours and work on figuring out a way to raise support for the mission. We can do it. We can create a new beginning."

I stared at her, amazed at her enthusiasm. "You've been thinking about this, haven't you?" I said with surprise.

"I just know that God turns all things for good. Besides, I know how to cook and clean, and it's clear the mission can use that."

"The men...uh..." I hesitated, treading carefully, "the men are not used to having a woman around."

She huffed again. "Yes, I can see that. But the place definitely needs a woman's touch."

I sighed deeply, thinking of the mountain of work ahead of us.

Ada must have read my mind. "We take one step at a time," she said, and tenderly touched my cheek. "Let's pray together and then get out of bed and get to work."

14

SUPERINTENDENT

September 21, 1909

I lugged two bags of garbage over my shoulder to the cans in the alley behind the mission and hefted them up and over with a crash. I stood by the receptacles to catch my breath; two weeks had never passed so fast yet seemed so slow. We were all exhausted. I looked at my hands and picked at the blisters on my palms. New pink skin formed underneath, and just like the mission itself, we were peeling back the old and seeing the beginning of new life. Dr. Loar had sent Ada with two hundred dollars for the mission, so we bought new mops, cleaning supplies, and aprons.

Ada demanded that we serve only one meal a day for two weeks. She had wanted to close the place down completely, but Joseph and I pleaded with her that there would be men that might actually starve during the fortnight. We convinced her we needed to serve at least one meal, a hearty lunch. We swore that for the rest of the day we'd be on our hands and knees cleaning and repairing—and we were.

One of the other helpers had stormed out on the third day, unable to handle the work and accusing Ada of having a tongue like a whip. We easily replaced him with another, willing and able to work and clean for his room and board. Even the Italian returned and with humility reconciled himself with my wife. In return, she promised to teach him how to cook.

Ada had thrown herself into the monumental task of rehabbing the mission, but I noticed a brewing storm of annoyance, often directed at me.

I exhaled a deep sigh. Someone had left a smoldering cigarette butt, and I squashed it with the toe of my shoe.

The back door creaked open and Ada stepped out onto the landing and glanced from side to side. Seeing that I stood alone, she shut the back door hard behind her and walked up to me. She crossed her arms and turned sideways.

Misunderstanding, I said. "Sorry, I just needed to catch my breath."

She ignored my comment, and in her silence, I wished I still smoked and had something to do with my hands.

A large tear rolled down her cheek.

"James Goodheart, why did you abandon me in the hospital that night?" A flood of emotions erupted, and she held her face in her hands as her body trembled.

I stood frozen for a moment, but then reached for her and wrapped my arms around her. "Ada...I am so sorry." I wanted to recount all the excuses and apologies I had written in my letters, but she knew all that. I loosened my embrace and held her by her shoulders. She would look no further than my chest. "Ada, from the moment we met, I knew you were the one. My heart became instantly bound to you...like my heart knew before my head, that I loved you." I tried to bend over to catch her gaze. When I finally did, her eyes puddled in tears. "That night in the hospital, when I thought I lost you, my mind went crazy. I couldn't live without you. I truly am sorry."

I held her face in my hands, kissed her forehead, and the tears running down her cheeks.

"Ada, please forgive me."

She nodded like she'd just been waiting to hear it from my mouth and used the edge of her new apron to wipe her face. She reached out and put her hand on my chest and then reached with her other to brush off some lint.

I leaned in and kissed her on the top lip, and she raised on her toes and returned a passionate kiss.

As I pulled her close, the back door creaked open. "My, oh, my." Joe hung out the door with a wide grin. "Carry on, you youngsters." He snickered, saluted us with his fingers, and closed the door.

We could still hear him laughing through the closed door and Ada slapped me on the chest. "I guess we're going to be the talk of the town."

"I sure hope so," I said and pulled her close and kissed her again.

I stretched my back, and the chair squawked under my weight, threatening to fall apart. I looked at Joseph, who sat across the table. "Looks like we missed one," I said.

Joseph and I had spent a good part of the week repairing the furniture with horse glue.

"I'll get to it as soon as we're done," Joseph said and gave me a thumbs-up with his bad hand.

With the other tables and chairs stacked neatly on one side of the room, the mission seemed like an empty, lonely space. I missed the swarming buzz of bums preparing for supper's grace and an ear beating. At least now the room squeaked with cleanliness.

The eclectic group sitting around the table included Ada and me, Reverends Gravett and Driver, Joseph, the Italian cook, Mary, and three men who worked for the mission. Donny played in the background with a train set Reverend Gravett had given him.

The best and most unusual part of the last two weeks was when Ada met Mary. I had dreaded the meeting, but by some miracle, the two hit it off splendidly. From the very beginning, I'd written to Ada about Mary and how she had as much to do with saving my life as anyone. The women met at the mission on the second day when Mary stopped by with a present for Ada, a small bottle of perfume. I doubted Ada would ever use it, but I noticed it had a place of honor on her bedside table with some of her prized possessions.

Ada responded with a gift for Mary. I couldn't believe my eyes when Ada detached the pearl cross from her collar and attached it to Mary's dress. It was the second time I'd seen Mary burst into tears.

Looking at the two of them today, I had to resist chuckling out loud. Ada, a head shorter, wore a gray blouse with a white collar, a black skirt under a full-length apron, and her auburn hair tightly pulled into her signature bun. Mary, on the other hand, had dressed to the nines. Her long red curls tumbled down her shoulders over her blue silk dress. Each woman seemed to hold a mutual respect for the other, and everything Ada suggested, Mary endorsed with a loud "Amen."

"I'm not sure the place has ever smelled so good," Reverend Gravett said to Ada. "Or looked so good." He swallowed another bite of Ada's pound cake. "Or tasted so good."

He took a sip of coffee and turned to me. "James, I'm sorry I've been out of town, and we haven't been able to install you properly, but I see that the lack of a ceremony hasn't mattered one bit." He smiled and turned back to my wife. "I am so thankful you're here, Ada. You know that in business, there can be only one head, and here at the mission, we've marked James as the superintendent, but we all know who the real boss is." He winked at her.

"That's fo'sho," Joseph spoke up, and everyone laughed.

"I'm afraid I'm giving you a heck of a mess and asking for a Herculean effort," Reverend Gravett said to me, "but I also know we serve a faithful God who will provide."

He reached into his leather briefcase on the floor and pulled out some papers.

"Before we do a proper installation and lay hands on you, I thought I better give you full disclosure," he said and spread the papers in front of Ada and me.

Reverend Driver leaned over to Joseph and said in a stage whisper, "Better go lock the doors, Joe." A man of little humor, I couldn't tell if he was teasing.

"I'll start with the good news." Gravett cleared his throat and shifted in his chair. "We own this place, and, like it or not, this is what we got. We purchased it during the heydays of '93, and we paid way too much for it, but at least it's completely paid off. I'm not sure it's worth much more than these papers, but we own it."

"Used to be a bar, pawnshop, then gambling parlor," Reverend Driver said, counting prior establishments on his fingers. "Until we came along," he added with pride that suggested they had reclaimed the building for a higher purpose.

"So here's the bad news." Gravett leaned back in his chair and sighed. "We're as broke as an Indian pony."

I tried deciphering the fine print on the papers.

"How broke?" Ada asked without hesitation.

"Broke, broke," Gravett said. "Five thousand dollars in the hole broke."

I looked at Ada, worrying she might beat me to the door, but she continued to sit calmly.

"It's like a drain without a stopper," Driver added. "There are more mouths to feed than we know what to do with, and the measly amount we collect in the plate after my sermons hardly pays for a loaf of bread."

"Galilee has given as much as they can," Gravett said, "and I'm getting pressure from the church elders to slow, if not stop, the support altogether. Everyone, everywhere is hurting." He wiped his brow.

I leaned back in my squawking chair, feeling the weight of a ton of bricks on my shoulders. The room fell silent. I'd been at the mission long enough to know that this place and the other ministries up and down Larimer relied on the generosity of their fellow citizens, but the city itself had gone broke. Many of the silver kings had lost their fortunes, died, or killed themselves, making it harder and harder for social services to have their hands out.

I knew I couldn't sell enough mustard to make a dent, and besides, I couldn't be working two full-time jobs. But then, out of nowhere, inspiration filled my head, and I just blurted it out. "What if we sell advertising?"

The entire group looked at me, convinced I had gone mad.

Driver spoke first. "You mean to put an ad in the *Denver Post* or *Rocky Mountain News*? I don't see how that would work."

"No, no." I shook my head. "I mean sell advertising to people."

Everyone still had a look of confusion.

"It's like this," I tried to explain. "We make our own newsletter and sell advertising to business people and at the same time market the mission."

"Newsletter?" Gravett asked.

"Yeah…I don't know," I said, not sure I'd thought it all the way through or even understood what I meant. "Some pretty fascinating fellas come through here." I rubbed my chin. "Let's help Denver see our clients as real people, not derelicts. Show folks what we're doing here. Maybe once in a while, we could post a sermon from one of you."

Now the Reverends were interested.

Other than agreeing with Ada, Mary hadn't contributed an opinion of her own. Now she spoke up for the first time. "I'd talk Mr. Gahan into placing an ad."

Reverend Gravett scratched his head. "I don't know. And, please, no offense to you, Miss Mary, but we'd have to be careful about what we're advertising."

"You mean I couldn't place an ad for my services?" Mary inquired with irony. She fluttered her eyelashes behind her Chinese fan, making everyone erupt with laughter. Out of the corner of my eye, I saw Ada squeeze Mary's arm. Mary smiled at her and continued to make her point. "Well, if you don't want the saloon's business, I know a few other businessmen I could persuade."

I held my breath, and my stomach churned as the good Reverends processed my idea.

Finally, Gravett nodded and said, "What would you call this newspaper?"

"Well, I wouldn't call it a newspaper. It'd be more of a simple two-page handout," I said.

"How do you plan on getting the funds for the first printing?" Driver asked, putting a dark cloud over my idea.

I didn't have an answer, but Joseph did. "Oh, I 'spect God will provide," he said with his wide grin.

Bolstered by his faith, I spoke up, "There is something else I've been pondering, and you'll have to grant me forgiveness up front."

The Reverends looked at me with concern, but I continued, "I've been wondering how beholden you are to the name of the mission, Living Waters. Reverend Driver explained to me what it meant and all, but if we're freshening up the place, maybe it would be a good idea to choose a fresh name."

Driver looked at Gravett, and I hoped I hadn't tipped over the Holy Grail.

The wheels in Gravett's head were spinning. When they stopped, he nodded and said, "Look, James, you're the new super. If you can turn this dying dog around, I suspect you can call it whatever you want...within reason, of course."

Driver's eyebrows elevated while his chin nodded. "You have something in mind?" he asked.

"Not yet. I wanted to ask you first to see how committed you were to the name, Living Waters."

The front door of the mission swung open, and the autumn wind blew in leaves from the street. Behind them walked a man in a tall cowboy hat and mud-caked spurs that jangled as his boots clomped across the floor. He removed his hat and slapped it against his thigh. A cloud of dust billowed throughout the clean room.

Joseph stood. "I'm sorry, sir, we've already served lunch, and there ain't no supper tonight."

But Joseph's kind announcement did not stop the man's advance. He walked across the room like he owned the place and stood over our table. My heart skipped a beat when I saw the full revolving cylinder of his six-shooter hanging from his side. I first thought that the Italian or one of the other men were in trouble, and Ada would experience her first shooting up close. I peered around the stranger to check on Donny. He had stopped playing and stood staring at the cowboy with his mouth gaping.

I looked into the cowboy's eyes and couldn't tell if I saw anger. Even without his hat, he towered over the table. We all remained silent, waiting for him to speak.

I saw a tear in his eye just before he found the words. "You men…" he began, then paused at the sight of Ada and Mary. "Pardon me, ladies." He started again, "You may not remember me, but this last July, my favorite horse, Sunshine, was shot outside these walls. You were awful kind in helping me with her." He turned to the Italian. "You told me how poor off the mission was and asked if I'd consider letting you cook the mare up for the bums. I just couldn't do it…nearly broke my heart." He brushed the tear away. "You fellas understood and helped me give her a right, fine burial."

I remembered the incident and the dead horse vividly, and I glanced at Ada and wondered if she recalled the story I'd described in a letter.

"No one else has treated me with such kindness," the cowboy said as another tear started down his cheek.

He reached for his side, and I flinched. But instead of grabbing his revolver, he reached into a leather satchel hanging from his belt. He took a fist-sized leather pouch from it and tossed it in the middle of the table.

"Thanks to my lucky stars or whatever you believe in," he said, "my mine in Salida is producing again, and I wanted to repay your kindness to me."

Our group sat stunned, our eyes fixed on the pouch. By how hard it had thudded on the table, I hoped it contained gold and not silver.

The cowboy didn't make us wait. "Just checked at the

bank," he said. "Gold weighs in at 252 ounces. It's yours if'n you can put it to good use."

Because gold buyers were a dime a dozen on Larimer and openly advertised their buying price, I did the math. I'd seen this morning they were purchasing it at twenty dollars and twelve cents an ounce. This man had given us over five thousand dollars in gold.

Joseph was right about God providing. I turned to him as he flashed his enormous white smile.

Reverend Gravett stood first. "What's your name, sir?" He extended his hand.

The cowboy took it firmly. "My name is Horatio Preston," he said.

Joseph laughed. "We's just trying to decide on a new name for this place. Maybe we should name it after our first benefactor. Preston's Place is as good as any."

We all nodded, but Horatio shook his head. "Oh no, I don't need no notoriety around these parts. People come begging once they know they could get a handout." His face turned red with the irony of his statement. "I don't mean no disrespect." He fidgeted with his hat between his hands. "I suppose if'n you want to honor me, then honor my horse Sunshine, the best dang mare a guy ever had."

"The Sunshine Rescue Mission," I announced.

"Well, there's our answer. Jehovah-jireh…the Lord will provide," Reverend Gravett said as we all sat in disbelief around the table for some time after Horatio Preston took his leave.

I'd seen nothing like it but felt nervous that the bag of gold still sat on the table. This wasn't the kind of neighborhood where you could just leave precious commodities out in the open. But if God can provide, God can protect as well.

We all agreed the Sunshine Rescue Mission sounded like a pretty good name. After all, Denver had more sunshine than most parts of the country, and Mary suggested everyone yearns for a ray of hope.

Donny whined at Ada's side, telling her he was hungry and tired. I guessed we all were, but I wasn't ready to quit the meeting. I had a burning question that needed squaring up before the Reverends officially installed us.

Driver never missed a chance to ask anyone if they wanted to know Christ as their Savior. So he asked Horatio Preston if he wanted to pray the sinner's prayer of salvation for himself, but Horatio said he'd come from England and needed no more religion. Driver had prayed over him anyway, that he and his family and all the generations that followed would live in prosperity.

I remembered the night I'd stumbled into the mission and prayed. "The sinner's prayer...I guess I don't understand it," I said to the Reverends. "Is it a magic formula or something?"

Driver looked like he had swallowed a pickle whole.

I think once he got over the shock of my question, he attempted to be kind in his explanation. "James. I guess all men," he nodded to Ada and Mary, "and women, of course, have to come to a choice in believing in God or not. The next decision comes in believing that Jesus *is* God."

Driver pulled out a small leather-bound Bible from his inside jacket pocket, flipped open the pages, and read, "'He,' meaning Jesus," Driver said, "'is the image of the invisible God, the firstborn over all creation. For by Him all things were created that are in heaven and that are on earth, visible and invisible, whether thrones or dominions or principalities or powers. All things were created through Him and for Him.'"

When he looked up from the Bible, he recoiled, as I must have looked like a deer in headlamps.

Reverend Gravett put his hand on my arm, smiled, and tried to reassure me. "I suspect the heavenly Father may laugh at our efforts, as He can turn people's minds to Him in many ways, but I think of the sinner's prayer as a means for people to confess their belief in Jesus."

I was glad Gravett intervened, as the more straightforward of the two.

"Jesus existed in the beginning. The scriptures say, 'He is the Word made flesh and dwelt among us.' God wasn't there first and then made Jesus. Jesus is God...you can't separate one from the other," Gravett said. "Accepting Jesus as our Savior through prayer, in whatever form it takes, is not some sort of ritual that we have to say so God will change His mind about us. It's not about changing God's mind about us...it's about changing our mind about God."

I looked at the others around the table. They all seemed to pay close attention to the Reverends, and my face flushed. It embarrassed me I had so much to learn.

Everyone nodded and Gravett added, "Part of the sinner's prayer is repentance, but some folks think this is just being sorry for their sins. Of course, that's okay as well, but repentance suggests taking on God's thoughts about ourselves. Where the scriptures say 'the goodness of God leadeth thee to repentance' it means that His kindness leads us to have a radical mind shift...to think together with God's thoughts toward us. Many people have turned it around. 'My repentance leads to God's goodness,' as if somehow we are changing God's mind about us."

"Amen," Joseph said.

By now Gravett squeezed my arm hard. "I know you have been chosen, James and Ada. And, James, I know you well enough by now, I suppose, that you don't feel worthy of this anointing. You worry about your fidelity to God. But my biggest hope and strongest prayer for both of you is you get to know yourselves as the one that Jesus loves—who you truly are in Christ."

"God desires that *all* men be saved," Reverend Driver told our group. "This is the foundation of the mission, no matter what we call it."

15

FIRE AND ICE

December 5, 1913
(Four Years Later)

I sat alone at a table in the corner, looking over the records of our finances for the last four years. A large group of men gathered around Ada and her pump organ, singing Christmas carols. The others sat at the tables sipping hot coffee and playing cards. The mission allowed no gambling, but that didn't make the games any less competitive. With the record snowstorm, we weren't asking anyone to leave after lunch as usual, and with the caroling and conviviality, it might as well have been Christmas day.

I glanced at the newspaper that Jimmy had brought in through the storm. The headline read: "Denver in Mantle of Shimmering White Stops Activity and Everyone Jollifies." *Well, that's certainly true for the Sunshine Rescue Mission.* The subtext read: "No Trains, No Schools Open, No Taxis, No Mail Coming into the City, No Noise, No Deliveries, No Funerals, Nothing but Snow, Snow, Snow and Still Falling."

I looked out the window at the white flakes drifting down. *Also true.* I worried for the people of skid row, and glad we kept the mission open for shelter from the storm. Given our resources, we probably should've closed, but if we did, people would die from hypothermia.

We also decided we'd better have plenty of extra coal to distribute and a hot meal on the stove.

"Lord have mercy," I said to no one.

When the storm hit yesterday evening, Ada and I spent the night at the mission along with Donny, who had made his way to the mission before dark, after Denver North High School wisely shut down early with the rest of the schools. He was a fine boy, even for a teenager. Ada wrestled with starting him in high school at thirteen, but he'd turn fourteen in a couple of months and showed great aptitude in his learning. He helped at the mission on weekends, and I paid him a small stipend for doing so.

"'God rest ye, merry gentlemen, let nothing you dismay…'" Ada's voice sang out, accompanied by the choir of men.

Seeing her content and entertaining the hobos made me happy. I wondered if her short legs were getting tired pumping the pedals, but when she glanced at me and winked, I smiled over her satisfaction with our station in life.

I'd bought the organ first thing with what we'd endearingly called the "Preston Miracle," the seed that had kept the doors open for the last four years. But like a man lost in the vast ocean, bobbing helplessly adrift and barely keeping his head above water, so too was the Sunshine Rescue Mission.

Joy and glad tidings at the merriment of the carols and the delicious aroma of Christmas cookies baking in the oven should have filled my soul. Instead, looking over the reports depressed me. I wondered if it was all worth it. The books came in and out of the red more often than the inebriates visited Hop Alley and the opium dens, but I'm sure these illicit places didn't share the same financial burdens as we did. Just when I thought we might squeak ahead, there would be an influx of need or some unexpected expense. Most days, I thought we might just have to give up and close the doors.

Joseph came through the swinging door of the kitchen with a cup of coffee and set a plate of cookies in front of me. "Here you go, boss." It was both a name and habit I was unsuccessful in breaking him of. He never missed a chance to remind me he predicted I'd be running the place. I'd push back and give him credit for getting me into this mess.

I took a cookie. "Thank you, Joseph."

"You look a little down in the mouth for such a joyful day," Joe said.

"Yearly finances," I said grimly. "Don't leave me out of your sight today. No telling what I might do."

He nodded. He knew I wasn't joking, and I wasn't talking about finances. I shared openly my daily struggle to fight off the craving for a drink. Some days it weighed on me worse than others, but during this time every month when I had to work out the finances, the unrelenting thirst struck. He'd told me that God installed me here for that reason. "You know what the men are going through," he'd said and added, "'God's grace is sufficient for thee: for My strength is made perfect in weakness.'"

I knew from all my Bible study that this passage came from the second book of Corinthians. And even though Gravett had ordained me as a Baptist minister, the knowledge didn't make me feel much better.

"The Lord will provide," he never tired of repeating. "Besides, I don't think you're goin' anywhere today." He shot me a smile and pointed out the window.

"I'm guessing you're right." I lifted the front page of the *Post* to him. "Says here that it's a hundred-year snow storm, forty-one inches…heaviest in the city's history." I read to him, knowing he couldn't.

"Better bring some more coal in from the back," he said and walked off, shaking his head and rubbing his shoulders.

A chill frosted the room even with the revelry, and I turned my jacket collar up around my neck. Ada and the men started in on another song—one of my favorites, "The Cherry Tree Carol":

"When Joseph was an old man, an old man was he.
He married Virgin Mary, the Queen of Galilee.
Joseph and Mary walked through an orchard green.
There were cherries and berries, as thick as might be seen.
Mary said to Joseph, so meek and so mild:
Joseph, gather me some cherries, for I am with child."

I'd always loved cherry trees and decided this spring I would plant one in the backyard of our new house.

The thought gave me a glimmer of hope as I watched the snow coming down even harder. As bleak as the snowstorm and the finances were, happiness bubbled up that I had put Ada and Donny into a proper home. It, too, became one of the ripple effects from the Preston Miracle. The owner, who had supported the mission, gave us special compensation in the price for an excellent home on Newton in North Denver.

I looked down at my handwritten notes and pecked away on my typewriter, a barely used Underwood I purchased from a hotel that closed its doors—the second thing I'd bought with the leftover monies from Horatio's gold.

I'd include this report in the Christmas edition of the

Sunshine Messenger. The monthly publication had gone from a two-page newsletter to a twenty-page newsprint magazine that included interest stories from the mission and a sermon by Driver or me. Its popularity had soared, and it amazed me it had taken off like that.

But it also included mundane items like these blasted financial reports. The end-of-year report would show that the total income for the mission in 1913 amounted to just over five thousand dollars. Of that, nearly four thousand, five hundred came from subscriptions and advertising for the *Messenger*, but there was only a measly five hundred from basket collection and just over one hundred in donations. *Like trying to squeeze blood out of a dead turnip.* We would end the year three hundred dollars short. Gravett and Driver said they were proud of that, but this brought me no satisfaction. One of these years I wanted to see us in the black. Plus, when we were short, my salary suffered first, which was meager to begin with. Ada and I had decided that we would not exchange gifts this Christmas, and all we could afford was one small book for Donny. My anger matched the lyrics the carolers were singing:

"Then Joseph flew in anger, in anger flew he.
Let the father of the baby gather cherries for thee!"

I agreed that the Virgin Mary's news had to be shocking for Joseph.

I stopped typing and picked up one of the newly printed three-by-five cards that I'd titled "Rays of Sunshine" after Mary's suggestion. It had been my idea to produce a simple promotional pamphlet to circulate among potential donors. The cards were easier and cheaper to hand out than the magazine, and they gave a quick overview of the mission. The card read:

1. It is clean.
2. Refined people attend.

Guess that's a stretch, but knowing the group includes Ada, I guess that's okay.

3. We hold clean, sane services every night of the year.
4. We agree with the Bible and with churches and are not into fault finding.
5. Are endorsed by the Ministerial Alliance.
6. We ain't affiliated with other missions.

I took my pencil and crossed out *ain't* and wrote in *aren't* for the next printing.

7. Our books are properly kept and regularly audited.
8. Our books are open to public inspection anytime.

Reverend Gravett had suggested the last two lines, "People are darn fickle," he'd said. "You can feed the entire city and do good works, but they love finding fault with godly people—maybe it makes their own miserable lives more tolerable."

I turned the card over and looked at the statistical report on the back:

1. Garments given 4,769
2. Employment given 754
3. Literature distribution 9,476
4. Visits to homes 1,831
5. Visits to hospitals 55

6. Visits to reformatories and jails 68

7. Bed and meals furnished 6,188

8. Legal and medical aid 2,091

9. Total attendance 37,532

10. Convert dealt with 2,091

11. The number fed at last Christmas dinner 956

12. Testaments given away 3,091

13. The number of people given coal 140

14. The number of people given transportation 19

I put the card down and sighed. I wanted to be doing more. So much more should be done. I looked at the number of visits to the hospitals and jails and vowed to triple that next year. We needed more space, and we were serving only men while the orphans on Larimer seemed to multiply like rabbits. The verse from the first chapter of James leapt from my head to my tongue, and I said out loud, "'Pure religion and unde-filed before God and the Father is this, to visit the fatherless and widows in their affliction, and to keep himself unspotted from the world.' Jesus help us."

I leaned back in my chair, watched the snowfall and listened to the rest of "The Cherry Tree":

"Then up spoke baby Jesus, from in Mary's womb:
Bend down the tallest branches, that my mother
might have some.
And bent down the tallest branches, it touched Mary's
hand.
Cried she: Oh look thou Joseph, I have cherries by
command.
Oh look thou Joseph, I have cherries by command."

"Lord, if it's just a matter of asking, then I pray you

deliver us from our need. Pour out Your finances and resources to us," I asked.

I turned back to the table, picked up the most recent envelope from my father, and pulled out the letter to reread. His shaky handwriting had gotten worse in the last month. His handwritten penciled note was in response to my most recent message to him, bemoaning our rotten situation as some churches had withdrawn support. I thought I might as well throw in the towel. "Seemed like the wealthy people had the least to give," I'd written him. I read his response once again:

Dear Jim,
After a night's sleep and awaking to surroundings, I am saying this: it is an impossibility for me to indicate what you should do. One thing is sure, the church preachers and their advisors have it in their hands to sidetrack any mission on the side, as is the Sunshine Mission, when they will and may hope their will is governed by the money demanded and the supply at hand.

And these automobile times when theaters and riding costs so much and causes a great pullback on the laymen's liberality. Which in a shrinking of preachers' salary there is crinkling taking place in the preachers. And so you see you are between the reaper and another millstone. Now the rub comes in, how to keep sweet and beat the blue devil back if you sour or give place in any degree to envy, which is another name for covetous, which again is idolatry. Then the devil has you where the hair is short. That is the way it is here, I see it.

Churches are often more interested in building their buildings than helping the poor. When in prosperity, just like all of mankind, they forget the fellow in the hole when surrounded and comfortable.

But the only way out for you and for me is to let patience have her perfect work in developing in us, the perfect mind of Christ. The patience problem is the biggest thing of all in the Christian life. I am adding this morning this line to help you consider carefully what you do, as great doors turn on very small hinges sometimes. And may God add His blessings to aid in your determine what to do. The old Book says in prosperity—rejoice in adversity. Consider now I am in full sympathy with the situation of your surroundings and it may be pivotal times in your life. But God will certainly lead you right if you trust the leadings of the Holy Spirit.

You are right in saying that liquor traffic is the curse of curses. Be strong in the Lord. But be most careful of pride, self-sufficiency, and arrogance. These are of the flesh, and that part of us must die in order that God may produce good fruit in our lives.

Your mother and I are proud of you, son, and long to come to Colorado for a visit and to witness first hand your good works. We chuckle to ourselves thinking of you as a minister of the Word and give thanks to the Lord for His redemption. (Even though He decided you should become a Baptist.) Give our love to Ada and that good boy of yours.
Your loving father, James Goodheart

I held the letter to my nose and inhaled, hoping to get a whiff of his pipe. Then I noticed something he'd scribbled at the bottom of the page. I squinted to read the scripture: "In the world you have tribulation, but in Me, you shall have peace." Matthew 16:30.

Ada and the men had started another song, and one of them had produced a fiddle from his belongings and another, a harmonica. The instruments and vocalists were creating such a sweet sound that it gave me a brilliant idea. With all the down-and-outers that floated through here, there had to be other musicians. Why not form a band? The Sunshine Band! Rich folks were always clamoring for things to do on weekends. What if the mission offered them concerts? We'd put on a world-class Sunday program with tasty snacks and fine music.

I leaned back in my chair and wondered if I really had gotten an inspirational whiff of my father's pipe when Ada and the men stopped in the middle of a song. I looked up to see what had happened. Everyone turned to the kitchen, where a great commotion erupted. I figured the Italian had flown into one of his infamous rampages, but when one man burst through the kitchen doors followed by a plume of smoke, I knew we were in big trouble.

"FIRE!" the man from the kitchen yelled.

The room filled with the black smoke along with the instinct to escape, but there was no place to go except out into the snow. By the time I got to the door, flames swirled from the kitchen. I hoped the cooks had bailed out.

"Ada! Donny!" I yelled, pushing through the men.

Then I saw them both. Some men must have escorted them out. A few more men tumbled through the door, allowing black smoke to escape into the afternoon sky. Icy flecks of snow hit the top of my head, and I shivered.

"Is everyone out?" I cried. The men stomped the snow and looked around, not knowing who to look for, and they gave more shrugs than acknowledgments.

In my wildest dreams, I hadn't even considered this scenario. I remembered the old brass extinguisher in the sleeping area but did not know if it even worked. I understood one thing clearly: if the Sunshine Rescue Mission went up in flames, this entire section of Larimer would likely go with it. We all stood frozen with indecision. The closest fire station stood blocks away, and with only one lane of traffic cut through the snow, the fire would incinerate the neighborhood by the time help reached us.

I surveyed the ragtag bunch of men, and my worst fear struck. "Where are Joseph and the Italian?" I screamed.

No one knew, and I started inside—I'd walk through flames for the man. Just as I opened the door, Joseph, with the Italian draped over his shoulder, burst through. He handed the cook off to the two men closest to the entrance, turned, and ran back inside.

When I tried to follow, someone held me back. "Reverend, you don't want to go in there," he said.

It took me a moment to shake free of him, and as I raced through the door, I heard Ada yelling for me to stop. I ignored her plea. The room collapsed in thick, dark smoke, and I couldn't see. I got on my hands and knees and crawled in the direction of the kitchen.

By the time I pushed open the kitchen door, my jaw gaped in horror. I knelt in the fiery furnace of hell, and Joseph stood in the middle of the flames.

I trembled in fear like the day I'd sat in the hospital with Ada. The antiseptic smell nauseated me as much now as it did then. No wonder I always sweated when I entered an infirmary and had to will my queasiness away. I looked up and down the hallway, praying that someone would come with news.

I stood in front of a statue of the Virgin Mary holding baby Jesus. The artist had depicted her angelic face, full of love for the divine baby, and I shook my head and sighed at the mystery of it all. No wonder people struggle with the concept of God, who created the universe and holds all things in balance, sending His Son, Jesus, to teach us love.

"Father, in your mercy, hear my prayers," I whispered, although I didn't need to. Well past midnight, the dark hallway of Saint Joseph Hospital echoed with emptiness. I knew Ada sat with Mary in the chapel. Mary had come as fast as she could as word of the fire spread quickly.

I leaned in and squinted at the placard above the statue. "The Love of Christ Impels Us," it read. I had to look harder to make out the carved text below it: "In 1873, Mother Xavier Ross of the Sisters of Charity of Leavenworth, Kansas, sent four Sisters to establish a hospital with only nine dollars and the challenge that the sisters, 'Look forward for what good there is yet to be.'"

I knew their courage to be true. Those nuns were fearless. I'd seen them walk boldly into the most rambunctious saloons and solicit handouts from miners and cowboys. Even seen them carrying heavy rocks from Cherry Creek to build the hospital's foundation.

"James, what a louse you are," I told myself. When the nuns had asked the mission for money, I had refused. At the time, I couldn't believe they were asking. Didn't they know we struggled to survive and competed for donations? I looked at the plaque again and realized how stupid I had been and pledged to make it right somehow. "You have sure been feeling plenty sorry enough for yourself," I murmured.

A nun dressed in white from head to toe stepped through a door but turned away from me, her heels clicking on the tile.

"Come on, Joe, we need you." I couldn't hold the tears back any longer, and my shoulders quaked as I recalled how awful he'd looked when we pulled him from the smoke and fire. We thought we'd lost him. It had seemed to take an eternity to commandeer a wagon and sludge through the storm. He was barely breathing when we got him to the door of Saint Joseph's Hospital, where the nuns took him from us.

Joseph had saved the mission for sure, and the entire city owed him a debt of gratitude for stopping the fire, even though it might cost him his life. He probably didn't give it another thought as he stood there fighting the blaze.

I'd learned so much from Joseph about unconditional love. If I was the head and Ada was the hands, Joseph was the heart, the love that held us all together. I looked at the eyes of Mother Mary looking at her baby. Yeah, that love…that divine love.

"Come on, Joe, fight!" I yelled and slammed my fist against the wall.

16

GOOD NEWS BAD NEWS

Christmas Eve 1913

The reporter from the *Denver Post* wore a straw skimmer hat with a black and red ribbon, like the hat worn by comedian W. C. Fields. He even had chubby cheeks and a shiny red nose like Fields, and between questions he chewed on a large intimidating cigar.

Sitting across from him, I kept glancing over my shoulder, double checking that the men weren't spoofing me.

"So, tell me about yourself, Mr. Goodheart," he said.

He sounded precisely like Fields, and I couldn't resist echoing the comedian's voice. "A woman drove me to drink, and I didn't even have the decency to thank her," I quipped out the side of my mouth. I considered it to be an excellent impersonation.

But the reporter looked at me as though I had gone mad. So I did another Fields. "Always carry a flagon of whiskey in case of snakebite and furthermore always carry a small snake," I said, flicking an imaginary cigar by my mouth.

He finally got it and cracked half a smile. "Yes, yes, I've been told I bear a resemblance to that man. 'I am free of all prejudice. I hate everyone equally,'" he recited Fields.

I laughed heartily, but the reporter didn't join in. I had to wonder if it represented less a quote and more his philosophy of life. I understood he wasn't in the mood for jokes, so I turned serious and told him the story of the Sunshine Mission. After all, I wanted a proper story in the *Post*, feeling honored that the *Post* had elected to write us up for their Christmas edition.

He jotted down notes on a small flip pad, tilting his head one way and then another. When I started on the statistics of how many men we serve, he stopped writing.

"I understand the fire from three weeks ago badly injured one of your negroes," he said.

I hesitated as the hair stood up on the back of my neck. "Yes, unfortunately, one of our *men*," I emphasized, "suffered burns. His name is Joseph Jackson," I said, pointing to his notepad that he should write it down. He didn't.

"I imagine you're taking more precautions to see that this sort of thing doesn't happen again," he said.

I crossed my arms over my chest in self-defense. This was not a friendly man.

He continued with his agenda. "I talked with the fire marshal yesterday, and they're saying someone set the fire on purpose."

My eyes squinted at him. "Yes, that's what they are saying—"

"Sure it wasn't one of your men?" he interrupted.

"Look." I glanced at the business card he'd given me. "Mr. Colbert. We were all inside. The fire marshal thinks someone stuffed rags down our oven pipe."

"Why would someone do that?" He wrote more than I verbalized.

"I have no idea, but there are some real vagrants in the neighborhood if you haven't noticed." My annoyance turned to anger.

"Suspect there are those that would like to have seen the place burn to the ground," Colbert said, surveying the room with disdain.

Now my anger boiled. After all, we'd spent weeks scrubbing black smoke stains off the walls and ceilings. I stood and looked him square in the face. "Why would you say that?"

"I know there are folks in the city that think places like this attract the undesirables—rather see them just pass on through to California. Maybe the money spent here would be better off going to hard working folks. From the looks of things, the mission is doing well financially. You own the building. Got plenty to eat." He shifted his cigar to the other side of his mouth. "Sure nothing illicit is going on here?"

This had not gone as I expected. I had it in my head that we were finally getting the recognition we deserved, and here this man blatantly insulted me. I realized the reporter, who searched for more gossip than truth, had duped me. I wanted to throw him out on his big fat nose, but such violence wouldn't do the mission or me any good.

I took a deep breath and sat back down in my chair. "Mr. Colbert, what you see here is just plain hard work and elbow grease. I suppose there are those that think Denver would be better off without our kind. I imagine you've never been in this situation—"

"I uh—" He tried interrupting me again, but I just talked over him.

"Until you've seen the dark end of the pit, it's hard to understand. Look around this room, Mr. Colbert. I don't know a single man in here who doesn't wish he lived somewhere else. What I've learned is that we're all simply one day away from calamity, and when we fall, we need someone to give us a hand up."

Colbert stood and flipped his notebook closed. His affect remained as flat as a record, and I couldn't tell if I'd offended him, or he discovered he would not get some salacious headline out of me.

"I just ask in the Christmas spirit that the *Post* runs something kind about us," I said and offered my hand in peace.

"We'll see what we can do," he said and turned to the door.

I escorted him, thanked him, shut the door, and, proud as a peacock, I swaggered back to the men who had watched the exchange. I pursed my lips and checked their expectant faces. Then I put my thumbs under my jacket lapels and drummed my fingers against my chest. "It ain't what they call you, it's what you answer to." I did my best Fields.

The men laughed, and I bowed deeply, imaginary hat in hand.

Colorado gave us a beautiful day for a visit to the hospital. We took as many people and musical instruments as we could squeeze into the wagon for the trip. Huge piles of snow remained from the historic snowfall, but we'd survived. The sky shone a brilliant blue, and the bright sunshine dazzled off the white powder causing me to squint against the splendor. We had much to celebrate and a day to rejoice.

Joseph had survived...by the skin of his teeth. He had second-degree burns on much of his face and neck, and a nasty third-degree burn on his left arm that had required two surgeries for grafting. Smoke inhalation almost killed him. The doctors had forbidden him to talk, so healing could take place.

I would have preferred to visit tomorrow, on Christmas Day, but we were expecting to feed over a thousand men, and we needed all hands-on-deck. Donny remained at the mission to help the cooks prepare. Ada baked a Christmas pound cake for Joseph, and Mary bought him new clothes for when the nuns discharged him. Plus, we had some special music for him.

The quality of musicians who came forward surprised me when I'd announced the formation of the Sunshine Band. We had two violin players, a flutist, a clarinetist, and three men who could play the piano almost as well as Ada. We even had a drummer; we just needed a drum set.

The nuns would allow us to see Joseph for the first time since the fire, not wanting visitors transmitting infections to him. But that hadn't kept us from holding an around-the-clock vigil in the waiting room.

As we unloaded from the wagon in front of the hospital, I noticed a placard off to the right of the stairs that said: "Built 1876, on land donated by Governor William Gilpin. Administrative building, 1899, by the generous donation of flour baron, John K. Mullen, and Margaret Brown." I nodded, reminded of the woman some were calling "The Unsinkable Molly Brown" for surviving the sinking of the *Titanic* last year. The community also knew her for the monster whist parties she'd throw. I wondered if she'd recovered enough to consider doing one for the mission. The card games would be right up our alley.

We trouped through the modest lobby and up the stairs to the men's ward. At the top of the staircase, three older nuns in their signature white tunics and even whiter aprons met us.

They covered their heads with white veils that cinched around their necks. The sister in the middle stepped forward and offered her hand to me.

"Reverend Goodheart?" she asked.

"Yes, ma'am," I said and took her hand.

"I'm Mother Marion, the head of Saint Joe's. These are Sisters Diana and Caroline. We are so glad we could finally meet face-to-face."

I smiled at the other two nuns and asked, "Have we met? How do you know me?"

"We've been expecting you today, but more importantly...we all know you," she said and turned to the nuns behind her. They nodded enthusiastically. "We pray for you and the Sunshine Rescue Mission every day during chapel. We have cared for many of the same men as you and they hold you in such high esteem we thought you might actually walk in on water today."

The other nuns chuckled, and my cheeks warmed.

"I'm afraid these darn feet of clay keep me from doing that," I said, making light of her compliment. "It's you, Sisters, who do the heavy lifting and to whom we are so grateful. We brought you all gifts."

I handed her an envelope containing a check I'd written from the mission for a hundred dollars. It would put us four hundred short for the year, but I trusted God to make up the difference somehow. She thanked me, took it without opening it, and slipped it into a pocket of her tunic. It hurt my feelings a little. I'd hoped she'd make a big deal of it, as it amounted to almost ten percent of my salary.

Ada and Mary stepped forward. Ada handed the nuns a box of pound cake she'd made, and Mary gave each one a colorful scarf and a box of scarves to distribute among the other sisters.

Mary seemed uncharacteristically shy. She had stewed all the way over that the bright colors might offend the nuns and now, standing in the midst of their white uniforms, she blushed with intimidation.

I stepped in to rescue her. "Mary has worried herself to an ulcer thinking you might not like the colors, but her, eh... friends made all these beautiful scarves." Now I blushed.

Mother Marion rescued us both. "Then we are honored to have them. We need a little color to brighten up the holidays." To reinforce her statement, she wrapped a bright red and green scarf around her neck, making the other nuns giggle.

"Mary has always wanted to be a nurse," I said, and immediately wished I hadn't because Mary turned bright red, redder than I'd ever seen.

But Mother Marion reciprocated with kindness and stepped forward to her. "I think that is a wonderful idea, my dear. We are starting a nursing school here next year, and we would love for you to apply." She rested her hand on Mary's arm.

Mary regained her composure and her sense of humor. She curtsied in her new emerald green Christmas dress and grinned. "I suppose I can't go to school wearing this?"

Everyone laughed, especially the nuns.

"I'm afraid we might give the Holy Father a stroke," Mother Marion added, making us laugh harder. "I imagine you would look wonderful in white," she said, settling the merriment and lowering her voice to hospital decibel. "Come. Joseph is probably champing at the bit to see you all. Follow us."

The nuns had moved Joseph out of isolation and into the men's ward, so we squeezed into the room filled with thirty men on cots. No one seemed to mind this Christmas Eve distraction.

I stood at Joe's bunk. "Glad you made it, my friend," I said, wanting to hug him tight but afraid I'd hurt him. The only bandage that remained was one on his left arm where they had done the skin grafting. The second-degree burns on his face and neck had erased the brown skin and replaced it with new, pink skin. "Aren't you a sight for sore eyes."

He reached for me, wanting a hug. "I ain't no china doll. Come on and give me a right hug and help me sit up."

As I embraced him, my finger brushed his bare back, exposed by the hospital gown, and I wondered if the fire had burned his back as well. I stepped to the head of the bed and grabbed his shoulders to ease him up to a sitting position. I couldn't help looking at his back, and I realized why I'd never seen Joseph without a shirt. Even cleaning up in the bathroom, he'd go from towel to shirt. I thought it was modesty, but now I knew the truth. The scarring on his back had nothing to do with the fire. Large keloids traced whip marks across his back. I wanted to ask him about the scars but decided not to in front of the ladies. The nurse came to the other side of the bed and adjusted his gown, covering his back, and nodded a knowing smile at me.

Joe invited everyone to embrace him, and they did, generously, making him radiant with holiday smiles.

"We were afraid we'd lost you," Ada said.

"Miz Goodheart, I trust the good Lord with my life, I trust Him with my death," he said. "The Father knows I'm ready to see my family any time now."

Joseph rarely talked about losing his wife and son in his thirties, but now, maybe after this brush with death, he'd be willing. We had lots to talk about when he got back to the mission.

As the others in our group were lining up against one wall where the sisters had made space, I realized that my run-in with the *Post* reporter still brewed in my chest. I figured Joe needed to know. "There are rumors going on that someone set the fire on purpose. May have stuffed rags down our stovepipes."

Joseph nodded like this came as old news to him. "Thought I heard footsteps. So it wasn't Saint Nicholas after all, huh?"

I watched his eyes—they contained no malice or hatred. He seemed to have settled it in his own mind.

"Lots to pray for, I reckon," he said.

I knew Joe had so much more to teach us about forgiveness, but our group grew eager to perform.

I looked at the men standing near the wall and smiled—we didn't clean up half bad. Our choir formed a semicircle just as we'd rehearsed, and I took my position in front of them. The sisters had wheeled a piano into the room, and Ada took her place on a chair at the keys.

"And now," I announced with pride, "I give you the Sunshine Band."

I nodded and smiled at Ada, and her fingers glided over the ivory, while the other musicians joined in.

I raised my hands. The choir followed my cue and sang:

"What child is this
Who laid to rest
On Mary's lap is sleeping?
Whom angels greet with anthems sweet,
While shepherds watch are keeping?"

The musicians accompanied them, then played a chorus on their own, and the singers joined in on another verse. The patients smiled and clapped.

I conducted the Sunshine Band with joy, but I couldn't stop thinking about that officious reporter and the rumors he helped to circulate. I needed to get past it. It was Christmas Eve after all, and I felt pretty darn good about myself. My family served with me, and I hadn't had a drink in six years. I had become well known in the city, even to these beloved sisters, and built one of the finest ministries in town. And imagined I looked especially dapper in my new brown suit as an ordained minister. I was doing pretty darn well, indeed.

I laughed out loud and swung my arms in rhythm as though I led the New York Symphony. I glanced over my shoulder at Joseph lying on the bed, and he smiled back.

***

After we sang all seven carols in our repertoire, the nuns convinced us to entertain in the women's ward as well. While the singers, musicians, and piano moved to the women's ward, I walked with Mother Marion.

"Please forgive me, Reverend," she said. "I overheard your discussion with Joseph about your building being set on fire. Lord have mercy on their souls."

I nodded.

"Forgive me..." She stopped walking to gather her thoughts. I turned toward her, and she put her hand on my arm. "As the youngest of the original sisters who came here from Leavenworth in 1873, I was a mere baby at twenty-two. Those were some pretty rocky years. Probably one short step up from where we are today." She smiled. "Caring for the poor will take every bit of you, as you pour yourself out. Only in heaven will we see the harvest." She wiped a tear. "Reverend Goodheart, I can see the wear in your eyes, and I want to encourage you with this verse. 'And let us not be weary in well doing: for in due season we shall reap, if we faint not.'"

I nodded. "Thank you, Mother—" Donny, still wearing his kitchen apron, came bounding up the stairs and interrupted us.

Every hair on my neck and arms snapped to attention. I could see by the look on his face that something was wrong. I thought the scoundrels must have lit the mission on fire again.

"Father, this came for you."

I looked at the telegram he thrust at me. I knew bad news followed before I read the words:

JAMES...stop...YOUR FATHER HAS DIED...stop

17

NOT-SO-HAPPY NEW YEAR

January 1, 1918
(Four Years Later)

I studied my son: tall, skinny as a rail, with a full head of hair—a clear reflection of my younger self. The suit that Ada and I bought him in August before he started at Colorado University in Boulder crept up an inch short in the trousers. *Where did the time go?*

It had been four years since I lost my father. *Well, he wasn't lost.* I knew exactly where he was, in the loving arms of Jesus, but I still shuddered at the memory of his casket being lowered into the grave. I missed him terribly. Near his last days, he wrote weekly with letters full of advice and encouragement. As we continued to build the mission, I'd pull them out every so often to remind me why we were making this sacrifice.

Mom died a year after Pop. My surviving brothers and sisters and I gathered in Bloomington for her funeral. I'd buried the hatchet with my brothers as Mom would have wanted, although I suspected John would never accept me as a pastor.

With my hand on the mission doorknob, I checked my pocket watch for the third time. "Donny, we better get you to the station. Your train leaves in forty minutes." Not that I was eager to see the boy go. Having him home for Christmas break filled an empty hole in Ada's heart, and he'd been a tremendous help with the mission's biggest Christmas dinner to date.

"Father, now that I'm in college, I sure wish you'd call me Donald," he said, picking up his suitcase.

I opened the door, but before we stepped outside, Joseph stopped Donny to give him a hearty handshake. And not to be outdone, the other men did likewise. Finally, Ada pushed through to our son. She grabbed Donny's shoulders, looked into his face, then hugged him so tightly I didn't think she'd ever let him loose. She told me having him leave felt like losing part of her soul. Truth be told, I'd miss him just as much. I hated to see him go, but at least he'd avoided shipping off for Europe.

When the United States declared war on Germany last April, Donny, Ada and I had gotten into a battle of words over whether it would be prudent for him to sign up for the army. But by the time the first American combat forces arrived in France in June, we'd already enrolled him in the university and were glad for it. Like the rest of the nation, we thought the conflict in Europe might pass us by, but the Germans sank the British-owned *Lusitania*, killing 1,128 passengers, including 128 Americans, and dashed those hopes. I'd insisted Donny stay in school and wait to see if his number came up for the Selective Service. I told him he'd be better off getting an education than volunteering to carry a rifle.

The waiting taxi driver blew his horn, and Ada released her grip. Coming from large families, Ada and I were both surprised and disappointed that the Lord had given us only one child. It made us all that much more protective.

Cold January air met me as I swung open the door of the mission and walked out to the taxi. I opened the back door and reached across the seat to pay the driver. Then I stepped back to hold the door open for Donny. He put his suitcase on the taxi floor and then offered his hand to me. I shook it firmly. Emotions threatened to overwhelm me: joy, pride, sorrow, fear—all converged in my gut. I released my grip, took him by the lapels, and smiled. I smoothed the lapels back down and ran my hand over the new Sigma Chi pin on his jacket pocket. Against my advice, he'd pledged to a fraternity. It lessened the sting when I found out their symbol incorporated a white cross. "You mind your p's and q's with the boys in the fraternity. Don't go and get caught up in their drinking games."

"Father, you know I won't."

"And watch out for those college girls." I grinned and winked.

He looked at his shoes and blushed.

I wanted to say so much more—to warn him about this or that, but I could only hope I'd raised him with the knowledge of who he was. Finally, I couldn't stand this man-to-man formality one more minute, and I grabbed him and hugged him tightly. "I love you, son."

"I love you too, Daddy."

He climbed into the taxi. I closed the door and waved the go-ahead to the driver, who put the car in gear and sped off with Donny down Larimer Street. "Lord, be with him."

"Stinking *Post*," I said, and slapped the newspaper down on the table. "Their news is not worth the paper they print on. Always looking to create conflict and division."

Ada looked up with furrowed brows.

I picked up the paper and read an article to her: "One thousand more arrests in 1917 than in 1916. Eleven thousand jailed. Two thousand and six drunks—a larger proportion than in 1916." I glanced up to see if she followed their argument. "They're using these statistics as a made-to-order argument for the anti-Prohibitionists. They even quote one, 'Ha! Ha! shout the champions of booze and beer. Does Prohibition prohibit? It does NOT!'"

I flung the paper down in disgust. "Stupid Colbert. I detest that cursed man. He and his liberal stances go against what folks want for the city."

"James Goodheart." Ada scowled. "You put your hat and coat on and take a walk to get your mind right before you preach tonight."

"Ada, you know as well as anyone how hard we've worked to chase out the blight of alcohol. The Women's Christian Temperance Union and the Anti-Saloon League won't stand for this kind of nonsense. The city's been dry for two years. Thank God for the scoundrels in the legislature for seeing fit to tighten the law banning all forms of alcohol last month."

She nodded.

"Then the wretched *Post* goes and reports something like this, making it sound like our efforts aren't working." I rapped my knuckles on the paper.

"Well, it doesn't help to send your blood pressure soaring."

"I guess you're right," I said, getting to my feet and putting on my jacket. "Think I'll stroll down to make some calls on Mary's patients. They've set up a temporary ward in the old Chever Hotel." I covered my head with my hat. "Also, I might stop by and confront that scoundrel Gun Wa."

"Gun Wa? Isn't he in jail?"

"Yes…he is. I don't know what the new fellow is calling himself, Lee, or something. I just call all these imposter doctors Gun Wa. It's like you chase one off and two more take their place."

"You be careful, James. Some mighty shady characters behind those doors. No need going and getting yourself killed over this." She looked back down at her prayer card and picked up her pencil. She palmed the small card with all the names of people she interceded for.

"Don't be going and adding that Colbert to your list," I said. "He deserves no mercy."

She glanced at me as though I should know better and continued to write in defiance.

I put my hands on my hips. "You wrote his name down?"

She gave me a smug grin. "No, I wrote your name down a second time. Figuring you need it right now. You get owly every time Donny leaves home."

I laughed sarcastically and bent to kiss her on the forehead.

She tenderly patted my chest. "He's going to be okay, you know."

I squeezed her hand and left the mission, knowing she spoke truth.

I wrapped my scarf over my face. The sun had warmed Larimer by a degree or two, but the cold stung my cheeks. The neighborhood appeared relatively quiet for New Year's Day, and I imagined most celebrants were nursing their hangovers. As much as I hated to admit it, Colbert was probably right. We weren't making much headway in curbing the moral decline of skid row. Like sitting on a dang balloon—as soon as you squashed one immorality, another popped out the other side. Larimer danced to the rhythmic beat between righteousness and the follies of the flesh.

As soon as the city had gone dry, reprobates found the loopholes. They could still drink alcohol designated for religious and medicinal purposes. All they had to do was get their hands on it. Judging by the number of drunks who stumbled into the mission last night looking for a warm place to sleep, there were a whole lot of men praying or in need of medical relief. I remembered a recent headline: "Pious Congregation Nabbed for Consuming 400 Gallons of 'Sacramental Wine' This Month."

I crossed Larimer and stepped onto the curb as a man stumbled out the door of The White House, probably one of the oldest watering holes on Larimer. It had declined from its claim to be a "first-class, legitimate house" to an inebriated dive and a haven for pornography. Men in the mission would describe men *and* women lined up at the pornography viewing machines, frantically turning the cranks, getting their jollies watching lewd acts while drinking alcohol. Even though Colorado banned alcohol, the bar served stuff smuggled in from Wyoming. Of course, the coppers raided the place often, but somehow the doors stayed open—the establishments greasing palms with generosity.

"Howdy, Reverend," the stumbling man slurred and saluted with his fingers.

"Hi, Eddy."

Eddy had become one of our regulars, repentant one day and drunk the next. He'd swear up and down he had his last drink and pledge his life to God, only to stumble into the mission inebriated the next day. If he couldn't kick his vice, we'd need to commit him to the asylum—the only safe place for a severe drunkard.

I thought of preaching to him, but I let him stagger down the street as I remembered a recent discussion with Reverend Gravett that I still processed. He tried to get me to look past the sin and see the person underneath. He said, "The true self, our authentic self, is the *who* God formed us to be—made possible by the indwelling of Christ—He in us and us in Him. The more you learn to see *that* in people, the more you will look beyond their failures. Our job is not to point out all the bad in people, but to help them understand the divine in themselves."

Gravett's words probably made my father flip over in his grave, as he believed in a more prudent lifestyle and the need for people to curb their fleshly desires. But I understood Gravett's point: "Look beyond the sin to the true light of that person, and you'll see some remarkable brilliance."

Two cats clawing and hissing between my feet almost made me fall and jerked me out of my thoughts. I steadied myself on the side of a building. "Stupid cats." I kicked at them, but they had already run away.

Truth be told, I felt kind of sorry for them. Cats were one sector of the population that Prohibition had greatly affected. There were now hundreds of stray cats that once had homes as saloon pets to beat down the rat population. With most of the saloons closed, a new organization, the Dumb Friends League of Denver, stayed busy corralling the cats and finding homes for them.

Two doors down, a small sign hung over the doorway: DR. WING LEE. Like the Caucasian man who preceded the fake Chinese doctor Gun Wa, Lee appeared as Chinese as an Irish leprechaun. He wore a wig and silks to make people believe he came from Asia. The authorities had shut down Gun Wa twenty years ago, but his scam lived on. Folks were frantic for relief from their daily ails, and the fake doctors could sell horse piss just by saying he imported the ancient medicine from China. The principal thing Lee sold now was prescriptions for "medicinal" wine.

Hesitating at the door, I wondered if I had enough restraint to confront the fraud without getting into an outright brawl. I read the claims posted on the entry: "Chinese medicine cures: tiredness, rheumatism, headaches, sleeplessness, women's hysteria, and men's incompetence." I laughed, sure it represented a misspelling of *impotence* or *incontinence* or a devilish pun on the foolishness of anyone who would purchase it. Then I heard the door lock click and saw a thumb and a finger flip the sign from OPEN to CLOSED.

Dang it, he must have seen me standing here. He knew I wasn't one of his gullible patients. I shrugged. Maybe it was a good thing he didn't open his door. No telling what he'd do to me—these cons were ruthless men.

I heeded Ada's advice and moved on. The Chever Hotel stood at the end of the block. Its porch covered the old stomping ground of Soapy Smith, who once ran a profitable soap scam. Soapy would insert a ten-dollar bill between a bar of soap and its wrapper and drop the soap bar in a barrel. Then he'd use a megaphone to gather crowds. His shills, partners in crime, would give him money for a bar of soap and reach into the barrel, seemingly at random, to claim their prize. They'd pluck the baited bar with the bill in the wrapper and whoop and holler like they'd found their weight in gold. The amazed crowd would line up to buy soap, expecting to find bars wrapped in bills. Of course, there were none. It was a clever, if not exactly a clean con, and it sold a lot of soap. They killed old Soapy a few years back, but many other scammers took his place.

I pulled open the front door to the Chever and started up

the stairs. I flinched at the potent smell of antiseptics. *Lord, how I hate infirmaries.*

Mary had told me she volunteered at the makeshift hospital ward here. Between the war and the flu, her business hadn't exactly thrived.

The city had turned the third-floor ballroom of the hotel into an infirmary for soldiers returning from Europe with the Spanish Flu. Mary had asked if I'd stop by to pray for some fellas. The world had seen some deadly touches of the flu before, but this particular year it struck healthy young people with deadly force, making the war in Europe a breeding ground for the rampaging disease that scared the world and the patients. Mary had told me that fear filled the ballroom as much as illness.

Halfway up the stairs, I heard men coughing. When I got to the third floor, I saw a box of cloth face masks at the door. I speculated that Mary and her fellow workers had made them. I knew God would protect me, but it seemed unwise to not use a mask, so I put one on.

I'd never worn a mask before, and it trapped the pungent odors of the ward around my face and caused the walls to close in as I stepped into the room. It shocked me to see how many occupied cots they'd squeezed into the space. No wonder fear was epidemic—they could admit no one until someone else died.

I caught sight of Mary and three other workers huddled around a cot in the corner at the back of the room. They were pulling a sheet over the patient's face, then wrapping it around him. Fear hit me as well.

I waited at the door until two men rolled the dead man onto a stretcher and hauled him out. Mary saw me and waved me over. My shoes felt nailed to the wood floor, but I forced them to move, and I joined her at the back of the room.

She nodded to me as if to say, "I told you so."

I shook my head in revulsion at the situation.

"The sisters tell everyone to wash your hands well and try not to touch your face until you do," she said.

Instantly I wanted to scratch my nose.

"Let me introduce you to some of the men," Mary said.

She turned and pointed to a frightened young man who looked to be the same age as Donny. "Samuel, this is Reverend Goodheart." She smiled. "You can trust him."

Another boy across the room went into a coughing fit, and Mary excused herself to go to his aid.

"Hi, Samuel. I'm Jim Goodheart," I said and offered my hand.

"Not sure you want to go shaking my hand right now, Rev." He grabbed a towel at his side and wiped his blood-streaked palm where he'd been coughing.

I stood leaning over the boy and felt awkward. He understood, moved his legs over and patted the bed, inviting me to sit. I perched gingerly on the side of his cot.

"Where you from, son?"

"California…sir," he stammered.

"Who're you with?"

"First Division, sir."

"One of the Doughboys, huh?" I had read in the papers the adventures of the first troops landing in Europe.

"Yes, sir." He straightened, but then seized with a coughing spell.

I helped him sit and patted his back until the attack calmed.

His eyes reminded me of Donny's when he'd wake with a night terror.

"How's it going over there?"

The boy looked me in the eye and then glanced from side to side.

He lowered his voice. "It's pretty…awful." He continued to search the room as though he might be in trouble for betraying the truth. "I was afraid." His lower lip quivered.

I held his arm. No words came to my mouth.

"Not sure here's any better," the boy said, as tears pooled in his eyes.

I looked up and down the room. "I imagine every man here feels the same way." I pulled my small Bible from my inside jacket pocket. "Do you know Jesus as your Savior?"

"Yes, sir."

I thought I saw a glimmer of hope in his face. "Then let's pray together, son."

18

VALENTINE'S DAY

February 14, 1918

"Why don't you all come on up and shake hands with ol' Jim and take Christ as your Savior?" I exclaimed to my congregation at the conclusion of what I deemed as a particularly wonderful sermon.

Under fifty men joined the service that evening. Attendance at the mission had dropped, and the age of those we served increased, most likely because of the war. Many of the young homeless men had volunteered for the army, knowing they would be fed and paid, even though the roof over their heads would most likely be a tent.

But I couldn't complain. Most of the men tonight were awake and had listened to my apologetics—an argument for Christ. Of course, some preoccupied themselves with survival, but because it was Valentine's Day, I suspected others wished they were smooching a sweetie back home. I didn't blame them.

Three men accepted my invitation and stood, but a man

in a handsomely tailored suit walking through the door interrupted my intentions. He looked familiar, but he certainly didn't look like the usual clientele of the Sunshine Rescue Mission. He removed his top hat, smiled, and waved an envelope at me.

"You who stood," I addressed the three men, "please stick around. I promise you an extra piece of cake and eternal life."

Two more men stood, probably for the cake.

I smiled at my flock and made my way to the well-dressed gentleman, admiring his morning suit of gray striped pants, white silk vest, and black tailcoat—complete with a walking stick.

"Can I help you, sir?" I inquired.

"Reverend Goodheart. Good to see you at the lectern."

I looked him in the eyes, trying to place his face and voice.

He could tell I struggled and thrust out his hand. "Horatio Preston."

"Oh my Lord, Mr. Preston. I am so sorry, I didn't—"

"Please, no apologies needed, Reverend. I'm just glad my little gift kept you going."

I looked him up and down, remembering the trail-dusted cowboy and his spurs. He'd shaved his beard, but his bushy mustache remained.

"Yes, I 'spect I appear different from before, but no less grateful for what you are doing here. My claim has continued to produce, and I imagine your prayers have had something to do with that. I'm now president of the First National Bank of Salida," he said and tapped the side of his head with the cane.

"Please…please, Mr. Preston, come in and let us get you a cup of coffee and a piece of cake."

"Call me Horatio, and I can sit for just a minute. Besides,

I have a request of you saints," he said and waved the envelope again.

His request and the mysterious envelope puzzled me, and I wanted my wife to be in attendance when he explained. "First," I told him, "let us make you comfortable. Please sit." I held a chair out for him. "Ada is in the kitchen with the rest of the staff. Let me fetch them…and your coffee and cake."

Soon we gathered at the table around Horatio. Many of the men had hung around within earshot, but Horatio didn't seem to mind and talked loud enough for everyone to hear.

"Blasted Krauts." He fumed, opened the envelope, and spread the handwritten letter on the table. "This here's a letter from my brother, Percy. He's fighting with the boys of Company A, 138th Infantry of the 35th Division. They're some of the first Americans to draw German blood in a trench raid at Hilsenfirst." Horatio looked around at the homeless men listening in. "It's in the Vosges Mountains in southern France."

They all nodded as if they knew the location of where he indicated. They were probably just acknowledging that our troops were kicking some butt.

Horatio pulled a tube from his jacket and unrolled a poster with portraits of three soldiers over the US flag. It read: "The First Three! Give till it hurts—They gave till they died." Under that, a large red cross highlighted the words: "War Fund Week—One Hundred Million Dollars."

He made sure everyone saw the poster before he continued. "These three heroes are the first to shed their blood on France's soil. Sure glad my brother's mug ain't on it, but God rest their souls and give peace to the families."

"Amen to that," Joseph said, examining the poster.

Horatio picked up the letter from his brother. "Says here,

the fighting is awful horrific. I'm afraid we're not getting the accurate picture in the papers."

"Not surprised," I said.

"Says here that they're scraping alongside the French, hardly a stone's throw to the Kraut border." Horatio poked the letter he'd pretty well memorized. "They're dug in mighty deep, but the Germans shell them with artillery at night, and then cut through the barbed wire and storm our trenches. Killed the three men and captured a handful more." Horatio pointed to the poster. "The commander of the French 18th Division spoke at their funeral and said, 'Having traveled so far to defend justice and liberty they...'"

Horatio paused, put a finger over his lips, and looked at all of us, making sure we understood the sacrifice. Satisfied, he solemnly withdrew a postcard from his other pocket. "The boys they captured are serving as curiosities to the Germans—their planes are dropping these postcards on our troops." He showed me the card and asked me to pass it around. The card depicted the dejected men behind bars on a wagon. "Dragging them around like caged animals," Horatio said, "the bastards."

The room fell silent. I could feel the weight of Horatio's news and the anticipation of the men expecting me to say something. Horatio's update contained information we were afraid of and hoped wasn't true, but it was. We knew that the Brits and the French would not beat the Germans back to submission.

"Percy says the morale of the boys is mighty low," Horatio continued. "They're out-gunned, out-trained...cold and hungry..." He swiped a tear and went on, "Percy is my only brother. Besides that, I owe him my life. We were prospecting for gold in the Klondike twenty-some years ago. Headed up White Pass Trail above Dead Horse Gulch. The mare we'd bought for two hundred dollars in Skagway had a heart attack going up the steep trail and fell off the edge. I had tied myself to the saddle and would have gone down with her if it weren't for Percy. He got a lasso around me and kept me from falling off the edge and down to decay with three-thousand dead horses at the bottom of the cliff."

Some of the surrounding men gasped. They'd heard the stories of Dead Horse Gulch and were astonished that this man had been there and lived to tell the tale.

Finally, Horatio explained why he came to the mission. "I'm here thinking you all have a direct line to The Man Upstairs. I ask you all to pray for a safe return of my brother." He picked up the letter and pointed to the last line. "Also," he said, staring directly at me, "says here they could sure use some moral support live and in person."

I couldn't stop thinking about Horatio's comment. A few days later, I talked with the Denver Rotary Club, who knew of my work in the city. They wanted to support my effort to visit the boys in the field to lend emotional support. But I hadn't mentioned my intentions to anyone else, including Ada. After my night sermon, I knew the time had come, especially since Reverend Gravett was present. I heard laughter coming from the kitchen.

I hesitated at the door, afraid to tell Ada and the staff, especially since I didn't know why I wanted to go, except that Horatio's story probably represented the tip of the iceberg. If the *Post* reported only half the story, the war on the Western Front must surely be terrifying. There may be a chance I wouldn't come home, even though I couldn't imagine they'd put a chaplain in harm's way. But perhaps, even though going to war petrified me, this was something I needed to do to prove to myself that I was a good man.

My father always warned me about my wanderlust, this need to search the other side of the hill where things were going to be better than what I already had. Maybe my desire to serve in the army would satisfy my craving for excitement and my constant struggle with restlessness. "Jim, somewhere along the way you need to learn to be content." My father had said it like it indicated a character flaw.

I pushed the door open. "Hey, what's all the commotion in here?" I yelled, making everyone jump and then fall back into laughter.

"James, you almost got me to droppin' the bread," Joseph said, pulling loaves out of the oven.

"You'll be giving an ol' man a heart attack," Gravett said and threw a wet dish towel at my head.

I took up the gambit and opened with Shakespeare. "I would challenge you to a battle of wits, but I see you are unarmed." I laughed and grabbed a broom and started toward them, brandishing it like a sword.

I poked Ada in the butt, making her whirl around with hands on hips. "James, you go and stop that right now."

I snapped to attention, holding the broom at my side like a rifle, and saluted the troops. Ada looked at me as though I had gone mad, but the men laughed.

"Your fearsome leader wants to talk with you," I said, turning serious.

The men looked at me with smirks on their faces. Even Ada rolled her eyes. I figured they thought I had some gag up my sleeve, and they waited for the punchline. But as soon as I mentioned Horatio's name, everyone sobered up.

I leaned the broom against the counter and crossed my arms. "Like I was saying, ever since Horatio showed up here talking about Percy, I'm afraid I can't get the boys in the field out of my mind." I hesitated but blurted out. "I'm thinking of going to France."

It was prudent I hadn't become an actor, as my timing always seemed off. Now I'd blown Valentine's Day, as my announcement silenced Ada. Like many other bad decisions I'd made in my life, proclaiming my desire to go to France in front of the entire group before talking with her was stupid. Everyone verified my oblivion when they turned to see her reaction. Stoically, she didn't make a scene but hadn't said a word to me since we'd left the mission for home.

In my study, as I fumbled with a gift box, pans rattled in the kitchen under her anger. The clock would turn midnight soon, and I couldn't imagine what she fussed with after our long day.

I'd put her in a sour disposition. I'd saved for six months to buy her this gold locket, but she wouldn't be in the mood for receiving a gift. Heart-shaped, with a small purple amethyst on top for Donny's birthstone, I hoped she'd put his picture inside. I made my last payment on it two weeks ago and had a hard time not giving it to her early. Now I'd gone and ruined the moment. I figured she'd be mad anyway since I spent more money than I should. We hardly had a pot to pee in.

I finished tying the red ribbon around the box and stood. Time to go face the music.

I approached the kitchen and waited in the doorway. She had her back to me, sternly mixing dough in a bowl. I pulled my pocket watch from my vest—quarter to midnight.

"Dear, what are you doing? Aren't you exhausted?"

She ignored my question, so I stepped to her and put my hand on her shoulder.

"Ada?"

Her stirring intensified, but she finally said, "This bunch of bananas will go bad if I don't make some bread tonight."

Strands of hair fell from her bun, and perspiration glistened on her neck. Her glasses needed cleaning. I sighed and smiled. I knew God heard my prayers by giving me such a strong and frugal wife. With everything that I'd put her through, here she worried about thirty-one cents worth of bananas. Despite it all, she loved me.

I held out the jewelry box. She ignored it until I said, "Happy Valentine's Day, my love."

She glanced at the gift but stirred more vigorously.

"You better open it, we've only got a few more minutes of Valentine's Day left."

She settled the mixing bowl on the counter, dropped the spoon, and pushed her glasses up with the back of her wrist. Then wiped her hands on her apron and took the small box.

She held the gift but said nothing.

A faucet of emotions opened and tears quickly filled her eyes. It unlocked a flood, and she turned and buried her face into my suit. I wrapped my arms around her.

"Please don't go to war," she said finally.

I gently rocked her in my arms.

When her body's quaking waned, I pulled back and held her by her shoulders. "Ada, I'm sorry I didn't talk this over with you. I'm afraid what started out as a thought has turned into a full-blown plan. I went to talk with the Rotary club about the possibility of going and before I left, the men were shaking my hand and writing checks to support my effort. If and when I get your permission, I'll go down and talk with the army recruiters."

"Why would you do this?" Anger returned to her voice.

"I didn't want you to worry. They are lowering the age of the selective draft to eighteen soon. Donny's birthday is in two weeks."

Ada, a smart woman, quickly put it all together, and more tears filled her eyes and dripped off her cheeks.

"I'm hoping if I volunteer, he won't have to go, at least not overseas. Some men I've talked to say it's unlikely they'd make both a father and son serve on the Front."

She continued to weep, but finally got more words out. "Where do you think they'll send you?"

"No one can tell me for sure, but I'm thinking a chaplain will be safe behind the lines."

"You don't know that!" she gasped.

I pulled her to me as my own tears flowed. "You know I would give my life for my son. I'm not afraid to do that."

She hugged me tight around my waist.

I pressed a kiss onto her forehead. "I know we have a lot to talk about and plans to make, but can't we put that aside for the evening? It's Valentine's Day after all, and the banana bread can wait."

ACT THREE

19

THE THIRTEENTH

March 13, 1918
(One Month Later)

"The thirteenth. I guess I should have picked a different day to travel," I said to Ada, wincing at my throbbing fingers. I'd just pinched them in the doors of Union Station. I blew on them to cool the pain as another ache flared in my right little toe, which I'd smashed into the bedpost that morning.

"James, don't be going and getting superstitious. It's just another day."

"Except it's not every thirteenth that I head off to war."

"Well, you ol' fool," she huffed, "you shouldn't be heading anywhere at your age."

"I'm only forty-seven."

"Well look around, you're twice as old as anyone else here in uniform."

She was right. I looked out of place, but I stood just as proud as the young'uns. The campaign hat, with a flat brim and Montana Peak crown completed the uniform. It might become my favorite hat, even replacing my beloved porkpie. My uniform bore no insignias, as the army station didn't know how to label me. I hadn't enlisted but registered as the Rotary club chaplain. All the same, the army insisted I wear the garb. The *Post* reported that the US military had gone from just under a hundred thousand men to nearly a million. *Guess they'd let anyone in, even an old fool like me.* But thankful they did, as I was proud to serve.

I stopped in front of a vast mirror on the wall of the station. My uniform appeared crisp and pressed, and I patted the front pocket where I had placed a letter from Horatio to Percy. Europe sprawled as a large continent, but he hoped our paths would cross.

While I admired my reflection, a group of soldiers knocked into me—pushing and shoving each other, full of piss and youthful vigor, eager to fight the Krauts.

"Excuse us, sir," one boy apologized. He examined me up and down, shrugged, and went on his way, probably wondering why an older man in uniform was not an officer.

I noticed Ada giving me the eye. This turn of events had not pleased her, nor had it been an easy month. Between arguments, we settled the affairs of the mission. I wished Donny could have come home to help, but the Selective Service Act passed last year required all men between the ages of twenty-one and thirty to register for military service, with rumors swirling it might drop to eighteen. I preferred to keep Donny tucked away at school in Boulder. If someone in this family had to serve and sacrifice, I'd rather it be me.

The biggest fight between Ada and me had been over whom to hire to help her and the men at the mission. Both Gravett and Driver declined to step into my position as super-intendent, so Ada became the natural choice to run the day-to-day operations, but the Reverends would come to preach. Even so, she'd need help. The afternoon of our biggest argument, Ella Pettit walked into the mission asking if she could help us, as if God had heard us bickering and sent an angel.

Now at the station, I looked back at Ella, Joseph, and Reverend Gravett and smiled at them. Ella, thirty-four and single, was still an enigma to me. Her mother and father were a rather prominent family in Denver, having made their money in the paper business. Her father had died of tuberculosis a year ago, and Ella still grieved. She thought that helping others might relieve some angst.

Ada wasn't convinced of her intentions. I suspected partly because Ella was not a Baptist, but mostly because of her young age and relative attractiveness. "She shows her ankles," Ada had scoffed, then fumed when I jested that Ella might increase our numbers.

I stole another glance at Ella. Her last name nearly matched her small stature, and on her first day of work as our new bookkeeper, I purposely teased her on that point, introducing her as Miss Petite instead of Pettit. As a good sport, she laughed at my jokes. Even though Ella showed her ankles —the style for young women—Ada promised to look past it.

As usual, Ella wore a black skirt and pastel-colored blouse this morning underneath her gray woolen overcoat. A floppy black hat covered her head, and round glasses adorned her fair-skinned face, which always shadowed a hint of sadness. I believed Ella would do a good job, but mostly appreciated that Ada had the help.

"Are you limping?" Ada interrupted my thoughts.

"Darn toe," I said, glancing at her. "Hurts like a son-of-a-gun in these new boots." I tried forcing myself to walk without a limp.

Ada looked tired. I knew she loved me but worried herself

sick. I put my hand on the small of her back, and she looked at me with such concern it nearly broke my heart. Tears welled in her eyes and mine.

It was probably a good thing alcohol was scarce right now. Had there been a pub in the station, I'd have rushed through the door and ordered a shot to steady my nerves. My greatest fear of going turned out to be the unknown. No one could tell me where I would serve or who I would be with. The army recruiter had laughed and said, "Your soul belongs to God, but your butt belongs to the good old US Army... they'll find a place to use it." All I knew was to report in Newport News, Virginia, and they'd assign me to a transport on one of the many troopships sailing back and forth to France and England.

A commotion caught my eye, and I looked past Ada.

"Oh God, it's Colbert," I whispered in Ada's ear.

The *Post* reporter interviewed departing soldiers while his photographer took their pictures. Because of Denver's war on alcohol, I'd had some heated conversations with Colbert. He saw me before I could adjust our course, and he turned away from one of the hundreds of young men pouring out of the station to the train.

"Reverend Goodheart," Colbert said and waved his photographer over. He stepped up to us and turned to a fresh page in his ever-present flip notepad. He shifted his cigar from one side to another, and I thought for sure he'd say something snarky. Instead, he said with a familiar comic inflection, "Once during Prohibition, I was forced to live for days on nothing but food and water."

The Fields joke surprised me, and Ada covered her mouth with her hand to suppress a giggle. I couldn't believe that even Colbert turned jovial on this patriotic and sacrificial day. I smiled uneasily, still not sure I could trust him.

"Glad to see you supporting our boys, Reverend. Can we take your picture for the *Post*?"

He said it more of a statement than a question, and as the photographer steadied his camera, I straightened my spine and crossed my arms, trying to look more confident than I felt.

Colbert asked me a few quick questions, then surprisingly offered his hand. "Good luck to you," he said sincerely.

I shook his hand, thanked him, and looked at Ada, who glanced down at her prayer card and smiled. I guessed that war could make strange bedfellows—like Japan joining the Allies.

We followed the stream of soldiers onto the train plat-form, and I turned to my colleagues from the mission. "Well, it's mighty kind of you all to see me off." Ella's eyes were red and swollen. I guessed with the loss of her father and me, her mentor, leaving caused tears of grief. I shook her hand and heard her sob. "Take care of yourself, Miss *Petite*." I smiled, trying to lighten the mood. "Thank you for looking after Ada."

I turned to Joseph and held out my hand. He ignored it and hugged my neck tightly. "God be with you, James."

Gravett held out his hand, and as I took it, he prayed over me, "Lord, hold James in your loving arms of protection and watch over him and keep him..." He uncharacteristically stumbled over his words and couldn't finish.

"Thank you." I nodded and let go of his hand.

I turned to Ada, who dabbed her eyes with a hankie. She looked up into my eyes and stood on her tiptoes to kiss my cheek. "Please come home to me, James."

20

USS POCAHONTAS

March 29, 1918

The closer our train got to Newport News, the more the patriotic cheers and revelry swelled. But now, standing at the docks, our mood sobered. Never had the US mobilized a fighting force to wage war on another continent, so the fundamental logistics of moving men and machinery to Europe proved staggering. I'd never seen such organized chaos —thousands upon thousands of men in motion with no better idea of what to do than I had, somehow trying to get to where the military assigned them. The sergeants barked orders to the enlisted men and struggled to organize them in rank and file.

As I watched soldiers dutifully march into gigantic ships that bellowed black smoke—like dragons swallowing their prey—my legs refused to carry me forward. Maybe until that moment I hadn't realized I entered something unfathomably bigger than myself. I would become a cell in a gigantic organism, but cells in any organism had their function. Mine was as a chaplain somewhere in France, but the army hadn't assigned me to a unit.

Two lines snaked along the docks. Many of the men in line flirted with the cheerful Red Cross servicewomen who gave us hot coffee, sandwiches, and cigarettes. They readily offered their smiles, like prayers, to the young men who might never return home.

"Which line you in?" said a man behind me, poking me in the back.

"Uh…" I turned around and looked down to see a short, squatty man with jet-black hair curled under his officer's cap. He had bushy eyebrows, an even bushier mustache, an engaging smile, and green eyes that were full of life. During the train ride, I had learned enough about rank to know that a man with a silver bar with two stripes placed him as a first lieutenant. But I still wasn't sure if I should salute.

The squatty Lieutenant examined me up and down, making me feel embarrassed. "What are you?" he asked with curiosity and not contempt.

"Uh…" I stumbled over my words. I had a heck of a time telling the young men on the train what I was doing there and why I was in uniform. They didn't know whether to salute me or ignore me.

"Cat got your tongue, eh?" He nodded and smiled. Looking around at the logistical frenzy, he reached into the front pocket of his military jacket and pulled out a pack of smokes. He thumped it on his palm and flicked the container, so one single cigarette stuck out toward me. I had watched the men on the train do this countless times. I reached out dutifully, took the smoke, and put it to my lips as I'd seen the men do. The Lieutenant flicked open a lighter and offered me the flame.

I inhaled as the flame struck the tip of the cigarette. It had been years since I'd smoked so when heat suddenly filled my chest, it ripped every ounce of oxygen from my lungs. I burst into a coughing fit, and in the midst of the attack, I thought I might not make it to Europe. I saw Colbert's headline: "Goodheart Gassed: Killed on Docks of Newport by Cigarette."

My coughing fit caused both the Lieutenant and the surrounding men to erupt in laughter. "First time?" the Lieutenant asked and took the fag from my hand. He put it in his mouth, took a long drag, and blew the smoke out the side of his lips. "Well," he said, "don't start. These things will kill you." Then he laughed. "What's your name?"

"Goodheart," I choked, "Jim Goodheart."

"Who you assigned to?"

I looked around and lowered my voice. I didn't want to be any more fodder for their humor. "Frankly, I don't know." I pulled out the papers the recruiter had given me to report to the docks in Newport News for immediate transport to France.

The Lieutenant took them, scanned them from top to bottom, then handed them back and shrugged. He looked at my uniform for a patch or an insignia. "Can't tell if you're army or air corps—you's neither fish nor fowl." He chuckled.

The clamps around my lungs released, and I found my voice. "I'm a chaplain from Denver…the Rotary club sent me."

He smoothed down his mustache, examined my eyes, nodded, and pursed his lips. "A man of the cloth, eh?" He reached into his front pants pocket and fished out a small cross made from a strip of palm leaf. "My mama sent me this from Palm Sunday last week. She said to be on the lookout for angels protecting me." He smiled. A small safety pin stuck through the cross, and he used it to pin the cross to my chest in the spot where all soldiers wore their insignia. He stepped back, examined his addition to my uniform, and thrust out his hand. "That will do until we can get you detailed properly. I'm Lieutenant R. D. Chapman. My friends call me Chappy." He let go of my hand and snapped a salute at me. The enlisted men behind us chuckled.

The Lieutenant's spine straightened, and he rolled his shoulder to shoot a glare at the men, who stopped laughing and looked away.

"Welcome to the army, Jimbo. Let's go find us a ride."

Truth be told, Chappy—Lieutenant and, as I learned, pilot Chapman—became a gift sent to me from God. Whenever someone questioned my identity, Chappy would say, "He's with me," and no one asked further questions. His words were as good as a general's orders. The crew assigning ships and bunks would admire the pair of wings on Chappy's chest and nod in respect. I was his shadow, and he didn't mind. He even got me a bunk under his in the officer's quarters on an upper deck with a porthole. They stuck the enlisted men on the lower levels. Not that it mattered much which deck you ended up on. We were all equal in the eyes of God and in the storm that churned the Atlantic.

I clung onto the sides of my bunk, my ears ringing and my body jolting in time with the roaring quadruple-expansion steam engines of the USS *Pocahontas* as the twin-screw propellers dug into the angry seas. The ship's bow rose like it climbed Pikes Peak, and just when the engines threatened to burst into violent vibrations, shaking every rivet, the vessel would crest the wave and come crashing down the other side, slamming me into the hull. The ship would pitch and roll, gearing up to begin its climb once again...and again and again. I hugged my inch-thick mattress, trying to keep from breaking any bones. Thank God I had nothing left to give but dry heaves.

I'd never been on the ocean, never even seen the ocean, and dearly wished I never had. I'd never been so sick in my life. If I could stand, I would have commanded my legs and feet to march directly to the captain and respectfully demand that he turn the blasted ship around or, at the very least, let me off this carnival ride.

The condition of the ship did nothing to allay my misery. When Chappy and I boarded the *Pocahontas*, I couldn't help noticing how poorly they had maintained it—rust streaking from every porthole, vent, and anchor. It didn't take me long to realize that with all the signs in German, the *Pocahontas*, with its two funnels and masts was a Deutschland ship. The US, ill-equipped for moving troops, either commissioned all available ships or, like this German ship, seized and interned them forcefully. When we boarded, I saw where the crew had hastily painted over the ship's original name, the SS *Prinzess Irene*, and replaced it with the USS *Pocahontas*.

We sailed with the Third Convoy Group, twelve ships in all, including the fleet of six transport ships, escorted by one cruiser and five destroyers. That seemed like a lot of ships in one place, and I hoped their navigators knew how to keep them from smashing into each other in these rough seas. I shuddered at the thought of a massive pileup, or the *Pocahontas* breaking in two as we crashed over the next wave.

The next upsurge caused such spasms in the ship, I thought for sure the engines had quit. Everything had gone still except my heart pounding in my ears. Then, with a shudder, the roar of the engines returned, and we came crashing down with such force I thought I could hear metal give way.

Chappy leaned over his bunk, smiled and said, "That was a bad one."

"God, just take me now," I moaned.

"Hang in there, pal."

I couldn't believe seasickness hadn't swamped this man like the rest of us. Maybe with the experience of a pilot came immunity to motion sickness. I should be so lucky. But regardless of what happened to me, I hoped we'd make it to France so he could join his unit and test his skills. At that moment, I wasn't so sure.

Even if we made it through the storm, the danger wouldn't be behind us. The ship's crew warned us about the German U-boats that were waiting to sink us the closer we got to Europe. The fact that the *Pocahontas* now made her third round trip gave me a glimmer of hope. Nevertheless, I reached for my life preserver belt and panicked when I couldn't find it. I thought I'd lost it and searched frantically until I finally recovered it from the end of my bunk.

Yeah, this would really keep me safe. Oh, God, have mercy.

After leaving Newport, we'd spent three days outside the port drilling—fire, abandon ship, and lifeboat drills. When they assigned us our bunks, they gave us the lifebelt and a scrap of paper with a number on it. The number, it turned out, matched the lifeboat they assigned us to in case of an emergency. Half the enlisted men had misplaced the paper after setting sail, so we spent the first day sorting out the confusion. We'd drilled day and night until most men made it to their respective stations, and the crew lowered some of the life rafts. Because the ship carried a thousand more passengers than the standard ratio of wooden lifeboats to passengers, the sailors haphazardly tied rubber rafts to the upper decks.

Even though we carried out the drills in relatively calm waters, with Virginia in sight, it became abundantly clear that if a call to abandon ship became necessary, we were doomed. The sailors scuttled one lifeboat when it caught on its rigging, swung wildly, and smashed into the side of the ship. Afterward, I overheard one of the ship's crew telling some wide-eyed men that it usually took less than ten minutes for ocean liners to sink into the cold depths of the sea. The men started calling the maneuvers "Drowning drills." Chappy called them "Bend-over-and-kiss-your-ass-goodbye drills."

Now, clutching my mattress, I didn't know if I could take another minute of the thrashing. "Lord, calm the storm...but if you don't, take me now," I prayed under my breath.

"Attention, attention," called the crackling voice of a crew member through a megaphone, the usual alert before the announcement of a drill. I couldn't believe the captain would make us report to stations during the storm. The announcement continued: "All able-bodied men should report to the lower deck to help with the bailing efforts."

Scrunched with a thousand men on the deck of the *Pocahontas*, I'd never felt more lonely or afraid, but our time to perish hadn't arrived. We'd learned the water flooding the lowest level of the *Pocahontas* came from a popped rivet. A single rivet nearly sank the ten-thousand-ton ship—all five hundred and sixty feet of rust.

Looking over the railing of the ship, the water turned flat as a Kansas cornfield and the rising sun painted the clouds red. Some comedian yelled in a pirate's brogue, "Red sky at morn', sailors take warn!"

Yeah, thanks. Just what I needed to hear. I had decided I was not ready to die, and I'd better be careful what I pray for. Shivering on this ship and afraid, I wished I'd bided Ada's harping: "James, don't go putting yourself in peril. You have a family." Still, I reasoned that the other thousands of men had families also, and they were putting themselves in harm's way too. Why should I be the exception? I was glad she did not know what we were up against, and I wasn't about to tell her, at least not until safely back on Larimer Street. If I came back.

At day eight of the ten-day sail, a bugle's reveille awakened us. I took a sponge bath for the first time since we'd left port and marched through the cafeteria. The mess hall crew slapped some sort of mystery meat mush and a chunk of bread on our plates, and we had ten minutes, standing at the stainless-steel tables, to get it down.

Then came the call for all hands on deck. The Captain ordered everyone to look for enemy submarines since we were now between the Azores Islands and Europe, where other ships had spotted German U-boats.

I realized that when I tried offing myself eleven years ago, my inebriated state gave me no understanding of my mortality. But now that my life hung in the balance of rusted rivets and German U-boats, the possibility of my own death became real. *Father, are you here?* I didn't want to die and wanted to know He was with me.

"What'd ya think?" Chappy asked. He'd used his clout to get us along the rail near the bow and starboard of the ship.

I looked out over the expansive ocean, feeling as small as a grain of sand. The only thing visible was the occasional coal smoke from the destroyers as they weaved in and out of the fleet.

"Unbelievable," I finally said. "Never in my life did I picture this vast nothingness. Makes me feel tiny and insignificant."

Chappy drew a long drag on his cigarette and exhaled, the

smoke disappearing in our sixteen-knot headway. "True, Jimbo. It's really something."

"What are we looking for again?" My eyes had gone buggy, and I feared missing whatever we searched for.

"When the Kraut submarines attack, they have to come up to periscope depth to set their sightings and distance. You will see two little antennae stick out of the water for a few seconds. They do that three or four times, then surface and fire torpedoes. But if you haven't seen the antennae by then, it's too late."

"Yeah, thanks," I said, squinting at the sea, trying to focus on the oblivion.

He laughed. "If the torpedoes don't get us, the mines might."

I just shook my head but didn't take my eyes off the water. *Father, I am not ready to die.*

A blimp's engines overhead scared me enough to look up for a moment at the flying curiosity. I'd never seen such a thing, but glad it was up there looking for enemy submarines as well.

I shivered as the fresh morning air blew across the bow. Chappy had told me the ship pushed maximum speed, zigzagging constantly to throw off the U-boats.

I looked down at the water lapping at the side of the ship and then back out at the emptiness of the ocean. A black speck appeared. Perhaps I imagined it, but I grabbed for Chappy's arm. "What is that?" I yelled and pointed.

My announcement caused all eyes around us to focus on where I pointed. I hoped I hadn't made it up.

"What do you see?" The men pressed me. "I see nothing."

I squinted at the end of my finger. Yes, something floated out there. My heart raced, but words wouldn't come. I pointed with certainty, shaking my finger for emphasis.

The blimp hovered over the area. I expected to hear the blare of "ARUGA"—the call to battle stations. I stared at my quarry. It was difficult to judge perspective, but the speck did not move, and our ship did not change course. Whatever the object, we were going to pass right by it.

When the speck came into view, it stirred, not with the flash of a periscope, but with the flapping of wings. My sighting turned out to be a large bird, standing magically on the surface. As our ship sailed past, the head of a huge sea turtle popped out of the water under the bird.

"Well, I'll be," Chappy guffawed. "That tired bird found himself a perch to rest on."

A scripture verse instantly came to mind, and I shouted it to the surrounding men, "'Behold the fowls of the air: for they sow not, neither do they reap, nor gather into barns; yet your heavenly Father provideth for them. Are ye not much better than they?' God is with us, boys."

The men returned a spontaneous shout of thanks. Turned out I wasn't the only one needing a sign of the Lord's omniscience.

But the moment didn't last. The battle station alarm blew, and the bird spread its wings and took flight.

We stood frozen, with nowhere to run. I grabbed the strap on my life preserver belt and snugged it tight.

Except for her battery of two old-style guns on the top deck and one on the stern, they did not equip the Pocahontas for war. Yet it was upon us—the screaming repetitive fire of the guns echoing off the steel hull of the ship and decking, and three thundering booms from destroyer cannons. With our ears ringing, we could see nothing and guessed the action erupted on the port side.

I looked to the sky, praying for God's help, only to see our ship's funnels bellowing clouds of black smoke that told me the captain coaxed every ounce of power from the steamer.

Chappy elbowed me and pointed into the water. The unmistakable bubble trail of a torpedo zipped past the bow of the ship, missing us by a few feet. The captain's efforts to urge the ship forward had thankfully failed, and the U-boat missed us by a fraction of a calculation.

The men saw what had happened and erupted with a cheer.

I lay on my bunk catching my breath and thanking God that the U-boat had missed, and the destroyer had foiled the Germans' attempts at getting off another shot at us. God's message became obvious to me. I was not in control, never had been, and if He provided for the birds of the air, I better let go and put my trust in Him. Easier said than done.

I looked up from my bunk. Chappy came down the aisle between the rows, accompanied by two men I didn't know. Officers in their bunks fell out like dominos and snapped to attention.

I decided I'd better do the same.

Chappy and his companions stopped in front of me. When I saw them, I broke into a sweat. Chappy had told me I shouldn't salute, but I recognized the silver eagle on the insignia bar of one man, and I stood at attention and raised my hand to my forehead.

"At ease," the man said.

"Colonel Fitzgerald, Reverend Goodheart," Chappy introduced us, and the colonel extended his hand and got right to the point.

"I'm afraid we're in need of your services this afternoon,

Reverend. I'm told you're the only man of the cloth on the ship. Several soldiers have come down with the Spanish flu and are filling up sickbay." He lowered his voice to a near whisper and continued. "One man died today, and we need a minister for his burial at sea. Will you help us?"

It came as a command more than a question.

"Yes, sir, of course."

One hour later, the ship's bell tolled, the boatswain's pipe blew, and the captain's voice boomed, "All hands bury the dead."

The troops and ship's crew mustered on every open deck of the vessel, arranging themselves in inverse order of rank. We would give the young man from Texas who died as much respect for his sacrifice as if he'd lost his life at the end of a bayonet or enemy bullet.

I stood aft, starboard, next to the boy's body wrapped in a flag, praying and trying to concentrate on the small booklet the colonel had given me to read for the church service.

The other ships in the fleet had pulled together in tight formation and lowered their ensigns to half mast. We were thousands of men, unknown to each other, thrown aboard these vessels, but losing a shipmate brought us together. I looked over a sea of solemn faces lost in reflection, including Chappy, who stood next to me, regarding the floor in contemplation.

The flapping of the US flag flying from aft mast, as they lowered it to half, became the only sound to be heard over the engines.

The men carrying the young man's body marched forward in slow time. Chappy motioned for me to keep step with the escorts. We advanced slowly to a bier mounted outboard and draped in flags.

"Present arms," one escort shouted, and everyone, troops and crew, snapped to attention as they placed the body on the bier.

Chappy nodded to me to read the benediction. I read as loud as I could and followed with the Lord's Prayer.

A haunting verse of "Nearer, My God to Thee" rose from the ranks.

The boatswain blew his whistle from low to high and back to low, and the roar of the engines stopped. A solemn silence fell over the ship as the escorts committed the young man to the deep.

21

AMANTY AIRDROME, TOUL, FRANCE

April 17, 1918

W hen we had arrived at the port of Brest, my official assignment was still unclear. I had thought Newport News throbbed with craziness, but once we hit the shores of France, the congregation of thousands of men turned into hundreds of thousands, and the chaos multiplied accordingly. It immediately became clear to me that my best bet was to stay close to Chappy.

As far as my exhausted brain could reckon, Chappy and I might as well have been on the far side of the moon. Although I have to admit, except for Paris, the countryside of France looked a lot like Illinois: relatively flat, with a patchwork of forest and farms. When our train from Brest arrived in Amanty, a farmer leaving for his property offered us a ride in his hay wagon. He spoke little English, but that didn't hamper his warm enthusiasm for us.

The farmer dropped us off at the entrance to an expansive field that the army had cleared for an airstrip. Filled with men and airplanes, the area buzzed with activity. Never in my wildest imagination had I pictured flying machines like the ones that zipped around overhead, coming and going from dirt strips that Chappy called runways.

As Chappy and I walked across the field toward buildings set back into the forest, four men approached us. We stopped to talk, and I couldn't help noticing the one-piece suits with fur collars the men dressed in. They strapped belts at their waist and wore heavy boots. Even though they looked alien, they were friendly and pointed us to the hangar and barracks of the 96th Aero Squadron, where the military had assigned Chappy.

We entered a large wooden structure with massive sliding doors that stood open. A man who appeared to be Chappy's age, in his late twenties, smiled when he saw us. He threw down his cigarette, crushed it with the toe of his boot and welcomed us.

"It's about time you got here, Chappy."

He wore a one-piece suit like the four men we'd encountered, but he had gold leaves on the insignia bar. The two men hugged each other tightly with loud slaps on the back. "How was the trip?"

"Pretty uneventful, Red." Chappy smiled at me and winked.

I wanted to add: "Yeah, about as uneventful as a hellacious Atlantic storm, one near miss by a torpedo, chaos in Brest, and a jaw-rattling ride on the train."

"How's your family?" the man asked.

"Everyone's good. Julia hated seeing me leave—hard leaving the boy. How's Claudia and little Claude?" Chappy asked his friend.

The man pulled a photo from his front pocket and

handed it to Chappy. "Growing like a weed. I can't believe he's one already."

Chappy turned to me to show the picture of a young woman with a child on her lap, then handed it back to his friend. "Our wives are best friends," he told me. "Our sons were born a month apart."

"Just goes to show the questionable judgment of our wives," the man said.

He and Chappy laughed.

"How long you been in country?" Chappy asked.

"Seven months, but who's counting?" The man pointed his thumb at me and smiled. "Who's your friend?"

"Major Harry Milford Brown, this here is Reverend Jim Goodheart."

Major Brown shook my hand until it hurt. "Nice to meet you, sir," I said, easing out of his grip.

He looked my uniform up and down and tilted his head at the homemade insignia that Chappy had pinned on my chest.

"Believe it or not, this man volunteered to be here," Chappy intervened. "He's a minister from Denver."

The Major nodded. "Well, the first line of order is to get you a proper chaplain's bar. No need confusing the rest of the men," he said and chuckled. "Hell, it's good to see you, Chappy," he said and hugged his friend again. Then, apparently deciding I was okay, he turned to me to explain. "We got our wings together in the Signal Corps at the Aviation School at Rockwell Field in San Diego." He thumbed at Chappy. "Best darn pilot there is in the sky. Almost as good as me." He slapped Chappy's back.

The Major turned to a small desk laden with papers and grabbed one from the top stack. "Look at this, we're about to become legitimate." He waved a sheet with an official-looking header and then read, "Effective Immediately, the Aviation Section of the Signal Corps is to become the United States Army Air Service of the American Expeditionary Force." He looked up. "I guess we're now known as the Air Service."

"I imagine we all get raises, huh?" Chappy asked.

"Yeah, that and a kick in the ass." Major Brown laughed. "Where are my manners? I got reassigned to the 96th myself, and I just moved into my office." He looked at the cluttered desk and shook his head. "What an office, huh?"

As he rummaged around in some boxes stacked on the ground, I looked around. We stood in a large wooden building with dirt floors that reeked of gas and oil, like a mechanic's garage. There were six airplanes in different states of repair, each surrounded by men, presumably fixing them. Pinned to the wall above the desk was a large map, various documents, and many photos of women in various states of undress.

"Aw, here it is." He stuck his hands in a box and pulled out a bottle of dark, golden fluid and three glasses. "You'll find out that the French have the best cognac in the world." He poured two glasses and started to pour a third when he looked over his shoulder at me. "Reverend, you care to join us in a little toast?"

I wanted to say yes so badly, feeling exhausted both physically and mentally from the long trip, but managed to stutter out, "No...no thank you." He didn't seem to mind and probably figured it was for religious reasons.

Instead, he asked, "Since you're not regular army or air corps, what do you want us to call you? Surely, we can't call you Reverend all the time."

"Just don't call me Shirley," I said and laughed. "Just call me Jim."

"The boys call me Red while we're flying. On the ground,

they call me Major Brown." He shrugged, "You know the army," he said as if I knew.

Chappy and Red raised their glasses and slugged back the drink. I swallowed hard, almost tasting it. Then Chappy said, "Jim is trying to meet up with Company A, 138th Infantry of the 35th Division. He has a good friend's brother serving with them. Any idea how we can get him there?"

Major Brown turned to the large map on the wall. "We're here at the Amanty Airdrome in the Toul Sector," he said, pointing to a spot in the northeastern part of France. It surprised me to see how close we were to Germany's border. "They just reassigned me from the 12th Observation Squadron. We were providing reconnaissance for the 138th Infantry." His tone turned somber. "Rev, you don't want to go there...in fact, I will not let you go there." His tone got darker. "It's a small step-up from Hades. The French and the Brits have been fighting for that area for a couple of years with enough artillery and trenches that it looks like the worst hell you can imagine. Poison gas has killed everything green and alive."

I thought I might vomit as my heart sank for Horatio and his brother, Percy, who fought in that hell.

"Are the Germans really dug in?" Chappy asked.

"They have trenches dug in from the Alps to the North Sea. Some places they have trenches four or five deep, and the Krauts have had time to reinforce them with concrete and machine-gun nests...it's a real crapshoot out there." He looked at me and frowned. "I'm sorry for your friend, Jim, but no way you're getting out there."

"I told him he should stay with the 96th," Chappy added.

"I reckon that's a good idea," Brown said. "We could sure use you around here. The boys don't know it yet, but things are about to get ugly. Except for days of training and reconnaissance, they have seen no real action, and everyone is restless. Besides, the last commander gave them too much leeway, and they've grown accustomed to going into Amanty and offering comfort to the French ladies." He paused and looked me in the eye. "The boys could use a better moral compass. What'd you say?"

"You sure there is no way to get me to my friend's brother?"

"We could drop you out of an airplane, but I'm not sure you'd do anyone any good once you bounced a time or two." He smiled.

I understood taking Horatio's letter to Percy was impossible and extended my hand to the Major. "Sounds like the 96th has a chaplain."

Brown had ordered his squadron to wheel two planes out of the hangar. While I stood out of the crew's way, Chappy and Brown walked around the aircraft with the Major pointing to various and sundry things. I had seen pictures in the *Post* of the Wright brothers' original plane and the next few versions, but they were nothing like the machinery that sat before me. The biplane, as Chappy had called it, stood on two rubber wheels in front and a skid plate in the back. It looked to be around thirty feet long, with a longer wingspan. The body of the airplane laid between two wings, top and bottom, and capped with a large metal casing where the engine sat. The plane's large wooden propeller nearly touched the ground when vertical. The body had two seats and ended in a tail of adjustable rudders that they had painted red, white, and blue. One plane had a large red number eighteen, and the other a fifteen, marked on their rears. Brown told us the squadron

TIMOTHY BROWNE

comprised only ten airplanes, but he hoped to get ten more soon.

Chappy and Brown were laughing with their arms around each other when they walked back to where I stood. I couldn't believe Chappy would crawl into one of these contraptions and fly. The assembly of wood, canvas, and wires looked hopelessly fragile. I couldn't imagine them getting off the ground, let alone staying airborne.

"You ready to go up?" Chappy smiled at me.

"You're never going to get me into one of those things," I protested. I could feel sweat dripping down my back at the thought of it.

"Never say never," Brown warned.

"What are these called?" I asked.

"Well, technically they are French Bréguet 14 B2 bombers powered by the 300-HP Fev Renault engines." Chappy grinned. "In reality, they are the biggest kick in the pants a man can have with his clothes on."

He and Brown laughed until the Major turned serious. "To the enemy, they are flying demons with their forward Vickers machine guns and two Lewis guns on the ring mounting of the observer's pit," he said, pointing to the guns. "They're death on wings."

Two men joined us from the hangar. One handed Chappy a one-piece flight suit, a leather cap, and a pair of goggles.

Brown introduced them. "Chappy, this here is Lt. Harold MacChesney—better known as Mac and Cheese—and this is Lt. James Duke."

"Duke," the man carrying the flight suit added.

Brown introduced me as the new squadron chaplain. For the first time since leaving Denver, a genuine sense of belonging enveloped me.

As Chappy put a leg into the one-piece suit, Brown said,

"Mac, you're with me. Duke, you're with Chappy. Boys, hope you've digested your lunch, 'cause you're in for a real ride."

I watched these brave men climb into the flying machines, pilots in each of the front seats and Duke and Mac in the rear or observer seats, while the crew pulled away the ladders. The powerful engines fired, and I shielded my eyes from the clouds of black smoke that blew toward me as the whirring propellers churned the air. I grabbed my hat before it blew off, and the planes moved onto the road leading to the field.

The planes accelerated down the runway and like giant birds lifted off the ground, one after the other. I'd overheard Brown tell Chappy they could fly over a hundred miles an hour and carry six-hundred pounds of bombs to an altitude of four thousand meters in thirty-five minutes. I shielded my eyes from the afternoon sun and watched them climb rapidly into the blue sky.

I thought for a moment I'd lost sight of them, but they had circled around and raced over me, and I reflexively ducked even though they were well overhead. I couldn't tell who chased whom, but the lead plane took a sharp right, then left, and rose in a steep climb but couldn't seem to shake the trailing aircraft. The pair looked like two massive birds engaged in a mating dance in the air.

I surveyed the vast airfield where I'd been told potatoes used to grow. Instead of crops, the field now had nine squadrons of men and machines disrupting the tranquility of the French countryside. I imagined this place without war; a perfect spot to enjoy a picnic with Ada and Donny. I thought about the men who had already given their lives, and I wondered what lay ahead for the soldiers battling the enemy I knew little about. One thing was for certain, I stood farther from Larimer Street than I ever thought I'd be.

I looked into the sky again, and my head spun trying to follow Chappy and Brown. When my stomach churned with conflict, it puzzled me. Yes, I was exhausted and hungry, but there was something more—I honestly felt like sitting down in the middle of the field and weeping. It occurred to me I struggled with a contradiction between homesickness and adventure. I missed Ada and Donny something fierce, but how exciting to be here to see men fly airplanes, a marvel of man's ingenuity. Yet my brain wrestled with the realization that they designed these machines to kill. A strong dose of inadequacy merged with pride for the US boys willing to fight and give their all for their country and for the foreigners, our allies, whom they had never met. I shivered. *What am I doing here?* I did not belong. I shivered again, but deep down I knew I did.

I swiped a tear running down my cheek and prayed the only words that came to me, "Lord, help us."

22

BOMBS AWAY

June 12, 1918
(Two Month Later)

Realizing I needed some privacy to meet with men who wanted pastoral care, Major Brown assigned me an office that turned out to be a broom closet. A tiny space, but adequate, considering fewer men wanted pastoral care than I would have liked. Only a handful of the enlisted men who battled homesickness or had received a "Dear John" letter sought my counsel, but until today I had not met with one officer. The officers were decent and respectful, but many were self-sufficient and cocky and claimed to have no need for God.

Today was different. I could feel it in the air, and even the officers' confidence waned. I had been at Amanty Airdrome for two months, and I'd watched the days drone on between training flights and rainstorms—mostly rain. The men of the 96th Bomb Squadron had been here much longer and grew restless, like caged fighting dogs unable to perform what they had trained for.

That morning, five good Catholic boys came for confession and two Protestants visited, seeking prayers before their bombing mission at four thirty this afternoon. The other nine pilots and observers believed in their own skills and flying machines to bring them back safely. One pilot confided in me that the Brits and the French had refused to provide them with a fighter escort, and because the Germans scrambled as many as twenty planes at a time, the odds stacked against their return to base. On top of that, only two of the entire squadron of pilots had ever crossed the enemy line before today.

The US Air Service didn't match President Wilson's boasting and all the hoopla that Ada had reported in her letters. The USAS had trained thousands of pilots, but truth be told, not one American aircraft had made it to foreign soil yet, and therefore, only a few pilots had planes to fly. The rest performed menial tasks, like cooking and cleaning latrines. Those lucky enough to fly, piloted old, leftover French trainers that the US teams patched together the best they could with limited resources. Three of the planes flying today had parts salvaged from a local farmer's harvester, and telephone wire held the wings together on two others. The only mishap the 96th had in the two months of intensive training at Amanty had turned into a blessing. Number fourteen crashed, and both pilot and observer walked away unharmed, and the crews salvaged the plane's pieces for parts for the squadron's other ten planes. If they had ordered me to fly one of those Frankenstein machines, I'd have been on my knees until they ached.

"Lord be with these boys today," I prayed.

I held the tension the pilots refused to acknowledge in my

five-by-five-foot claustrophobic space, and it became oppressive, no matter how I arranged the closet. Piling all the brooms and mops in one corner, I'd found a tiny desk and two chairs to do my counselling. I'd straightened the shelf behind me that held large containers of cleansers and disinfectants—aware of the bottle of carbolic acid surveying me from the top ledge. Its red skull and crossbones seemed to taunt my fidelity, reminding me of my past failures and begging me to give in to the surrounding temptations—the booze, cards, and female companionship meant to comfort the boys as they waited for orders.

I pulled out my pocket watch. It read three o'clock. The squadron would take off in an hour and a half, and I would be no help to them out there, so I pulled a sheet of paper and pencil out of the drawer of my desk and wrote:

My dearest Ada,
I received your letter yesterday with much joy and
appreciation. It took four weeks to arrive, but I can't
tell you how much it helped fill my loneliness for you
and for my friends at the mission. I am so thankful to
hear that everyone is well, especially you, my sweet
wife. I worry daily and pray for you all, moment by
moment.

I say THANK GOD that Donny is not being shipped
overseas. I have literally held my breath, thinking that
he might. Although I fret as much concerning his
assignment as an aide at the armory in Boulder, where
people are suffering from influenza and tuberculosis.
Please remind him that his father said to wear a mask
and wash his hands often to protect himself. Your
reports of the Spanish flu from the *Post* are frightening

as the army appears to shield us from such news. What we saw in Denver before my departure was the tip of the iceberg. PLEASE be careful, my dear Ada. I am saddened to hear your news of severe outbreaks in Europe, but so far, thank the Lord, it has spared our base.

I was concerned from your previous letter that Mary fell sick with the flu, and I thank the Lord that He restored her to good health. Please send her my regards.

Ada, I am troubled about the financial state of the mission and am truly sorry that you had to take money out of our measly savings to cover this month's debt. I trust you to make wise and prudent decisions and am so pleased to hear that our work at Sunshine continues under your care. The mission has been in worse straits and deeper debt. I will send a letter to the Rotarians and see if they would consider increasing their support. You make for a steady rudder.

Give my love to Joseph and the others. I am pleasantly surprised that Ella Pettit is working out so well for you. It sounds like she is doing a fine job.

Please tell Horatio when you see him that I am pained to say I have not been able to deliver his letter to Percy, but we have heard news that the 138th Infantry may move north, and I am keeping a close eye out for any chance to contact his division.

You asked me in your latest letter how I find the people of France. The dear French people, after four years of hardship, are all in mourning but do not take time for tears. Instead, they wear a smile through all the discouragements. You also asked about the army base. The runway here at Amanty Airdrome on Saint-Dizier field is a muddy meadow cut from a farmer's ground. We have nine squadrons of the Air Service, with approximately eighty men in each, but I find I spend most of my time with the 96th. Our barracks are wooden, dirty, and flea-infested, but don't feel sorry for us, as we live in luxury compared to the poor souls fighting along the Western Front, where dead bodies are outnumbered only by rats. Tell people to pray.

I find that my mission here is not primarily religious, but I do what I can to make it harder for the boys in the field to do wrong. I remind them daily that it is worthwhile to keep themselves in hand, especially while on foreign though friendly territory because the eyes of the homefolk are on us. I find what the army needs most is a friend as well as a leader. Also, here in this blood-soaked soil where our boys are separated from all home ties, I try to be both a father and a brother to them.

My dearest Ada, I long to hold you in my arms. Lord willing, I will see you again at the end of September. It cannot come soon enough.
Faithfully yours, James

I started to include a drawing of the new squadron logo

that Lt. Harry Lawson had designed but thought better of it. She wouldn't appreciate the large black triangle with a red devil thumbing his nose at the ground as he held a bomb in the other hand. The crew had freshly painted the logo on each of the ten Bréguet bombers. It wouldn't please her that they now affectionately referred to the squadron as the Red Devils.

I spread my hand on the letter to seal it with all the blessings I could muster when I heard music out at the staging area. The Brits had put together a small military band. I folded the letter, put it in an envelope, and slid it into my front pocket behind the chaplain pin that Major Brown had given me. Patting the pin and letter, I then pulled my new officer's hat from the desk and set the cap on my head. I liked the campaign hat better, but the Major thought it best that the men give me the respect of an officer, even though I was neither fish nor fowl, as Chappy said.

I followed the music through the empty hangar, wishing Chappy had let me pray over him. He was my best pal on base, and I wanted to pray for his safety. But I didn't push it. I knew some pilots believed that discussing the danger or petitioning God somehow jinxed them. I had learned to respect their superstitions. A few wore lucky socks or sweaters or carried some memento they thought would keep them safe. Some walked the same exact number of steps to their planes and insisted the crew move the aircraft if they were going to be off on their count.

I joined a large gathering where General Trenchard, commander of the British Air Force, and many other French and American dignitaries were on hand to bid farewell to the first US bombing raid. I'd heard at lunch that only eight planes were airworthy for the first flight into combat. Brown had grounded two crews, who fumed at missing out.

The closer I got to the planes, the more menacing they

appeared, heavily laden with bombs and Lewis guns locked and loaded for air-to-air combat.

Major Brown and his observer, Lt. Rath, climbed into the lead plane, number eighteen, while Chappy and the others climbed into their aircraft. I suppressed an urge to salute the brave men who were, for the most part, unafraid to die. My heart trembled in terror for them as they strapped into machines that were barely held together, tasked with a mission to bomb a rail station they had never seen, and the real possibility they could get lost along the way. Besides their rickety aircraft, they faced countless dangers, including anti-aircraft fire and German fighters that were faster and more maneuverable. I had the hardest time wrapping my mind around the fact that the pilots rarely spoke malice of the enemy. If anything, our pilots saw their German counterparts as competitors and were not setting out to kill them, but to slow the war machine and protect the other Americans on the ground.

The British band struck up the popular song "It's a Long Way to Tipperary," and the ground crew joined in patriotic enthusiasm. But when they cranked the propellers on each bomber, the Renault engines turned over, and the roar of the aircraft swallowed the song and sent hats flying.

I looked at my pocket watch again. It read four-twenty, and the planes thundered down Saint-Dizier field, circled overhead into a large V and headed northeast.

"Lord, bring 'em back safe," I prayed and waved at the planes.

The wait for the return of the squadron continued the agony. Two of the eight returned within the first hour. They had mechanical problems but landed safely, despite sputtering engines. Three more returned in the fading light of late evening. Major Brown arrived with them, but Chappy and his observer were one of the three planes that hadn't returned. Brown seemed confident that they had made it over enemy lines into France and simply put down with fuel or mechanical problems. But I wouldn't believe in Chappy's survival until I saw the whites of his eyes.

The band and the dignitaries had long departed, and of the eighty men of the 96th Bomb Squadron, not one man had dozed off to sleep. At precisely three in the morning, Chappy and the rest of the crews waltzed in, no worse for wear. We gave them a hero's welcome as the ground crew boosted each of the six men onto their shoulders and celebrated their safe return. In order not to miss a single detail, Major Brown gathered the eight pilots and eight observers for a debriefing at the tables reserved for meals and cards.

To my surprise, Major Brown began the debriefing by asking me for a prayer of thanksgiving.

I bowed my head and started with, "Father…" when a jumble of emotions made my eyes water and stole my words. I honestly didn't know where to begin. It had been such a tumultuous journey for each man to get to this moment. And just maybe our efforts would turn the tide in this awful conflict, and every man would come home safe. "Thank you, our dear Father."

Apparently, it was all that needed to be said, because the men erupted with a loud "Amen," and cheered again for the crews' safe return.

"Okay, okay," the Major said. He stood and silenced the room.

"Clapp and Dunn…Codman and McDowell, your planes lost rpms once we got to twelve thousand feet, and you had to turn back." He turned to the squadron's chief mechanic, James Sawyer. "Master Sergeant, you have any comment?"

"Yeah, bloody French," he said, and then strung together his typical obscenities for the outdated aircraft.

Everyone nodded, knowing he was the best mechanic a squadron could have. His skill and ingenuity were the reasons they had any success at all.

"The French keep promising us new planes," the Major said. "We'll see. For the rest of us, I estimate we dropped four thousand, two hundred pounds of goodwill at Dommary-Baroncourt rail station, and I believe we scored direct hits on the marshaling yards."

A loud cheer erupted again. This time Brown had a hard time quelling the enthusiasm.

"We were just over Étain when we started getting antiaircraft fire," Brown shouted.

"Yeah, archies all the rest of the way," one pilot said to the ground crew.

Fortunately, I'd heard the term before, so I didn't have to ask. The pilots called the antiaircraft bursts "Archibalds," and when someone had shortened it to "archies," the nickname stuck.

Brown turned to the ground crew. "As we made our turn to home, archie fire ceased, and three German planes rose up out of nowhere with guns blazing. Grundelach and Way, you seemed to have the first shot at them."

"That's right, sir," Way spoke up. "They came below and to my right, putting some holes in our canvas, but nothing more."

"You get a good look at them?" Brown asked.

"Yeah…the wide-eyed look of the pilot when I blasted him with my twin Lewis's was as clear as the big, fat iron cross on his fuselage."

A howl of laughter came from the crew as they leaned in.

"What were they flying?" one man asked.

"Pfalz D-IIIs," Chappy answered.

I saw the nods and raised eyebrows of the men.

Chappy leaned into me. "They're squirrelly, fast little buggers." Then he said to the others, "Even though the Germans followed us to the Allied lines, they seemed to keep their distance, knowing we outgunned them. Right before we crossed over the line, they gave us one more go. I caught two explosive rounds in the motor."

Now I leaned in.

"That tough ol' bird maintained its rpms just long enough to let me set her down gently in a field."

Another cheer went up. It was impossible not to feel the enthusiasm of the men.

Brown turned to the other two crews that were forced to set their planes down. "You men take damage as well?"

"No, sir," one pilot answered. "We simply ran out of petrol."

All the men laughed, and I laughed with them. There was so much to pray for.

23

TRAGEDY

July 6, 1918
(One Month Later)

S tanding outside the hangars waiting for Chappy to pick
me up, I watched the ground crews pick and shovel at
the large ruts that plagued the runways. The heavy rain
muddied the tarmac, threatening to bog down the Bréguets'
tires and occasionally snapping propeller blades during takeoff
and landing.

The local farmers of northeast France couldn't remember
such a wet summer, and the cold, damp weather made the
entire squadron edgy. Recently, there were two fist fights over
ridiculous arguments—one man accused another of using his
fork and another accused his bunk mate of breathing too
loudly. Inevitable, I suppose, with hundreds of young men
confined together with surging hormones and no appropriate
way to express them.

Still, despite the rain, the squadron successfully completed
four more bombing missions over Conflans and Longuyon with

no casualties—dodging the archies and German air assaults. The German fighter pilots were well aware of the heavy defensive fire of the observers and their Lewis guns and resigned themselves to one or two side pass attacks. Mac claimed the first confirmed kill on the third outing and the Major awarded him a certificate.

Reports that Germany's commanding General, Erich von Ludendorff, referred to the flying yanks as "the wild cowboys" fueled our boys with confidence and determination. The soubriquet sparked great enthusiasm throughout the Allied theater and spurred the call for the much-needed repair parts for our planes. New Bréguet bombers arrived as well.

Still, the chronically inclement weather dampened the gusto, and they aborted all missions for two weeks. Today marked the first day the clouds opened on a blue sky, and the crews took full advantage of it.

Chappy flew an early morning reconnaissance, but sat his plane down twenty miles from Amanty after running out of gas. When the pilot landed a plane down prematurely, it was a matter of driving gas to the aircraft and flying it home. Chappy swore Sawyer had put a brick in his tank, causing him to have less fuel than the other planes. But the other pilots razzed him for being heavy on the throttle.

I waved at Chappy and Mac as they bounced toward me in the Model T army truck. The vehicle didn't appear to differ greatly from the new Model Ts driven in Denver, except the military painted them green. They sported bigger tires, and the back half of the passenger carriage had been chopped off and replaced with a wooden bed to carry supplies. Chappy and Mac had gone to the fuel station to pick up a barrel of petrol and strapped a wooden ladder to the passenger side. Chappy had assigned Mac as his permanent observer, or rump-man, as they were nicknamed.

With the rest of the crews busy flying or fixing planes, Chappy promised he'd teach me to drive so I could take the truck back to the base while he and Mac returned the plane to Saint-Dizier field.

The truck squealed to a stop, and Chappy jumped out. "You ready for this, Jimbo?" He slapped me on the back.

"Yeah, today a truck, tomorrow a plane." I laughed.

"Maybe now I should pray," Mac said, leaning out of the truck and smiling.

Chappy bowed into the cab to show me the mechanisms. "You have three pedals on the floor. The brake, backward, and forward." He pointed to each, right to left. "This here is the handbrake lever," he said with his hand on a metal stick. "When it's all the way back like this, it locks the brakes. When it's halfway, the truck is in neutral, and you push the left floor pedal to go forward in low. With the handbrake all the way forward, the truck is in high gear, and you can really fly."

"Yeah, but the idea is to keep the wheels on the road," Mac added.

"How do you give it more gas?" I asked.

Chappy pointed to the small lever arms coming off the steering column near the wheel. "This right one is the throttle. Push it down and you accelerate, pull it up and you slow down. The left lever is the spark advance. As you increase speed, advance the timing, and it will smooth out the engine. Easy peasy."

"Like falling off a log," Mac said.

"Yeah, but you guys are used to piloting an aircraft," I said with hesitation.

We squeezed into the bench seat, and Chappy took me through the start-up sequence of pulling out the choke, turning the key to the battery, advancing the throttle slightly, and hitting the starter button on the floor.

As soon as I hit the starter, the truck lurched forward with a sharp jolt. Chappy reached for the key and turned it off. "Oh yeah," he said, "make sure you pull the brake lever all the way back."

I followed his advice while he and Mac laughed at my jerky start.

I soon got the hang of it, and the feeling was wonderful, having never experienced anything as exhilarating as driving this vehicle. What would my father have thought? I grinned at the memory of our ride to Bloomington.

Mac caught my grin and nailed it. "A man has to spend a better part of his life in a truck."

When we passed two pretty French girls strolling down the road, Mac leaned over Chappy and me and pushed the horn button. The girls turned and waved, and one lifted her skirt ever so slightly, flashing shapely calves. I have to admit, I sat up a little straighter.

We bounced across the field where the Bréguet sat idle, and with my newly acquired skill, I slowed the throttle, retarded the spark, released the forward pedal, and applied the brake.

"Well done!" Chappy said.

"So amazing," I said, not caring that my grin soared from ear to ear.

"Next, you'll be wanting to fly," Mac added.

Chappy's back straightened, and he looked at Mac with a peculiar look, but not of the comradely fun we had shared. Alarm bells rang in my head.

"That's a great idea, Mac. You mind if Jim takes your seat for the ride home?"

"Not in the least," Mac said. "Give me the chance to see if the girlies are still on the road, needing a ride." He jumped out of the truck, jogged around to my side, and opened the door.

I sat stunned, like they were deciding the fate of my life without even giving me a voice. "Uh…"

"Oh, come on, Jimbo," Chappy said. "What man can say he learned to drive and fly on the same day? Besides, it's a quick flight home, and you don't have to worry about any Germans." He nudged me off the seat.

I wiped the sweat from my upper lip and couldn't believe my mouth said, "okay," as I got out of the truck with Chappy right behind me. Mac handed me his leather cap and goggles.

Without thinking, I pulled on the cap and rested the goggles above my forehead as though I'd done it all my life. Then I helped Chappy and Mac set up the ladder next to the plane's propeller and haul buckets of petrol from the barrel to the plane. Mac stood at the top of the ladder, pouring the gas into a funnel stuck through the engine casing. He replaced the cap, climbed down, and held the ladder for Chappy to climb into the pilot's hole.

"Your turn," he said to me, pointing to the observer's seat behind the pilot.

I forgot about the pleasure of driving when it became clear I was about to fly, and I mounted the ladder with reluctance.

Mac climbed up behind me to offer advice. "Because these older Bréguets are trainers, you can control the plane from back here if something happens to the pilot. But I'd advise you to keep your hands off the controls." Then he grabbed the handles of the large guns level with my face. "If you see any Germans, just look down the sights and pull this trigger." He winked at me.

I crossed my arms over my chest. "I'm not touching a thing."

"But hold on." He moved my hands, one to each side of the ring mount where the Lewis guns sat.

Chappy leaned back and said, "It's going to be a little bumpy getting up out of this field."

I looked around frantically for some sort of strap or rope to keep me in place. When I saw nothing, I clutched the ring mount, my knuckles turning white.

"You'll be fine." Mac smiled and pulled my leather cap down. "Don't forget to put your goggles on."

"Hope we put in enough gas," Chappy said and laughed.

"You're such a pal," I said, pulling my goggles down.

Mac took the ladder back to the truck and went to the front of the plane, where he spun the propeller. The engine sputtered and kicked over. He returned to the truck and snapped a salute with a broad smile.

I think I hollered that I didn't want to go, but when Chappy slammed the throttle all the way forward, whatever I yelled got lost to the roar of the engine. We bounced and thrashed from side to side, hitting every bump in the field. I hung on for dear life until, suddenly, we smoothed out, and the ground below separated from us.

I looked down at the field in astonishment. "Yee haw!" I yelled. *If Larimer Street could see me now!*

"Now you know," Chappy yelled back.

How thrilling! The perspective of the ground from our rising altitude was unbelievable. Fields and trees blended into a patchwork of browns and greens.

"Pull the rope by your right hand," Chappy yelled back.

I did what he asked, and a trapdoor opened under my

feet. The earth moved below, and I quickly released the rope before I fell into oblivion.

When I caught my breath, I yelled at Chappy, "What in the world is that for?"

"It's so we can see what we're bombing."

It came as a sobering recognition that they built this marvelous airplane to be a killing machine.

"There's Saint-Dizier field to our right," Chappy said.

The realization we neared the base both relieved and disappointed me that we returned so soon.

"Looks like Clapp and Dunn finally got their plane up," Chappy yelled.

I could make out the red number seventeen on the tail of the plane. I had seen them working hard on the motor the last few days in the hangar. They hadn't flown for two weeks, and Clapp fell into a foul mood.

"Let's go pay 'em a visit."

Our plane glided to the right as Chappy accelerated to make the turn. The cool blast and ear-splitting din were invigorating as we pulled into formation alongside number seventeen. To be hundreds of feet off the ground, but seemingly close enough to reach out and shake hands struck me as strange. I kept my eyes on the tips of the wings to make sure the planes didn't touch, and I gritted my teeth. Chappy held my life in his hands.

When Clapp and Dunn recognized me in Mac's seat, they waved enthusiastically and gave me two thumbs-up. Dunn spun his Lewis guns toward us and shook his arms like he fired them at us. I could imagine how the German pilots felt.

Suddenly, a loud bang and a large puff of black smoke billowed from Clapp's exhaust chimney above the motor. Their plane appeared to stall. After a moment, the engine sputtered to life, and the propeller continued to turn until another piercing pop and black cloud exploded from the engine casing, and the prop stopped.

Chappy banked our plane sharply to the left, giving Clapp and Dunn plenty of room to maneuver. Losing an engine did not always mean a death sentence, as many of the Bréguets had been set down safely in silence. But Chappy told me that when the engine went dead-stick it flew like a rock. He positioned us so we could observe their landing.

Six hundred feet off the ground and aimed toward the runway, it looked like Clapp and Dunn were in the best shape they could hope for. Clapp kept the craft nice and level, and they appeared to have plenty of airspeed to make the strip.

But the rains of the last two weeks had softened the ground, and when the plane's tires hit they augered in, and the aircraft cartwheeled, erupting into a fireball.

———————

"Can you be faithful to God even when you don't see Him, and what you are experiencing doesn't match your expectations?" I spoke to myself as much as to the men of the squadron. We packed the local YMCA building full of solemn men, many wiping away tears. I stood between two handmade pine caskets draped in US flags. My emotions were still raw, and I couldn't stop seeing the terrible visions of the two men's bodies, charred and stiff, as we removed them from the burned wreckage like grotesque, ashen mummies frozen with permanent expressions of agony.

I put a hand on each casket. "Clapp and Dunn were great men. You are all great men, involved in a horrific conflict. It is okay to be sad, fearful…angry." I sighed and shook my head. "I'm afraid I have more questions than answers right now. And I say in this time of grief that we share…that we pull together…take time to be kind to your brother. I've just had one of my best days and one of my worst days. When Chappy took me up in the plane, I experienced the thrill you men risk your lives for. It's like seeing our existence and God's creation from the edge of heaven."

I extended my arms from my sides, palms up, like the scale of justice. "Death and life. One just as much part of the other. I think down deep we all know there is something beyond this life. Otherwise, we'd lock ourselves in a box and never risk the light of day. So, let us all hold on to that hope that death is a transition, that when our time comes, the Father will take us home. When each one of us reaches our allotted days, and we enter into eternal love, we can say…the Lord has brought us home."

I turned to the soldier in the corner holding a bugle and nodded.

He started the haunting tones of taps, and I knelt by the caskets and prayed under my breath, "Father, forgive me for my unbelief, for my own fear of death." I remembered the turtle perch provided for that bird to rest his tired wings out on the massive ocean. "Forgive my always asking for more, even after You give me glimpses of who You are. Father, give me the strength to be faithful when circumstances change— even for the worse—when things happen that appear opposite of Your goodness."

24

DISASTER

July 10, 1918

As I pulled out onto the road from the Saint-Dizier field, the stagnant gray clouds hanging over the Airdrome mirrored the deeply depressed morale of the men. Major Brown canceled morning reveille and roll call—a wise decision, considering that the men had consumed every drop of alcohol on base shortly after the funeral for Clapp and Dunn. By the time I hit the sack, even Chappy and the Major were sloshed.

I appreciated the dank morning weather that had grounded the planes and spared more lives. During the previous day, drunken courage and anger had swelled to the point of resolve to go on a raid today to avenge the death of their comrades. Of course, the Germans weren't directly responsible for the demise of Clapp and Dunn, but the Germans sure the hell were the reason we were here in the first place. Burning up was a terrible way to die, and no one could erase the image of the bodies pulled from the wreckage.

At any rate, Chappy couldn't go anywhere until they rein-stalled his motor into the casing. What he'd been swearing to, that he had less gas than the rest, turned out to be the truth. The day after the crash, they discovered a small leak dripping into the dirt from his plane. If they had not found it, Chappy could have suffered the same fate, but the repair required that the engine be completely removed.

I had to get out of Dodge, and the Major, in his condi-tion, could barely moan an affirmative when I asked him if I could take the squadron's truck. At least, I think he said, "yes." In any case, I figured I'd be back before his stupor wore off. Only officers drove the truck, but after Chappy had given me my first lesson, my new *modus operandi* had become taxi driver for the enlisted men, and I got plenty skillful with the crazy machine. I didn't mind driving the boys, as it gave me a chance to connect with them on a personal and deeper level. After the crash of Clapp and Dunn, twelve had come to me to give their lives to Christ. Their shield of invulnerability had shattered.

But this morning I drove alone, which suited me just fine as the smell of alcohol in the barracks and on everyone's breath drove me nearly insane with longing and regret. Besides, I had a special mission.

We'd continued to hear rumors that Percy's 138th Infantry had moved north out of the Vosges Mountains and possibly hunkered down near Nancy. The city stood twenty clicks away from the base and only another ten to the Western Front. I'm not sure the Major would have let me go if he knew I headed east, but ever since hitting the shores of France, Horatio's letter burned in the pocket of my jacket. He'd told me what the letter said: "Percy and I always had a love-hate relationship, and I'm afraid at times in our lives I haven't always been kind to him. I used to call him all sorts of terrible names and slug his arm until it hurt so much, he couldn't use it. I need to let him know I'm sorry and I love him. If he gets killed over there, I'll never forgive myself for not telling him how I really feel about him."

I understood the powerful desire to gain forgiveness—I had needed it many times over in my own life.

I swerved around a large hole and slowed as the motorway narrowed.

Coming around a bend in the country road, a brigade of soldiers marching in formation startled me. From a distance, I couldn't discern if they were friend or foe, and I realized I probably should not be out here alone. But when I saw a large Canadian flag on the back of a Jeffery armored car with its large disc wheels and central turret on top that escorted the men, I blew out a sigh of relief. They weren't my US boys, but they weren't Germans.

Each man carried a rifle and a large pack on his back and wore a steel Brodie helmet, which differentiated the Allied soldiers from the Germans, who wore the Stahlhelm with its distinctive coal-scuttle shape. But I noticed straight away how worn and tired the brigade looked. Mud and dirt caked their uniforms. These men had seen action and had it hard. I pulled to the back of the formation, and the Jeffery blew a horn for the men to separate and let me pass.

As I motored through, a few men waved, but mostly, these bloodied and bludgeoned troops stared with dead eyes or ignored me completely. I regretted looking so crisp and clean. Even though I was in France helping my boys, my cushy assignment seemed to fall short when I saw the walking wounded. The French and British, along with its colonies including Canada, had lost hundreds of thousands of men before the US finally engaged. And if reports were as erroneous as those of the Spanish flu, they had drastically under-stated numbers.

When country homes grew closer together, I assumed I entered the outskirts of Nancy. The scene grew frighteningly stark, with partially destroyed and bombed-out houses and buildings. The town appeared abandoned, and I slowed to turn around when I saw a large structure a few blocks ahead with signs of life. I slowly motored up until I saw troops wearing Brodie hats coming in and out of an old cathedral.

I pulled to the front and jumped out of the truck. The cathedral stood as one of the few buildings still intact.

Men carrying stretchers with freshly wounded patients rushed past me. As the last man passed, he yelled over his shoulder, "Sir, you better get inside. They're hitting us pretty hard today."

With that, a distant boom thundered, and a massive explosion hit a few blocks away, raising a cloud of dust. I hightailed it into the building behind the stretchers and entered a hall of horrors. Massive columns supported a high Gothic ceiling of what must have been an ornate cathedral. The army piled rubble on one side and injured and dying men on the other. One side wall of the transept and part of the ceiling had collapsed. The central nave remained intact, but where I imagined had been pews, men lay in rows of organized states of brokenness. Instead of a heavenly choir, a drone of pain and suffering echoed. At the far end of the church, above the altar, the apse displayed a large painting of Jesus ascending from the cross.

"Oh, Lord."

"Can I help you, sir?"

I turned to a private, who sat on the baptismal font puffing on a cigarette. He had both legs wrapped in bandages.

He saluted me. "Forgive me for not getting up." He waved at his injured legs.

I smiled and offered my hand. "Jim Goodheart. I'm the chaplain from the 96th."

"Looks like you've come to the right place, Rev." He shook my hand and raised his arms to the high ceiling and gargled some notes mocking a choir. "But you will not find much of God in here." He took another puff of his cigarette and blew it out defiantly to the ghosts of past parishioners. "Just lots of suffering and death."

"What is this place?"

"This here's the Fourth Corps field hospital."

I heard a boom of artillery that hit close enough to shake the building and knock more plaster off the walls. Instinctively, I ducked.

It did not faze the young private. "They got Big Bertha taking shots at us today," he said nonchalantly. "It will be over soon, one way or another."

I looked into his eyes. I understood what brings a man to where he doesn't care if he lives or dies. For these young soldiers, if they survive, how do they go back to a normal life?

I wanted to pray for this boy or hug him, but it seemed like such a trivial gesture and probably one he'd shun.

"Can I help you with something?" he asked, bringing me back to reality.

"Yeah, uh…thanks. I'm looking for Company A of the 138th."

"Oh, they're up there, all right," he said, pointing east. "Right in the worst of it, I'm afraid."

"You happen to know Lieutenant Percy Preston?"

"Sure I do. One of the most popular lieutenants of the division. I'm from a different company, but most of the guys know him. He'd give you the shirt off his back."

"I've got a communication for him. Can I get to him?"

The young soldier looked me up and down, then laughed. "I don't think so."

"Pardon us," came a voice from behind.

I didn't realize that I blocked the doorway, and I stepped aside. A field medic led a line of twenty men with their eyes covered in bandages. Each held the shoulder of the man in front of him.

"Damn Krauts." The young soldier swore. "Using chlorine gas again. Unless you have a gas mask under that starched uniform, you won't make it a mile toward the line. Take my word for it, Rev. You don't want to go anywhere near no-man's-land."

I guessed he was probably right.

The boy looked past me and said, "Hey, Lieutenant, you anywhere near Company A?"

I turned to see a young lieutenant following the line of the blinded men. "Who's asking?" he said.

I extended my hand. "I'm Jim Goodheart."

"He's a chaplain," the young soldier added.

"Dr. Lewis Browne," the lieutenant said. "We're at the aid station behind a big chunk of the 138th."

"You happen to know Lieutenant Percy Preston?"

"You bet...Perc is one of the best. What can I do for you?"

I pulled the letter from the inside pocket of my jacket and handed it to him. "It's a letter from his brother."

"Death in the family? He needs no more bad news right now."

"No, nothing like that," I said. "More of a reconciliation letter."

The doctor put it in his pocket. "I'll make sure he gets it."

He then looked me up and down. "Mighty important letter for you to put yourself in harm's way."

I looked at the floor. "I made a promise."

"Roger that, Goodheart. Living up to your name." He smiled and patted me on the shoulder. "I'll make sure he gets it," he repeated.

———

I had accumulated images I knew would never leave my mind. Men with missing limbs and nauseating wounds. Maybe the blinded men were the luckiest of all, because they'd be on their way home soon. I knew Major Brown would be angry and worried if I didn't get back to base before dark. Still, I stayed longer at the field hospital than I should have and prayed for as many men as I could. It was the least I could do. I knew there would be hell to pay, but I prepared to face the consequences.

When I finally started back, the weather had improved, though my mood had become gloomier. I tried to buck up, knowing I had delivered Horatio's letter, and the clouds seemed to promise a beautiful sunset.

Summer solstice had just passed, so sun lit the Airdrome in lengthening shadows when I pulled into base. I had missed chow and steeled myself for an ass-chewing by Brown. But as I turned toward the barracks and hangar, my heart dropped. Planes were rumbling out to taxi. I could see six in all, each loaded down with bombs. I yanked out my watch—five minutes after six—I'd never seen planes leave for a mission this late in the day.

I pulled to a stop near the ground crew that saluted them off. Chappy stood with them. I parked the truck and walked over to him.

He leaned toward me. "Glad to see you're okay, Jimbo." He wiggled his eyebrows and then dropped his salute.

"What in the world is going on?" I asked.

"The Major woke in a hangover huff. The ceiling lifted, so he called for a raid. We couldn't convince him otherwise," Chappy said and shook his head.

"Probably didn't help that I had gone MIA."

"I don't think he even noticed. He was so damned determined."

I looked for Mac and didn't see him. "Where's Mac?" I asked.

"Brown's usual rump-man has been puking all morning. Mac took his place."

"But it's so late," I said.

Chappy shrugged. "Maybe they'll catch the enemy at Conflans by surprise." He paused and wiped his face with his arm. "But I'm not sure I have a good feeling about this one. Wish I'd gone with 'em."

———

My pocket watch read eight thirty, and we had another hour and a half before the sun set. But a light drizzle fell, and the sky turned dark. Typically, the mission to Conflans took three to three and a half hours, depending on encounters with German aircraft. The Bréguet's maximum fuel capacity could keep a plane aloft for four.

Rain clouds had converged on the sky an hour after they left. If everything had gone as planned, they should have dropped their bombs and headed back by now.

Chappy and I stood with some of the men, willing the clouds to part. "Better break out the fire pots and line up the runway for them," he told Sawyer.

The men did what they were told. We waited. When ten o'clock rolled around, they added more powdered sulfur to the pots. If any of the planes were going to make it home, it had to be now.

A half an hour later, complete darkness engulfed the Airdrome, and we realized our worst fears—not one plane would return home tonight.

———

No one slept. If by some miracle the men had completed their mission but landed short of the Saint-Dizier field, they would have made their way home by the time reveille sounded. We sat at breakfast in silence, barely lifting a fork, only hungry for news. Cigarettes came out and before long, the room filled with the frantic puffing of smoke.

One young man with exceptional hearing called our attention to the droning of a single aircraft. We leaped from the table and ran outside. But even I could tell it was not the rumble of one of our Renault engines.

As we shielded our eyes from the rising sun, an orange, single-engine plane lazily circled overhead.

"Holy smokes!" Sawyer yelled and ran into the hangar.

I looked at Chappy. "Son-of-a-gun!" he yelled. "It's a Kraut Rumpler reconnaissance plane."

Sure enough, as the pilot turned and dipped his wings at us, the big, black iron crosses on the body and tail were visible.

Sawyer came out of the hangar, blasting one of the spare Lewis guns at the plane, but by then the German passed well out of range. The plane dipped its wings one more time near the end of the runway and dropped an object with a long yellow streamer.

A couple of men took off in a sprint as the Rumpler buzzed nonchalantly back eastward. The men raced back to us carrying a metal canister and handed it to Sawyer.

Sawyer opened it, pulled out a piece of paper, and gave it to Chappy.

I looked over Chappy's shoulder to see a message written in perfect English. He read it out loud: "We thank you for the fine airplanes and equipment which you sent us. But what should we do with the Major?"

25

SEARCH

July 12, 1918

I had closed the door to my tiny closet office. Depression hammered us all, and I needed to catch my breath before saying one more prayer. I wanted to be alone. The leadership respected my input and trusted my Godly counsel, and I wrestled with the notion that I'd missed the opportunity to advise Brown against his impulsive decision. I may not have talked the Major into delaying the mission, but somehow I felt responsible for the entire unit.

Chappy became inconsolable with his friend Red missing in action, and he regretted allowing Mac to go. The bond between pilot and rump-man was stronger than a blood tie since each depended on the other for survival.

A month ago, Mac had brought a little terrier to the base. Tyge, as we called him, had become the squadron's mascot, but when Mac disappeared, the pup adopted me. I glanced at the dog in the corner. He looked at me with his big brown eyes, figured all was well, and went back to chewing his toy.

I turned back to the blank piece of paper on my desk. I tried to decide how much to reveal to Ada. Somehow, I knew in my heart that even thousands of miles away, she had a pretty good idea of what was happening. By some invisible heartstrings, I figured she knew things were bad. I just wasn't sure I was ready to let my emotion flow onto the paper:

Dear Ada,
My beloved wife. Pray for the boys and me. I know you do, but I ask that you step up your diligence and request that the entire mission pray for us. In Otto von Bismarck's own words, "God has a special providence for fools, drunkards, and the United States of America."

I have seen some awful things. The boys have just experienced indescribable loss, and I'm afraid I'm at a deficiency for words. I wish I could go into greater detail, but for the safety of the men, I cannot say more.

I have faith that I will return to you in the fall but am afraid this experience has left me with more questions than answers. I am guaranteed to come home a changed man.

Ada...I'm afraid my words fall short of what my heart feels for you. Please forgive me for where I have failed you and when the pressures of office crowd out my deep devotion to you. When gazing at the brilliant stars over France last night, I could only think of you. I love you more than there are stars.

Please give my love to Donny, saving plenty for yourself. The one thing that war has taught me is to hold
tighter to the ones you love. War truly is hell.
Your loving husband, James

A knock at the door startled me, so I quickly folded the
letter and sealed it in an envelope. I wanted to make sure it
went out today. I lied about being certain I would return to
Ada's loving arms. I had no faith in that at all, but there was
no need to cause her worry, considering all she had on her
plate.

"Come in," I shouted.

Chappy poked his head around the door. "You ready,
Jimbo?"

"As ready as I'll ever be," I said, feeling both shocked and
honored that Chappy had asked me to fly with him this
morning. After yesterday's disaster, I knew that only two
planes remained of the shattered 96th, and one of them
required an entire wing to be replaced before it could fly
again.

Chappy had convinced Sawyer and his crew to work
around the clock to get his Bréguet airworthy. We still had no
idea if they had shot down the missing six planes and the
teams were dead, or if the Germans indeed held them captive.
It might be possible to gather some intel by sending out a
reconnaissance.

Rath, Brown's rump-man, still couldn't hold anything
down. Whether it originated from the alcohol or food poison-
ing, he would not be of any help. Chappy sent him to the
medical station in Champagne.

Since Chappy was determined to fly, Rath's illness left
him in the lurch. As temporary commander of the 96th,
Chappy refused to split up the other flight team, and he knew

that regulations forbid taking an enlisted man up. That left me.

"Are you ready?" Chappy repeated.

I took a deep breath and shrugged, "*Savoir-faire.*" I knew little French, but I'd heard the men say it often enough to know that it was the right thing to say and do.

Chappy nodded and handed me a flight suit. I slipped it on when he added, "Today you're going to need this as well." He handed me a large fur coat that the pilots wore for high altitudes. "Going to keep us at reconnaissance altitude. Gets mighty cold up there."

As I stretched the coat over my arm, a metal flask fell onto my desk. I picked it up with two fingers as though it were a snake.

"Sorry. Didn't know it was in there," Chappy said. "We use a little cognac to take the chill off. All the pilots carry one."

I closed my lips tight and held the flask to him. He took it, apologizing again. We'd become close enough that he knew my aversion to alcohol was more than religious.

I finished getting suited up, and we walked out to the bomber that the crew had readied for us. I climbed up the ladder. As I jumped into the observer's seat, I gave the ground crew a thumbs-up, and they cheered.

I glowed in their affirmation. It may have been the proudest I'd felt in my life, to be a pilot's rump-man about to take off in wartime in service of my country.

Chappy climbed up after me. "I'm keeping us at high altitude so we should be free of archie fire," he explained, "but there's no guarantee we won't see a German flyer or two. Keep vigilant at all times. We'll get the hell out of there if you spot one, but if they get close, you're going to have to fire on them. Think you can do that?"

"Sure," I said with little confidence, "look down the sights and pull the trigger."

He nodded. "If it runs out of ammo, unclip the empty steel drum here"—he pointed to the clips—"and snap another in place." He rapped his knuckles against the other canisters by my knee. "We only have a quarter rack of bombs, so it's not such a struggle to keep altitude. I'll climb to our max ceiling of twelve thousand feet before we cross over the Front. But just so you know, if we see any of our planes on the ground in German hands, I'm required to take us down and destroy them. No good having our own planes used against us."

I nodded, and he gave me a pat on the head and a thumbs-up. He climbed down so the crew could move the ladder and hold it for him as he jumped into the pilot's seat.

I pulled on my cap and goggles. The goggles fogged with hyperventilation, and I tried to slow my breathing. My pride dissolved, and my confidence waned. But it had become too late to change my mind. Besides, a significant part of me didn't care. I'd heard the men who flew the planes say, "*Je m'en fous*." Right now, it was good enough for me. I didn't give a damn either.

The ground crew cranked the prop, and Chappy taxied us to the runway. It was one of the few cloudless days we'd had in weeks, but I was already glad to have the heavy fur coat as the recent rains cooled the morning air.

The Renault engine blasted us with wind as Chappy pushed the throttle forward. We zipped down the dirt runway and quickly lifted off. We climbed steeply, and my stomach rose into my chest. The blood rushed from my head, and for an instant, I thought I might black out.

The feeling passed, and I could feel the plane continue to rise as Chappy piloted us in lazy circles.

After twenty minutes, he leaned back and said, "We're right at twelve thousand. You might find the air pretty thin up here. Just remember to breathe deeply."

I nodded at his reminder. I promptly exhaled and gulped air in, sure that I'd been holding my breath the entire time. The heavy fur collar of the jacket kept the chill from my neck, but my gloved hands sweated as I tightly gripped the handles of the Lewis guns.

"I'm pointing us toward Conflans. We'll be over no-man's-land in five minutes. If our men set down, I'm figuring it would be between there and the rail station. Look for the red, white and blue roundels on top of the wings, but always monitor the sky for iron crosses."

"Roger that." I pushed myself up to standing as the crew had instructed. I had a much better view in most directions, and I searched frantically. The wind off the upper wing blew hard and cold at my back, but I would not let the discomfort halt my mission. I reached down and pulled the trap door rope. It slid open so I could see below us.

Soon the ground color went from greens and browns to deadly grays marking the Western Front—a few miles wide and stretching from horizon to horizon, as though a demonic giant had inserted his fingernail and split the earth, leaving a wake of destruction.

News from the Front reported that the line had changed little in the four years of fighting, but thousands upon thousands of men had died here, creating a stalemate as both sides dug in deeper and deeper—success and defeat marked in feet rather than miles. The future didn't look good because the Germans were developing larger tanks, artillery, and planes to penetrate our defenses. It would be only a matter of time before they broke through.

Flying safely at twelve thousand feet, I could not see the

death and destruction, but just knowing what ensued below made me sick to my stomach, and I swallowed down the bile.

"See anything?" Chappy yelled, reminding me of the mission at hand.

"No...Unfortunately, no!"

"I don't either. We have about twenty minutes to Conflans."

I knew that meant to keep a sharp eye out to the sky.

No-man's-land soon gave way to greens and browns again. War was a ridiculous effort of maniacs and madmen—there are women, children, and families hacking out their survival on either side, for God's sake, wishing the nightmare would pass them all by.

The farmers' fields faded from countryside to industrialized city. Large smokestacks bellowed black smoke from German war factories.

"That's Metz to the right," Chappy yelled.

The large city extended along the La Moselle River, the same river that flowed past our base.

I saw white puffs of smoke under the aircraft, followed by explosions well below us.

"Archie fire," Chappy said. "They know they can't reach us. They're just letting us know they see us. Here you go, you bastards, chew on these."

I saw our bombs drop from the lower wing. I had seen hatred for the Germans grow throughout our team, and now I felt it in my own heart.

It took many minutes before I saw explosive blooms and one huge blossom of smoke.

"Hit something worthwhile," Chappy said.

I sighed and tried to ignore the possible casualties of the indiscriminate destruction.

"Holy smokes!" Chappy yelled. "You seeing what I'm seeing?" He tipped the plane to the right.

It took me a minute to understand, certain my perspective was off. It looked like a giant flying dragon surrounded by toy planes. "What is that?"

"I've heard rumors." Chappy caught his breath. "It's the new Zeppelin-Staaken R-VI. They estimate its wingspan at close to 140 feet."

"It looks like it has four engines."

"Yeah, and it can drop as many bombs as our whole squadron. I suggest we skedaddle."

As the words left his mouth, Chappy sped up the engine and glided left, but not before one of the German fighters broke formation and turned toward us.

In less than ten minutes, the pilot caught up to our Bréguet. I saw flashes from his forward guns, and I froze until shots ripped our right wing fabric.

"You better shoot back, if you don't want to be target practice," Chappy yelled and dipped the plane.

I didn't hesitate. I aimed at the iron crosses on the bottom of the aircraft, grabbed the handles with all my strength, and pulled the trigger. The Lewis's recoil hit hard. I lost visual of the fighter for a moment, but quickly readjusted and fired again and again.

I thought I'd made contact and watched as the Kraut swerved and abruptly pivoted away.

"Attaboy!" Chappy yelled.

We hightailed it home in silence and landed smoothly. The crew helped us down with jubilation, but when we reported no sign of our squadron and the sighting of the monstrous plane, the mood grew somber, and the crew dispersed. Chappy and I ducked under the lower wing to inspect the damage. Multiple bullet holes had zipped harmlessly through the fabric, but Chappy pointed to a spot where a bullet nicked a support wire.

"You did good up there," he said, squeezing my shoulder.

But my shoulders trembled, and I wept.

Two weeks after our flight, the new commander of our squadron, Major J. L. Dunsworth, walked into the mess area carrying some papers and a large map that he spread out in front of us. I pushed Tyge off my lap and stood at attention with the rest of the men. Dunsworth, a no-nonsense officer, tried shaking our squadron out of its slump with military precision. He'd put an end to the late-night drunken poker games and stopped issuing weekend passes. Cigars were the men's only guilty pleasure.

On the plus side, the new commander brought eleven new Bréguet bombers and the replacement pilots and observers needed to fly them. The men practiced formations and bombings on flying days while Sawyer and the crew prepared the planes for over-the-line runs. Now we had lucky-number thirteen planes and crews. Even so, and despite my best efforts, Chappy's affect continued to darken.

"At ease," Dunsworth commanded.

We gathered around him as he pinned the map corners flat with drinking glasses. "We just got this correspondence from Colonel Billy Mitchell," he announced. "Our men are alive, but they are in German hands."

A collective cheer and groan erupted.

"The Krauts were nice enough to send us proof of life,"

Dunsworth said, holding up a picture of all twelve men, alive and in uniform, looking ashen and defeated. He passed the photo around, and I watched Chappy stare at it and sigh.

"Apparently, they got into high-altitude winds, and it blew them way off course." He pointed to Koblenz, 150 miles northeast of Conflans. "They all put down after their petrol ran out."

"Holy crap," one pilot said.

Dunsworth frowned at him. He didn't allow swearing. "The men are being transferred to the POW camp at Land-shut. The Spanish Red Cross has visited them and report they are in reasonably good health."

"Bloody Krauts," one of Sawyer's men said.

Dunsworth ignored the comment and continued, "I talked with Colonel Mitchell myself, and he gave me an outright tongue lashing even though it happened before I'd arrived. He's as mad as hell that the Germans have intact aircraft. The Colonel wants to remind us that if any of you set down in enemy territory, your first responsibility is to destroy your aircraft...no matter what." He aimed steely eyes at each man in the room.

"Easy for him to say," someone in the back muttered.

Dunsworth glared in the voice's direction, but the men remained stone-faced. No one would admit to the comment or reveal who had said it.

"The colonel said that after this lapse in judgement, Major Brown was better off in Germany than he ever would be with us."

I saw Chappy's face turn beet red as he excused himself from the room.

26

ZEPPELIN R-VI

August 31, 1918
(One Month Later)

I wrestled my body around, trying to find a comfortable place on my bunk in the officers' barracks. I kept reminding myself that we had it good, but this darn mattress had every lump and bump of an Illinois country road. Tyge snored softly between my cot and Chappy's as I finally found the sweet spot.

"Sure you want me to read the letter?" I asked Chappy.

"If you don't mind. I need some sort of news from home. Can't figure out why Julia has stopped writing."

"Okay, here goes." I adjusted the lantern. "But I'm skipping over the intimate parts."

"Come on, Jimbo, throw a dog a bone, will ya?"

We laughed.

I proceeded to read my letter from Ada:

"Dear James,

I am enclosing a picture at your request. I'm not sure
why you'd want a picture of this near half-century old
woman for your wall, you old fool."

I feigned offense. "She just called me an old fool," I
interjected.

"Well, she got that right," Chappy said, and we laughed
again.

"I've seen the girly pictures the war produces for the
homesick boys, but don't you go thinking I'm the
kind of woman to show that much skin. My bare
neck is all you get, James Goodheart."

I fanned my face with the letter. Chappy's face streamed
with tears from laughter. Then, with a flourish, I pulled the
photo from the envelope and examined it. I liked what she
had done with her hair, loosening the bun slightly. I knew
she never smiled for photos, but I caught a glimmer in her
eyes that fueled my longing for her. Her dress must be a
new fashion because it revealed her bare neck. She'd always
worn high collars pinched under her chin. She looked good,
and I felt a twinge of jealousy toward those who got to see
her in person. I figured the male photographer had enjoyed
a beautiful view in addition to his task. I felt guilty and
wondered if I had asked Ada to do something against her
moral code.

"Come on, Jimbo," Chappy shouted. "You going to share
the photo or just lie there drooling over it?"

I hesitated, then handed it over. "But don't go coveting
another man's wife."

Chappy studied the photo and shrugged. "Fine-looking
woman. Kind of reminds me of my mother."

I had to smile. Ada and I were old enough to be parents to most of these boys.

"How many years you two been married again?" he asked as he handed the photo back.

"Twenty-five this last July."

Chappy whistled through his teeth. "That's a long time. What's the secret?"

I thought about it as I studied my wife's face. "Probably the grace of God and the love of a good woman," I said finally. "She's had to put up with all my shenanigans."

"Well, twenty-five years is something to be proud of."

I nodded and kept reading:

"They are now calling the flu an epidemic and thank the Lord that neither Donny nor I have come down with it. I have passed on your strict instructions to him and added a few of my own. We have a firm policy at the mission not to accept any man coming off the street with a fever or cough. Mary has been quite helpful in making bed space available at the temporary hospital for our men."

"Who's Mary?" Chappy asked.

"Who?" I asked, although I'd heard him correctly. *How do I answer that?*

"Mary, the one making room at the hospital."

"Uh...a friend...and a nurse." I left it at that and continued reading:

"A fight broke out the other day, but Joseph stopped it before they shed too much blood. Otherwise, we continue to bump along. I'm afraid we are in much need of your fundraising skills, as Ella says our books

are getting mighty short. She's a whiz with the
numbers, but at times she's a thorn in my side. She
thinks she always knows the best way to do things.
I'm trying to be patient. I am grateful to the Rotary
club for their help, but we are now nearly five thousand in debt. I have talked with our creditors and
they have promised to extend grace until your
return."

I stopped reading and dropped the letter to my chest.
Putting such a burden on Ada had been unfair.

"A noble thing you all are doing there in Denver," Chappy
said. "I imagine there's going to be lots more men in need
once this blasted war ends. Maybe when I get back home, I
should start a mission in Seattle."

I looked at Chappy and saw he had turned serious. "I
think that's a wonderful idea, Chap. I'd help any way I could."

He put his hands over his face. "Gotta figure out some
way to get the war behind me."

I nodded. "You and me both, brother." I pulled the letter
back up and read:

"The *Post* says you men are making significant
headway against the enemy and we may win the war
by Christmas."

I slapped the letter on my chest, looked at Chappy, and
gave a raspberry. "They have no idea what it's like here."

Chappy just shook his head, and I went back to the letter,
ad-libbing now:

"My dearest James, I can't wait to hold you next to me
again and feel your muscular body next to mine. Lord

knows, you make me feel things that a woman shouldn't—"

Chappy shot up to sitting and stared at me. "What?"

"Oh, there's plenty more," I teased. "You want me to keep reading?" Then I burst into laughter loud enough to make Tyge raise his head and stare at me.

Chappy realized I kidded and threw a dirty sock at me. "You're such a horse's ass. I knew when you said *muscular* you were pulling my leg."

"Hey, watch it." I shot the sock back.

I decided not to read the rest of the letter aloud. It would just make of us both sad, so I read it to myself:

"If I understand correctly, you will leave France on September 13 and be back to me on September 29. The days can't pass quickly enough."

I couldn't wait to be back with my family. But the thought of abandoning my boys brought unbearable sorrow. I couldn't believe that six months had passed so miserably slow and so incredibly fast at the same time, and that I departed in two weeks. Chappy and the rest of the team did not know when this hell would end for them. *Lord, let it be over soon.*

I folded the letter and looked at Chappy, who rested on the edge of the cot. His face had darkened as though he knew what the remainder of the letter said. His shoulders drooped and his head slumped.

"You think God will ever forgive me for what I've done here?"

I sat up on the side of my bunk. I guessed what haunted him, and I owed it to my friend not to give some glib, off-the-cuff answer, so I waited.

August had been a successful month for the squadron. The boys were making a real dent in the German war machine. But, during the thirteenth and final mission of the month, their formation got turned around in the clouds, and they ended up dropping their payloads on Bühl, a Hansel and Gretel fairytale village. The German authorities reported the incident as a war crime because the bombing occurred during a market day in the nonmilitary hamlet, killing countless civilians and livestock.

"Stinking, Bühl," he said, and his body shook.

I reached over and put a hand on his shoulder. He suffered guilt from the boys' failed mission, and I didn't know what to say.

"I suspect I've done too much wrong to be forgiven."

I watched his tears hit the floor. Tyge rolled over and draped his head on Chappy's foot in sympathy.

"Chap, each one of us has to account for our lives. But the way I understand it, Christ came to pay the price for all our sins. Every last one of them. Now and forever. I suspect we're all gonna have to deal with our guilt and find ways to forgive ourselves."

"I just can't see how He'd let me into heaven." He wiped his tears on his sleeve.

"Some days I feel the same, but then I have to lean into His promises. If we confess our sins, He is faithful and just to forgive us our sins and to cleanse us from all unrighteousness."

He nodded.

Tyge lifted his head and perked his ears. He stood and barked.

Chappy and I and the other men in the barracks stopped conversing and listened. We looked at each other and shrugged.

Conversations started up again, only to be interrupted by a soldier bursting through the door yelling, "Bombers!"

They trained us that it didn't matter what we were doing or how we were dressed, the last place we wanted to be during a raid was in a building or near a plane on the ground. We hightailed it to the door and fled.

As we ran to the forest in the fading light of the last day in August, the undeniable distant drone of aircraft hummed. It grew louder and impossible to know if it was friend or foe. Surprisingly, the enemy had rarely attacked the Airdrome, but in case of a raid, the Major instructed us to run into the forest behind the barracks. No pilot sat on the runway with his engines revved, and with no time to scramble the aircraft, the safest bet was to move away from any potential targets.

Someone pointed to the origin of the noise, and everyone saw the monster apparition in the sky. It came not from a squadron of planes, but from a single, massive bomber. I recognized it straightaway—the Zeppelin R-VI.

The four-engine giant roared overhead, and bombs whistled down at us.

Everyone dove for cover as the Germans unleashed their military might onto Saint-Dizier field.

Thunderous explosions and blinding flashes of light erupted, convulsing the ground. I hurled face down and covered my head with my arms.

"Oh God, oh God, oh God!" I screamed.

The acidic smell of ammunitions burned my nose and throat, and the roar of the detonations ripped at my eardrums.

Clutching for life, I hugged the base of the nearest pine tree but feared the sturdy pine might topple in the wake of the blasts.

A wave of heat bellowed, searing my face and hands, surely hot enough to set the entire forest on fire.

My body shook with fear, and I buried my face in the moss surrounding the tree, screaming at the Germans to stop.

Bomb after bomb exploded. I thought for a moment to run. But where? I imagined the entire area erupting in a fireball. My terrified body wouldn't move.

And then all fell still.

I remained frozen in silence, my fingers embedded into the bark of the tree. Screams and yells pierced the ringing of my ears, and my mind imagined the worst. I didn't want to lift my head or open my eyes until I realized the shrieks were cheers. They came from the other side of the barracks. I forced myself off the ground and ran toward the commotion.

Torch beams flashed and more cheers erupted.

"They missed, they missed!"

It was indeed true. The blasts heavily marred and pocked the fields and runways, but spared every barrack, hangar, and airplane except one. The monster's bombs fell and exploded harmlessly forty feet in front of the hangars—the darkness was bad for the Germans and a blessing for us.

As quickly as it came, the threat left, headed east, swallowed into the night.

Rumors had swirled that other squadrons were trying to pin the 96th with derogatory nicknames like "The Bewilderment Squadron" after Major Brown and crew were lost over enemy lines, or "The Original Child of Hard Luck" after the bombing of the village.

Maybe the error of the Zeppelin R-VI had broken those curses. One thing was for sure, however: I'd lost my taste for war.

LOSS

September 13, 1918

Chappy and I were packing our belongings—Chappy for a mission, me for home.

"I don't think I can leave," I said and sat on my bunk. "I can't say goodbye."

Chappy looked up from filling his small flight bag. "Jimbo, you get out of here while the getting is good." He saw my frustration. He smiled and said, "That's life, I suppose, a series of goodbyes. Just look at the 96th—one goodbye after another, hardly recognize it anymore. Lindsay and I are the last of the original Red Devils. The teams have turned over two or three times by now."

I wanted to add, *not by leaving, but by dying*, but I didn't. Chap was right—hard to even recognize the group. Even Dunsworth had moved up to group commander with the formation of the First Day Bombardment Group, and Captain James A. Summersett, Jr. took command of the 96th. The closeness and camaraderie of the original group had long faded, and fresh faces arrived weekly, full of fresh enthusiasm to fight the Germans.

"We need to get you home to your wife and son," Chappy said.

"Yeah, you as well."

"Don't worry about me. We've all picked our poison. I knew what I had gotten into when I climbed inside a plane."

I'd been too embarrassed to tell my friend about my near suicide by carbolic acid. He did not know how close he'd struck to home. Chappy had become the friend and brother I'd always longed for. Even though twice his age, he'd taught me more about courage and fidelity to country and his friends than I'd learned from any man. I blinked a tear.

"Oh, you're not gonna go and get sappy on me, are ya?"

I dug inside my front pocket and pulled out the palm cross that he'd first pinned on my uniform. I handed it to him, "I know your mama would want you to have this."

He took it and put it in the top pocket of his flight suit.

"Chappy, I can't tell you how much your friendship means to me. I look forward to seeing you in the States when the dust settles—to meeting your wife and son."

He nodded and changed the subject. Then pulled some papers from his flight bag. "You see the latest?" He handed them to me.

It contained the confidential report that only the pilots were privy to, but he often shared these with me. I read it back to him:

"The Hundred Days Offensive, began on 8 August
1918, with the Battle of Amiens. The fight involved
over 400 tanks and 120,000 British, Dominion, and
French troops. By the end of its first day, we created a
gap fifteen miles long in the German lines. Allied

command has shifted tactics to strike-withdraw, strike-withdraw. Punching many holes in the Western Front like sticking a pin in the Zeppelin war machine."

"Zeppelin?" I looked up.

"I think they're referring to that massive balloon airship, not the plane. The Germans have been dropping bombs on Paris with the dang thing."

I nodded and kept reading.

"US air support making advances possible. British and Dominion forces launched the next phase of the campaign with the Battle of Albert on 21 August. The assault was spread by French and British troops the following days. The next week, the Allied pressure along a sixty-eight-mile front against the enemy was substantial and merciless. From German accounts, 'Each day was spent in bloody fighting against an ever and again on-storming enemy, and nights passed without sleep in retirements to new lines.'"

"Sounds like you men are kicking some heinie," I said. "Maybe Ada is right. You all keep this up, you could be home by Christmas."

Chappy just shrugged.

I read the last line in bold print:

"September 12th starts the St. Mihiel offensive."

"St. Mihiel?" I asked.

Chappy looked around and lowered his voice. "It's the

first major ground offensive of the US boys. They're trying to take back Metz. We may have the Germans on their heels."

I nodded. I remembered seeing Metz from our flight and knew how far the city sat behind the Front. "That would be impressive."

"I hope it's worth the cost."

He didn't have to continue. We'd lost eight aircraft and three pilots and their rump-men just yesterday. A terrible southwest wind along with fast-moving clouds had made flying extremely dangerous. They had lost all those men and machines on or over Saint-Dizier field, making the losses that much harder to bear.

Chappy closed his flight bag and looked at his pocket watch. "Time to go."

I followed him out of the barracks. The crews were busy preparing the nine remaining bombers that were airworthy. Eighteen, our luckiest aircraft and the last of the original ten planes of the 96th, took the formation's lead for the nine flying today.

"You flying lead today, huh?"

"Yeah, most of these boys haven't been over the line yet."

I stood back as Chappy inspected his plane with a new observer and the ground crew. Satisfied, he climbed up the ladder and jumped into the front seat. Before the crew removed the ladder, I climbed up to see him off.

"I'm leaving for the train station at one. You should be back in time to see me off. Don't be late!"

"Yes, mom," he smiled.

I started to climb down, but he grabbed my hand. "Hey, Jimbo...thanks for being here." His expression turned serious. He reached into his heavy flight jacket and pulled out his silver flask. "I know you have no need for this, but maybe you can put some sacramental wine in it for communion."

I pushed it back at him. "No, Chap…I can't take this."

"Well, it's too late. It's yours. Besides, if I don't come home from this blasted war—"

"Don't even say those words," I commanded.

He gave the thumbs-up for the crew to spin his prop. The engine roared to life.

I stuck the flask in my jacket and climbed down.

Chappy turned and yelled over the drone of the engine, "Tell my son about me if I don't come back."

I lunched with the ground crew until we heard the drone of the Bréguet's Renault engines.

"Thank God," one man said.

We all pushed back from the table and ran outside.

I frantically counted the planes as they circled overhead and began lining up for landing. The lead plane pilot always landed last—to make sure all his men were down safely. I tracked them with my fingers. "Nine," I yelled.

I looked at Sawyer standing next to me. He counted as well. He sighed, apparently not agreeing with my number. Pressure filled my chest.

We watched the planes land. Sawyer was right, one was missing. It was Chappy's.

I'd lost count of the times that Chap had set down in another field. The ground crew had joked about his multiple farm runways, calling them "Chapman's Landings."

When the other eight bombers landed safely and taxied to the hangar, the wait grew unbearable.

I saw Sawyer talk to the first crew to deplane, then shake his head. My heart sank.

The rest of the crews jumped from their cockpits and

gathered around Captain Summersett. Lieutenant Lindsay explained, "We were turning for home when ten Fokkers came a-blazing. We fought 'em off as best as we could, but their BMW engines made 'em swarm like bees. Chappy broke off formation and took 'em on. He had no chance to escape but allowed us to get over the line." Lindsay shook his head, unable to continue.

His observer, Lieutenant Anderson, finished for him. "Number eighteen took the Spandau gun's full fire...it burst into flames. Chap bailed out at 300 feet...there's no way..."

My knees buckled.

If they said anything else, I didn't hear. My ears quit listening, and my heart sank. I felt a hand on my shoulder, but my sense of smell was stronger—the smell of alcohol as the men toasted to their lost comrades, as they always did.

I pulled out the metal flask with the large C engraved on the front. It shook with liquid, filled with pilot's courage.

I opened the flask and raised it to my lips. "To Chappy," I said and took a long drink.

ACT FOUR

28

BLINDED

September 30, 1918

I t felt like I'd been dreaming—a really lousy dream—when the train pulled into Union Station in Denver. I'd seen more men die in the last six months than I'd ever imagined anyone could see in a lifetime. I figured by now the good ol' US Army would have informed Chappy's wife that he was killed in action. I was done with the army, and I was done with the war. I was even done with the pain. It had been a long trip from France to Denver. The heartache that battered my brain at the start of the journey blew itself out, and now my mind seemed numb to it. I swallowed my own pain— dazed with the grief of the families that had lost fathers and sons and husbands.

I patted my army jacket pocket for Chappy's flask. I didn't know when or how I'd get to Seattle to talk with his wife, Julia, but I'd made a promise. Chappy's son, only a year old, would not have a single memory of his father. I hoped I'd live long enough to sit down with him face-to-face and tell him we all hailed Chap as a hero.

I shifted in my seat and pulled at my hot, wrinkled, and soiled uniform that stuck to my body. I'd been wearing it since before I boarded the troopship at Brest to sail home. They filled the ship with the wounded, the sick...and me. They might as well as numbered me among the sick as I'd puked most of the way back, which probably kept me from drinking the rest of Chappy's cognac. With my nausea left on the sea, I thought now would be a good time for a swig of courage, but I knew that if I did, Ada would smell it on my breath—and what a fine reunion that would make. I shivered involuntarily and couldn't shake the remorse of abandoning my boys in France.

I tried to set my mind on the bright side. There were three things I looked forward to—hugging Ada and Donny, getting out of this stifling uniform, and taking a bath...a really, really long soak. After traveling for two weeks, I reeked, but it hadn't mattered, as no one paid any attention to me. I got a few glances, but I figured they wondered why an able-bodied man came home while the rest of the boys were fighting on. My guilt followed as a constant travel companion. Only one person spoke to me—an elderly man in New York stopped me on the train platform and asked me how it had gone. *Terrible* was the only word that came to mind. I wanted to curse but thought better of it when I remembered I'd returned to civilization.

I bent down, gazing out the windows looking for Ada, but couldn't see her. My arrival came a day later than expected because of the ocean voyage. I had sent a telegraph from New York with an updated itinerary. Maybe if she didn't pick me up here, she'd be waiting at the mission.

I never expected to feel so conflicted about coming home.

The homesickness that I'd felt for Denver I now held for the boys at Amanty, and as much as I hated my uncomfortable cot in the barracks, I longed to be back.

So much rage boiled in me. As my heart pounded in my chest, I wanted to stand up and let a verbal assault roll off my tongue, lashing everyone within hearing distance. The other passengers chatted and laughed. *How dare they?* Didn't they know what happened over there? Didn't they care?

I stood and grabbed my bag from the overhead rack before the train lurched to a stop. I had to get out before I vomited or hit someone. I caught a few annoyed stares as I jostled to the train door, not bothering to excuse myself.

I leaped out before the conductor could get the step in place, then took a long, deep breath of Colorado's crisp air. How I'd missed that.

Then I saw them. Ada and Donny walked arm in arm down the platform. Dropping my bag, I raced forward and threw my arms around them both. The tears came.

"Oh, my Lord, you two are a sight for sore eyes," I blubbered. I let loose of them and then grabbed Donny by the shoulders and held him at arm's length. I inspected my boy, still skinny as a rail, but had a shiny gold chain draped across his vest.

"I bought it with my salary from the Armory," he said quickly, probably fearing it would upset me.

"It's very handsome, son." I pulled him close and hugged him tightly. His body stiffened, embarrassed at the public display, but I squeezed him tight anyway. "I missed you."

Then I turned to Ada, who had been waiting patiently. I hugged her and with one grand gesture, whirled her around. She huffed, but when I set her back down, I kissed her neck, and she let me.

"I missed you so much, my ever-loving sweetheart," I said

and noticed she wore the dress in the picture she'd sent me. In her favorite colors, black and gray, the seamstress cut the dress short which showed her ankles. When I admired them, she blushed.

"It's the style these days." She smiled and fanned herself. It had been a long time since I'd seen that smile. Then she stood on her toes and kissed my cheek. "Thank you for coming home to me."

I noticed Donny turn away, embarrassed by his parents' outpouring of affection. As happy as I was to see them, I searched the platform in both relief and disappointment that no other welcoming party accompanied them.

Ada must have noticed. "We have a little surprise waiting for you," she said.

As we started down Eighteenth Street, I thought we headed to the mission, but the driver of the fancy Essex Coach passed Larimer Street, turned on Broadway, and stopped in front of the Brown Palace Hotel, one of the finest establishments in Denver.

"What's going on?" I asked.

"You'll see," Donny said and looked at Ada, who smiled again.

When we arrived at the front doors, the doormen opened them wide. As two more doormen took our jackets in the entryway, I remembered how beautifully the Palace shone with its decorative sunburst lights in the Florentine arches of the mezzanine—like stepping inside a jewel, glowing with the Mexican gold onyx of its lavish central atrium.

But the luxury hotel appeared mostly empty and abandoned, except for a giant American flag that hung down the nine-story foyer. As soon as we entered the atrium, however, a brass band hidden in the corner struck up "The Stars and Stripes Forever," and a joyful cheer came from a crowd that appeared from every nook and cranny, including the balconies above.

"What…?" I looked at Ada.

"I know you told me not to make a big deal out of your homecoming, but the Rotary club insisted, and it just grew from there." She yelled over the music. "We're all very proud of you." She hugged my arm.

I hoped the band would stop at one verse, but they did the second and then repeated the whole song. Sweat dripped down my back, and I resisted running from the hotel. When the song finally ended, I raised my arms and waved. A loud cheer erupted, and well-wishers quickly surrounded me.

"Thanks for serving," a man said and slapped me on the back.

Someone else said, "Way to kick those Krauts."

I nodded, smiled, and shook hands until I saw Joseph with Mary and the rest of the mission staff standing off to one side. I waved to them, trying to resist the crowd of well-wishers that edged me toward the stage.

As the mob continued to push me forward, the band played John Sousa's "Semper Fidelis," and I stopped for a moment to hug Joe and Mary. Ella Pettit broke through the crush to hug me tightly around the waist. Her intimate gesture embarrassed me, and I gently peeled her away with Ada's help. They pressed me up the stairs to the platform, and Ada and Donny followed.

The president of the Denver Rotary Club stood with the elderly and frail appearing Mayor Speer, held erect by his walking stick. They greeted me warmly and shook my hand.

The president indicated the chairs for Ada, Donny, and me and stepped to the podium.

He held out his hands to settle the rambunctious crowd, and when they finally fell silent, he said, "We welcome you home, Jim Goodheart." The multitude erupted in jubilation again making it even harder to quell. He waved his arms to silence them. "I asked Mayor Speer to say a few words."

Mayor Speer tottered to the podium and spoke. The mob quieted to hear his weak and raspy voice.

"My fellow Denverites. It brings me much pleasure to welcome our local hero."

Hero? I didn't like the sound of that and thought I might be sick.

The mayor coughed into a hankie and wiped his mouth. "Even before this brave man headed to Europe to support our boys overseas, he worked as our city chaplain, making rounds through the jails, hospitals, institutions, and flophouses. He's helped many young men get out of jail and back on their feet."

The people applauded loudly.

"Today, I make it official. I am naming James Goodheart the City Chaplain of Denver with all the duties and rights..." he continued through coughs and mumbles I couldn't hear.

The blood drained from my face. Ada squeezed my arm.

Fortunately, the Rotary president took over. "Now let's welcome our man, Jim Goodheart," he said, as someone behind me shoved me to the podium. I saw the reporter Colbert standing below the stage, frantically writing notes. The president put his hand through the crook of my arm. "James, say a few words to the good people of Denver."

I could hardly breathe and thought I might have a heart attack in front of everyone. "Uh…"

He tried helping me out. "I bet you're glad to see your family."

"Yes." I smiled at them. "Ada and Donny—" Donny titled his head. "Uh...Ada and Donald were kind enough to meet me—"

The president interrupted. "We're all dying to hear how all our boys are kicking the Germans' behinds." The comment brought a roar from the crowd, a drum roll, and cheers for the US echoed throughout the hotel.

Images flashed through my mind: the young soldier's body slipping off the plank into the sea, Clapp and Dunn's burned bodies, the Major and his crews in the POW photo, the field hospital in Nancy full of injured and dying men, the line of men blinded by the chlorine gas, and most of all, Chappy's smile as he waved to me from his bomber the very last time.

My senses rang with emergency alarms. The deadly Zeppelin R-VI might as well have been flying directly over Denver with its bombs whistling. All this attention fueled my sense of guilt and failure. I knew if I didn't get out of here, my heart would explode.

I don't know if I excused myself when I ran from the stage, but I could hear the president making light of my departure. "I'm afraid our guest needs to use the bathroom after the long trip from France. How about another tune?"

I heard the band oblige with "It's a Long Way to Tipperary."

———

Miraculously, I found my way to the men's room. Breathing hard, I leaned against the tile wall and slid down until my butt landed on the floor. Joseph entered the room, locked the door, and sat down beside me. When I pulled Chappy's flask from my pocket and took a swig, he didn't say a word.

The cognac burned my throat as it went down but relaxed my body and mind enough that I didn't think my heart would burst.

Joe held my arm with his deformed hand. I couldn't look away from the keloid that had replaced his fingers. His eyes were closed, and his body swayed. I figured he prayed silently.

I took another drink.

He still said nothing.

"I'm sorry," I finally said.

"Sorry?"

I raised the flask in a toast and lowered it back onto my lap. "I guess I'm just blinded by the attention. How do I get this all behind me?"

Joe looked at me with his compassionate gray eyes but stayed quiet.

I worried he judged me, and desperate to hear him speak. I needed his help.

"I know your life has been hard, Joe. How did you get past the loss of your wife and son, the whippings, your hand?"

He let go of my arm and wiped his brow. "Yes, siree. Life can throw lots of misery our way. Not sure I've seen anyone escape it."

"So what do you do?"

"You work through it. Have people who will love you out of it. I suspect the key ingredient in healing is forgiveness."

I took another drink. "I'm sorry, Joe. I feel like I'm letting you down."

He shook his head. "No need looking for forgiveness from me. Look to yourself." He squeezed my arm tight. "I suspect the first place you need to extend forgiveness is to life itself... for being so screwed up...for being so damaged."

29

SURRENDER

November 11, 1918
(Two Months Later)

Water roiled around the fly, but when the large trout sucked it under, I reacted too slow to set my line. My mind drifted elsewhere. I'd found a new passion and stress reliever—fly fishing—dry fly fishing, to be exact. It was as much of an art as a skill, like painting or playing music. Yes, with practice you could improve, but mostly it seemed like God distributed the talent, and you either had it or you didn't.

These darn brook trout with their pea-sized brains seemed to be smarter than most men I knew, including myself. But they acted like a fastidious woman, insisting that the fly is presented just so, laid out silky smooth on top of the water with the right size and color, like shoes from Paris.

Come on, Jim, concentrate. I whipped my new bamboo rod up to three o'clock, letting the thin line lash behind, then flicked the pole forward to nine. The Royal Coachman flew through the air. As floating line landed first, the leader gently unfurled on the water and set the fly down in the middle of a deep hole behind a rock. The Coachman's red body and white parachute top hovered on the water, then swirled, and pulled across the hole as the current caught the line.

Ada had given me the bamboo rod as a belated birthday gift, and I hoped she'd seen my eloquent cast. She'd told me the fly shop owner regarded the Royal Coachman as the fly of kings.

Bam!

A fish jumped clear out of the water, taking the fly. I tugged the line, trying to give the fly the perfect pressure to set the hook but not pull it out of the trout's mouth.

I shouted to Ada as my rod flexed and the fish tugged. It dove deep, and I lifted the arcing rod above my head, trying to clear him from getting snagged. He broke the surface again and danced momentarily on top of the water with his tail.

"That's a beauty," Ada cheered from the picnic blanket.

For me, dry fly fishing is like patting my head and rubbing my belly. I carefully kept tension on the line while giving the fish enough play so as to not break the leader. This was the largest fish of the day, and with one amazingly powerful pull, the fish dove deep, pulling line from my reel and causing the handle to rap my knuckles. The darn thing enacted its revenge.

Then the line went slack, and the pole straightened. I thought I'd lost it, but with one more burst of display, the green and gold fish with its glowing red spots danced on the rapids. Our eyes seemed to meet, and in a final act of defiance, the fish spit out my fly.

Just like that, it ended.

"Oh, that's too bad," Ada said.

"You win some, you lose some." I shrugged, almost glad

the big guy got away and lived to fight another day. Besides, we had plenty of fish to take home to fry.

"You give him too much of a jerk?" Ada asked.

"Actually, I think it's the jerk at the end of the rod that's the problem." I laughed.

I glanced around at the beautiful stream and the mountains surrounding us and inhaled. During these moments, I could forget my nightmares and the friends I'd lost. I could even forget my craving for alcohol.

I turned back to Ada, who smiled. She patted the blanket, inviting me to join her.

I hopped from one rock to another, slipping as I hit the wet bank and almost going down. I recovered quickly and bowed. "Ta-da!" I tipped my newsboy cap, also part of her present to me.

Ada giggled.

This glorious November day cooled enough for a light jacket but was not chilly enough to keep us from enjoying the solace. The sun shone brightly, warming rocks and battle-scarred souls alike. I reached for my stringer of fish, lifted it out of the ice-cold water of Coal Creek, and held it toward Ada. "Your man has caught you dinner."

"Aren't you something?" She smiled, almost sounding seductive.

I put the string of fish back in the water and joined Ada and the picnic she had spread out.

"You better eat something, James."

I sat down, bit into a red apple, and reclined with my head on her lap.

The last six weeks, whenever weather permitted, we'd come here to "our spot." Ada had suggested that I take off plenty of time from the mission. "It can run itself," she'd say. She seemed to understand I returned in a fragile state. She hugged me tenderly when I wept and held me close when I woke up in sweats from night terrors. Joe was right—love was the salve, and forgiveness was the key. I'd told Ada about it all —the victories, the horrors, and especially the men, probably to the point she felt she knew them all personally.

But now the war had ended, and later today we were going back to Denver for the celebratory parade. Truth be told, I wasn't in the mood to celebrate and afraid it would get my head all riled up, fueling the nightmares. That's why we'd gone fishing. Ada realized I needed a distraction from the hubbub of the city's preparations.

Secure in our spot, I picked up the *Post* only to see a jumbled mess with boldface headlines all over the front page. Across the top, it read:

"VICTORY. WORLD AT PEACE."

The editor had exploded with excitement and ordered more headlines down each side of the page:

"WAR'S OVER"

and

"SURRENDER."

There wasn't much room for text, but what else was there to say?

I reread the article under the headlines and turned the front page to Ada. "Did you read this?"

"Yes." She laughed. "Those newspaper fools are probably just mad the war is over, so they're starting a headline war with each other."

She was probably right. Four days ago, the *Denver Times* had headlined:

"PEACE! ARMISTICE IS SIGNED; GERMANY GIVES UP."

The *Times* had posted it well before the *Post* and sold a ton of newspapers. The only problem was it wasn't true...at least not until today.

"The *Times* jumped the gun," I said.

"Yeah, and the *Post* took no time in using their misreporting to blast their rival."

I read part of the *Post* article:

> "This fake news was a deliberate,
> premeditated and mercenary
> newspaper crime..."

I laughed. "Maybe the *Times* will be prosecuted along with the Germans for war offenses. Just remind me to never get on the *Post's* bad side."

"That's for sure, James Goodheart." She gave me a look that said I should behave with Colbert, who still looked for a salacious story about the mission.

I pulled my cap over my eyes and snuggled into her warmth. "Wish Donny could be here with us today."

"Donald," she reminded me.

"I know, I know. I guess he'll always be Donny to me. But I'll try."

"He's become a man, you know. He has a lady friend."

I sat up. "Really? Why haven't I met her?" I felt hurt that Ada knew something that I didn't. "Who is she?"

"You've actually met her. Josephine," she said.

"One of his friends from North High School?" I put my head back in her lap.

"Yes. They've been friends for a long time, but I've noticed some changes lately."

"Changes?"

"Oh, the way they talk or look at each other. Just things a mother would notice." She pulled off my cap and rubbed my head. "I'm thinking we might have an engagement by next year."

"Oh, go on," I scoffed in disbelief.

"Remember, I'm the one that predicted the boys would be home by Christmas." She smiled and kissed the top of my head.

"That is true," I said.

"The kids are meeting us this afternoon."

I raised my eyebrows. The babbling rapids filled my ears, and I yawned. The sun and Ada's touch made me sleepy. I folded my arms on my chest, and we stayed put, enjoying nature's beneficence in silence.

Ada spoke first. "What are you thinking?"

I sighed. "I'm just thinking about the certificate of commendation Captain Summersett sent me. Awful nice of him. Just makes me sad that so many of my boys who signed it aren't coming home."

She wiped at a tear that rolled down my cheek. I knew enough to let them come. They'd either flow now or in a fit of rage at some dumb thing.

"The captain also wrote a letter saying they'd lost another batch of pilots and observers after I left, four in one day and five in another. I should have been there for 'em."

"You think you could have stopped the loss?"

"No, of course not," I said in anger. "Sorry." I sighed. "I just wish I'd been there for the boys."

I sat up and pulled out my pocket watch. "Maybe we should get going. The parade is in three hours. Let's go celebrate with the rest of Denver."

Once we got back to Denver, we picked up Donny and Josephine near Union Station, and he helped me take the top down from the touring car I'd borrowed from Reverend Gravett. The Model T had a full carriage, and I blew out a sigh of relief to discover it had the same controls as the truck I'd driven in France. I enjoyed impressing the family with my driving expertise, a skill I needed to navigate the large, boisterous crowd. Even though the city remained in Prohibition, the liquor-soaked frivolity spilled out onto Sixteenth Street.

The entire population of Denver showed up. Mercantile houses, stores, and all other businesses dismissed their employees for the day and placed delivery trucks and vehicles at their disposal for the parade. Mayor Mills, who had replaced the recently deceased Speer, declared a holiday and lifted the ban on city gatherings, originally instituted because of the global influenza epidemic.

People were sick and tired of the awful war news, and it was time to cut loose and rejoice. Once the sun went down, the temperature dropped, but the crush of the parade crowd kept everyone warm. Ada and I waved and shouted with the throng until our arms were stiff and our throats were sore.

Finally, we walked into the mission half-froze to death but full of excitement. What a jubilee it had been. I helped Ada off with her jacket, and she headed for the coal stove in the corner to get warm. Donny did the same for Josephine, and she joined Ada.

"Josephine have fun today?" I asked him.

"Oh my gosh, yes. Thank you."

"Well, I'm glad. See that she and your mom get something warm to drink."

I walked over to Reverends Gravett and Driver sitting in the corner sharing coffee and conversation. They smiled at me, and I held out the Model T keys to Gravett.

"Thank you for letting us use your car," I said.

It puzzled me when he didn't take them.

Gravett looked at Driver and then at me. "It's actually your car now, Jim."

"Well, the mission's car," Driver corrected.

Gravett shrugged. "We think it's high time the Sunshine Rescue Mission had an automobile. We've chipped in, along with the Rotary club. It's all yours."

My jaw dropped, and the words tumbled out. "Oh my Lord, this is something."

"We're glad you're home, Jim," Gravett said. "The last few days, Billy and I have been looking over your five-year plan for the mission. It's ambitious, to say the least. But if any man can do it, we have faith that it's you."

"With the Lord's help," Driver added.

"If we don't get the finances turned around, it will all be for not," I said. "My first task is to visit our faithful donors and try to get out from under this blasted debt. It's like a chronic abscess waiting to burst and kill the mission."

We looked up when the door swung open, and Horatio Preston walked in. I was so glad to see him. I'd sent word that I believed Percy had received his letter. I had just been thinking about Percy during the parade and hoping he'd be home soon.

But as Horatio walked over to us, I knew he carried bad news.

Gravett and Driver stood while Horatio fought for words.

Finally, he said, "Percy didn't make it," and handed me the letter from the army that all families dread:

Dear Mr. Preston,
It is with great sadness that I relay to you that your brother Percy has died in the field of battle. My name is First Sergeant Clyde Heath of Company A, 138th Infantry of the 35th Division. I served under your brother, Percy. Lieutenant Preston was one of the most popular men in our division. He was liked by the men outside our company as well as by his own men. He was a brave, manly fellow and considerate of his men.

South of Shippy at the Argonne on September 26th, Lieutenant Preston and his men advanced across the line. They encountered a machine gun nest, and the men fell thick. They hit your brother in the leg, but he fought on. A shell broke near him, and he died at the hospital a few hours later.

I am genuinely sorry for your loss. Percy was my commanding officer, my friend, and my brother in arms. I am shipping the contents of his belongings to you. One thing he held dear was your letter, which he often read to us when we were down.
Sincerely, First Sergeant Clyde Heath.

I handed the letter to Gravett and hugged Horatio. He wept on my shoulder. "I'm so sorry, Horatio. I prayed he would make it."

He stepped away, pulled a handkerchief from his pocket, blew his nose hard and wiped his eyes. "Stinking war," he said. "Kind of had a gut-feeling it would turn out this way."

"I'm so sorry," I said again.

"Well, thank you for getting my letter to him. I guess I have some comfort knowing he got it and that he's in a better place now."

We all nodded.

He handed me a fist-size bag—heavy enough that I knew it was another Preston miracle.

"Figured you'd be needing this. Lots of men coming home needing a warm meal and a place to stay."

30

WEDDING

April 9, 1921
(Two and a Half Years Later)

How do I move past the despair? I guess by throwing myself into the work and service of others. This wedding helped as well. I should have listened to Ada. Donald and Josephine got engaged last year during New Year's; he'd just turned nineteen, and she eighteen. I said they were too young and made them wait a whole year to marry. Donald became despondent and to my disappointment, he didn't return to the university. Fortunately, he'd secured an excellent job at Western Electric, a subsidiary of Mountain Bell as a yellow pages salesman. He seemed to have marketing skills in his blood—a chip off the old, aging block. I couldn't believe I'd turned fifty this year.

I'm sure for Donald, this day of nuptials couldn't have come fast enough. I watched as my son fidgeted through his vows, almost dropped the ring, and finally put it on his bride's finger. Josephine and her parents were staunch Episcopalians at St. Barnabas. I loved teasing her about being among the "frozen chosen," churchgoers more reserved in their practice of religion. I guess that's what Donald will become now. I was learning about Episcopalian ritual, although I still didn't understand the bell they rang before and after the service. Perhaps they were announcing the arrival and the departure of the Divine. I'd asked Ada, probably a little too loudly, about the things near the altar that looked like spittoons. "Is that where you spit out the wine?"

She'd elbowed me so hard my arm still ached.

"You may now kiss the bride," the priest pronounced.

I thought the smooch lasted too long, so I cleared my throat loudly, even if it meant another elbow in my side.

The priest turned the smiling newlyweds to the congregation. "I introduce to you Mr. and Mrs. Donald Everett Goodheart."

We stood and cheered as the organist pumped out the recessional hymn.

I turned to exit from the pew, but Ada grabbed my arm and held me in place. When the bride and groom, priest, and candle bearers had made their way to the back of the sanctuary, the priest turned and pronounced a blessing over the congregation. Everyone fell silent, and an altar boy went to the brass bell and struck it.

"Guess we can go," I whispered. "God's left the building."

That brought such a hard jab to my ribs that I moaned. "James Goodheart," she whispered, "I swear. You better behave on your son's wedding day, or you'll be sleeping on the couch for the rest of your miserable life."

"Okay, okay," I added. "I promise." I couldn't help grinning. I loved to tease her, and she knew it and forgave me.

Ada was the love of my life, and today she looked stunning. Mary had convinced her to shed her usual blacks and grays and fitted her with a silky midnight blue dress with lace draped over her shoulders.

"James," she said, breaking my reverie.

"What? Oh. You go on ahead and ride to the reception with Donald and Josephine, and I'll meet you there."

"I'm sure they'll love that," she huffed. "Don't be late."

"No, it's all right. I won't be long. Joseph has asked me to visit a young boy in jail to see if we can help, so he doesn't have to spend another night. Besides, it won't kill the kids to wait a few more hours to be alone."

"You forget what it's like to be young and in love."

"I may have forgotten the young part, but I'm still very much in love." I kissed her on the cheek. "You look wonderful."

"Okay, with that, you're excused. But don't be too long."

I walked from the church and met Joseph at our Model T.

"Sorry to take you away on such an important day," Joe said.

I waved it off, and we got into the automobile. "We'll be back before they know we're gone. I probably should skip the toasts, anyway."

By sheer will power, I'd been able to keep from drinking every day. But occasionally, when my nerves got the best of me, I needed a shot to get me through.

I glanced at Joe, who stared straight ahead and seemed to ignore my comment. He looked the same at eighty-one as he did when I first met him at sixty-seven, though he rubbed at his joints more often and didn't push the mop as quickly.

As we drove toward the jail, I asked him, "Sometimes, I don't get why there seems to be two sides of me, the part that communes with God and is at peace, and the other part that screws up and does bad things."

He held his tongue for a long time as we turned up Park Avenue.

Finally, he said, "I guess someday we'll see clearly," and smiled at me through his cataract-clouded eyes. "I think it's okay that we don't have it all figured out."

"It's just that some days…well, maybe most days, I don't feel worthy of my calling."

That made Joe laugh. "Oh, James, now don't go playin' the worthiness game. Only God is worthy. He doesn't love you because you're good…He loves you because *He* is good."

I nodded. He was right, of course.

"James, you *are* a good man. Maybe you just don't know that yet." He patted my arm. "Hey, you know what you're called when you have perfect contentment? When you can sit quietly through lousy news and money problems? When you eat happily whatever is put on your plate, and fall asleep after a long day without a drink?"

"Dead?" I asked.

Joe chuckled. "No…but that's a good one." He paused before answering his riddle. "A dog," he laughed.

I laughed with him. "A dog's life for sure."

"James, you just need to take the pressure off yourself. I pray you can someday find peace with not being perfect. Quit beatin' yourself up over your weaknesses. God is faithful to finish what He has started."

I wanted to believe that as much for the mission as for myself, but the finances were a constant worry. We'd made gains this year and increased our salaries over pauper's wages. We socked a bit of money away into our savings and even contributed a small amount to Donald and Josephine's wedding.

I pulled to the front of the county jail, trying to absorb his advice.

We walked inside and greeted the guards, who knew us well and escorted us to the crowded cell block.

Horatio had been right. After the war ended, men flooded the city, licking their wounds and trying to find meaning in their lives. Between the war and the influenza epidemic, the mission whirled busier than we could handle. The Wilson administration had given little thought to the fact that vast numbers of returning war veterans couldn't find work, and probably the reason the Democrats had lost the last election. That and the Republican candidate, Harding, had become more popular with the women who voted in their very first election.

Joe stopped at the second cell on the block and introduced me to a young man.

"Alex, this is Reverend Goodheart. We're going to see what we can do for you," he said.

I smiled at the jailer, Officer Mallone, and shook his hand. "You mind letting us take him to a room to talk?"

Because I made my weekly rounds here, Mallone didn't hesitate to unlock the cell and escort us to a small interrogation room.

I waited until the officer closed the door behind us.

The three of us sat in the chairs around a small table, and I got right to it. "So, Alex, tell me what happened."

Maybe because I called him by his name, or he read my sincerity, or due to the reassuring presence of Joseph, his emotional dike broke. The young man dissolved into tears, and his nose ran with snot. "I'm so sorry, Reverend...I'm so sorry," he could barely get the words out as he wiped his eyes and nose on his sleeve.

I put my hand on his arm and let him sob, and Joe gave him a hankie that seemed to help him find his composure.

"Truly, Reverend. I's not a bad person, I swear. My mama is a good Christian. Raised me as one as well. 'Spect I'll be going to hell for what I've done." He sobbed again.

"Joe tells me you stole a car."

The boy put his head in his hands in shame. "I knows it was stupid, but I just didn't see another way. I didn't think it through, and now they're telling me they've charged me with a felony, and I could go to prison for years."

"Why'd you steal the car?"

"My wife, sir. I swear. She's in the hospital with our baby, and I's not sure how I's going to pay the bills. I left the hospital, and the stupid car idled out front with the keys in it. I don't know what I thought." He wiped his face with the hankie.

"Joe tells me you drove it back and turned yourself in."

"Thought they might forgive me. Guess'n I was wrong."

I looked at Joe and smiled. He'd already told me the boy served.

"Where'd you fight, son?"

"In France, with the 35th."

"*Vive la France*," I said.

"Yeah, *vive la France*. We go fight for them and then come home to nothin'," he snapped with anger.

I understood and thought about Chappy's wife, Julia. I owed her a letter. I'd visited her in Seattle two months after I'd returned. We'd shed many tears together, but then quickly ran out of things to say. Ada kept steadfast at praying for her and their son daily. I just hoped Julia would find a way to rebuild her life without Chappy.

I looked at Alex and caught his eye. "Yes…I understand."

"We got married when I got home, and she got pregnant straight away."

"In that order?" I teased.

"Yes'n, I swear, Reverend."

"I have a good friend that says the first baby can come at any time," I said, "but the rest take nine months."

Joe laughed, but I'm not sure the young man understood.

"How much is your fine?" I asked.

"Fifty-two dollars." He cried again.

"Is your wife still in the hospital?" Joe asked.

"As far as I know."

"Which one?" I asked.

"At St. Joseph's."

I looked at Joe. He understood that would be our next stop on the way to the reception. I hoped Donald and Josephine would understand.

"What if we pay your fine?" I asked him.

"You'd do that for me?" he stopped weeping and looked at me with shock. "I would be forever grateful."

"Then what are you going to do?" I asked.

"I'm going to find a job to support my family."

"We'll talk with the sisters. If they know what you're up against, they'll find a way to make it square. Probably even find you a job in the hospital that can put a few dollars in your pocket."

"I don't know what to say," Alex said. I could hear new life in his voice.

"We'll go pay your fine, take you to the hospital, and talk to the nuns."

I stood, and the boy flung his arms around my neck. "Thank you, Reverend. How can I ever repay you?"

I eased him back and held him by the shoulders. "This

ain't from me. It's from your Father in heaven. Sometimes we just need a reminder that He loves us."

Alex looked at the floor. "I didn't think He'd ever love me again."

I laughed and said, "As a wise man recently told me, 'He doesn't love you because you're good…He loves you because He is good.'" Alex hugged my neck again, and I winked at Joe.

31

GOD IS GOOD

July 9, 1922
(One Year Later)

I bounced my foot to Karl Hoschna's "The Love Dance" that the Sunshine Symphony Orchestra played so well. It may have been a stretch to call the mission band a "symphony orchestra," but we had two violins, a viola, a cello, two flutes, a clarinet, and a tuba, and we thought that sounded pretty symphonic and cultured.

As a typical Sunday evening at the Sunshine Rescue Mission, a concert preceded the service, pleasing me with our accomplishments. I always sat in the front row on the far right in the auditorium at our expanded mission. I liked to steer some of our wealthiest donors to the best seats in the center.

I looked over my shoulder and smiled. What an eclectic mix of the nearly three hundred people—some of the most established and richest in the city mingling with the most destitute. There were no reserved seats, but the homeless always gravitated to the back.

On Sunday mornings, we went through a case of soap and buckets of coal to heat the water so the men could shower and become presentable. Not that I wanted them to feel ashamed, but they knew the score. They understood where the finances came from to pay for their meals and beds and why it held importance to look their best. Besides cleanliness, we strictly enforced two other house rules—no panhandling and no booze.

I didn't think the men realized I broke both those rules. I panhandled, so to speak, in a sophisticated way. I used my charm to schmooze the wealthy for contributions to the mission. And I didn't hesitate to take a shot from Chappy's flask in my office when I needed to settle my nerves. Ada knew, but she didn't nag as long as I behaved myself.

At any rate, the Sunday concerts were excellent times to mix the two aspects of society. I wanted especially for the wealthy to see that my men weren't much different from themselves. The gatherings even helped some of our more motivated occupants to find jobs. Unlike what the *Post* reporter Colbert claimed, that "giving free aid just fueled a man's laziness," our goal remained to give our friends a hand up. I was smart enough to know there would always be some bad apples, but just like life, I took the bitter with the sweet.

The orchestra finished beautifully, and Ada stepped to the piano. She nodded to the cellist, who smiled back. Then she began Goltermann's "Cantilena," while the cellist slid her bow in harmony. As my daughter-in-law's favorite, I looked back to where she and Donald sat and smiled. Josephine had their four-month-old baby in her arms, rocking her to the rhythm. Shirley, my first grandchild, was born March 5, almost a year after their wedding, so I couldn't tease them about her being born too early. I had a hard time believing I'd become a grandpa. Mostly, I couldn't believe I slept with a grandma.

I looked at Ada and smiled. She caught my gaze but continued to play—which she did so delightfully. She didn't miss a note, but she probably wondered what made the wheels in my mind turn so quickly.

The Sunshine Rescue Mission had prospered along with the rest of the city. New industries were flourishing: electric power, movies, automobiles, gasoline, tourism, and housing. Denver finally rose out of the slump of the silver crash, and the war and influenza epidemic were behind us.

I looked to my right at Ella Pettit to see if she enjoyed the music. She'd proved herself a whiz at the numbers, but also stingier than Ebenezer Scrooge. Ella fussed at me more than Ada did when it came to the mission's spending. She'd tell me I'd become generous to a fault and that if the books didn't balance, it was because I'd forgotten to make a recording. And reminded me that every penny had to be accounted for and groaned whenever I asked her for the checkbook. Nevertheless, she looked pretty tonight, sitting still and attentive. She'd cut her black hair to a shoulder-length bob and wore a fashionable red dress that I couldn't help but notice hiked up almost to her knee. It occurred to me that the length of women's skirts edged up every year, and I wondered what another forty years would bring. As if she knew my thoughts, she shifted and pushed her dress down. I looked away embarrassed, then back at Ada and the cellist, trying not to feel the warmth of Ella's shoulder next to mine. I still couldn't understand why she hadn't married. Maybe her frugality put suitors off.

The mission spent as much as we brought in, but we used it on necessities. Our annual budget had risen to over thirty-five thousand dollars. Nearly fifteen thousand people attended our services, and we provided three thousand beds each month. To accomplish that, we had expanded our footprint from one storefront to three—from 1822 Larimer Street to 1820-1824 Larimer Street. One space functioned as an auditorium for concerts, community gatherings, and special performances. In addition, we opened the new Sunshine House at 1640 Market Street as a dormitory for transients. Our prosperity also allowed us to hire talented union musicians for special programs.

Ada and the cellist continued. I was up next. I opened my small, leather-bound Bible on my lap to see if the Lord had any word for me tonight. My mother had given me the Bible for Christmas in 1888 when I turned seventeen, just before I first came to Denver to work with my brothers. It had become tattered around the edges. The book fell open to Isaiah, probably because I turned to this verse so often: "And if thou draw out thy soul to the hungry, and satisfy the afflicted soul, then shall thy light rise in obscurity, and thy darkness be as the noon day."

"Yes, Lord, shine light through the darkness of my soul," I prayed under my breath.

The music stopped, and the audience applauded. I took a deep breath and headed to the front of the room. I moved the small lectern to the center, placed my notes on it, and smiled at Ada as she took her seat.

"Everyone, please give another warm applause to our talented musicians."

The crowd clapped and cheered, and I tried using the energy of the room to boost my confidence.

I pulled today's front-page news from my Bible and unfolded it as a prop. "I don't know if you saw today's headlines, but I thought I would share them with you."

I shook out the newsprint. "Now I know that you all are

aware of the robbery of two hundred thousand dollars from Denver's mint in December." Everyone nodded. "Well, the *Post* reported today that they have found the perpetrators."

A grin spread across my face. "The police found them smoking cigars and writing legislation…at the state capital."

The crowd roared, and I laughed with them. Then I flexed the paper again.

"Here is another article. Congress is releasing funding for a thing called a highway bill—whatever that is. They want to build a road that goes from Chicago to Santa Monica and call it Route 66." I put the paper down and tilted my head. "Maybe they're all high on the sauce." I brought my thumb to my mouth as though taking a swig, and everyone laughed. "For goodness' sake, we can't even get the horse-sized potholes fixed on Larimer, and they're telling us we need a road across the country."

This brought guffaws and cheers.

I let them quiet while I closed and folded the paper, then opened my Bible to read from Matthew: "'And so he that had received five talents came and brought another five talents, saying, Lord, thou deliveredst unto me five talents: Behold, I have gained beside them five talents more. His Lord said unto him, Well done, thou good and faithful servant. Thou hast been faithful over a few things. So I will make thee ruler over many things: Enter thou into the joy of thy Lord.'"

I closed the book, set it back on the lectern, and nodded.

"I recently read about a prince in Spain whose success was something everyone admired and which all envied. His ship had come in like the galleon of old, loaded with riches, and his castle became a glorious edifice in the realm of actuality. He had everything, but he had nothing! You see, the prince was described in the most unflattering of terms: angry, arrogant, bitter, and the unhappiest of men. Forever in his quest for riches, he felt self-sufficient, and the man who felt that way writes with a trembling hand a sorrowful 'finis' at the close of the last chapter of his activities. He wrote; My life is all for naught. For no man attains happiness without God."

I looked up and cleared my throat, making sure I had everyone's attention.

"All manmade pathways lead to one terminal—darkness! The world expects that we attain success, but strictly along the path of righteousness. But only he who believes in Christ, attains success through Him and walks with God!"

I picked up my Bible again and turned to a page in John and read: "Then spake Jesus again unto them, saying, 'I am the light of the world; he that followeth me shall not walk in darkness, but shall have the light of life. Abide in me and I in you. As the branch cannot bear fruit of itself except it abide in the vine, no more can ye except ye abide in me.'"

I put the Bible down, paused, then stepped in front of the lectern. "Before I make my altar call, I wanted to wish a happy birthday to our Mary McDougall." I smiled at Mary, who sat beside Ada. I held my hand next to my mouth and asked her, "Can I share your news with everyone?"

Mary shrugged and then nodded.

"Mary has decided to fulfill her lifelong dream of going to nursing school in California," I told the crowd. "We're working on finances for her tuition. Anyone who is so inclined can help."

As was my custom, I looked around to see if anyone had anything to add.

When no one did, I said, "Please stay and have birthday cake with us after the service." Then I concluded with my usual invitation, "Please, come on up and shake hands with ol' Jim and take Christ as your Savior."

Summer solstice had passed two weeks ago, and a brilliant full moon rose in the east. But the summer sun's warmth still radiated in the evening, and I removed my jacket as I said goodbye to people outside the mission.

"Thank you for coming." I shook hands with a man and his wife.

"Good service tonight, Reverend," he said.

"I wish it could have been a bit longer," she added.

I smiled and nodded and greeted the others. It had been a wonderful night. Fourteen people came to receive the loving grace of Jesus.

A man in a top hat and expensive suit came through the door and extended his hand.

"Exemplary service tonight. Could have been a little shorter."

I laughed and said, "One man's meat is another man's poison."

He frowned, then laughed with me. "I suppose so," he said. "You see the Yanks are planning on building a new stadium in the Bronx? May have it ready for next year. That is, if Babe Ruth can hold it together."

"Yeah." I nodded. "Heard that he threw dust at the ump and then climbed into the stands and engaged in fisticuffs with a heckler."

"People are booing him when he doesn't hit a home run every time," the man said.

"I feel kind of sorry for Babe. Never understood what makes people feel good about the demise of a man."

Mary and Ella had been eavesdropping on our conversation. "Just makes their own lives not feel so miserable," Mary said.

"'O beware, my lord, of jealousy, it is the green-eyed monster which doth mock the meat it feeds on,'" I quoted Shakespeare's *Othello*.

The man in the top hat laughed. He turned to Mary and tipped his hat. "Mary, congratulations on your schooling," he said, then headed down the street.

I watched him go. Even though one of the wealthiest men in the city, he never missed a Sunday evening service. But he was also the tightwad of tightwads, often putting only two bits in the collection plate.

I looked back through the door and saw no one else coming, so I visited with the ladies. Mary lit a cigarette and shared it with Ella. Ella was five years older than Mary, but with Mary's hard life, time had not been as kind to her.

I turned to Ella as she blew smoke out the corner of her mouth. "Any contributions to help Mary's schooling?" I asked.

She shook her head. "I can see why people get stuck by their circumstances."

"I thought Mr. Ellis there might come through," I said.

Mary looked at the ground. "Probably not unless he received something in return."

"I'm sorry, Mary, we'll figure out a way."

She took a drag and handed the cigarette back to Ella. "Maybe I should just give up on my dreams and go back to…work."

"Don't do that," I said. "I have faith that God will provide."

"I wish I had trust like that. I think it's easier to believe for someone else than it is for myself."

"So true," Ella said.

32

MARY MCDOUGALL

August 24, 1924
(Two Years Later)

I sat in my office at the mission. It contained a small wooden desk and two chairs and only slightly larger than the broom closet I had in France. That was okay with me. I may have been in charge, but I didn't need executive trappings.

I had covered the walls with war memorabilia and movie posters that people had given me. One war poster depicted a butcher, a woman in blue, and a plate of fish, captioned with: "Buy Fresh Fish, Save the Meat for our Soldiers and Allies." Another poster showed an army nurse holding one end of a stretcher with the caption: "Hold up Your End—War Fund Week." Besides the posters, magazine articles and newspaper clippings, I had thumb tacked to the wall a couple of personal items from the war: a picture of me standing in front of a bomber and the certificate of commendation signed by the men of the 96th.

Joseph stood near my desk, squinting at a movie poster. "Who's the pretty lady?" he asked, inspecting the fair-skinned woman wearing a lamé headscarf and holding a basket of flowers.

"That's Claire Windsor," I said. "She's one of the leading ladies in the moving pictures. Ada and I went to her latest one, but Ada deemed it too risqué even without one spoken word. All the same, she let me have the poster."

Joe's vision had continued to fail, so he moved his face closer to the image. "Trying to figure out if she has anything else on besides the scarf."

"I think that's the point," I said and laughed. "Darn flowers."

He turned to me and grinned, then sat in the other chair. "May have to go see one of those cinema things. You think they'll catch on?"

"Who knows? Might be just a fad."

I handed him a piece of paper from my desk. He tried reading it but gave it back.

"What is it?" he asked.

"Reverends Gravett and Driver have sold all the assets and properties of the Sunshine Rescue Mission to Ada and me for one dollar."

Joe whistled through his teeth. "One whole dollar, huh?"

"I think they believe we're doing such a good job that we should have full fiduciary responsibility."

"Fiduciary?" Joe asked.

"They trust us to make moral decisions with the money and assets."

"Well done, good and faithful servant. You have been faithful with little things. I will now make you ruler over many things." Joe spread his arms as wide as the room permitted. "All this is yours now."

"Yeah. Lucky us—all this and a bellyache."

We laughed. Then I said, "In all seriousness, I must admit that I feel the weight of it, the responsibilities and the possibilities. Maybe now we can search for a place for the orphanage. I feel terrible that we haven't been able to help the kids. That makes me feel like a failure."

Joe shook his head. "Why'd you even say that, James? Look at all you're doin'."

"I know. It's just that there is so much more to do."

"James, I knew from the first day you stepped into the mission you had a plan, but I don't reckon I ever met a man as driven as you. It's okay to be satisfied with what you got done today."

"I just feel like the Lord is calling me to greater things," I said.

"James, this'n you know, but even Jesus said we can give everything we's got to the poor. We can serve and give out our lives...but even that ain't enough. We can go to church and associate ourselves with godly people, and that falls short. We can live holy and righteous lives, and that's still lacking. Look at the Pharisees and Sadducees. Jesus called them vipers."

I nodded.

"The only way in livin' is our believin' in Jesus and what he did for us on the cross...nothin' else," Joe reminded me. "I think our Lord was tryin' to open our eyes to the truth of who we are—God's children."

"I guess I know that in my head, but I'm not sure my heart always believes it," I said.

"James, you know I love you, and I don't mean to hurt your feelin's, but sometimes you seem to keep yourself pretty occupied with livin' how you think everyone else thinks you ought."

I looked into his eyes and saw no malice or disappointment. Joseph was a good friend and knew me better than anyone in the world. I owed him and Mary my life.

Joe continued, "God's promises give us reassurance of the final day, the final hour when we stand 'fore Him and found blameless. Oh, what peace we can find in that fact…in that reassurance…in that hope."

I leaned back in my chair, put my hands behind my head, and sighed. Joe had been talking about heaven more and more, and I wondered if he thought that his final day approached. I didn't want to think about that and wasn't brave enough to ask if he suspected it. I wasn't sure what I would do when that awful day came.

So I changed the subject. "You going to Mary's going-away party at Gahan's tonight?"

"I'm not sure I'm up to it," Joe said. "Feelin' a little tired today."

I nodded. I had been trying to talk him into living with Ada and me, but he'd laugh and say the mission was his home.

"No one wants an old black man at their party, anyway."

"You know that's not true, speaking of living in the truth," I said.

"Mmmm, mmm. You sure know how to turn a man's words on him." He laughed. "What did the Reverends think about the mission buyin' Mary an automobile?"

"I showed Gravett and Driver that we had the funds and even enough to pay for her tuition. Joshua readily approved it. Billy took a bit more convincing. But Joshua reminded him I now held the purse strings, and if I thought that was the best use for those funds, then so be it."

"I'm sure they knows how much Mary has meant to the place—and to you," Joe said.

"Well, I'd hoped it wouldn't have taken two years to raise

the funds, and I wish you'd be there to see Mary's face when we present her with the keys." I encouraged. "You see the Essex Coach sitting outside? She'll be so happy."

"Beautiful piece of machinery," he said.

"I talked the automobile salesman down to just over a thousand. It's not the top of the line but will get her to California safely."

Ada and Ella came to the open door and knocked on the frame.

"Ella asked me about some checks," Ada said, "and I don't know what they were for, so I thought we'd come to you."

Ella slipped past her, placed the ledger on my desk, and pointed to two charges—one written for twenty-seven dollars and the other for five dollars sixty-two cents. I knew what each represented, but pretended I had to think about it.

Finally, I said, "I spent the twenty-seven for mattresses from the Barth Hotel. They got new ones, so I bought some of their old ones for the Sunshine House." This was true, but my upper lip sweated, and I could feel heat in my face.

"And the other?" Ella asked.

"Uh...oh yeah, now I remember. I bought some sheets from them as well." This was a lie. I'd talked the hotel manager into letting me write the check for "sheets" in exchange for a couple bottles of moonshine I knew he'd stashed under the counter. A kind of gentlemen's agreement.

I had the bottles well tucked away in the back of the bottom drawer of my desk. The subject of the checks had never come up...until now.

Ella seemed satisfied but added with petulance, "Would you *please* mark down in the ledger what the checks you write are for?"

I looked at Ada and then Joe. I had a feeling they both knew I'd lied, and my cramped office seemed to shrink.

I stood and said, "Ada, you ready to head to Mary's party?"

"I don't want to go into that smelly devil's den," she huffed. "I've already given my hugs and blessings to Mary."

"Joe doesn't feel up to it either," I said. "So no one's going with me?"

"I'll go," Ella volunteered, and we all turned to her in surprise.

I hadn't been in Gahan's since I'd sneaked in smelling like a wet dog, hoping to have a last drink to drown my pain. The saloon hadn't changed. Even the same player piano plunked away in the corner. When I saw Mary standing with friends at the bar, it reminded me of the first time I'd seen her with her red hair and blue eyes that could stop a man's heart and frenzy his brain. But unlike Gahan's, she had changed. Tonight, she'd wound her hair in a bun, and she dressed conservatively with no cleavage showing.

The kindness she'd shown me at my lowest point kept me from ending my life. She knew my weaknesses and struggles, and I knew hers, but we held no judgment between us. I thought about the story of Jesus talking to the chief priests in the temple courts and saying, "Truly I tell you, the tax collectors and the prostitutes are entering the kingdom of God ahead of you." I knew this would be true for Mary.

I was so proud of her. She could tame the vilest person with her intelligence and charm—she'd make an excellent nurse. I still didn't understand how I could love this woman as much as I did, with a love not driven by lust—a chaste affection. She made me feel comfortable with myself, and it was okay to be me.

I hated to see her leave, but at the same time, it filled me with gladness for the divine glory to see her realize her girlhood dream.

"I'm going to get some punch," Ella said, interrupting my thoughts. "You want some?"

"No, that's okay. I might have a piece of cake later."

Ella walked through the crowd to the table filled with beverages and treats, and I walked to the bar where Mary had just said something to make her friends laugh.

As I joined them, a few turned around in surprise while others looked away or excused themselves. *Nothing like a pastor to throw a wet blanket on the party.*

"Hi, darlin'," Mary channeled Pixie with the Irish accent. "You new around here, stranger?"

"Aye, lass, I just got off me boat," I said with my best attempt at an Irish brogue. It made her laugh. Comfortable, I continued to play the jester and turned to her friends remaining at the bar. "You hear about the Irish priest driving along a country road when a copper stops him? The policeman smells alcohol on his breath and sees the empty wine bottle in the car. He says, 'Father Mulcahy, have you been drinking?' The priest says, 'Just water.' And the copper replies, 'Why do I smell wine?' The priest looks at the bottle and says, 'Good Lord! He's done it again!'"

Mary and the others laughed.

I removed the jester cap. "You ready for your surprise?" I asked.

"What have you done now, Jim? You and Ada have done so much for me already."

I smiled. She had cried buckets when we told her that the mission paid her tuition and we'd get her to California. I'm sure she assumed we'd got her a train ticket, but I knew she'd need transportation once she got there.

"We have to go outside," I said.

"You got me a horse?"

"Something like that."

The entire party followed us. I'd parked the Essex Coach by the front door, but as soon as we got outside, Mary looked up and down the sidewalk and turned to me with a furrowed brow.

I turned her shoulders so she faced the Essex Coach, pulled the keys from my pocket, and dangled them in front of her face. It took her a moment to understand. She looked from the keys to the automobile and back to the keys. Then her face lit up.

"Noooo!" she yelled and then began jumping with joy. "Oh my God, Jim Goodheart! I hope this ain't no joke." She let out a gleeful scream. "This is a joke, right? You're pulling my leg."

I continued to smile and jiggled the keys again. "No, this is real. This is your new automobile."

———

After sharing the joy of the mission's gift, I leaned against the bar, sharing a moment alone with Mary. Everyone else enjoyed the cake and punch. After the jubilation, she'd confessed she didn't know how to drive. I said I'd teach her— that it would be a snap. After all, I was the best driver in the army. "You'll have plenty of time to practice before you take off in a few days," I added.

She looked at the floor and blinked back tears. "I'm going to miss you, James Goodheart. You're a good man. You've always been a good man."

"I wish I could believe that," I said. "You know the night I stumbled in here, I suffered from a severe case of rejection. I'm still not sure I've recovered."

"Jim, I wish you knew how other people see you."

"As a rascal?"

She put a hand on my arm. "You're one of the most likable men I know."

"Well, all I know is that it's exhausting always trying to please people."

I realized Ella stood next to me. Her chest pressed against my arm, and I stepped away and turned to her. Her face flushed.

"You okay?" I asked.

"I'm great," she bellowed. "Never been better." She swayed as though her legs had turned to rubber.

I looked at Mary, not sure what happened.

Mary shook her head. "Someone musta spiked the punch with moonshine."

"And it's the best punch ever," Ella slurred, waved her arms, and started to fall. I caught her before she lost her balance. "Thank you, James." She giggled.

She'd never used my first name.

"Oh darling, we need to get you home to bed," Mary said.

Ella hiccuped loudly and covered her mouth. "What a good idea," she burped, crumpling into my arms.

Mary tried to take her from me, but I said, "I'll walk her home. She just lives a block from us. You can't leave your party."

Mary kissed my cheek. I put Ella on her feet and tried to steady her. I took a firm grip of her arm above her elbow and escorted her outside.

"Why we leaving?" She tried to protest, but her words swam together. "I need more punch."

I started moving us in the direction of her apartment,

having to support much of her weight. "Come on, Ella, you got to help me out here—try walking."

"I am walking," she slurred. "See?" She swung her leg back and forth and would have fallen if I hadn't caught her. "I'm walking."

I supported her for more than a block and the crisp evening air revived her enough, so she regained some balance but lost some inhibition. She clutched my arm tightly. I felt her face on my sleeve as if she were hiding. Without looking up, she murmured, "Thank you, James. You are such a kind man." I felt her mouth moving and couldn't tell if she kissed my coat or wiped her nose. I glanced down to see her peering up at me. "How you care for everyone around you makes me want to be a better person."

I admit it peeved me when she interrupted my time with Mary, but I couldn't stay angry. I patted her hand and said, "I'm so sorry, Ella. I had no idea someone spiked the punch."

"I'm not." She stopped, stood up as straight as she could, and looked at me with unfocused eyes. "I think I love you."

"I love you too, Ella. You are part of our family."

"No, Jim. I love you, love you." And with that, she vomited over my shoes.

33

BENEDICTION

September 11, 1924

Fluffy, luminous clouds drifted over Denver as I walked down 14th street with leaves crunching under my feet. Fall was always one of my favorite times of the year as nature began a long roll back to prepare for winter's slumber. Maybe as a professional melancholic, I found comfort in the harvest season.

But my melancholy threatened to get the best of me. It had been two weeks since Mary's farewell party, and Ella turned as cold as an icebox. Right after the incident, I had hoped she'd have some booze-inspired amnesia and forgot it all. But as time went on, I was sure she remembered and terribly embarrassed by her behavior. That night, I got her into her apartment and onto a couch and left, but not before she tried to kiss me. I pried myself loose and skedaddled without hesitation.

Alcohol can make the sanest, most sober-sided person crazy and stupid. I should know. Her confession of love shocked me—having no idea she felt that way. Her father died when she was young, and she'd always treated me like a father-figure. Was it romantic love? I shuddered at the thought. She probably just needed to heal from her father's premature demise.

When I told Ada the whole story, she had some choice words to describe my stupidity for escorting Ella home and especially for being alone with her in the apartment. No amount of justification appeased Ada, and the worst part was that she thought we should let Ella go.

"I never trusted that girl," she said.

But as an excellent bookkeeper, we could not easily replace her. I suggested just letting the whole thing blow over.

"If we don't talk about it, it never happened," I told Ada, who'd frowned.

My pocket watch read eleven o'clock, and I quickened my steps from the jailhouse to Larimer Street. The street clocks confirmed the hour as they chimed the time. I ran late. With prisoners filling the jail to capacity again, I'd spent more time than I intended counseling the defendants. As the city chaplain, every day started this way, but this morning, I hadn't wanted to leave the mission with Joe feeling so poorly. When he began coughing up green sputum, I'd sent for the doctor, who indicated there was little he could do except give him codeine to make him more comfortable. With the end in sight, I wanted to be with him.

But I had to make one more stop before returning to the mission for the noon sermon. I still did not know what I was going to preach on for either the noon or the evening service. I hoped it wouldn't be about Joseph's passing.

I nearly collided with a woman pushing a baby carriage and jumped out of the way. I excused myself and tipped my hat. So much to do, so much to think about. *The candle prob-*

ably doesn't know it's getting short when it's burning at both ends. I wasn't sure I could continue at this pace, but how could I deny a person in need? I hurried to see a young family I'd already put off for days. They were in a world of hurt because of no fault of their own.

The husband had a good job as a delivery man, and he and his wife had three adorable children under the age of ten. When he had stepped off a curb, twisted his ankle, and broken his leg, their idyllic life had come to a screeching halt. They laid him off, and like so many of us, the family had little savings. With his leg not yet healed and the bills continuing to roll in, they'd lost their home and their way. Now they were staying in the old, rat-infested Chever Hotel and were about to be evicted since they couldn't afford even fifty cents a night. I still didn't know what we were going to do for them. The mission and the Sunshine House weren't meant for families. It reminded me that practically all of us were one step away from disaster. One day we have all we need, and then, just like that, we slide into skid row.

"Reverend Goodheart." I heard a familiar voice from behind.

I turned to see Colbert trying to propel his colossal frame to catch up to me.

Lord, just what I need.

"Reverend Goodheart," he said around his cigar and between gasps. "Can I ask you a couple questions?"

"Do I have a choice?" I quipped, but it didn't get me so much as a smile. I noticed he had the latest edition of the *Sunshine Messenger* under his notebook.

"I looked over your financial records," Colbert said. "Looks like you are doing quite well."

I looked at him, waiting for a snide question, but he didn't have the courtesy to look at me. His eyes were on his ubiquitous notebook, and he poised his pencil to write, regardless of what I said. *Go take a flying leap. I don't have time for this* is what I wanted to say.

"I imagine you and your wife sit at home enjoying the profits of the mission." He looked up with a self-satisfied smirk, expecting a response. I said nothing and scratched my ear. He hadn't actually asked a question yet. He tapped his pencil on the notebook.

"The mission finally has adequate funding for our current needs," I said. "There is so much more that we could do. I'm about to visit upon a young family that has fallen into hard times. The city could use a safety net for folks like this." It came as a perfect answer for publication, had Colbert been an honest reporter.

"What do you tell the people of Denver that say you're just attracting the derelicts to the city?" He puffed his cigar, blowing smoke in my face.

I waved it away and took a step back. *Doesn't this man have anything else to do, anyone else to bother?* "I'm not sure we could consider this young family with their three young children, who have lived and worked in Denver for some time, vagabonds."

I watched him scribble. Was he interested in the young family? Nope. I continued as his quarry. "You just going for a visit to spread your religion?" he looked up and sneered. "Making them jump through hoops before you help them?"

When I laughed in his face, he looked down, preparing to scribble. I cleared my throat and said with as much civility as I could muster, "Look, I make no apologies for my faith. I believe in the two hands of the gospel—one for generosity and the other for the message of hope. I can't imagine getting through the hardships of life without both."

He stopped writing and looked up to thrust another jab. "You feel you need more converts?"

"Mr. Colbert, I know we don't see eye-to-eye. You see my belief in God as a disability and a crutch. I wish people like yourself would see that God is offering much more than belonging to a club—it's about coming into freedom. It's all about waking up to who we truly are, not joining a secret society with tons of rules."

"You seem to profit from this freedom," he snarled. "Aren't you getting paid as the city chaplain as well?"

"As a matter of fact, the salary is one dollar a year, so I guess no one needs to worry about my making money too fast." I laughed. *Why am I wasting my valuable time on him?*

"That's not the rumors I hear swirling." He pursed his lips and rolled his eyes.

I frowned and replied, still trying my hardest to be civil. "I have no idea who you're talking too, but as you well know, our books are open for inspection at any time...by you or anyone else."

I guess he realized he would not get my goat when he flipped his notebook closed and walked away.

"Mr. Colbert," I called to him, and he turned. "What do you believe in?"

He took the cigar out of his mouth and spat. "I believe in nothing, except that man has a rotten streak in him and the world is going to hell in a handcart. I'll be glad to be worm food someday." He spat again. "Look around. We're at the center of a rotten world where men, greedy for gold, lure others into lives of debauchery. You can't tell me you're much different."

I don't know why I asked him, and I certainly didn't expect that answer. If I'd thought about it, I wouldn't have guessed that Colbert lived a sad and bitter life. If I'd been a better man, I would have counseled him. But he made me angry, and I had things to do.

I made a quick stop at the Chever Hotel and gave the destitute young family ten dollars so they could stay a few more nights and get the kids some food. I promised I'd get back to them with a solution, and then I returned to the street, fueled with anger at Colbert for taking up my time.

Still fuming when I walked through the mission door, I saw Ada's beautiful but worried face. I forgot about that blasted man and followed her to Joseph's bed. We'd hung a sheet at the end of the bunk room to give him some privacy during his last days. We'd begged to let us take him to the hospital, but he'd refused. He'd lived at the mission the past twenty-five years, and he wanted to die here.

Ada retreated, knowing I'd want to be alone with Joe. When I pulled back the curtain, I worried I'd see a dead man. But when he opened his eyes and managed a smile, I blew out a sigh of relief.

I sat on the chair next to his cot and held his hand. "How you feeling, Joe?"

He wheezed and coughed but caught his breath. "I think it won't be long 'fore I see my beloved wife and son," he said and smiled broader than before.

I bowed my head and prayed.

Joe's other hand covered mine. "How ya doin'?" he wheezed.

I looked up and smiled. "It's just like you, my friend, to ask after me when you're down and out."

"I's worry about you, James. I's not sure what you're gonna do without me."

He ribbed and turned serious at the same time. His jocular tone brought tears to my eyes. Truth be told, I wasn't sure either. I smiled. "I ran into that ornery Colbert today. He's determined to find fault in me. Lord knows I have many faults, not the least of which is an occasional shot of booze, but I'm not about to reveal any faults to that pathetic excuse for a newspaperman."

"You know, James, havin' people see how you handle your failures speaks louder than your successes," he began, then paused to catch his breath.

He'd turned the topic back to me. I guessed he wasn't just talking about Colbert. He knew this would be our last conversation.

"You don't be needin' to hide from anyone," he said. "When you pretend to be someone perfect to make a gain, you might as well be rearrangin' the deck chairs on the *Titanic*."

I sobered at the thought of when that ship went down— a vivid image that reminded me of how I arranged for the rich people to sit in front at the Sunday concerts. Did I really pretend to be a big shot? Had I forgotten how I'd crawled into the mission, a drunken wretch with plans of suicide?

"It's okay, Joe. Don't talk so much. You need to save your strength."

"No, James, you're needin' to know this—" He coughed up a plug of mucus.

"Joe, *please* save your strength," I pleaded.

But he continued, "God knows all about us…our flops, our weaknesses…like the woman at the well. Remember?" He gasped for air.

"Yes, Joe. I remember."

"Take off the mask and don't pretend. God will not reject

you." He fought for a breath. "Better to let go and say, God help me. That's when He breaks the chains and cuts you free."

This was his benediction. But there was so much more I needed to know. Losing him filled me with fear. "But what if everyone knew the truth about me?" I asked. "What would I do? I feel like I have to hide my failures." Tears streamed down my cheeks.

"James," he whispered, "...you don't be needin' to have it all together."

———

The Lord provided a beautiful sunset, full of reds, oranges, and yellows, as though the heavens sang, "Well done, good and faithful servant."

We held vigil the rest of the day and into the early evening. Ada played Joe's favorite hymns, and the rest of us prayed or sat quietly in reflective solitude. Joseph had been the foundation of all our lives. He showed as much grace and strength in his death as he did in his life—quick with a kind word, never judging, always pointing the way to the Father.

I sat with him as he took his last breaths, hoping for one more lesson from the man who had so much to teach. The transition between life and death continued as such a mystery, the final stripping away of all ego and self, and Joe revealed the way. Joe showed us that death and life are not opposites, but the wholeness of the mystery of God—a transition into the fullness of God.

I'll never forget Joseph's final heavy sigh that released his earthly life. It wasn't the sigh so much as the smile that crossed his face. Like he met with the one love that carries us across the threshold. I opened my Bible to First Corinthians and read, "For now we see only a reflection as in a mirror, then we shall see face-to-face. Now I know in part, then I shall know fully, even as I am fully known."

Joseph had crossed over, and I rejoiced for him. I tried to imagine what he saw: his wife and son and Jesus—a joyful occasion for him.

But not for me. I ached, and I didn't know if I could stand it. I remembered holding fast to the ship on the raging ocean headed for France. I was drowning without a life vest or an anchor. Now I'd lost Mary and Joseph in one seismic wave.

34

ADDICTION

May 29, 1926
(Two Years Later)

I thought that two years would have been enough time to grieve Mary's departure and Joseph's death, but I thought wrong. I continued to suffer heartache, even on this warm spring day when I hoped fly fishing would bring me out of my slump. But I felt as raw today as when I'd lost them—worse, in fact. I was drunk. And I couldn't stop drinking. The poisonous cure and constant companion no longer helped.

Coal Creek ran high and muddy with an early spring runoff—not the best conditions for dry-fly fishing. But I needed a distraction and fervently hoped dipping my line would help. I stood ankle deep in the creek, trying to change flies because the Royal Coachman hadn't brought a bite. The ice-cold water made my teeth chatter and hands shake. But it wasn't just the cold causing my hands to tremble. Last year I'd noticed a tremor that I didn't want to admit may be from the alcohol.

Although she said nothing, Ada knew about my daily drinking, and I suspected the men at the mission knew too. Donald certainly knew. He had to come get me from the Empire Hotel a few times when I'd been unable to drive home. But he'd said nothing. I was so embarrassed and ashamed that my son had seen my weakness. I didn't try to hide my lapse in judgment, but I doubted Joe had that in mind when he said I should stop pretending. I was used up, overwhelmed, exhausted, unmoored, and I had no desire to change. I just didn't care.

I had really believed I could keep up the schedule from dawn until well past dark—preaching, serving, and giving until there was no more to give. I saw myself scrambling around and around on a giant hamster wheel, wanting to jump off. Maybe I hoped the booze would make me fall off.

I squinted at the fly in my hand. Along with everything else, my eyesight had gone to pot, at least close-up—either that or my arms were getting shorter. The leader finally found the eye of the elk hair Caddis. I twisted the fly around, pulled the end through the loop to secure the knot, then chewed off the extra length with my front teeth.

I glanced over my shoulder to make sure Ada hadn't checked on me. One benefit of Donald's marriage to Josephine was that her mother owned a summer place on Coal Creek. Because Josephine's father had passed, Nancy often invited Ada and me to stay, and I always tried to help with the chores. Ada and Nancy had become good friends and were sharing tea when I'd told them I was going fishing. Ada warned me about the conditions of the creek. She'd certainly be upset if she saw me drinking out here.

When I didn't see hide nor hair of her, I opened my split-willow creel, empty of fish, and pulled out Chappy's flask. I took a long drink. *How did I get back to this miserable place?*

"The best thing for a case of nerves is a case of scotch," I quoted Fields and toasted the pesky fish.

I put the flask back into the creel and inspected the creek, which flowed like a raging river today. Its typical tranquil babble rose to a deafening roar. Angry rapids rumbled over boulders hiding deep holes. I wondered how the fish survived the roiling water whirling over the top of them. They were probably tucked safe and sound in the depths below the fray. "Yes, Lord, that is my prayer, that someday I find the same stillness within me."

A boulder split the creek about thirty feet downstream—just the place for trout to hide. That's where I headed, using willow branches overhanging the stream to steady myself on the slippery rocks as the current tugged at my legs. When I stood within striking distance, I wedged my foot between the stones and supported myself with the upstream foot. The willows behind wanting to snare my line made for a tricky cast, but it made good practice to flick the fly overhead instead of back and to the side.

I slung the creel around to my hip and carefully stripped out line to make my first cast. It hit a foot short of the hole and the current yanked it downstream. I tried again with the same results. "Shoot."

Inching forward with my left foot, the water lapped at my knee. I slipped, but my foot dug in and wedged between rocks. I'd seen some rubber waders at the fishing store but had rejected them as they were quite spendy. I sure wished I'd sprung for them now. I wouldn't last long if I fell into this icy water.

I pulled another few feet of line from my reel and cast toward the hole. Then, I don't know how it happened, but an enormous fish came at my fly as my feet slipped out from under me. My lungs filled with glacial water, and the current washed me under and downstream. I tossed and turned violently, head over heels, with my rod in my right hand and my creel in the other.

Thinking I would die, I fought to right myself. I tried flipping my legs downstream as it held my best chance of survival, but my head smashed against a boulder, and the curtain came down. For a moment, all went black.

But as fast as it had swept me under, my head bobbed out of the water and I gasped for air. My hands clutched the rod and creel. I couldn't hold on to both and survive. I had to choose one or the other. I saw Chappy smiling and asking me to make sure his son got his flask someday, and I released my rod.

The water sucked me back under, but I hugged my creel with one hand and paddled and kicked like mad. I stopped with a thud as my body slammed into a fallen tree. With my free hand, I grabbed a branch to stop my cartwheeling and hung on tight. The angry water nearly pulled me under the log. If that happened, I was dead for sure. I fought with every ounce of strength. Miraculously, my foot found leverage to push, and I clambered onto the log.

Ada screamed and Nancy fainted when I opened the door. I had no idea what a fright I looked like. I clutched the creel and shook from hypothermia while blood drained from my scalp and covered my face. My clothes hung wet on my body.

Once Ada recovered from the shock, she revived Nancy and took her to her room to rest. While they were gone, I got the bleeding stopped and cleaned up the best I could.

Ada returned, stripped me of my clothes, wrapped me in blankets, and set me by the hot stove in the living room.

After handing me a steaming cup of tea, Ada went to check on Nancy. I took the flask from the creel and added a shot of whiskey to the drink.

When Ada came back to the living room and saw that I settled into comfort, I knew a butt-chewing followed.

"I told you," she began, "you shouldn't have gone fishing and especially by yourself." She added some choice words under her breath. "Nancy told me that two people have drowned this year in the high waters."

"Sorry I lost my pole," I mumbled.

"I'm sorry I lost my pole?" she repeated. "You damn fool. Is that what you're sorry for? How about the fact that you're back to drinking? That alcohol makes you stupid, like telling Nancy she has cute legs. How about the fact that you're not doing your job well?" Her eyes filled with tears, but she continued to list my faults. "How about the fact that I saw you standing too close to Ella the other day, acting way too familiar? How about the fact that Ella is saying we're over ten thousand dollars in debt?"

I swallowed hard. Ada had been preparing this speech for a while. I wasn't sure I'd ever seen her this angry.

"I lost you once to alcohol," she said, "and I'm not about to stand around waiting for that to happen again." She cried a river of tears.

She glared at me, her face red and wet, and said, "Donald talked with me about it last week. He's worried as well."

Now she had me. This confession stabbed my heart, as Donny was the last person I wanted to burden. I covered my face with my hands. *How did I get here again?*

I had to stop drinking.

When I dropped Ada at home and told her I was headed to the mission, I didn't lie. But when I got to the corner of Larimer and Eighteenth, I bypassed the mission and turned on Eighteenth to Glenarm, aiming for my favorite watering hole in the basement of the Empire Hotel.

When I rounded the corner, my emotions waffled between hurt and anger. Ada had refused to talk to me all the way home from Coal Creek, and she wouldn't listen to an apology. It upset me that she and Donny talked behind my back. At the cabin, Ada told me about Donny's concern with my "alcohol inebriety"—my alcoholic habit. We'd even argued over this as the newspapers were talking about the new term *addiction* and whether they should consider it a weakness of the will or a physical disease.

Shakespeare used the word in *Henry V*: "Since his addiction was to courses vain," meaning he had strong inclinations to activities of no value. If the word was good enough for Shakespeare, it seemed good enough for me. I prided myself that even in my inebriated mind, I remembered the Bard.

But whether they called it inebriety or addiction and considered it physical or mental—it continued as a problem, and I knew it. What I felt seemed like a yearning beyond control, a desire, a strong pull that even with the strongest of wills, I had become powerless against. Maybe it really manifested like a demon, as my father had said. I just didn't know. But I knew that my addiction kept me from doing my job at the mission. How could I be an example to the poor souls when I lived like a wastrel smelling of whiskey?

Pressure pounded between my ears—something like nervousness or pain, to where if I didn't get relief, my mind might explode. I knew my internal struggles and agony caused me to turn to lesser comforts. I fought the urge to blame it on God. Still praying and asking Him to take my desire for alcohol away. If I didn't know better, I could soon talk myself into believing He'd turned His back on me or was mad at me and inflicted punishment. But that was not His character. I had no one to blame but myself, and I just didn't see a way out.

As I turned the corner toward my relief, the increasing pressure inside my head released like air out of a tire. Even though Denver strictly enforced Prohibition, the drinking establishments had simply moved underground. The Empire speakeasy was no exception. On this Monday evening when I strolled in, it sat practically empty—just the way I liked it. The bartender saw me coming and poured my usual: a shot of whiskey and a mug of beer. "Thanks, Levi," I said and straddled the stool.

My hand shook as I tossed back the shot. I wasn't sure if the anger and hurt or the hypothermia made my bones still ache.

I took a swig of the beer to relieve the burn of the whiskey. Levi left me alone to serve a beer to the only other man at the bar. That suited me fine. I wanted isolation with my thoughts and didn't want to talk with anyone.

On the ride home, I had tried talking to Ada about Ella and the money, but she'd just huffed and turned away, so I quit trying. Yes, I had probably let the boundary slip slightly with Ella, but I sensed nothing more between us and I didn't see any harm in being friendly. None of us ever discussed the events surrounding Mary's going-away party, and I figured Ella had forgotten about it. It made me sore that Ada thought I had flirted. Okay, sometimes Ella and I yakked it up, but sharing a laugh made life worth living.

I took another drink of beer and wiped my mouth on my sleeve. Was Ella dallying with me? Maybe she did, and maybe I liked it. Anger steamed the back of my neck. Ada and I would celebrate our thirty-third anniversary this July. Perhaps our marriage had gotten too comfortable, or maybe it had just grown stale. Ada had gone through the change two years ago and wasn't always pleasant to be around. Certainly, menopause didn't help at all with her desire to be intimate. "Maybe I do enjoy Ella's attention," I said in a moment of clarity. But I certainly had no plans to act on it, and the thought of Ada's accusation brought more heat.

Besides alcohol, money had become another problem, one I didn't have an easy answer for. The mission constantly flipped in and out of debt depending on donations, but ten thousand dollars missing from the books? It couldn't be that much. I knew where three thousand of it went. I'd bought Ada and Donny new cars. The cars hadn't arrived yet, but I planned on giving them both on our anniversary. Donny did plenty for the mission, so I didn't think anyone would gripe. A car for Ada came as a no-brainer. "It was my money, by God," I said so loudly that Levi looked at me.

He walked over and poured me another shot, which I gladly accepted and drained.

"Might as well leave the bottle," I said.

He did, without judgment. He also left me alone.

Maybe I'd go get my money back from the dealer. I knew I'd siphoned money from the account to buy booze, but not seven thousand! In one generous drunken mood, I'd bought drinks for the house, but that only amounted to a few hundred dollars. Ella could be the one stealing from the kitty. Maybe that's why she treated me so sweet.

I'd ask Ella to audit the books, but first I'd have to figure a way to explain the multiple checks I'd written to the Empire to pay for my drinking.

I poured myself another shot and slugged it down. The booze deadened the pain but never took it away. And when the buzz wore off, the shame and suffering were worse. So the cycle went on. I couldn't talk about it with Gravett or Driver. Driver, especially, believed such problems were due to a weak nature and solved by prayer and Bible study. The truly devout could pull themselves up by their bootstraps and quit sinning. If only it were that easy. I didn't exactly enjoy the abuse of alcohol.

Maybe I should've let the Coal Creek current suck me under the log. When that thought came, I realized dying didn't scare me. In fact, I'd welcome it. Sadness and anger swelled in my chest again. After all, I'd survived. With all I'd done for the city, the demon of suicide had slithered back into my life with his mouth to my ear, whispering about the joy of carbolic acid.

I took another shot.

35

THE BOTTOM

January 18, 1927
(Eight Months Later)

"Hail, king! For so thou art: behold, where stands.
The usurper's cursed head: the time is free:
I see thee compass'd with thy kingdom's pearl,
That speak my salutation in their minds;
Whose voices I desire aloud with mine:
Hail, King of Scotland!
Hail, King of Scotland!"

I recited the scene where Macduff reenters holding
Macbeth's head. My audience erupted with cheers and
chanted the last line: "Hail, King of Scotland!" I waved my
arms in jubilation and nearly fell from the homemade stage in
a room on the top floor of the Empire.

I jumped to the floor with a grand gesture, and my friends
slapped me on the back and offered congratulations.

"Good one, Jimmy."

"Best Shakespeare yet, Rev."

Someone started the phonograph, and the record spun with Ben Bernie's "Ain't She Sweet." The phonograph belonged to the mission and probably the reason they always invited me to the Tuesday night variety show. I'd cemented my position by springing for a case of moonshine from Wyoming the last couple of Tuesdays. The popularity of the illegal shows had grown so much that now people came by invitation only, and everyone had to learn a secret knock and pay two bits at the door. It was all on the hush-hush. No one wanted to end up in jail.

The owner of the Empire had no objection since the entry fees paid for the space. It didn't matter how noisy the shows got. The Empire had fallen into disrepair, and most of the rooms were unoccupied or rented by the hour. The post Great War attitude had become eat, drink, and be merry for tomorrow you may die.

I took a seat at a congenial table and a friend handed me a full shot glass. "To the Roaring Twenties," he said, and we clinked glasses.

"Yes, indeed," I said, and we gulped the liquor down. I laughed. Prohibition had done nothing except to spurn a new culture of short-skirted flappers, jazz, and the loosening of moral standards.

Our self-appointed emcee, in a comically loud tweed suit, jumped onto the stage. "Okay, folks, how about another hand for our very own Jim Goodheart!"

My friends, seventy people strong, cheered so loud I feared the coppers would hear, but it sure felt good. Maybe I should have pursued an acting career after all. I chuckled, knowing I'd just made my father turn over in his grave, so I took another shot for dear ol' Dad.

"Up next we got Scrappy singing 'I'm Looking Over a Four-Leaf Clover.'"

Scrappy leaped onto the stage and nodded to the girl running the phonograph. She lowered the needle, and Ben Bernie's Hotel Roosevelt Orchestra played. Scrappy belted out the song, mostly in tune.

Three flappers in knee-high dresses danced, and some of the younger men quickly joined in.

As I enjoyed the spectacle, Mrs. C. H. Ellis swanned up to me with a long cigarette holder. She sang along with Scrappy and blew the words at me. Her dress looked like something Ada would call a slip, her shoulders bare. A long string of pearls hung from her neck. Instead of a hat, she sported a sparkly headband with a red feather.

"I'm looking over a four-leaf clover
That I overlooked before
One leaf is sunshine, the second is rain
Third is the roses that grow in the lane
No need explaining, the one remaining
Is somebody I adore."

She took a drag on her cigarette, blew the smoke over my head, and kissed me on the cheek. "Hey, Jim, you're looking handsome tonight."

My brain flashed on Pixie, but I took a drink and made the image dissipate. I smiled at Mrs. C. H. Ellis.

"Thanks, Charlie. You don't look half bad yourself." Everyone called her Charlie because she excelled at the Charleston.

"Oh, I'm one hundred percent bad. I guarantee that," she said and brushed my cheek with her hand. She smelled delicious.

We both laughed.

She blew a smoke ring that floated to the ceiling along with her smile. She leaned in and whispered in my ear, "Jim, you saved me and my kids last week, and I wanted to thank you again. You were so kind to help us."

I whispered back, "I see Willy's still in jail for what he did to you." I noticed the bruising around her eye had faded. "He should stay in there a while longer and think about how to treat a lady."

"Me and the kids would be out on the street if you hadn't intervened," Charlie whispered and kissed my ear.

"The folks that took you in say you can stay for the month. We're using mission funds to support your stay, but we gotta figure things out by then," I said.

A burst of applause interrupted our discussion of her situation as Scrappy finished the tune.

"Okay, folks," the emcee said, "while the girl is changing the record to the Varsity Eight's 'Doo Wacka Doo,' let's hear it for Charlie."

The loudest applause of the night came after Charlie shimmied her chest at me and trotted to the stage. She struck a seductive pose, and then, as the music played, she shook and wiggled around the stage to great fanfare. The men whistled and yelled, and even the women egged her on to be more provocative.

I poured another shot from the bottle on the table and drained it. My head spun like a top, and I felt like I sped at a hundred miles an hour standing still. I wondered if I was going to pass out. It wouldn't be the first time for a Tuesday night.

Somewhere in my inebriation, the music changed to the Charleston, and before our very eyes, Charlie whipped off her flapper's dress, revealing shorts and a top that left nothing to the imagination. I saw her underthings when she kicked her leg up, turned, and shook her bottom.

My mind reeled, and I shut my eyes only to have my ears assaulted by a noisy commotion and a thudding crash at the back of the room.

I hoped when I opened my eyes it had been a nightmare, but by the familiar smell of the urinals and the clanking of doors, I knew it wasn't. As the city chaplain, I'd been in the county jail almost daily for over ten years, so I had no trouble recognizing the odors and sounds, although I never expected to wake up on this side of the bars again.

When I finally opened my aching eyeballs, that's precisely where I found myself. I tried rolling onto my side, but the metal bench hurt my shoulder. I moaned and turned back. When the pungent smell of vomit burned my nose, I figured I must have puked on myself. I attempted to sit up but had to hold my head with my hands when images from the night before flashed through my mind. Charlie...yes; she danced around, and everyone cheered. Oh, then the crash. Yelling. Yes, then lots of screaming.

I touched my scalp. It felt damp, and I wondered if someone had cracked me on the skull. In any case, my head pounded like a freight train barreling down the track.

Did I fall or get pushed to the ground? And how'd I get here? I had no clue.

I forced my eyes open again. No others accompanied me in the small cell—the one in the back the police reserve for the insane. At least no one witnessed my shame.

The jail door opened, and I heard footsteps approach. I thought my father strode in to bail me out like he did twenty years earlier. Then I remembered he died long ago and maybe I really had gone insane.

I looked up. A man stopped at my cell, whispering.

His lips were moving, but I couldn't hear him and stood to stagger closer to the bars.

"Reverend Goodheart, you doing okay?"

Officer Mallone, one of the policemen I knew well, stood outside the cell.

I nodded.

"Reverend, we gotta getcha out of here before the newspaper men show up. I don't know what the hell you were doing in the midst of all the shenanigans last night, but you were drunk and belligerent as hell. You got your butt hauled in with the rest of them, but I booked you as John White, fifty-five-year-old laborer."

I was not yet aware enough to understand how he had helped me, but I noticed he got my age right.

"One of the boys has gone to get your son," Mallone whispered, looking over his shoulder. "No one needs to know you were here. But we got to get you some help."

Over the last year, when I got too drunk to drive or even walk, Donald had rescued me, but he'd never picked me up from the jail before. I couldn't have felt more shame if I stood before the Lord himself. When I saw my son, I knew I'd wrecked every image of a good father or honorable man, and it broke my heart.

He paid the bail with his own money so as not to drag the mission into my cesspool. We sat outside the jailhouse in the car I'd bought him.

"I'll make sure you get paid back," I said.

He didn't speak when he came into the jail and hadn't said a word since. Even now, he only looked away and scowled.

I knew then I'd destroyed everything I'd worked for and strived for. I'd never felt so broken. I'd always needed my father to be pleased with me, but at that moment I realized how important it was to have my son proud of me. And I'd just shot that all to hell. My son now parented me, going against the natural order of things. I could only weep.

"You want me to take you home?" Donald finally said.

I didn't know what to do. Going home to face Ada was more than I could bear. I had failed her too. "I'm a man swinging by his noose."

"You need help." He turned to look at me.

I couldn't look at him and simply nodded. I knew I needed help, but just thinking about it brought chills up my spine. When alcohol stripped every last ounce of their dignity, we'd send some men to the Colorado Psychopathic Hospital. I guessed I had reached that point.

I looked at my son. "Judge and be judged," came to my lips. Donald looked at me with confusion. More aware now, I continued, "Even though I served them for years, I sometimes spoke critically of the men that were too weak to kick their vices. Now I am one of them. I guess you better take me to the asylum."

36

ASYLUM

January 19, 1927

Donald drove us to the front of the ominous-looking three-story Colorado Psychopathic Hospital. Traces of early-morning light accentuated its spooky gothic outline. I sat in the car staring at the structure. One lone lamp flickered at the door, and I half expected a flash of lightning to illuminate the place. Lights peeked from a smattering of rooms between heavy window slats that looked like cell bars. I imagined agonized faces of patients begging to be let out.

I'd never been in the state facility and had no desire to go there, either as a minister or especially as a patient. My heart raced, and my mind fought against the thought of being forcefully locked away in the depths of this hell. All those nightmares about the war and losing so many of the people I'd loved had brought me here to suffer and die by drowning in a vat of whiskey stirred by the demon of alcohol.

I knew I hadn't gone crazy but sitting here wasn't helping. I wanted to go back to the mission. I almost said so when

Donald opened the passenger door, took a firm grasp of my arm, and led me to the entrance. As I trudged along, I felt like I walked the green mile. Donald supported my weight to help me up the four stairs to the door. He rang a bell. I expected Igor the hunchback to greet me with wonky eyes. Instead, the door opened to a smiling nurse in a white uniform dress.

She escorted us through a modest foyer with leather chairs into a well-lit office with an exam table and desk. She invited us to sit down in the chairs facing the desk and asked if we needed some water. We both accepted.

The nurse questioned Donald. I guessed because I smelled of alcohol and vomit, she assumed I was the patient. After writing his answers on a form, she said, "The doctor will be in to see you shortly." She put the clipboard on the desk and exited the office.

I feared burly men in white coats would burst through the door at any moment and haul me off to a padded cell. My hands were shaking so severely that I couldn't get the glass to my mouth without spilling the water down my chin. Sweat beaded from every pore. Flashbacks of my delirium tremors flooded my mind, and I imagined Joseph standing next to me —smiling.

I jumped as the door opened and a young man with a beard and mustache entered. He looked like he'd just awakened as he blinked and smoothed his hair down. It surprised me he wore only slacks and shirt, and not a white coat. He plopped himself into the chair behind the desk and reached for the clipboard. Before acknowledging us, he settled back into his chair to read.

Finally, he looked at me. He said nothing, and that made me shake all the more. I looked at the floor with shame.

His chair squawked when he stood. He went to a cabinet in the corner and unlocked it with a key. He removed a bottle, closed and locked the door, came back, and handed it to me.

As I accepted it, I couldn't believe my eyes—a bottle of beer. I thought it was a joke or a test. I glanced at Donald, whose eyes went wide with alarm.

"Drink up," the doctor said. "It's going to make both of our lives more manageable."

I put the bottle to my lips, expecting the sour taste of medicine, but a genuine draft filled my throat. Warm, but beer nevertheless. It tasted good.

When I rested the bottle in my lap, the doctor furrowed his brows with exasperation and lifted his hand urgently. "Finish it," he said.

So I did, concluding with a large belch. When no one laughed, I excused myself.

Only then did he introduce himself. "I'm Dr. Eric Freeman. I'm a second-year psychiatry resident, and I'll be taking care of you. You are?"

I wanted to say, "John White, fifty-five-year-old laborer," but I had tired of lying to myself and everyone else. "James Goodheart," I said.

This seemed to surprise the doctor. He straightened in his chair, reached inside his pocket for a pair of glasses, and put them on. The doctor stared at me for a good long time. He finally nodded, and a smile spread across his face. He kept nodding as though working something out in his mind.

"God has a way of surprising us," he said.

I wondered which one of us had gone mad, until he added, "You remember telling me that?"

I shook my head slowly. "I'm sorry—"

"With all the people you've helped, I don't expect you'd remember everyone. Besides, I was just a young punk. Is this your son?" He glanced at Donald.

I nodded.

"I'm sorry," I repeated, trying to remember the doctor's name.

"You teased me when I sat behind bars," the doctor said. "You said 'You sure your name is Free-Man? You're looking more like a Not-So-Free-Man.'"

He looked at Donald and explained. "At seventeen, I came to Denver from New York to find work. I had visited my aunt in Cheyenne, and when I'd been in Denver for a whole hour and a half, the police arrested me for vagrancy. Still not sure why except that I'm Jewish."

"That and you gave the copper a tongue lashing," I said, the memory returning.

"Yeah, that's right." He laughed. "Forgot about that part. Anyway, the judge gave me no leniency, and he sentenced me to thirty days in jail. I had no money and no way to contact my folks." He turned to Donald. "Your father walked in and had me out of there in two shakes. Got me a job at St. Joseph's sweeping floors. Working at St. Joseph's was the reason I became a doctor."

"You won't hold that against me, will ya?" I ventured a laugh that he reciprocated.

The humor broke the tension in the room.

"You never asked what religion I held to," the doctor said. "You probably didn't care, and I'll never forget your charity. You told me, 'God loves surprising us with His kindness.' I'm so happy I can return the favor. It looks like you've gotten yourself into a bit of a spot, Reverend Goodheart. We'll get this figured out. It's all going to be okay…that sound familiar?"

With tears welling in my eyes, I smiled and said, "Just don't call me Not-So-Good-Heart."

When Dr. Freeman finished laughing, he turned to Donald. "Your father is truly a good man."

I'd been a patient for three days, and Ada visited for the first time. Dr. Freeman had prescribed a medicinal bottle of beer every afternoon, and every time I took a sip, Ada tightened her jaw. I looked out the window toward the Rockies from my bed on the third floor. I'd always thought they sent people here to the Colorado Psychopathic Hospital because they were too far gone. But instead of a nuthouse, I experienced a shelter from the storm—one full of compassion. Yes, they kept us locked in, and I'm sure there were wings of the hospital I wouldn't want to go, but they treated me well.

"I can't believe they're letting you have booze," Ada grumbled.

"Well, it's just beer, and they tell me it keeps me from the DTs."

"But that's what got you here in the first place." She sighed. "I'm not sure I can do this again." She turned away.

I tried to get her to look at me, but she'd been angry for a long time, and there seemed no way to change her mind.

"I fired Miss Pettit," she said finally.

I started to speak but thought better of it.

"I've always thought she was too pretty and too flirty with you for her own good," Ada added.

"How'd she take it?" I asked and finished my beer.

"She's fit to be tied. Hell hath no fury like a woman scorned."

I almost said, "Ain't that right?" but I held my tongue.

"She's had a thing for you from day one," Ada continued. "I should have never let you talk me into hiring her." She leaned down and pulled some papers from her purse. "And now she's saying that the mission is as much as twenty-five thousand dollars in debt—that it could be even more." Ada cried softly into a handkerchief. Then, as her tears dried, she spoke defiantly. "I told her we couldn't afford to pay her any longer, and she had to go."

I put my hand to my forehead and sighed. "Impossible. How can it be that much?"

"We feed and house hundreds every day. We're bleeding goodwill."

A knock came from the door. "Come in," I said.

Dr. Freeman opened the door. He wore a white coat and looked rested. "Is now a good time to talk with you both?"

He didn't wait for an answer. Ada dabbed her eyes and sat up straight as Dr. Freeman introduced himself to her and took a seat in the extra chair.

"Mrs. Goodheart, thank you for coming in today. I'm sorry we haven't let you see Jim before now. We consider it part of our drying-out protocol."

"Doesn't look like it's working very well," she said icily and indicated the beer bottle.

"Yes, I know it's strange to be treating the problem with the problem, but people can die from the delirium tremens, and we've found it most effective to wean patients off the alcohol gradually."

It was the first time I'd heard the explanation, and thinking about the DTs and getting weaned off made me sweat.

"We've been letting him have three beers a day," Dr. Freeman said. "Tomorrow will be two, then one. We hope that will be his last drink...ever."

"For Lord's sake, I hope so," Ada said, shivering reflexively.

"I don't know if Jim told you of our connection," the doctor said, "but I respect you both for what you have done for the city."

Ada nodded.

Dr. Freeman crossed one leg over the other. "There are two camps of thought for alcohol treatment," he began, "and they depend on if you think of the problem as a disease or a failure of willpower. Here at CPH, we follow the teachings of Dr. William Silkworth, who says, 'Alcoholism is an obsession of the mind that condemns one to drink, and an allergy of the body that condemns one to die.' Dr. Silkworth advises the Oxford Group, which is headquartered in my hometown at the Calvary Episcopal Church."

He reached into his jacket pocket, took out a card, and gave it to Ada.

"These are the tenets the Oxford Group adheres to." He recited them as Ada read the card:

"We admit we are licked.
We get honest with ourselves.
We talk it over with another person.
We make amends to those we had harmed.
We try to carry this message to others with no
thought of reward.
We pray to whatever God we think there is."

Ada frowned and handed the card to me. "That's it, Doctor?"

"Look, Mrs. Goodheart, I know this sounds simplistic, but this philosophy seems to work as well as anything else. Other doctors are trying morphine, but that just seems to switch one problem for another. Some institutions are prescribing aversive conditioning."

"Like givin' the wife a board to whap me upside the head every day," I said, attempting levity.

Only Dr. Freeman laughed. "Well, not exactly, but not any more pleasant." He turned to Ada. "Look, I'm not saying you have an easy road ahead. But just like that man in the black suit said to the dumb teenager behind bars...there is hope."

On my first day of sobriety, I beamed like a celebrity when the morning nurses congratulated me. But I'd felt just as much a celebrity a week ago sitting in the Empire, delivering Shakespeare, accepting accolades, and craving a reward of the stuff that drove me here.

They gave me my last drink yesterday, but if they offered another, I'd take it with pleasure. The doctor talked of letting me go home in a few weeks, but as much as I had feared coming to the asylum, I dreaded even more being sprung free. I couldn't trust myself. That's what had me worried the most when Dr. Freeman walked in for our morning session. He'd asked if I wanted to call him Eric, and I agreed as long as he called me Jim.

"Good morning, Jim," he said. "How are you feeling today?"

"Ahhh." I stuck my tongue out as if I were a sick kid.

"I assume you're feeling anxious about going back into the real world."

I nodded and fought back some tears.

"Well, you're not alone. That's how every recovering addict feels."

"I'm not sure I feel like I've recovered from anything," I said.

"Well, it's a relative term. In my experience, it's a moment by moment process. It's going to be important that you have a support system around you. I imagine there are men at the mission who you can be vulnerable with?"

I nodded without conviction. How I missed Joseph.

"I wanted to get back to our discussion about the war," he said. "You went through some awful things in France—lost a lot of friends."

"True, but I'm not sure what that has to do with my problem."

Eric laid down his clipboard and put his hands behind his head. "Jim, this is the problem. Alcohol is just the symptom. It's like someone coming in with headaches caused by high blood pressure. If we just treated the pain in the head, we'd be missing the point. Since the war ended, my specialty has been discovering and treating the many problems of returning veterans. My colleagues and I see a pretty clear pattern."

"Not everyone that goes to war ends up in here," I mumbled.

"True, but I believe that pain is pain, and in my short time in medicine, I have found no one who escapes it. Not even me. It depends on how you deal with the pain that matters."

The familiar sense of shame welled up in my chest. "I always thought that my battle with booze was strictly a character flaw."

"It's not a flaw, Jim…it's how you learned to cope with life. You started using alcohol early in life as a comfort from pain. Some people use booze, some sex, some power, some gambling…anything to cover up or mask the pain. And it doesn't always have to be what you would consider a vice. It can be good things as well: service to others, food, work, exercise—anything to distract from the pain. We all seek what comforts us. Everyone has a similar battle."

"Where is this pain coming from?" I asked.

"Life...it comes at us in all forms. Addiction is our attempt to cover the pain with more and more of what doesn't work."

"But I feel like this addiction disqualifies me from running the mission and preaching the gospel."

Eric laughed. "I think your job at the mission gives you the best view for helping people and yourself. Remember what you told me eleven years ago? 'Don't let this define you.'"

37

SPIRITUAL AWAKENING

February 14, 1927
(One Month Later)

I met with Eric every day for four weeks after my admission to the hospital. Sometimes we met in my room, other times in an office, and often, like today, we met outside. Even though it was February, the sun made it unseasonably pleasant. It had been a mild winter, which usually meant we could expect a late, heavy snow. Eric and I sat at a picnic table on the hospital grounds, warming body and soul, when I saw Reverend Gravett park his car and walk toward us. A nervous chill ran down my spine.

This would be the first time I'd seen Joshua since my fall, and the consequences of my sins still weighed heavily on me. Gravett would surely judge me and find me wanting. But since they would discharge me tomorrow morning, Eric thought we should meet today. Eric and I had become good friends, and I felt like I could tell him anything. In turn, he asked me for advice on some of his patients. I found we had similarly wicked senses of humor, so we got along splendidly and spent much of the time laughing. To me, his friendship had been the best medicine.

I waved at Joshua as he walked across the expansive lawn to where we sat. I wore street clothes today, and that made me less self-conscious than if I had met him in hospital-issued pajamas.

I had wondered all night what I would say to him, and more importantly, what he would say to me. I think that worried me more. While they had me locked in the hospital, Ada took charge of the mission, as she had during my wartime service. By all accounts, with the help of the staff, she held it together, feeding and housing hundreds of men every day. I wondered if she kept up with the books. I'd soon find out. In any case, the mission appeared to be running smoothly in my absence. While it thrilled me, it also bruised my ego knowing they got along so well without me.

I stood and extended my hand when Joshua approached. Rather than shake it, he embraced me with a bear hug. The icy chill left my body, and I melted into his acceptance and love. He held me while my body trembled and my tears fell.

When I finished, he backed off and held me by the shoulders. "James, thank God…I thank God you're okay. You look better than you have for years." He hugged me again.

I felt like the prodigal son whose father had run out to meet him. I was only a few years younger than Joshua, but I'd always looked up to him as a father figure.

He stood back and looked at me again. "James, you look ten years fresher."

"Amazing what straitjackets can do," I shrugged.

Joshua looked at me as though I might be serious, but when Eric and I laughed, he got it and chuckled.

I took the opportunity to make the introductions. "Eric, I

am so pleased to introduce you to Reverend Joshua Gravett.
Joshua, this is Dr. Eric Freeman."

"Nice to meet you, Doctor."

"Please, call me Eric."

"Only if you do the same," Joshua said.

"Okay, Eric," Eric said and laughed.

Joshua glanced at me and grinned. "Now I know why you
two get along so well."

Eric suggested we sit at the table where an urn of hot
coffee rested. He poured a cup for Joshua and refilled our
mugs.

Joshua started to speak, but I interrupted him.
"Joshua..." I had prepared a speech last night, but the words
I'd practiced vanished. All I could manage was, "Joshua, I am
sorry." Both emotional and physical pain overcame me. My
failures and shortcomings choked my chest and churned my
stomach. Like hot, burning coal poured on my flesh, it was
the pain felt by the sinner in the pit of hell. I swallowed hard
and tried again. "I'm so sorry for what I've done to you and to
the mission."

Tears welled in Joshua's eyes. "James," he said, "I am so
sorry. I feel like I've failed you. I knew you were working your
fingers to the bone and I should have stepped in. It is you
who needs to forgive me."

I shook my head in disbelief...and belief. I should have
known. Only a person who carries the love of the Father and
knows Him intimately can speak as Joshua did.

Eric and I had discussed at length the Oxford steps. That
day, addressing my friend, Reverend Gravett, I started with
step four: "Joshua, I must confess to you my infidelity...to
you...to myself...to God. I have not conducted myself as a
man worthy of grace. I've been self-indulgent—drinking,
partying, being in places I shouldn't, using mission funds for

booze and entertainment." The words were painful to say, but I had to say them. "I have become powerless to my desires and to alcohol."

Joshua listened patiently.

"I've tried being good. I've strived and strived to do right. I made a mess, but I'll make amends. I'm going to make it right again."

Joshua put his hand on my arm. "James, I know it's going to be right, and God will see to it." It surprised me when he emptied his coffee on the ground and examined his cup inside and out. He held it to my face and asked, "What do you see?"

"Well, a mug," I said.

"Yes, and a good-looking cup at that. It's nice and white and clean…a few scratches and dings, but, mostly, it looks pretty darn good." Then he turned the mug so I could view the inside, worn and stained with coffee.

"James, you are like this cup. You've spent a lot of your life working on how good it looks on the outside, but in reality, it is the inside that is in much need of care."

I looked at Eric, who smiled. I frowned and asked, "You guys talk before he came over?"

"No, I swear," Eric said and turned to Joshua. "This is exactly what Jim and I have been talking about."

I got it, I really did, and I remembered Joseph's dying words about being vulnerable.

"I get it," I said. "My insides are a mess, and I've been playacting as if they're not…I'm sorry and embarrassed."

"You shouldn't be embarrassed," Joshua said. "We all do that. Besides, that's just the ego talking…the shadow self. The part of us that is self-sufficient and dresses us up so no one can see our failures and weaknesses. I suspect what God is after for all of us is to come into the light and a sacred realization that we are all in need of Him to heal our internal lives."

He turned to Eric. "Forgive me, Doctor, if I'm stepping on toes here, but the way I see it, the craving for alcohol or any other addiction is merely trying to fill the desire that we all feel for something more...something greater. We turn to those things by a deeply frustrated desire for more. We're all in need of a spiritual awakening."

"Spiritual awakening," Eric said, and nodded. "I like that."

"What our thought life is like on the inside determines how we go through life on the outside," Joshua continued. "So many people consume time with the facade and forget they're longing for life on the inside. I'm no different—we are all radically egocentric."

"Now that you say that," Eric said, "I think most of the people I care for with addictions settle for abstinence rather than a real transformation—this spiritual awakening you mentioned."

"Yes, that's true," Joshua said. "We are all addicts of one kind or another, and often we are blind to what we are addicted to. We don't even realize we need emotional healing. It is why Jesus tells us to deal with the log in our own eye before thinking about the splinter in someone else's." He turned to me. "In my experience, we need something like what you have been going through to deal with the log." He patted my arm. "You cannot heal what you don't first acknowledge."

I sighed deeply. "I thought you were going to tell me to give up the mission."

"No, I'm not going to do that. But I am going to ask you to give up some of your responsibilities, so you don't end up here again."

"You don't think I'm disqualified?"

This made Joshua laugh loudly. "I think you are the most

qualified. You are in the best position to unbind others. You are growing...religion is lived by people fearful of hell, but the genuine connection with God is mostly found by people who have been through hell."

This had both Eric and me nodding.

"I told you he was wise," I said to my doctor friend.

"You should hang out with him more," Eric said.

I knew what he meant, because we'd talked about my tendency to hide my problems from those who were in the best position to help. The fear of rejection kept me living in bondage.

"Look, James," Joshua said. "Until you hit bottom, you will not hunt for another spring of life."

"Then what?" I asked.

"Keep doing what you are doing now. Going through these steps: getting honest with yourself, talking it over and making amends, praying to God that He removes your short-comings and strengthens your relationship with Him. I believe one of the most powerful prayers is: 'Let your will be done to me and through me, Father.'"

I nodded, trying to absorb what he said.

Joshua took his Bible from his pocket. "I have these two verses written in the back so I can look at them every day," he said and read to us: "Psalm 46:10. 'Be still and know that I am God,' and Ephesians 4:22, 'That ye put off the old man who is corrupt according to deceitful lusts and be renewed in the spirit of your mind by putting on the new man who is created after God in righteousness and true holiness.'"

He tucked away the Bible. "For me, the verses remind me daily to spend time in silent prayer with the Father and let Him heal me from the inside out. I ask you to be willing to let God change you and know that only those who have suffered truly can understand the afflicted."

We sat in silence for a long time. A small bird landed on the table, examined all three of us, and seemed to offer us a benediction before flying off.

It made me smile. *Okay, God, I'm listening.*

"God does not love us after we change, but loves us so we can change," Joshua said. "I think our spiritual awakening is when *that* goes from our head to our heart." He held out his coffee cup again. "Now can I have some more coffee?"

We all laughed, and Eric filled his cup.

Joshua sipped and swallowed with satisfaction. "Now for some practical matters," he began. "Once you're sprung out of here, I want you to take a couple of weeks for yourself. Go practice this contemplative prayer. We want you to come back to the mission, but we don't want you to overextend yourself. You need to think about your schedule, and when you're ready, let's talk about it. Lastly…and I don't bring this up to scare you, only to prepare you. That man from the *Post*, Colbert, has been around asking for statements. I'd be mighty careful around him."

38

SECRET PLACE

March 1, 1927

Nancy, Josephine's mother, graciously gave Ada and me the key to her cabin at Coal Creek. Typically, no one could access the place in the winter, but this year's mild weather made it a perfect retreat. Fishing was out of the question as the creek partially froze over, but with little snow on the ground, I could take walks in the woods and enjoy the winter's stillness—that matched perfectly with what I hoped for in my heart.

Every morning I wrapped myself in a heavy Pendleton blanket and reclined in a comfortable chair in front of a crackling fire. The flames licked at the logs glowing with shimmering embers.

"Here you go, James," Ada said, handing me a mug of steaming cinnamon tea.

"Thank you," I said and grinned at her. She smiled back and joined me by the fire, sitting in a rocking chair and pulling out one of her many prayer cards to begin silently interceding for people on her list.

I thanked God for the power of a praying wife—probably the reason I was still alive and reasonably sane. After many hours of venting and tears, her anger toward me slowly abated. I needed much more time to heal our marriage, but I knew the faithfulness of God. I did not expect her to forgive me or trust me any time soon, but I hoped she could access a divine deposit of both within her. In my solitude, I searched for that deposit in and for myself. I realized no amount of counsel could give anyone this gift. No one could do the work for me. Only by suffering the mortal blow to the ego could I be ready to discover forgiveness within.

I was uncovering grace in places I'd overlooked or taken for granted: Ada's embrace, the warmth of a fire, the solitude of my thoughts. Deep within my heart sat an island refuge from the raging sea—a secret place in my heart where no amount of angst, addiction or fear could topple me. To access the place where love dwells, where my deepest dreams and desires were stored, I needed to stop scrutinizing everything in my mind and open my heart.

When I said goodbye to Joshua at the hospital, he gave me one last piece of advice for my retreat. "Remember Jesus's words to His disciples: 'When thou prayest, enter into thy closet, and when thou hast shut thy door, pray to thy Father which is in secret.'"

I knew Jesus didn't want me to find the nearest actual closet, but to seek that place in my heart where I could be still and in silent contemplation, commune with Him. So here I sat by the fire, opening my heart to find that place—trying to ignore my mind's pull to continually draw me away with fears and lists of things I thought I should be doing.

In the hospital, during one of our lengthy discussions

about God, Eric had told me that the Israelites' sacred name for God, Yahweh, really couldn't be pronounced—it had to be breathed. He taught me some breathing exercises to help with my anxiety. I sipped my tea, closed my eyes, let the muscles in my limbs relax, and focused on my breath...inhale... exhale...Yahweh.

Words are inadequate to describe what I experienced, but they are all I have. I let go, surrendered. I couldn't do it by force, but by giving into it. My consciousness flowed into a secret room in my heart, pushed away fear and anger, and flowed out with joy and peace. I wondered if this garden of delight had been there all along, and whether I had walled it off and closed its doors somewhere along the way. Maybe we are born with joy and peace in God, and that's what we see in babies that makes us love them so much.

A loving sensation enveloped my heart like the blanket that wrapped around my body. I was aware of Ada taking the cup of tea from my hand as I turned and fell into a gentle sleep.

Just like my life, my recovery took a few steps forward and a couple steps back. I could feel my blood pressure rise the next day when we pulled to the front of the Sunshine Rescue Mission. Colbert stood out front, pacing back and forth. I turned to Ada as we exited the car, "Be sober, be vigilant, because your adversary, the devil, is a roaring lion and walketh about, seeking whom he may devour."

"Good advice for yourself, James. Go to him in the opposite spirit. Love destroys hate."

I faced him and extended my hand. "Good morning, Mr. Colbert. What can I do for you?"

He ignored my hand and focused on his pencil tip resting on his pad. "My sources tell me that there is someone in District Attorney Cline's office going over an audit of the Sunshine Rescue Mission finances as we speak. You care to comment?"

I looked at Ada. She had her eyes closed, praying, I assumed. I looked Colbert up and down. Walking the path of love followed a rugged trail. I knew nothing about the man, not even if he was married or had children. The haphazard way he dressed made me think he was not a family man and most likely wrestled with loneliness. I'm sure he had his own pain.

"We have always had our books open to the public," I said, "and we asked our bookkeeper to do an audit just recently." I said no more as I realized who was speaking to the DA. If Ella sought vengeance, she knew my character flaws as well as anyone, and I was in trouble.

"I understand you've been in the asylum," Colbert said.

I looked at Ada again, who remained deep in prayer. How could I explain to this man the blessings of my respite and recovery? "Yes, I'm afraid the pressures of the office were overwhelming me. But after some rest, I'm looking forward to returning to help the poor get their footing, hopefully with a better understanding—"

"You arrested?" Colbert interrupted.

It surprised me when Ada grabbed my arm. "That's enough, Mr. Colbert," she said, escorted me through the mission door, and slammed it behind her. "Bastard," she whispered.

I looked at her in shock.

"Well, if the shoe fits," she added.

When she flicked on the lights, a bodacious shout erupted. "Surprise!" The staff and clients had filled the room and started singing rounds of "For He's a Jolly Good Fellow."

Ada hugged my arm as they sang, and for a moment, I forgot about the challenging last year and Ella and Colbert, and I remembered my purpose in life.

I sighed. It was good to be home.

Ada didn't think I should preach after dinner, but I told her now was the best time to share. I was right. I talked from my heart without once referring to a written note, staying the most vulnerable and honest I'd ever been. I described my descent into depression and my dependency on alcohol. I talked about my war experiences and about other pains I'd held in my heart. Then opened up about how I'd hidden behind my self-reliance and external facade, only to have it crumble. But mostly I talked about God's faithfulness and the love I'd found inside myself—Christ in me and me in Christ. Then I asked the men if they wanted this for themselves. I don't think I saw one man who didn't raise his hand. Staff members held their hands high, and so did Ada. We prayed together to experience this spiritual awakening.

Afterward, an indescribable peace and joy filled the room and our hearts...that, and a lot of hugs.

The staff had made a cake that said WELCOME HOME, JIM. We enjoyed refreshments and each other's company. The hours passed, and yawns increased. It grew late, and the men headed to their bunks.

I sat musing in the afterglow of revival, sipping coffee and nibbling cake. I thought of Ananias baptizing Saul, when the Lord said to them, 'For I will show him what great things he must suffer for my name's sake.' I had suffered, and with

God's help, I had claimed victory in recovery. He had given me a new platform to see my own life and the lives of those around me.

I took another bite of the sweet cake and licked my fingers. *Yes, it was good to be home.* I yawned.

Speaking of home, I thought and looked for Ada. She stood near the door with her back to me, talking to three staff members in heated whispers. When she turned around with a newspaper in her hand, I read the terrible news on her face.

As she came to me, I tried accessing that secret place, that place of peace, but when she slammed the newspaper on the table in front of me, my heart filled with fear and anxiety. The headline read:

"DA Cline Hides Identity of Informant After Seizure of Jim Goodheart's Books at Sunshine Rescue Mission"

39

AVALANCHE

March 4, 1927

Three days later, I sat at my desk in my cubbyhole office with the door closed. With all the controversy in the *Post*, it became difficult for me to find my secret place. I needed the shelter of this physical one.

The competing newspaper, the *Rocky Mountain News*, had only reported on my hospitalization and wished the mission and me well, but the *Post*, itching for salacious news to increase its circulation, continued to harp at the DA until he released Ella's name. I did not know what she told them, but I didn't think it could be any worse than the current accusation —that of mishandling the mission's funds.

Any hope of finding that safe place in my heart evaporated when Ada opened the door without knocking, put a folded *Post* on my desk and left, shutting the door. I stared at it for a long time before opening it. Bold letters four inches high—larger than the headline announcing the end of the war—said:

DRUNKEN ORGIES CHARGED
TO GOODHEART
INVESTIGATORS FIND TRAIL
OF WINE, GIRLS,
AND WILD SPENDING

The room spun, and blood drained from my face. I slid from my chair onto my knees and sobbed.

"I'll have to leave Denver," I said to my friends gathered around me in the mission dining room. I had spread the newspaper article out on the table in front of us.

When no one said a word, I assumed they agreed with me.

The reported news had quickly spread up and down Larimer Street, and the rest of the men that filled the room eating lunch were exceptionally quiet.

I looked around the mission that we'd worked so hard to build for the sake of the downtrodden. I had screwed up. All this was my fault. I could get mad at Colbert and the *Post*, the DA and Ella, but this all came as the consequence of my infidelity. The knowledge of that crushed me. I thought I'd hit rock bottom a month ago, but it turned out to be only a ledge. I'd bounced and fallen another mile to land on piercing stakes.

I looked at the words we had painted on the wall ten years ago:

UNCHANGEABLE TRUTH
All we, like sheep, have gone astray:
we have turned, every one to his

own way and the Lord hath laid
on Him the iniquity of us all. – Isaiah 53:6

In my mind, I saw Jesus hanging on the cross with blood dripping down His face from the crown of thorns. His body bruised and broken from the beatings and His hands and feet so painfully pierced. I saw myself, my body sagging under the weight of my sin. The arrest, the hospitalization, the *Post*— had all laid me bare. I hung crucified. Christ with me, me with Christ. I'd never understood it until now.

Tears filled my eyes. "I am sorry, everyone."

A man with a bald head and gray beard set his coffee mug down hard and stood. We all turned to look at him. Frank, a widower, couldn't find regular work because of his advancing age, but had enough savings to live in a flophouse. He came for most meals at the mission and probably just as much for the companionship. For his part, we put him in charge of the mail room.

"I'm telling you; this slander is a pile of horse crap!" Frank loudly announced, the top of his head turning red. "I frankly don't care what you've done, Jim, and especially don't give a flying flip what the *Post* is saying. Look around, you're in good company."

Many of the men laughed.

"Not that the world or the *Post* care about any one of us, but look around, there's not one man in here who wouldn't lay down his life for you. You've believed in each one of us while we were down, and we believe in you."

A loud "Amen" resounded with applause.

Frank let the group cheer and then said, "Indicated by the near hundred letters you get a day, you got friends all over this country. Men thankful for what you did for them and how you helped get their lives on track. Jim, I know the last few weeks, you have read no mail, but I want you to hear one that came in a few days ago."

He pulled a letter from his inside pocket, unfolded it and read:

"Dear Reverend Goodheart…Jim.
It's been six months since I left the Sunshine Mission, and I wanted to thank you and Mrs. Goodheart for all you did for me. I now have a good job at a publishing company in St. Louis and a girl. We're getting hitched soon. You helped me find my dignity again, but maybe just as important, you pointed me back to the source of life.
Yours truly, Ernest

PS: I'm hoping someday to be a writer and I send you this poem:

'Famed is the name of the sculptor who can
Fashion mere earth to the pattern of man.
Greater is he who can shape shattered men
Into the form of the human again.'"

Frank folded the letter and slid it back into his pocket. "That's what you've done for all of us."

Another cheer rose from the men but quieted as the front door of the mission swung open. My five-year-old grand-daughter, Shirley, bounced in with her curly blond locks springing with each step. She marched through the tables of men without hesitation with Josephine steps behind, trying to catch up. Josephine grimaced and mouthed apologies to the men for the interruption.

"Grandpa, Grandpa," Shirley quickened her step when

she saw me and flung herself into my arms. She hugged my neck tight.

Josephine caught up and leaned in to kiss my cheek. "I'm so sorry, Grandpa Jim, but she insisted we come visit today."

I set Shirley on my knee and straightened some ruffles of her dress. "My, don't you look like a fine lady today." I held out my hand to Josephine, and she took it. "Jo, I'm so sorry…"

I wanted to say more, but she waved it off. "Now go on with you," she said. "You know I love you." She squeezed my hand.

"How's Donald?" I asked.

She smiled at me. "He'll be fine. He's had to work through some things."

I searched her eyes for truth, and she held my shoulder and said, "Truly, it's gonna be okay."

I looked at Ada and fought back tears as she nodded.

Shirley tapped me on the chest. "Grandpa…" A tear ran down her solemn face. "Daddy said you were sad, so I drew you a picture."

She unfolded the paper with a drawing of two stick figures in an embrace with a heart traced over top and handed it to me. "Oh darling, what a delightful picture. Thank you."

She leaned into me. "I didn't want you to be sad, Grandpa. Please don't be sad."

I smiled and hugged her tight. "Is that you and me hugging in the picture?"

"No Grandpa," she said with all the exasperation a five-year-old could muster. "That's Jesus hugging you."

I needed Shirley's reminder of who held me. The next few days of headlines were no more forgiving:

JIM GOODHEART CHARGED WITH RECKLESS ORGIES

Disclosures Result in Backers Withdrawing
Their Support and End Chance That
Sunshine Mission Will Be Reorganized
With Him in Charge.

I asked one of my coworkers what orgies were, and I cried when he told me. I thought they were rambunctious parties, and if that meant the variety shows at the Empire, I was guilty as charged. But the realization that everyone in Denver thought it involved lurid sexual free-for-alls got me sick to my stomach. How would I ever convince people otherwise?

The *Post's* assassination of my character continued with a headline claiming DA Cline also investigated a long list of questionable activities:

CONTRIBUTION OF $8,550 TO GOODHEART IS HUNTED

CLINE WILL AUDIT
MISSION'S BOOKS

Canceled Checks Show That Hundreds of Dollars in Funds
Were Spent on Purposes Not Intended by Donors

The mission had received the eight thousand dollars from the estate of the late Esther Lewis three years ago. We designated it for the general fund. And, yes, I had probably spent hundreds of dollars on booze and the variety show—one check for two hundred ninety, another for one hundred fifty and yet another for four hundred fifty dollars. But the *Post* made it sound like I'd misused every donation ever given to the mission.

The *Post* also described in detail my arrest amongst the most unsavory of Denver and claimed they had forcefully admitted me to the asylum. They said the police were in possession of the Sunshine Mission's phonograph.

But by the end of the week, all the accusations hung on the three checks. On the last day of the thrashing the text read —almost as an afterthought: Ella Pettit, not DA Cline, had done the audit.

By March 11, the final headline read:

CLINE ASSAILS GOODHEART
FOR WASTING MISSION FUNDS
AND ASKS TRUST AGREEMENT
BE BROKEN

The article said that the indebtedness of the mission had increased from ten to twenty thousand in the last year. This was correct, but the money had not gone into my own pocket, as the paper suggested. The final number they accused me of spending personally amounted to $5,662.85. This sum included the three automobiles I'd bought for Mary, Ada, and Donny, and the three checks I'd spent on booze. Still, it was nothing I was proud of.

Most of the backers of the mission notified me they were withdrawing support. I figured Denver residents who didn't like the idea of skid row saw it as a victory…good riddance.

The Rocky Mountain News printed a final article that said:

"It looks like District Attorney Cline acted with more haste than discretion in seizing the books of the Sunshine Mission. If, as indicated, he had no intention of making an investigation looking toward possible criminal prosecutions, then he had no business taking the records. It is only when investigating an alleged crime that he has authority to seize the books of an organization or individual. So far as Jim Goodheart is concerned, there could be no misappropriation of funds. He is the Sunshine Mission. He had the legal right to spend the mission receipts as he pleased. He didn't have to account to the District Attorney or anybody else."

The scurrilous *Post* found one more allegation against me: a disgruntled employee accused me of hiring union musicians instead of cheaper, in-house talent. *Everyone is ready to kick a dog when he's down.*

A week later, not one article appeared in the *Post* about the Sunshine Rescue Mission. As fast as the devastating avalanche had hit, it stopped. But our lives and the landscape would never be the same. *The Denver Post* had tried and convicted me. But with no indictment by District Attorney Cline, there was no case. Ada and I had full charge of the mission's finances. The DA was clear that there was no criminal intent, and they filed no charges. The matter was settled, but they had destroyed my life and the mission.

40

PLEA

March 13, 1927

From the mission's kitchen, I peered through a crack by the door. Only standing room remained in our meeting room, and I'd never been so nervous before a gathering. It's terribly hard to shed the facade and bare yourself. It would have been so easy to fall back on my acting skill and play the comedian. And easier still to take a drink, but I'd come so far that I didn't want to miss another moment of what the Lord had in store for me. Good or bad, He held it all in His hands. I took a deep breath and found the safe place in my heart. Whatever happened was going to be okay, because it just was.

I thought the Sunshine musicians played exceptionally well tonight, and I decided to go out at the end of the song. It meant so much to me that both Reverend Gravett and Dr. Freeman had come tonight and would speak on my behalf. When they'd offered to talk first, I told them I wanted to apologize publicly before anything else.

I caught my reflection in the stainless-steel cupboard. I

looked tired. My mind continued as my Achilles heel, unable to shut it off at night or stop wrestling with my thoughts. I would always need further renewing of my mind.

The music slowed. I took another deep breath and pushed the door open. When I walked through the crowd, the silence of the room struck me as funny, and I almost fell back into my old comedic self. I was tempted to gag it up and tip-toe down the aisle, but better judgment prevailed.

I went straight to the lectern and gripped both sides to steady myself. I had written no notes. I looked at the faces in the crowd, some with smiles, others with disapproval, most with indifference.

Tears threatened to come before the words—a hazard of speaking from the heart. I smiled and nodded to Joshua, Eric, Ada, Donny and Josephine, who sat in the front row.

"I stand before you a broken man…and a new man. And before I say another word, I want to say I'm sorry. I'm truly sorry for what I have done. I cannot tell you the depth of grief it causes me. I had been sober for over ten years. I thought I'd never drink again. But I did, and when I took another drink, I took one more, and then another, and another still. I did things I'm not proud of and hit rock bottom and spent weeks in the hospital. Now I find myself in front of you, ashamed."

I pulled a hankie out of my pocket and wiped my face.

"In a few days, I will have been sober for two months. What I have learned is that even as important as sobriety is, it is only the beginning. It is necessary to go further, to look below the surface at the heart. What I saw was dark and painful, but that is where the Lord touched me. He said, 'Come to me and find rest.'"

I wiped my face again.

"I confess my second fall and proclaim my repentance. And I promise you with renewed zest, more than ever, to labor in relieving poverty and the saving of souls. I ask not your pity. I have God to comfort me. I am not too proud to come back to you the same way others have come back to the mission. I fell once, I may fall again, but I don't want your sympathy, I have a Savior. I vow I am back for good and we will reorganize the mission. I will make this right."

I'm not sure what I had expected, maybe cheers or some encouragement. Everyone remained silent as I stepped from the lectern and smiled at Eric, who got up next. As I sat beside Ada, she patted my arm. I looked behind me to see if Colbert or anyone else from the *Post* had come—no one. I saw Irwin Harrison from *The Rocky Mountain News*.

"I'm Dr. Eric Freeman from the Colorado Psychopathic Hospital," Eric began, "and I took care of Reverend Goodheart while he recovered in the hospital. You all know Reverend Goodheart as Jim, and that is how I know him as well. You see, I would not be standing before you this evening without his love and support. As a young hooligan, I found myself behind bars in the county jail, and it was Jim's kindness and care that sprung me free and landed me a job at St. Joe's. I am forever grateful for his heart to serve us all—rich or poor. I want you to understand that there is nothing unusual about backsliding among reformed inebriates, but I believe Jim's horrendous schedule, unusual mental strain, and compassion led to his collapse. I also want to reassure you that Jim is undergoing continued treatment and counseling, and I know by the grace of God and strength of his character that he will overcome."

Eric sat, and Joshua took his place at the lectern as the awkward silence continued.

"I have asked Dr. Freeman to leave his contact information. Lord knows, many of you need his services."

This brought a few chuckles from the crowd.

Joshua pulled his Bible from his jacket and read from Matthew: "'Judge not, that ye be not judged. For with what judgment ye judge, ye shall be judged, and with what measure ye mete, it shall be measured to you again. And why beholdest thou the mote that is in thy brother's eye, but considerest not the beam that is in thine own eye? Or how wilt thou say to thy brother, let me pull the mote out of thine eye, and behold, a beam is in thine own eye? Thou hypocrite, first cast out the beam from thine own eye, and then shalt thou see clearly to cast the mote out of thy brother's eye.'"

He tucked the Bible back in his pocket and stared at the crowd, almost daring them to respond. They clearly received his message. Then he continued. "It is not what a man does that counts the most in his religious life, but what he overcomes. If, as I believe, Jim is truly repentant for his recent transgressions, his greatest work may lie before him."

Joshua had said that to me many times in the last month, and I thought for a moment he would begin and end there.

But he cleared his throat and went on. "Here at the mission, there has been so much to do and so little to do it with. Jim has worked day and night. He had no regular hours and placed no limit upon his endurance. It was a terrific pace he set for himself. If anyone in Denver is inclined to doubt that statement in the least, I want them to stay and spend some time here and acquaint himself with the multitudinous duties that must be performed. Most of us don't understand the courage this man has held in fighting off the struggle of his desire for alcohol, but he never had a criminal impulse in his life. When he backslid into periodical sprees in the last two years, it was his profligate kindness that involved him in money difficulties," he continued. "There is no more benevolent or kinder-hearted man on earth. He always wants to give all he has—to anybody and everybody. If he gave freely to bootleggers and unchaste women, that is only because of his natural characteristic of benevolence. To all these folks, he always has given all the resources of the mission. There was never any question about whether they were deserving. Quite often, perhaps, they were not. But they needed help, and Jim always found some way to give it. For the first five years of the Sunshine Rescue Mission, the treasury nearly always was empty, and many debts went unpaid."

Joshua stepped from behind the lectern and paced slowly down the aisle.

"Jim, our very own prince of charity and champion of the down-and-outer, has confessed his second fall, proclaimed his repentance, and renewed with zest his labors in the relieving of poverty and the saving of souls." Joshua addressed everyone in the crowd, looking from face to face. "For more than eighteen years the moral side of his nature triumphed, and Jim was happy with the wide respect he so highly cherished. Then, in a sudden unreasoning, fateful lapse of strength, he yielded, and his old foe dragged him almost to the depths from which he had risen so spectacularly in his early mission work."

He stopped and put his hands behind his back, looking from person to person.

"Jim will prove himself once again to those who have respected and trusted him and absolve himself for his straying into the paths he renounced two decades ago. We have prayed and studied the Bible together for many, many hours. I visited Jim at the hospital where we talked and prayed," Joshua concluded. "He is sincerely repentant, and the day of his greatest usefulness to God may be just beginning."

Joshua was right. I continued to preach every night, and more men came to salvation than ever before. The crazy thing was, men were coming up and swearing that their ailments and body aches were spontaneously going away. I had heard of such things at the hands of Smith Wigglesworth, John Lake, and other faith healers, but I had never experienced or witnessed it myself. One man claimed to have a tumor on his neck, and as we were worshipping, he felt a burning there, and when he touched it, the tumor had disappeared. I had no reason not to believe him. I knew through the scriptures such things were possible. Even Jesus said we'd see marvelous and wonderful things—things that made us wonder.

Throughout the summer, and with Joshua's help, we turned the financial operations over to ten newly established board members. For my part, I'd gotten a job as a stock salesman for the American Agency and Investment Corporation, and with my salary and money Ada and I had saved, I paid off the entire six thousand dollars that the *Post* said I owed the mission.

Despite all this, it was like a hand from hell rose up and turned off the spigot of contributions. Without donors, the mission bled money. It became clear it would not survive. I contributed what I could from my own salary, but it wasn't near enough. At first, the board members were full of good intentions and energy toward public service, but by the end of the summer, their interest dwindled, until one day not one of them showed up for a scheduled meeting.

Now, two days later, I paused on Seventeenth Street, looking up at the Equitable Building that I had a hand in capping with brick thirty-seven years ago. I stood under the spot where I had dangled by a rope, pranking my brother. What a tortuous path it had all been.

I had an appointment inside the Equitable and entered through one of the three arches that led into a polished onyx lobby with a vaulted ceiling. I found the directory and saw that Mr. Schuyler, an attorney and one of our board members, was on the second floor. The elaborate stairway looked like something from a royal castle. The first set of stairs split, and each half, lined with heavy brass railings, curved up to the second floor. The landing showcased a large Tiffany stained-glass window.

I found the office, and the receptionist escorted me into a conference room where Joshua, Ada, and the attorney waited. Without saying a word, I sat down and read the papers that Mr. Schuyler had drawn up. The words were hard to read through my tears, but I knew what the legal jargon said: I signed over the properties of the Sunshine Rescue Mission to my creditors and resigned as superintendent.

THE END OF SUNSHINE

August 27, 1927

O n August 27, the headline of the *Denver Post* read:

JIM GOODHEART RESIGNS
AS THE SUPERINTENDENT
OF THE CITY'S MOST FAMOUS
GOSPEL MISSION

Signs away the Property to
Satisfy Creditors

ACT FIVE

REBIRTH

March 20, 1946
(Twenty Years Later)

Indeed, my life reads like a sad story if the narrative ended there. But thanks be to God, my life has gone on for another twenty years. Not without hardship, mind you, but the thrashing I took in the Denver newspapers is a thing of the past. Joy and peace have soothed the trouble and strife, all because of the Lord. Of course, times have changed. They say it's progress—I'm not so sure. Modern life neither cheapens the price of living nor the cost of dying, but it sure adds excess baggage.

As I turn my brand new Chevrolet truck left from Alameda Avenue into the Fairmount Cemetery, I hear a horn honk behind me. I guess I forgot to turn my blinker on. Talk about excess baggage—I still can't get used to the darn turn signal. It's such a nuisance. "If you're following me that close," I say into the rearview mirror, "the inconvenience serves you right." I complete my turn, and the impatient driver speeds down Alameda.

I'm a little later than usual for my Wednesday visit, but I'm sure I'll be forgiven. I wanted to buy flowers, and I had to drive around to three different stores until I found spring daffodils, Ada's favorite.

I wave to the man in the guardhouse.

"Hi, Jim," he calls and waves back. He knows me by name since I've visited every week for the last twenty months, sometimes twice weekly.

A guard at a cemetery always strikes me as funny. Guess they don't want anyone sneaking out. That's what I thought until I realized they actually don't want someone slinking in. Just last week the paper reported the police arrested two grave robbers for digging up remains. Made me shudder. It takes genuine desperation to make a person do that.

I drive past the guard house down the wide lane and can't help but notice the ivy-covered archway and the Old Gate Lodge in the distance, looking forlorn like ruins from ancient times. Seems a shame that's no longer the entrance. I used to love riding down the narrow lane under the arch into a secret garden through the big stone castle. I suppose the change was inevitable. Wider roads are necessary as cars get bigger and faster.

I continue slowly down the lane on past the Ivy Chapel. Its ninety-foot-high steeple soars into the blue Colorado sky like a miniature Notre Dame, adorned with gargoyles, flying buttresses, and spires. The chapel's architecture and nobility are far removed from the simple pulpits I've enjoyed throughout my life, but it's hard not to pause and appreciate the reverence it inspires. The chapel was part of the city even before we built the Sunshine Rescue Mission.

Of course, it devastated me when the Mission closed. I

didn't know if I'd survive. The government announced the Great Depression soon after Sunshine closed its doors, but I claimed the term for myself, feeling that despondent. I hurt so badly that I could only fall on my face before God…and I've never been so thankful for that. Not for hurting. Only a crazy person would relish that. What I'm grateful for is when I fell before God, my spiritual awakening began in earnest.

Back when I stayed in the hospital, Joshua Gravett, Eric Freeman, and I talked about spiritual awakening. I've thought long and hard about it. I know my spiritual awakening came out of my pain and suffering. Of course, I haven't got it all figured out. There are days I am overflowing with peace and joy and others when I am bereft of either. Some days I walk in the cool of the day with the Father and on others I'm hot with rage and even question His existence. But I'm okay that my spiritual awakening is still, well, awakening, moment by moment, day by day, year by year. Right now, I walk in freedom more days than not. I've learned to let myself be vulnerable in order to experience the liberty of being my true self. Like my beloved brook trout, I find it easier to get to that safe place in my heart where stillness dwells, far below the chaotic current of the slings and arrows of outrageous life.

There's Shakespeare again. I can't get his lines out of my mind, although I make no more attempts at playacting.

More than anything, as I awaken to my spirit and my true self, I understand when it comes to faith, hope and love that I have found the greatest of these. Jesus's teachings and examples fill me with a greater understanding of love. His love wooed me home. I believe that this is the point, after all. Love your God with your whole heart and love thy neighbor. Life is a training ground on how to love. All life's trials and challenges point the way, always asking: Are you going to respond with love or fear? I am learning to respond with love.

I drive slowly around the labyrinth of roads through the jumble of grave markers and monuments. The miniature mausoleums are so elaborate you'd expect the eternal guests are dining on champagne and caviar.

When Josephine and Donny's second child, Joann, was stillborn, Ada insisted we buy a family plot. I wasn't much interested. She said it didn't need to be as grand as the Ivy Chapel, but it should be special, clean and tidy with a bed for flowers. I said I'd prefer a rock to mark my remains.

Then, twenty months ago, we lost Josephine suddenly. She was only forty-two. I still wrestle with God over her death. The doctors didn't give us many answers either. They thought maybe her heart gave out.

Josephine's death brought Ada and me to our knees and fell harder on me than anything I'd experienced. Our beautiful Josephine. Even now it pains my chest. How I miss her smile and boisterous laugh when something tickled her funny bone, and I was often the one doing the tickling. Everyone knows how much I love my son and thank God for him daily, but just maybe, in the Lord's loving kindness, he gave me a son so I could have a daughter-in-law. She was so easy to love and so easy to spoil.

I park the truck across from the family plot under a large red oak, its many buds bursting with foliage. Last fall, the oak's leaves blazed brilliant red and gold. For everything, there is a season. Back at the turn of the century, Reinhart Schuetze designed the cemetery and planted the abundant arboretum so giant guardians could watch over the deceased in all kinds of weather.

Now, the last week of March, the oak luxuriated in the Denver sun, stretching its branches in this early spring. I'd heard on the radio that the temperate spring, which caused the city's trees to bloom prematurely, concerned the city officials, because there's always a chance of snow in April—reminding me, I better check on my beloved cherry tree when I get back home. So goes the weather in this mile-high city.

When the mission closed, Ada and I moved from Newton Street to Adams. I planted a Montmorency cherry tree first thing in the backyard. It matured enough the last few years to provide an abundance of the tart fruit for the best cherry pies and jellies in the world. I swear, cherries also help me fight off gout, and that makes it a good excuse to eat a slice of pie a day all summer long.

I see the large stone that marks our family's final resting place, with "GOODHEART" engraved in large letters across the front of the gray granite. Both Josephine's name and Ada's name were carved below in smaller letters. I never thought Ada's name would be there so soon.

I grab the bundle of daffodils, get out, and gently shut the door. Two ring-necked doves coo and court atop a tombstone behind ours. I smile. Ada would love hearing the love song of the doves. Oh, my dear Ada…how I miss you.

What a terrible Thanksgiving we had fifteen months ago. I found nothing to feel thankful for. We knew it was coming, but death is never a welcomed visitor. They had diagnosed Ada with breast cancer. Looking back, I'm not surprised that she died only five months later, with the stress of Josephine's passing. For both Ada and me, the bone jarring pain of losing Josephine so suddenly and seeing Donny so distraught broke our hearts. We couldn't do anything to take the pain away.

I'd always thought my name would be on a gravestone before anyone in my family. Now only Donny, me, and his two girls, Shirley and Virginia, ages twenty-four and fourteen, remain. Unfortunately, between his longtime job at Mountain Bell and being a single parent, I don't see him much.

Maybe I should call him soon.

Loneliness. That is the real scourge of old age—not declining health or failing mind. I've got no fear of death. Thank you, Jesus. But loneliness, that's a cancer…something to be afraid of. More painful than the worst gangrenous sore.

I step to our plot. "Hello, my dear ones," I say and pull last week's flowers from the vase and replace them with the daffodils. I can almost hear the golden trumpets singing praises to the sun as I arrange them in the vase. "They're the first daffodils of the season," I say to Ada.

Ada used to rush into the house each year, announcing the arrival of the first flowers in our garden. Her excited voice was hope renewed after a long Colorado winter.

"Hello, Josephine," I say. "Your daughters are becoming almost as beautiful as their mother."

Our gravestone stands on a cement slab large enough to sit on the lip, which I do, resting my back on the granite. I close my eyes and turn my face to the sun, letting the radiant heat warm my body and soul. Spring had become my favorite time of year, with the crispness of the air still blowing off the snowfields of the Rockies and at the same time, the sun comforting my weary winter heart. I hear birds flitting and chirping, having returned from their journey south, and I inhale the scent of budding trees filling the air with sweetness.

"Thank the Lord Chappy's son has returned home from the war," I say to Ada. "He wrote me a letter."

I open my eyes, reach into my inside front pocket, and pull out the letter I received yesterday. I unfold it, and read:

"Dear Reverend Goodheart,
It is with such joy to inform you I have returned
home, but it is with extreme sadness that I received
your news of the loss of Mrs. Goodheart. Both my
mother and I are distraught and share in your sorrow.

You and Mrs. Goodheart have meant the world to us through the years. I apologize I could not extend my condolences until now."

"See, it's not just me who's missing you," I tell Ada. I let my hands and the letter fall into my lap and close my eyes.

Chappy, Jr., a true junior, prefers to go by his initials, RD, but doesn't seem to mind that I called him by his father's nickname. After all, he's the spitting image of his dad, although without the bushy mustache.

Julia didn't enjoy a close relationship with her parents, so Ada and I always felt we served as adopted ones. She never remarried. She told us there was no way she could ever replace Chappy, so she didn't even try.

One of the best days of my life was when we got to travel to Seattle for Chappy, Jr.'s eighteenth birthday, and I presented him with his father's flask. I think I cried all the way to Seattle and back. The boy had struggled with the loss of his dad and the lack of his guidance through a youthful rebellion. But when I told him the many stories about his father and then handed him the flask, it was as though I had passed Excalibur to the young man. Shortly after, he joined the military and became a pilot like his father and fought his own war. But unlike Chappy, he returned safely from Europe. "Thank God!"

I bring Chappy Jr.'s letter up and read:

"My mother is well and sends her love. She is, of course, relieved that I have returned from the war. Due to secrecy, I have been unable, until now, to share my part in the effort against Hitler. I flew the new P-51 Mustang fighter. I know you would be interested because of your own experience. But man, you should

see this aircraft. It is a one-seater, but it is as fast and
mobile as anything we got, except the Spitfire, and it
has a much longer range. They had us fly escort for
the bombers, but unlike what you experienced, we
flew miles ahead, clearing the way for our bombers to
strike the heart of the German empire. I'm sure Dad
never imagined that we'd have speeds over four
hundred miles an hour."

I put the letter down. I swear I can still smell the oil and
the sweat of the courageous men of the 96th, but I can't
imagine their planes flying three times faster. Losing those
brave men still brings me pain and I have to wipe my eyes
before I can read again:

"I have two bits of good news to share with you. The
first thing I did on my arrival home was to ask my girl
to marry me. I can't wait for you to meet her. Our
wedding is in July, and I will send you an invitation. I
hope you can come!

The other good news is they have promoted me to
major, and they have asked me to work on a particular
project for a new type of aircraft they are calling a jet.
(I wish I could tell you more.) All I can say is it's like
strapping a rocket to your shorts."

I smile. Chappy would be so proud. Church people
always say the departed are looking down from heaven. In this
case, I genuinely hope that's true. Chappy would enjoy seeing
his chip off the old block. "There's a little more," I tell Ada
and read:

"Reverend Goodheart, I'm not much for words, but I can't tell you how much the faith that you helped instill in me served me through the war. I could hold a weekly Bible study with the men in my squadron as we confronted the dangers. It helped us find strength in the face of our adversary. I find my words fall short to express my gratitude.

With much love and respect, RD (Chappy, Jr.)
Major R.D. Chapman"

On some of my darkest days, I swear my life is a failure, but when I get kisses like this from God, I think maybe I made a difference. People often ask me if their good works can balance out the sin in their lives. But I tell them it must be grace alone. On bad days, it's hard for me to understand God's grace, for if we base our salvation on our own merits, no one qualifies. It had been the hardest and longest lesson for me to learn: there is no way for me to reconcile the bad I'd done in my life with good deeds. Jesus had already paid the price. The only way I know how to survive this life is in believing Jesus and what He did for us on the cross. To trust anything else cheapens His sacrifice for us all.

"Wish I saw what you both are experiencing," I say to Ada and Josephine. We buried Ada with her prayer card in her hands. I know that she still intercedes for me now that she is face-to-face with God.

"I hope she's not nagging you too much." I smile, feeling Ada's elbow from the grave.

I push myself off the tombstone, turn, and pat the top of the granite. "Love you both."

"A man has to spend part of his life in a pickup truck." That's what Mac said at the airbase when he and Chappy picked me up, and I drove the army truck, then flew back to the base with Chappy.

I'd always told Ada the same thing, but she'd just scoff at me. But today I knew it was true. I breathe in and out, happy as can be. There is nothing like cruising the streets in a brand-new pickup truck on a March day in the mile-high city of Denver. Bluebirds sing and sunshine warms your bones. The crisp mountain air blows through open windows to refresh your spirit.

"Ada, you're missing a beautiful day. You probably wouldn't admit it, but you'd love riding in this Chevy. I know, I know. You wanted me to buy a conservative sedan, like the one we always had, but I think you're smiling with me right now."

I'd bugged her forever for a truck. Three years ago, she relented and let me put in for the lottery. I'm sure she thought I'd never see the light of day in one.

Years later, with World War II only six months from settled, the military still limited how many trucks civilians could purchase, so it surprised me as anything when the dealer called and said, "You're a lucky man, Jim Goodheart."

I told him luck had no bearing on it. I said, "The good Lord is a kind and gracious Father, and if he sees fit for these ol' bones to sit in a new Chevrolet truck, then no man could stand in the way."

We chuckled over that one.

But I knew it as truth. I just wish Ada had been here to see me pull up to the house in this fine two-toned truck. The body painted mint-blue with darker fenders, sported running boards and enough chrome on the grill to blind a righteous man, plus the whitest white walls you'd ever seen. I can see her shaking her head and saying, "Oh, James, you old fool, now why in heaven did you go and do that?"

I feel her beside me.

"I know what you're thinking," I tell her. "You're thinking I look plenty smart in my new truck."

I hear her huff and smile. I reach down and click on the radio. "Imagine, a radio in a car." The wooden knob turns easily, and I glance down to find my favorite station, KLZ. A snappy tune replaces the white noise as I adjust the dial to the 560 wavelength.

I veer off Alameda onto First Avenue, which becomes Speer Boulevard. We have so many parks and trees in Denver, thanks to the good-humored Mayor Speer.

Memories of being welcomed home from the war when I became so overwhelmed seemed like smoke from a distant fire.

Maybe it's because I just came from Fairmount, but nostalgia overtakes me. I remember so many old friends who poured their souls into the fabric of the city. Like Mayor Speer, who truly believed in me and the work that Ada and I did. I miss my visits to the hospitals, jails, and flophouses, but I sure don't miss the long hours.

Even after the mission closed, I stayed active in the moral oversight of Denver, helping wherever I could. For ten years, I preached at a small Baptist Church in the western part of the city. We had only seventy-five dollars a month in tithes, and my salary amounted to five dollars a week, but I loved preaching in the simple setting. I certainly didn't do it for the money.

I turn off Speer onto Larimer. The radio plays a snappy song, and my left foot taps the beat with the guitar and piano. "Lordy me, this cad can play." Even my hips want to sway to the rhythm. "Get your kicks on Route 66," the singer repeats the refrain.

"Now that sounds like a fine idea...a trip to California." What a perfect vehicle to do it in. My fingers drum the rhythm and beat on the gray steering wheel.

I shift down to stop for some young men in uniform crossing the street. Even though the soldiers lug heavy duffle bags, there's a skip to their steps, pushing and shoving each other with camaraderie.

I hadn't yet heard my truck's horn, and when I press on it, the sharp blast surprises me and the soldiers. I lean out the window and yell. "Hey, boys, welcome home! Where did you serve?"

The boys turn, smile, and one yells back, "France, sir."

"*Vive la France,*" I yell back and wave.

I watch the boys hop to the curb, and I honk again. Bet they're headed to Gahan's for a drink and a chance to get lucky.

It's been a long time since I've been to Gahan's. Forty years ago, Mary, with that flaming red hair, blue eyes, and contagious smile, waltzed into my life and gave me a slice of kindness that bumped my life's trajectory.

Talk about a redeemed life. When Mary trained to be a nurse, she caught the eye of a physician, and they wed and have two sons. She works the cancer ward at the hospital in California, still serving up her kindheartedness.

Strange. That day I met Mary and ended up at the Living Waters Mission seems like yesterday and a million years off, all at the same time.

The wail of a siren rattles my thoughts, and I turn down the radio. In the rearview mirror, I see Denver's Engine Two roaring up behind me, so I veer to the curb to get out of its way. Number Two's single red dome light flashes, and the chrome siren blares. I'd seen the truck before and knew it was a Chevy, but twice as big as mine, with large dually tires on the back, ladders hanging on each side, and a spool of red hose wound with military precision in the bed.

I expected the firetruck full of brave men to whiz past, but as I pull to the curb, the truck slows beside me, and the four men inside and the two hanging from the back lean in for a look at my new pickup. The driver tips his hat, and two others give me a thumbs-up.

I straighten my spine with pride. Like Mac said, a man and his truck.

I wave back to the men. Feeling brave, I gun the motor to follow the firetruck. Maybe I can help. Doesn't every man want to be counted among the brave? The few who will risk life and limb for others and rush in when others shrink back are the real supermen.

The firetruck squeals onto Seventeenth toward Union Station, and I turn as well. But as they speed off, I realize my valiant effort is misdirected and ease off the gas. I pull my pocket watch from my vest and see that it's noon, time for lunch and the twelve o'clock ear-beating at the mission.

Suddenly time doesn't matter, and I slam on the brakes to keep from hitting a man and young woman charging out of the Oxford Hotel into the street. The man tries to grab her arm, but she pulls away, folds her arms tight over her stomach, and turns her back to him. I want to hope it's a lover's quarrel, but I can see it's a business proposition gone wrong. The man wears bright blue slacks and a gaudy plaid sports jacket. He has no tie, his shirt is unbuttoned, and his shoes are blue wingtips that match his pants. I whistle through my teeth and wonder how much the shoes set him back. He's probably a pimp or something else illegal. After all, it isn't unusual for the Oxford. The hotel has seen better days. They rumored that if it didn't clean up its act, it would soon be a flophouse.

The man with the blue wingtips yells so loud that everyone on the street turns to look. He tries again to grab the woman's arm, and she pushes him away with both hands. I'm pretty sure he's a pimp, and I'm afraid he's going to slug her. I stop the truck, open the door, and start to speak when the hotel doorman rushes to the couple. The pimp sees him coming, turns in a huff, and he and his wingtips trot away.

I close the door, reach for the gear shift knob, and put my hand on the steering wheel when the woman turns to the truck and smiles. Pretty little thing. I feel Ada punching my arm and saying, "She's not smiling at you, Jim! For Lord's sake, you seventy-four-year-old fool." I know, dearest. I know she's smiling at the shiny new truck and the possibility of making a buck.

I stab at the pain in my heart with my fingertips. No, it isn't the Oxford's demise that's making me sad. It's the loneliness. John and Luke are both gone. Mother and Father are long dead. And Ada…I can hardly bear the loneliness. I glance at the passenger seat and wish she was there.

The young woman is making her way to my window. She leans in. "Hi, darlin'." She smiles and winks. "Looks like you could use some TLC."

I think of Pixie, a long time ago. How things change and stay the same.

I push back my sadness to reply, "God bless you, my child, for making an old man's day, but I'm a man of the cloth."

Her smile disappears, and she looks as if she might be sick on my new vinyl.

"I'm sorry," she says and steps away from the truck.

Before she gets out of earshot, I lean out the window. "You know child, Jesus loves you."

But that only speeds her exit, and I watch her reenter the Oxford.

I put my truck in gear, turn right on Wynkoop, and then again on Nineteenth. For twenty years, I have avoided driving by the mission. It was just too painful. But today is the day. I turn onto Larimer Street and pull to the curb in front of where the Sunshine Rescue Mission used to be and where Ada and I had poured out our lives.

After the mission closed, I not only ministered in the Boulevard Baptist Church, I went back to full-time work as an advertising executive, making good money. Selling was what I did well. From the dash, I grab one of my few remaining souvenirs from that time—a wooden Sunshine token that says: "Sunshine Rescue Mission will help you." The address is on the back. I flip the token over and over.

No one required it of me, but leaving the mission in such debt haunted me, and I became determined to pay it off. It took me ten years to settle the entire debt of the mission— $38,000. Even the *Post* wrote a nice article. Two years later and two doors down from the original, Reverend Gravett used the money to purchase space and the Denver Rescue Mission returned to Larimer Street.

Looking around, I see Larimer has changed little since the days when I sat at the door inviting the drunks, destitute and woebegone to join us for a meal. I remember their stories and hardships, and I'm sure the new mission fills with similar people and similar stories.

I think about killing the engine and going in, but it's still too painful. "God bless the people who continue the good works."

I'd heard that Colbert died the year after he pounded the

nails into the coffin of the mission and my reputation. Probably the hardest thing I had to do was to let go of the anger I held for him. I'd underlined a verse in Isaiah so many times it was hardly readable anymore: "For the Lord of hosts hath purposed, and who shall disannul it? And his hand is stretched out, and who shall turn it back?"

The Lord is responsible for my destiny, not any man, but betrayal seems to be a stronghold of strongholds that lays down a pit so deep with bitterness and unforgiveness that it could hold the entire world. For the first few years, my thoughts and prayers went like this: "I forgive you...grumble, grumble, grumble. I forgive...grouse, grouse, grouse." Again and again and again. So many years went by until finally I could say: "I forgive you."

I can't say I ever felt any remorse for his passing, but I came to where I could pray for God's mercy and grace over him. It pained me to sincerely ask God to bless a man like Colbert. I could do it only when Jesus's command became real to me: "I say unto you, love your enemies, bless them that curse you, do good to them that hate you, and pray for them which despitefully use you, and persecute you."

Ada and I never heard from Ella Pettit again. We heard rumors that she'd left Denver shortly after my crucifixion in the *Post*. I always wished I could've seen her and apologized to her. I knew what happened was not her fault, and that I had a hand in her misdirection. "God bless you, my child."

Joseph was right. Love is the salve, forgiveness is the key. Not that I do it correctly every day, but it probably started at my vital spiritual experience. Only then could I stop drinking the daily poison of bitterness, hatred, and fear.

Speaking of drinking, I wish I could tell you I have fought that battle perfectly as well. Occasionally, I take a drink or two as a prescription for my nervous condition and physical health, even though Dr. Freeman, who remains a good friend, wishes I would never drink.

Eric has become involved in a new movement called Alcoholics Anonymous. One of his patients, Bill W., who, along with Bob Smith, a colorectal surgeon from Akron, Ohio, expanded the Oxford Group's steps to twelve and encouraged alcoholics to meet regularly. I couldn't agree more with the Twelfth Step: "Having had a spiritual awakening as the result of these steps, we try to carry this message to alcoholics, and to practice these principles in all our affairs." For the recovering alcoholic, they describe two essential moments for lasting sobriety, a long-term spiritual awakening that happens over your lifetime and a vital spiritual experience that happens in a moment of time.

I hear hymns wafting through the air from within the mission. The old ego tugs on my mental strings, telling me I should be in there. But I know the mission is not me...the Lord has made that abundantly clear. Yes, service to others is the heart of Christ. But the most potent lesson of my last twenty years has been that the mission is not my identity. If we—mankind—misplace our identity in other people, places, or even ministries, we can be toppled. Our identity has to be in the One who made us. That is the true journey of life— discovering our true identity in the Lord. But what a difficult journey it is!

I probe my chest with my fingertips. This trip down memory lane has probably been as much as my heart can bear. I shift the truck into gear and head home.

When I step inside, I toss the keys to the Chevy on the entryway table next to the phone and decide to call Donny. I dial the number and the sweet youthful voice of my grand-daughter, Virginia Mae, answers.

"Hi, Virginia. It's Grandpa Goodheart. Is your father home?"

"Hi, Grandpa. No, he went to visit Shirley. Can I take a message?"

"No, just calling to say hi. Have him call me when he gets a chance. How is high school?"

"Oh, you know, same ol' same ol'," she says, chewing bubblegum.

"You meet any nice young men?"

"Oh, Grandpa, you know I go to an all-girls school."

I can tell she is blushing. "Well someday, I pray you find the perfect boy."

I hear her blow and pop a large bubble.

"So, Virginia, who's your Savior?"

"Oh, Grandpa. You ask me that every time we talk."

"Yes…because it's important to me."

There is a long pause before she responds. "Jesus," she says, but not very convincingly.

I smile. At fourteen, such talk was the furthest from my mind as well. But as parents and grandparents, we wish we could save our kids from all the lumps and bumps of life. We want them to know God is looking out for them. Knowing then what I know now would have saved me a lot of heartache, but I also know that this discovery is one treasure hidden by God for us to find for ourselves. It is critical to find it…because when you understand who Jesus is…you have everything.

"I love you, Virginia, and so does God. Please ask your father to call me when he gets a chance."

I hang up the phone and fold my arms, thinking of

Virginia and how very special she has been right from the beginning.

Dr. Freeman and his friends at AA talk about a *vital* spiritual experience. They say that for every man and woman, it happens differently. I remember mine clearly. It started three days after Christmas in 1932. The mission had been closed for five years. Donny and Josephine had settled into their lives and were wonderful parents to Shirley, who recently turned ten—full of energy and cute as a button, and Josephine was due with Virginia.

But on that day, I'd sunk to one of my lowest points—and that's saying something, considering all the trials my life had seen me through. I knelt alone at the Boulevard Baptist Church and prayed. They had stripped the gilding of the holidays—the wreaths and the tree were gone, and the festive flags and flowers taken away. But, maybe by accident or divine design, a wooden nativity remained on the side table near where I knelt. I gazed at each carved figure—Mary, Joseph, the Wise Men, the angels—who all looked adoringly at the Christ child. I'd seen the crèche many times, but that day it hit me in a different way. This God-Child was so remarkable and mysterious. As I prayed, a verse from Saint John came to mind: "Verily, verily, I say unto you, except a corn of wheat fall into the ground and die, it abideth alone: but if it dies, it bringeth forth much fruit. He that loveth his life shall lose it; and he that hateth his life in this world shall keep it unto life eternal. If any man serves me, let him follow me; and where I am, there shall also my servant be: if any man serves me, him will my Father honour."

A month later, with Christmas long past, Virginia was born. After Donny and Josephine brought her home, we all stood and admired this little one—full of innocence, full of life, every finger and toe perfect. It was nothing, and it was everything. The first time I held her is when I experienced my vital spiritual experience. No bright flash of light or a thundering voice from heaven. It was way more subtle, like a quiet whisper as I held the baby.

And just like when we look at the baby Christ, I could see all the promises of heaven and earth fulfilled in this beautiful little baby. It was like God said to me: Here is life. Here is *your* life: Christ in the baby, the baby in Christ—Christ in you, you in Christ. As Virginia looked at me, I saw a glimpse of heaven, and I prayed, "I will praise Thee for we are fearfully and wonderfully made. Marvelous are Thy works, that is what my soul knoweth right well."

A child pointing the way to the Father. Imagine that!

I knew in that vital instant I had lost my life to find it. All my life, I believed there was more, but seeing the divine in the baby, I realized I had everything in the beginning. But I lost it. Little by little, I became disconnected from the divine. That was my sin, and I'd spent all my life trying to reconnect. Through my failures and mistakes, I came back to Him. My true self was always there. I just had to find it. I understood at that very moment that the dwelling place of God was in our hearts at the very beginning—woven into our very DNA.

My vital experience erased years of bitterness and resentment. My eyes opened to my long-buried identity. Jesus had seen me through the trials and tribulations of life, and finally, I had come home.

"Dear Virginia," I smile at the memory and let out a long sigh.

I glance at the wall clock. It's past noon. I'm hungry and decide to make some lunch. But first, I need to check my cherry tree in the backyard. I push open the screen door and walk to the corner where my tree is in full, brilliant bloom. The sweet fragrance matched its beautiful blossoms. Soon the flowers will turn to fruit. Winter into spring, spring into summer; death unto life, suffering into hope. It's the ultimate metaphor for my life. "But the fruit of the Spirit is love, joy, peace, long-suffering, gentleness, goodness, faith, meekness, temperance: against such, there is no law." Jesus showed us the Way.

"Thank you, Lord, for opening the eyes of my heart to see the love and life all around me." I lift my arms in worship, bumping the tree branches, so a shower of cherry blossoms drifts over me.

As the beautiful blossoms fill my senses, pain stabs my chest. I cringe. I can't feel my heart beat. I wonder if I'm dying. I slide to the ground under my beloved cherry tree. I can't breathe. I know I'm dying.

The final curtain falls.

The rest is silence.

Strange…to be mindful of my own death. I am aware of my body, but it is as if my mind watches it slip into death. I lay under my beloved tree but observe the scene at the same moment.

My mind and my body contract and expand like they had become my breath.

Yahweh.

Jesus extends his hand. He helps me off the ground and covers my eyes with His hands. As He takes His hands from my eyes, He asks if I can see.

"I see silhouettes of people walking toward me."

He touches my eyes again and I then recognize the people.

I nod slowly. I'm surrounded by a huge orchard full of cherry trees blooming in brilliant shades of pink. I smell their fragrant nectar. They are all there—Ada, Joseph, Chappy... my father and mother...my brothers...Josephine.

I run to them, and we embrace.

Then thousands of people gather around us. The Lord says to me, "My son, these are the people whom you have helped. There will be many more."

I hear the angels and archangels worshipping and feel His hand on my shoulder. His love radiates through me.

"Well done, good and faithful servant.

Welcome home."

Faithfully Yours

Jim Goodheart

PHOTOGRAPHS ACTS ONE-THREE

Please visit https://www.authortimothybrowne.com/books/larimer-street/ for more photographs and historical documents.

ACT ONE

Goodheart Reunion- 1891

Ada Loar (Goodheart) - Age 16 (1889)

Jim (center) and his brother's Luke and John - 1888

QUIETLY MARRIED.

Mr. James Goodheart and Miss Ada Loar Wedded by Rev. Gilliland.

—Mr. James Goodheart, son of Mr. James Goodheart, one of the old citizens of Bloomington, and Miss Ada Loar, second daughter of Dr. and Mrs. N. Loar, of West Front street, were married yesterday at noon by Rev. Gilliland in the parlors of the Christian church. A few intimate friends of the couple were present, and to most of their acquaintances this announcement will be a surprise. On the Limited Mr. and Mrs. Goodheart left for Chicago, where they will visit for several days, and on returning will commence housekeeping at 701 West Washington street. Mr. Goodheart is engaged with the Ela Baking Powder Company and is a highly respected young man.

Jim and Ada's wedding announcement July 29, 1893

Ada and Donny - 1900

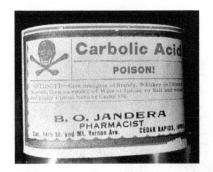

Denver - early 1900s

Line of men waiting for a meal at the Mission

ACT TWO

Loar Family- Donny in front of Ada - 1908

Jim Goodheart

Denver Labor Day Parade September 6, 1909

Jim, Ada, and Donny

Little girl entering Sunshine Rescue Mission.

Sunshine Rescue Mission Logo

Donald Everett Goodheart - 1917

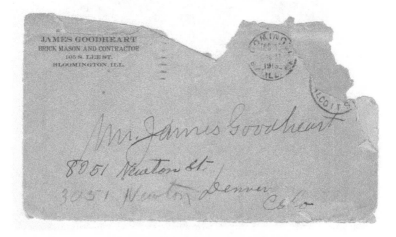

One of the many letters from Jim's father.

Dear Jim after a nights
sleep and awaking to surroundings
I am saying this it is an impossibility
for me to indicate what you should
do one thing is sure the Church
preachers and their advisers have it in
their hands to side track any mission
on the side as is the Sunshine mission
when they will and mayhap their will is
governed by the money demanded and
the supply at hand and these automobile times when Theatres and riding
costs so much causes a great pullback
on the laymens liberality which
if a shrinking of preachers salary
their is crinkling takes place in the preacher
and so you see you are between the upper
an neather mill stone now the rub
comes in how to keep sweet and
beat the blue devil back if you sour

Letter to Jim from his father

WW I poster - The First Three

Jim, Ada, and Donny outside the Sunshine Rescue Mission

ACT THREE

Jim Goodheart Now Is on His Way to France

JIM GOODHEART.

Jim Goodheart of Sunshine mission, who now is on the Atlantic on his way to France as the Rotary club's chaplain to the United States forces abroad, had his photograph taken the day he left Denver, clad in his new uniform. The photograph herewith is the first printed of Jim as he appears in his regimentals.

Jim Goodheart - 1918

USS Pocahontas

*Men and Bréguet 14 B2 bomber of the 96th Aerial
Bombardment Squadron - American Expeditionary Force -
Amanty Airdrome on Saint-Dizier field - Toul, France*

Jim Goodheart - Toul France 1918

Refueling Bréguet 14 B2 bomber

Clapp and Dunn's wreckage

Ada Goodheart

Field Hospital

Bréguet 14 B2 bomber of the 96th Aerial Bombardment Squadron

Men of the 96th Aerial Bombardment Squadron - American Expeditionary Force - Amanty Airdrome on Saint-Dizier field - Toul, France

Letter of Commendation to Jim Goodheart from the 96th Aerial Bombardment Squadron

Jim and Ada's catch

Coal Creek Cabin

One of MANY of Ada's prayer cards!

Sunshine Rescue Mission

Josephine and Shirley - 1922

Donald, Josephine, and Shirley - 1922

Orchestra Selection—Southern Melodies
.................................Sunshine Symphony Orchestra

Cornet Solo—....................................Gospel Hymns
John Leick

Quartette Selection—
If Christ Should Come..................................Meredith
Sunshine Mixed Quartette

Orchestra Selection—
Lamb of God...Bizet
Sunshine Symphony Orchestra

Tenor Solo—
We Shall Shine As The Stars.........Van DeVenter
Charles M. Howell

Sermon..Jim Goodheart

Orchestra Selections—
a. Chocolate Soldier Selection
b. When You And I Were Young Maggie
....Butterfield
c. Venetian Love Song............................Nevin

Quartette Selection—
I Love Him..Foster
Sunshine Mixed Quartette

Orchestra Selections—
a. Flute and Clarinet—The Merry Lark
....Theo. Bendix
b. Violin Solo—Meditation From Thais
....J. Massenett
Ed. Wurtzbach
Sunshine Symphony Orchestra

Quartette Number—
Old Rugged Cross....Sunshine Mixed Quartette

Orchestra Selection—
Cinderella's Bridal Procession.........S. Dicker
Sunshine Symphony Orchestra

Nov. 21, 1926   K L Z 7 P. M. to 10 P. M.
SUNDAY EVENING SERVICE
Service by Remote Control from the
SUNSHINE RESCUE MISSION
DENVER
Under direction of
JIM GOODHEART
(Please notice change of hour)

————

Orchestra Selection—
a. March of The Mannikins.................Onias
b. Face to Face........................Herbert Johnson
c. Intermezzo—La Rosita.................DuPont
Sunshine Symphony Orchestra
Ed. Wurtzbach, Director

Quartette Selection—
Beautiful Valley of Eden.................Sherwin
Sunshine Mixed Quartette

Orchestra Selections—
a. Mighty Lak' a Rose...............................Nevin
b. Gospel Hymns.......................Arrangement
c. The Love Dance...................Karl Hoschna
Sunshine Symphony Orchestra

Cello Solo—Cantilena.................G. Goltermann

Orchestra Selections—
Somewhere A Voice Is Calling.................Tate
Sunshine Orchestra

Congregaitonal Singing.

Prayer.

RADIOGRAMS
THE LITTLE HOUSE WHERE GOD HAS DONE SO MUCH

HE · HAD · EVERYTHING · BUT · GOD

HIS SUCCESS was something everyone admired and which not a few envied. His castle in Spain became a glorious edifice in the realm of actuality and his ship came in like the galleon of old, loaded with riches. He had everything and he had nothing! For ever in his quest of riches he felt SELF-SUFFICIENT and the man who feels that way writes with a trembling hand a sorrowful "finis" at the close of the last chapter of his activities. For no man attains happiness without God.

All man-made pathways lead to one terminal—DARKNESS! "Then spake Jesus again unto them, saying, I am the light of the world; HE THAT FOLLOWETH ME SHALL NOT WALK IN DARKNESS—BUT SHALL HAVE THE LIGHT OF LIFE."—John viii, 12. "Abide in me and I in you. As the branch cannot bear fruit of itself, except it abide in the vine; no more can ye, except ye abide in me."—John xv, 4.
It is expected of us that we attain success, but strictly along the path of righteousness, and he who believes in Christ, and through Him attains success, "WALKS WITH GOD!" "And so he that had received five talents came and brought other five talents, saying, Lord, thou delivereth unto me five talents; behold, I have gained beside them five talents more. His Lord said unto him, Well done, thou good and faithful servant: thou hast been faithful over a few things, I will make thee ruler over many things: enter thou into the joy of thy Lord."—Matt. xxv, 20-33.

Sincerely,

JIM GOODHEART.

Sunshine Rescue Mission Program

The Paid Circulation of THE DENVER POST Yesterday Was 173,52

2c by Newsboys—5c on Trains

Sunday paid circulation of The Denver Post
100,000 greater than total paid circulation of
all fourteen other Sunday papers printed in
Denver and Colorado, Wyoming and New
Mexico combined.

THE
DENVER POS

Daily   The Denver Post 8
172,592 Paid Circulation 2½
         for February
Denver's Population, 1927, Over

HOME
EDITION

THE BEST NEWSPAPER IN THE U. S. A.

DENVER, COLO., FRIDAY, MARCH 4, 1927

40 PAG

DRUNKEN ORGIES
CHARGED TO
GOODHEART

INVESTIGATORS FIND
TRAIL OF WINE, GIRLS
AND WILD SPENDING

Denver Post - March 4, 1927

PHOTOGRAPHS ACT FIVE

Jim holding Virginia - 1932

Shirley and Virginia Mae Goodheart - 1933

Jim and Ada Goodheart

REFERENCES

1. Vallier, Myron. Historic Photos of Denver. Turner Publishing. 2007

2. Graves, Albert. A History of the Transport Service. George H. Doran Company. 1921

3. Dorsett, Lyle. The Queen City - A History of Denver. Pruett Publishing Company. 1977

4. Goodstein, Phil. The Seamy Side of Denver. New Social Publications. 1993

5. Olsen, Margaret Hook. Patriarch of the Rockies. - The life story of Joshua Gravett. Golden Bell Press. 1960

6. Joseph, Frank. Last of the Red Devils - America's First Bomber Pilot. Galde Press, Inc. 2014

7. Stone, Wilbur Fiske. History of Colorado; Vol. 4. The S.J. Clarke Publishing Co. 1919

8. Barnhouse, Mark A. Denver's Sixteenth Street - Images of America. Arcadia Publishing. 2010

9. Bretz, James. Denver's Early Architecture - Images of America. Arcadia Publishing. 2010

10. Dorsett, Lyle. Denver Rescue Mission - A Brief History. 1983

11. Second Bombardment Association. Defenders of Liberty. 2nd Bombardment Group/Wing 1918-1993. Turner Publishing Co. 1996

12. Rohr, Richard. Breathing Under Water - Spirituality and the Twelve Steps. Franciscan Media. 2011

13. Noel, Thomas. Denver's Larimer Street - Main Street, Skid Row and Urban Renaissance. Historic Denver, Inc. 1981

14. The Reverend James Goodheart files, photographs, and sermons in possession of Virginia Goodheart Browne and Donald Preston Goodheart

15. Files of Denver Post and Rocky Mountain News. The Denver Library.

CALL TO ACTION

I can't tell you how much it means to me to hear from my readers. The best way to do this is to sign up on my website: AuthorTimothyBrowne.com (I promise not to bombard you with tons of newsletters or communications!)

As a thank you, I would like to give you a free eBook copy of *Maya Hope*. Just click the button that says, START MAYA HOPE NOW to get your free copy and to sign up. I look forward in connecting with you!

Also, I hope you enjoyed reading *Larimer Street*. I would so appreciate it if you would leave a review on Amazon, Barnes & Noble, Goodreads, and BookBub. You can simply copy and paste your review into each one. These reviews are so very important to my career as a full-time writer. Your honest reviews truly make a difference and so easy to do. Just go to the respective website:
Amazon: Amazon.com/review/create-review?& asin=B09JQBS2S2
Barnes & Noble: https://www.barnesandnoble.com/s/ Timothy%20Browne
Goodreads: https://www.goodreads.com/author/show/ 15623925.Timothy_Browne
BookBub: https://www.bookbub.com/authors/timothy-browne

Thank you!

AUTHOR'S NOTE

All through my life, I grew up with stories of my great-grand-father, Jim Goodheart. I have scrapbooks full of pictures, letters from Jim's father and other family members, and reams of newspaper clippings—lots of facts and figures—even a master's thesis written about Jim. Through the writing of *Larimer Street*, I began knowing him as great-grandfather Goodheart, then Reverend Goodheart, then Jim Goodheart, and then finally just Jim, as he wanted everyone to know him. Jim was beloved. There were volumes written on his life as the Superintendent of the Sunshine Rescue Mission but indeed, there were many gaps.

What has been missing in Jim's story is the why. Why is it that we do what we do, both good and bad? I've thought about this for my own life. You can read my CV and about me on the internet or other sources, but few know my heart. One might ask, why did a successful orthopedic surgeon sell everything and become a medical missionary?

In that same light, I dived into Jim and Ada's lives looking into the mystery—the why. I knew of all of their fantastic work and ministry, but why did Jim succumb to alcohol after he had been sober for so many years? And maybe, most importantly, after all that he went through, how did he finish so well? How did he find peace and joy that seems all too often to elude all of us?

As you read *Larimer Street*, know that Jim and Ada (my great-grandparents), Donald and Josephine (my grandparents), Virginia and Shirley (my mom and aunt) and Joshua Gravett are all real people. The men of the 96th are likewise as real and courageous as I've written. But, because of gaps in the story, many other characters are fictitious, including Mary, Joseph, Chappy, and others. The real people that come and go through Jim's story helped shaped these characters in the book.

Also, I want to honor the memory of the amazing young men of the 96th, many of whom sacrificed their lives. When I got to France with Jim, I was moved to tears at the bravery and sacrifice of the men who fought in WWI. I used the character of Chappy to represent these courageous men. Many of the other men are true-to-life. Brown, Clapp, Dunn, and others are men who gave it all for our freedom—may they be honored as we remember them.

Jim was a kind man, generous to a fault. One of the things I have pondered almost daily about Jim's life is how he finished so well. He went through hell and back. How, in the final analysis, did he find peace and joy? He found it, I found it, where it has always been: in turning to the One who made us.

I love these words of Richard Rohr: "The real authority that changes the world is an inner authority that comes from people who have lost, let go, and are re-found on a new level. These are the people who can heal, reconcile, understand, and change others. The pattern for this new kind of authority was taught by Jesus when he said, 'Simon, you must be sifted like wheat, and I will pray that you will not fail; and once you have *recovered*, you, in turn, can strengthen the brothers [and sisters]' (Luke 22:31-32, italics mine). This sifting and then recovering is Peter's real and life-changing authority, as it is for anyone. It is interesting to me that Twelve-Step programs have come to be called the 'Recovery' movement. They are onto something!"

The twelfth step is about spiritual awakening, and this is my greatest prayer for my children, their children and generations that follow and for you who read *Larimer Street*, that *all* may have a spiritual awakening and be touched in your innermost being by the Divine. That you understand, like Saint John, that Jesus is the mediator who stands between the Divine and our human existence and holds the two halves together.

DENVER RESCUE MISSION

I humbly ask that you consider a generous gift to the wonderful people of the Denver Rescue Mission who carry on the work of people like Jim Goodheart and Reverend Joshua Gravett.

May God bless them all!

https://denverrescuemission.org

ALSO BY TIMOTHY BROWNE

Available Now:

THE BOOK OF ANDY

In this modern-day Book of Job, Andy sits at the bottom of life's pecking order. Working as a honey-dipper (a septic truck driver) and living in a single-wide trailer in small-town Montana, Andy longs for love and a better life. His only solace is found on the wild side of the river amongst the ponderosa and bull trout. But when Andy is granted all that he desires, the peace he once found in his simple existence, and the serenity of dipping a dry fly into the Blackfoot River evaporates. A family secret that seems like a cruel betrayal emerges as a great blessing in disguise. The *Book of Andy* is for everyone who feels that life has beat them down…for anyone who prays for a breakthrough. Fans of *Walter Mitty, A River Runs Through It,* and *Forrest Gump* will enjoy this humorous family saga of finding faith, love, and contentment.

AMAZON: https://amzn.to/3vUJJ3g

THE DR. NICKLAUS HART SERIES

MAYA HOPE

A doctor stumbling through life. A North Korean bio- terrorist plot. The two collide in an unforgettable tale.

Dr. Nicklaus Hart, a gifted trauma surgeon, searches for meaning in his life. His self-reliant spirit is broken with the death of his missionary best friend, found sacrificed at the base of a Maya

Temple. Going to Guatemala to fill the shoes of his friend at the mission hospital, he discovers God's redemption and peace in the smiles of the children he cares for. But his own life is in danger as he and his team stumble onto a deadly North Korean plot.

Amazon: https://amzn.to/2IkM2TU

THE TREE OF LIFE

A massive earthquake hits Eastern Turkey, the ancient area of Mesopotamia, unveiling hidden secrets and opening an epic battle between good and evil.

Dr. Nicklaus Hart has lost his moral compass. As an orthopedic surgeon in a busy trauma practice, the cares of the world overshadow what Nick knows is true about himself. With his life unraveling, he falls into his old patterns of stress relief but knows they are a poisonous cure. Nick is shaken from his moral slumber when a massive earthquake strikes Eastern Turkey, and he makes the snap decision to respond. Thrown into the chaos and devastation, Nick must face his internal struggle head-on.

Amazon: https://amzn.to/2HqXUqD

THE RUSTED SCALPEL

A pharmaceutical company promises you hope and happiness in a pill. Would you take it if it cost your relationship with God?

Dr. Nicklaus Hart returns from responding to a massive earthquake that rocked the Middle East, allowing an ISIS terror cell to enter the ancient area of Mesopotamia. Captured, tortured and blinded by the hands of the radical terrorists, Nick arrives home a broken man. He has lost everything he holds dear—his sight, independence, profession and most of all, hope. But at the bottom of the pit, God sends him a lifeline and restores his physical and spiritual vision.

Amazon: https://amzn.to/2oXuTrW

THE GENE

Following their marriage, Dr. Nicklaus Hart and Maggie Russell enjoy the splendor and passion of a honeymoon in Hawaii. They learn that their union has brought new life, but the overflowing joy of Maggie's pregnancy and their romantic getaway is interrupted by the shocking news of a genetic disorder discovered in Maggie's family lineage—that both Maggie and the baby carry the mutated gene for the horrific Huntington's disease.

Nick and Maggie travel to Poland, where the top geneticist, Emmanuelle Christianson, has founded and operates BioGenics whose mission statement is: Advancing the Human Genome. Their journey reveals more than the fight for knowledge, it uncovers a simmering evil left over from World War II. One that puts their lives in danger. Amazon: https://amzn.to/2THnuwC

Dr. Timothy Browne is an Orthopaedic Surgeon and Medical Missionary who has served around the world with Operation Blessing, Mercy Ships, and Hope Force International. Browne has ministered in Guatemala, El Salvador, Honduras, Nicaragua, Panama, Brazil, Ukraine, Borneo, Malaysia, Singapore, South Korea, North Korea, Philippines, Sri Lanka, Haiti, and Sierra Leone. He now lives in Western Montana with his wife, Julie, who along with their three sons, served with him.